The Little Sparrows

OTHER BOOKS BY AL LACY

Angel of Mercy series:
   A Promise for Breanna (Book One)
   Faithful Heart (Book Two)
   Captive Set Free (Book Three)
   A Dream Fulfilled (Book Four)
   Suffer the Little Children (Book Five)
   Whither Thou Goest (Book Six)
   Final Justice (Book Seven)
   Not by Might (Book Eight)
   Things Not Seen (Book Nine)
   Far Above Rubies (Book Ten)

Journeys of the Stranger series:
   Legacy (Book One)
   Silent Abduction (Book Two)
   Blizzard (Book Three)
   Tears of the Sun (Book Four)
   Circle of Fire (Book Five)
   Quiet Thunder (Book Six)
   Snow Ghost (Book Seven)

Battles of Destiny (Civil War series):
   Beloved Enemy (Battle of First Bull Run)
   A Heart Divided (Battle of Mobile Bay)
   A Promise Unbroken (Battle of Rich Mountain)
   Shadowed Memories (Battle of Shiloh)
   Joy from Ashes (Battle of Fredericksburg)
   Season of Valor (Battle of Gettysburg)
   Wings of the Wind (Battle of Antietam)
   Turn of Glory (Battle of Chancellorsville)

Hannah of Fort Bridger series (coauthored with JoAnna Lacy):
   Under the Distant Sky (Book One)
   Consider the Lilies (Book Two)
   No Place for Fear (Book Three)
   Pillow of Stone (Book Four)
   The Perfect Gift (Book Five)
   Touch of Compassion (Book Six)
   Beyond the Valley (Book Seven)
   Damascus Journey (Book Eight)

Mail Order Bride series (coauthored with JoAnna Lacy):
   Secrets of the Heart (Book One)
   A Time to Love (Book Two)
   Tender Flame (Book Three)
   Blessed Are the Merciful (Book Four)
   Ransom of Love (Book Five)
   Until the Daybreak (Book Six)
   Sincerely Yours (Book Seven)
   A Measure of Grace (Book Eight)
   So Little Time (Book Nine)
   Let There Be Light (Book Ten)

The Little Sparrows

THE ORPHAN TRAINS TRILOGY

BOOK ONE

Al & JoAnna Lacy

Multnomah® Publishers *Sisters, Oregon*

THE LITTLE SPARROWS
published by Multnomah Publishers, Inc.
© 2002 by ALJO Productions

International Standard Book Number: 1-59052-063-7

Cover design by Kirk Douponce/UDG DesignWorks
Cover image of boy by Robert Papp/Shannon Associates
Image of orphans by Getty Images
Background cover images by Corbis

Multnomah is a trademark of Multnomah Publishers, Inc., and
is registered in the U.S. Patent and Trademark Office.
The colophon is a trademark of Multnomah Publishers, Inc.

Scripture quotations are from: *The Holy Bible,* King James Version

Printed in the United States of America

For information:
MULTNOMAH PUBLISHERS, INC.
POST OFFICE BOX 1720
SISTERS, OREGON 97759

Library of Congress Cataloging-in-Publication Data
Lacy, Al.
    The little sparrows / by Al and JoAnna Lacy.
        p. cm. -- (The orphan trains trilogy ; bk. 1)
    ISBN 1-59052-063-7 (trade pbk.)
    1. Homeless children--Fiction. 2. New York (N.Y.)--Fiction. 3. Orphan trains--
Fiction. 4. Orphans--Fiction. I. Lacy, JoAnna. II. Title.
    PS3562.A256 L58 2003
    813'.54--dc21   2002013130

04 05 06 07 08 —10 9 8 7

This book is affectionately dedicated to
Gail Messick of Montgomery, Alabama,
a faithful fan who has shown us much love.
We love you too, Gail. God bless you!

1 CORINTHIANS 16:23

Prologue

In midnineteenth-century New York City, which had grown by leaps and bounds with immigrants from all over Europe coming by the thousands into the city, the streets were filled with destitute, vagrant children. For the most part, they were anywhere from two years of age up to fifteen or sixteen.

The city's politicians termed them "orphans," though a great number had living parents, or at least one living parent. The city's newspapers called them orphans, half-orphans, foundlings, street Arabs, waifs, and street urchins. Many of these children begged or stole while a few found jobs selling newspapers; sweeping stores, restaurants, and sidewalks; and peddling apples, oranges, and flowers on the street corners. Others sold matches and toothpicks. Still others shined shoes. A few rummaged through trash cans for rags, boxes, or refuse paper to sell.

In 1852, New York City's mayor said there were some 30,000 of these orphans on the city's streets. Many of the ones who wandered the streets were ill clad, unwashed, and half-starved. Some actually died of starvation. They slept in boxes and trash bins in the alleys during the winter and many froze to death. In warm weather, some slept on park benches or on the grass in Central Park.

Some of the children were merely turned loose by the parents because the family had grown too large and they could not care for all their children. Many of the street waifs were runaways from parental abuse, parental immorality, and parental drunkenness.

In 1848, a young man named Charles Loring Brace, a native of Hartford, Connecticut, and graduate of Yale University, had come to New York to study for the ministry at Union Theological Seminary. He was also an author and spent a great deal of time working on his books, which slowed his work at the seminary. He still had not graduated by the spring of 1852 but something else was beginning to occupy his mind. He was horrified both by the vagrant children he saw on the streets daily and by the way the civil authorities treated them. The city's solution for years had been to sweep the wayfaring children into jails or run-down almshouses.

Brace believed the children should not be punished for their predicament but should be given a positive environment in which to live and grow up. In January 1853, after finishing the manuscript for a new book and submitting it to his New York publisher, Brace dropped out of seminary and met with a group of concerned pastors, bankers, businessmen, and lawyers—all who professed to be born-again Christians—and began the groundwork to establish an organization that would do something to help New York City's homeless children.

Because Brace was clearly a brilliant and dedicated young man, and because he was a rapidly rising literary figure on the New York scene, these men backed him in his desire. By March 1853, the Children's Aid Society was established. Brace was its leader, and the men who backed him helped raise funds from many kinds of businesses and people of wealth. This allowed Brace to take over the former Italian Opera House at the corner of Astor Place and Lafayette Street in downtown Manhattan.

From the beginning, Brace and his colleagues attempted to find homes for individual children, but it was soon evident that the growing numbers of street waifs would have to be placed elsewhere. Brace came upon the idea of taking groups of these orphans in wagons to the rural areas in upstate New York and allowing farmers to simply pick out the ones they wanted for themselves and become their foster parents.

This plan indeed provided some homes for the street waifs, but not enough to meet the demand. By June 1854, Brace came to the conclusion that the children would have to be taken westward where there were larger rural areas. One of his colleagues in the Children's Aid Society had friends in Dowagiac, Michigan, who had learned of the Society's work and wrote to tell him they thought people of their area would be interested in taking some of the children into their homes under the foster plan.

Hence came the first orphan train. In mid-September 1854, under Charles Brace's instructions, Dowagiac's local newspaper carried an ad every day for two weeks, announcing that forty-five homeless boys and girls from the streets of New York City would arrive by train on October 1, and on the morning of October 2 could be seen at the town's meetinghouse. Bills were posted at the general store, cafés, restaurants, and the railroad station, asking families to provide foster homes for these orphans.

One of Brace's paid associates, E. P. Smith, was assigned to take the children on the train to Dowagiac, which is located in southwestern Michigan. Smith's wife accompanied him to chaperone the girls.

The meetinghouse was fairly packed as the children stood behind Smith while he spoke to the crowd. He explained the program, saying these unfortunate children were Christ's "little ones," who needed a chance in life. He told the crowd that kind men and women who opened their homes to one or more of this ragged regiment would be expected to raise them as they would their own children, providing them with decent food and clothing and a good education. There would be no loss in their charity, Smith assured his audience. The boys would do whatever farm work or other kind that was expected of them, and the girls would do all types of housework.

As the children stood in line to be inspected, the applicants moved past them slowly, looking them over with care and engaging them in conversation. E. P. Smith and his wife looked at the quality and cleanliness of the prospective foster parents and asked them about their financial condition, property, vocation, and church attendance. If they were satisfied with what they heard, and saw no evidence that they were lying, they let them choose the child or children they desired.

When the applicants had chosen the children they wanted, thirty-seven had homes. The remaining eight were taken back to New York and placed in already overcrowded orphanages. Charles Brace was so encouraged by the high percentage of the children who had been taken into the homes, that he soon launched into a campaign to take children both from off the streets and from the orphanages, put them on trains, and take them west where there were farms and ranches aplenty.

When the railroad companies saw what Brace's Children's Aid Society was doing, they contacted him and offered generous discounts on tickets, and each railroad company offered special coaches, which would carry only the orphans and their chaperones.

For the next seventy-five years—until the last orphan train carried the waifs to Texas in 1929—the Children's Aid Society had placed some 250,000 children in homes in every western state and territory except Arizona. Upon Brace's death in 1890, his son, Charles Loring Brace Jr., took over the Society.

In 1910, a survey concluded that 87 percent of the children shipped to the West on the orphan trains up to that time had grown into credible members of western society. Eight percent had been returned to New York City, and 5 percent had either disappeared, were imprisoned for crimes committed, or had died.

It is to the credit of Charles Loring Brace's dream, labor, and leadership in the orphan train system that two of the orphans grew up to become state governors, several became mayors, one became a Supreme Court justice, two became congressmen, thirty-five became lawyers, and nineteen became physicians. Others became successful gospel preachers, lawmen, farmers, ranchers, businessmen, wives, and mothers—those who made up a great part of society in the West.

Until well into the twentieth century, Brace's influence was felt by virtually every program established to help homeless and needy children. Even today, the philosophical foundations he forged have left him—in the minds of many—the preeminent figure in American child welfare history.

Chapter One

I t was early April 1874, in southeastern Wyoming on a bright sunny Saturday morning. The prairie was golden with sunlight beneath an azure sky. White clouds rode the high wind, patching the land with drifting shadows. The air was clear and crisp, and from the *Circle C* ranch where rancher Sam Claiborne and his wife, Emma, stood on the front porch of their two-story white frame house looking westward, their range of vision extended all the way to the majestic Rocky Mountains some fifty miles away. The lofty peaks were still snow packed and filled the horizon. The Claibornes were looking for movement on the prairie, but the only movement in sight was a bald eagle winging its way southward on the airwaves.

The lanky rancher, who would turn thirty-five on his next birthday, sighed. "Honey, I can't wait any longer. I've got to get into Cheyenne for my appointment with Lyle Wilson. The bank closes at noon on Saturdays and I don't want to be late."

Emma, who was a year younger than her husband, said, "Go ahead and saddle Midnight, dear. I'll keep watch."

Sam nodded. "Okay. Be back shortly."

Emma observed her husband's form as he hurried around the house, then a small frown lined her brow and a shadow flicked across her blue eyes as she looked toward the west once again. She knew how much her child enjoyed riding and racing her bay mare across the prairie, but of late she had found herself ill at ease each time.

She whispered a prayer toward heaven, asking the Lord to bring both girls back safely. Betty Houston was Jody's best friend and a fine Christian girl. The girls were excellent riders, but out there on the prairie a lot of things could happen.

Emma took her eyes off the prairie for a moment to look around the ranch. She and Sam had worked hard over the years to make the *Circle C* what it was today. And even now, from sunup till sundown, their days were filled with chores and work of various sorts. Sundays always brought a nice break, with church services morning and evening, which invariably were a blessing.

Emma smiled to herself as she scanned the five hundred acres she could see from the porch, and thought how all the work was worth it. *After all,* she mused, *good hard work never hurt anyone.*

Two weeks ago, she and Sam, along with Jody's help, had put a fresh coat of paint on the house. Now it stood gleaming in the sunshine. Dark green shutters adorned each open window, making pretty frames for the lace curtains fluttering in the morning breeze. The grass around the house was beginning to put on its spring greenery, and the tulips and the daffodils made a bright-colored border around the front porch.

I couldn't ask for more, Emma thought. *You've been so good to us, Lord.*

Some fifteen minutes after he had headed for the barn, Sam came around the corner of the house, leading his big black stallion. She glanced at him and shook her head. "No sign of them, yet. I hope nothing's wrong."

Sam pulled Midnight to a halt at the porch steps. "I'm sure

they're all right, honey. Sometimes those girls just get wound up while racing each other and forget about the time."

"Mm-hmm. I know."

Sam flipped the reins over Midnight's head, looping them over the saddle horn, then moved up the porch steps. He took Emma in his arms and kissed her. "I'll be back by one o'clock or so." He moved down the steps, took hold of the saddle horn, and lifted his foot to put it in the stirrup.

"Wait a minute, Sam. Here they come!"

He dropped the foot to earth and looked westward.

The *Circle C* was located some thirteen miles north of Cheyenne on the south bank of the Lodgepole River. Sam's eyes focused on the two riders as they galloped along the edge of the river toward the ranch, bent forward in their saddles, their long hair flowing in the wind.

He smiled when he saw that the bay mare carrying the girl with the dark hair was ahead by two lengths. Sam was proud of his twelve-year-old daughter, who had become an expert rider. He flicked a glance at Emma. "Honey, those girls sure love to race each other."

"That they do," she said, descending the porch steps. "Strange, isn't it? About half the time Jody and Queenie win, and half the time Betty and Millie come out ahead."

"Yeah. I think those two mares have a secret pact to make it work like that."

Emma laughed. "Know what? I believe you're right!"

Soon the bay mare thundered up and skidded to a halt a few seconds before the gray roan. Betty Houston, who was the same age as Jody Claiborne, said jokingly, "You and Queenie cheated, Jody!"

While the horses snorted, breathing hard from the race, Jody laughed. "And just how did we cheat?"

"Well, you and Queenie made Millie and me ride closer to the riverbank. The air is thicker close to the water, so it slowed Millie down."

Sam and Emma both laughed at Betty's good-natured reasoning. "She's right, Jody!" Sam said. "You should've been the one riding closest to the river. It's only fair that you give your best friend the advantage."

Jody looked at her best friend. "Thanks Betty! I appreciate your letting Queenie run in the thin, dry air. Next time, it'll be Millie's turn."

Everybody laughed, and Jody dismounted. "Daddy, I'm sorry if I held you up. We kind of let the time get away from us. But thanks for waiting for me. I sure want to ride to town with you."

Sam smiled. "It's all right, Jody. I thought you girls might be a while getting back, so I went ahead and saddled up Midnight. Soon as Queenie catches her breath, we'll go."

Betty ran her gaze over the three faces. "I'll be going. See all of you later."

"Thanks for letting me win," Jody said, a wide grin spread over her pretty face.

Betty grinned back, wheeled her mare around, and trotted away.

Jody turned to her father. "Daddy, just give me two minutes to wash my face and get a drink of water, and I'll be all set to go with you."

"Sure. Go ahead, honey. Hurry, though. Remember I have an appointment with the bank president. I don't want to be late."

"Yes, sir!" she said. "Be right back."

As Jody took the porch steps two at a time and plunged through the door, Sam took Emma in his arms and kissed her. "Thank you for giving me a daughter like that, sweet stuff. What a girl! She's so much like her mother."

Emma crinkled her nose. "My, hasn't God blessed you? Just think what a fortunate man you are to have two such marvelous women in your life."

"Don't I know it!"

Emma clipped his chin. "And don't you forget it!"

"Oh, how could I? How blessed I am!"

Sam stepped to Queenie, took hold of the reins, and said, "Hey, ol' gal, let's get you a drink of water."

He led her to the nearby watering trough and let her drink all she wanted. As he was leading her back to the front of the house, Jody came out the door and put her arms around her mother. She asked if there was anything else her mother needed from the general store other than what was on the list she had given her that morning.

Emma said there was nothing else. Jody told her she would see her later and moved up to her father. "Thank you for watering Queenie for me, Daddy, and thank you for waiting for me."

Emma looked on with pleasure as Sam kissed Jody's forehead and squeezed her tight. She was glad that Sam and his daughter were very close. It pleased her that they spent so much time together. Jody had made herself a tomboy, knowing her father very much wanted a son too. She worked with him on the ranch and helped with the chores. She also helped her mother with the cooking, washing, ironing, and the housework, which she enjoyed more.

Father and daughter mounted up and rode toward town, where he would take care of his banking business while she purchased a few things at the general store.

As Sam and Jody rode into Cheyenne and were moving past the railroad station, they saw a train with several coal cars. The coal was being unloaded into wagons owned by Cheyenne residents, town merchants, the town's blacksmith, and several ranchers and farmers.

Jody glanced at her father. "I guess we don't need coal this time, do we, Daddy?"

"No. We're set till the middle of next fall."

She ran her gaze over the coal cars. "Those Rocky Mountains must really be full of coal. They just keep digging more out all the time."

"Yes. When God created the earth, He knew that man would need the coal to heat his homes and business buildings; that the blacksmiths would need it to do their work, and the factories would need it for melting alloys of iron, carbon, and other elements to make steel."

"Well, I'm sure glad we have coal to heat our house in these cold Wyoming winters, Daddy. The Lord sure has been good to the people He put on this earth. I wish more of them would see how good the Father was to send His Son to provide them with salvation. But most of them seem to have no interest in Jesus. They want religion, but they don't want Him. Or they want to mix what He did at Calvary with human works, which is to say that what Jesus did when He shed His blood on the cross, died, and rose again was not enough to save lost sinners."

"You've got that right, sweetheart. Anything added to His finished work at Calvary is human works, and as you well know, the Bible says salvation is by grace, not of works, lest any man should boast."

"That's what my Sunday school teacher was saying last Sunday, Daddy. When human works are added to the gospel, it takes the glory from Jesus and puts it on those who do the works."

"Right. And because Jesus paid the full price for our sins on the cross, God the Father wants all the glory to go to His Son."

"And that's the way it should be."

"Amen, sweetheart."

Soon Sam and Jody were in Cheyenne's business section. As they drew near the general store, Jody said, "Daddy, I'll be sitting on one of those benches in front of the store when you come back from the bank."

"All right, honey. See you later."

Jody veered Queenie toward the hitch rail in front of the store as her father headed for the next block where the Bank of Cheyenne was located.

She dismounted, patted Queenie's long neck, and entered the general store.

Twenty minutes later, Jody came out of the store, packages in hand, talking to a teenage girl who was in her Sunday school class. The girl headed down the boardwalk, and Jody stepped into the street and drew up to her mare. She began placing the small packages into a canvas bag that was attached to the rear of her saddle. When she got to the last package, she reached inside and took out a long stick of licorice candy. Her favorite.

Jody's mother always gave her permission to purchase a nickel's worth of candy whenever she went to the general store for her. She patted the mare's neck again. "Daddy will be back in a little while, Queenie."

The mare bobbed her head and whinnied lightly as if she understood Jody's words.

Jody went to one of the benches and sat down to wait for her father.

She relished every bite of her licorice stick. Since it was Saturday, farm and ranch families were in town for shopping, which made for a constant stream of people moving along the boardwalk. Jody sat in complete contentment, for people watching was one of her preferred pastimes. A few minutes had passed when Jody looked up and saw Pastor Dan Forbes, his wife Clara, and their two sons coming down the boardwalk. Peter Forbes was Jody's age, and Paul was ten years old. Clara Forbes spotted Jody first, and pointed her out to the rest of the family. Jody put the licorice stick in her purse.

"Your parents in the general store, Jody?" asked the pastor.

"No, sir. Daddy's over at the bank doing business with Mr. Wilson. Mommy didn't come to town with us. I just finished a little grocery shopping for her."

"Oh, I see."

Clara smiled. "Well, it's nice of you to do the shopping for her, honey."

"I enjoy it."

Jody noticed Peter and Paul as they stepped across the boardwalk to the hitch rail and stroked Queenie's long face, speaking to her. Queenie nickered her own greeting.

The pastor looked at Jody. "Have you and Betty had a good race lately?"

"Oh yes. Just this morning, in fact."

"And who won?"

"I did."

"Well, that's good. The last time I asked about you girls racing was at church a couple of weeks ago. Betty had won."

Jody giggled. "Oh, we trade off as to who wins."

"Really? So you two plan on who's going to win before you race?"

"No. Millie and Queenie plan it out."

The pastor and his wife both laughed. "Come on, boys, we have to be going. We don't want to be late for your dentist appointment, Paul."

The boys left Queenie and moved back to the spot where their parents stood. Jody said, "Tell Dr. Miller hello for me, Paul."

Paul chuckled. "Tell you what, Jody—I'll stay here, and you go see Dr. Miller in my place. Tell him hello in person."

"Nice try," said Clara.

Paul made a mock scowl. "I don't want to go to the dentist, Mom."

"Nobody does," said Clara. "But with all of us it's necessary from time to time."

The pastor told Jody he would see her and her parents at church tomorrow, and he and his family walked away.

Jody sat down on the bench again, took her licorice stick out of her purse, and went back to her people watching.

A short time later, she saw her father riding down the street toward her. As he pulled up to the hitch rail, he looked at her and smiled. "Get your shopping done, honey?"

"Sure did," she said, putting the last piece of licorice in her mouth and rising from the bench. "I already loaded the sacks into the canvas bag." She ducked under the hitch rail and mounted Queenie. "Pastor Forbes and his family came by, Daddy. Paul has an appointment with the dentist."

Sam screwed up his face. "I'm glad we have dentists in this world, but I sure don't like to go to them."

"I never met anyone who likes to go to the dentist."

As father and daughter headed north on Main Street, they soon found themselves drawing near the railroad station. They saw that the coal train was gone and a passenger train stood in its place.

Jody's attention was drawn to a long line of children who were standing on the depot platform next to the train. Men and women were talking to them. "Daddy, look! It's one of the orphan trains."

"Sure enough. I read the announcement about this train in the *Cheyenne Sentinel* last week. It told that the train would be in today for prospective foster parents to pick and choose the orphans as they wished."

"I've heard you and Mommy talk about the orphan trains at times, Daddy, but I never understood about these foster parents. Do they adopt them legally after a while?"

"Well, from what I've read, most of them remain foster parents, even though the plan is to raise them until they are adults. But some do adopt them right away. They simply go to a local judge to get it done."

"Well, Daddy, here's your chance to get that boy you've always wanted!"

Sam laughed. "Tell you what, Jody Ann Claiborne, since you're such a tomboy, that's enough! I don't need a boy."

"Then I guess I'm not going to be replaced."

"You're sure not!"

"Daddy…"

"Yes?"

"Could we go in there to the depot and just watch for a few minutes?"

"Why, sure. Since my meeting with Mr. Wilson was shorter than expected, we have time."

They left their horses at hitching posts in the depot's parking lot and moved up to the platform beside the train. Jody's eyes were wide as she beheld the scene from close up. She quickly counted sixty-three children in the line. Adults were moving slowly along the line, looking them over, and talking to them.

The children ranged in age from about four or five to their mid-teens. The boys were dressed in black or gray suits with white shirts and neckties, and the girls were in red or blue dresses that were all styled similarly. The hems of the dresses came down to the tops of their black lace-up boots.

Jody noticed similar expressions on the pinched faces of both boys and girls. The apprehension they felt showed in their eyes, and it was obvious that turmoil was racing through their hearts as they stood as spectacles on display before the adults. They fidgeted and continuously watched the faces of the adults who were taking measure of them.

Young as they were, some of the children looked beaten down with wary eyes that appeared much too old for their age. Some of the older boys tried to mask their fear with a facade of bravery while the older girls often glanced at each other, eyes round and huge as they felt the gaze of the scrutinizing adults on them.

Jody's tender heart went out to them and her green eyes filled with tears. She looked up at her father. "Daddy, what will happen if the train arrives at its destination on the West Coast and no one takes them?"

"Well, sweetheart, from what I've read about it in the newspapers, the children that are not chosen are taken back to the Children's Aid Society in New York. Some of them are so discouraged that they go back to the streets. Others wait till they can get on another orphan train and try again."

"Do the ones who are chosen always get into good homes?"

Sam shook his head. "Unfortunately, no. Though the Children's Aid Society people don't like it, many of the boys and girls are chosen just to be made into servants and field hands. And some of those are abused. It's so sad. If this is a typical group, some of those you see right here are not actually orphans, but have run away from homes in New York City where they were mistreated and abused. And then they end up in homes just like the kind they had run away from."

Jody wiped tears from her eyes. "That's awful, Daddy."

"Yes, but thank the Lord, the majority of the children do find good homes where they are loved and given the care they deserve. I'll tell you, sweetie, life on those New York streets is appalling and very dangerous. At least those who are chosen—even if it is to be servants and field hands—will have food and clothing supplied, a warm, comfortable bed at night, and many of them will be sent to school."

Jody ran her misty eyes over the line of children. "Daddy, I wish we could take them all home with us."

Sam put his arm around her shoulders and drew her close to his side. "I do too, darlin'. I do too. But we can't."

"I know, Daddy, but it doesn't keep me from wishing."

Chapter Two

While Sam and Jody Claiborne observed the proceedings on the depot platform, they spotted a couple named Hap and Margie Lakin, who owned a small ranch near the *Circle C*. The Lakins were in the line of prospective foster parents, talking to the children and looking them over.

"What do you think of that, Daddy?" asked Jody. "Hap and Margie are looking for a foster child."

"Well, she did have that miscarriage two years ago, and another one last year. Maybe the doctor told her not to try having any more babies."

"I imagine that's it."

Father and daughter continued to watch the line. One by one, couples were choosing a boy here, a girl there, and the Children's Aid Society men and women in charge of the orphans were questioning the prospective foster parents. Papers were being signed on clipboards, and couples were walking away with the children they had chosen.

Jody elbowed her father. "Look there, Daddy. Hap and Margie have been talking to that little girl for several minutes. I think they're interested in her. I heard the girl say she is nine years old."

At that instant, Hap spotted Sam and Jody and smiled at them. Margie asked him something, and after he had answered her question, he gestured toward Sam and Jody looking on. Margie looked at them, gave them a tiny wave, then went right back to talking to the little girl.

Jody noticed that standing right next to the nine-year-old was a girl a couple of years younger, who strongly resembled the nine-year-old.

Jody elbowed her father again. "See that little girl right next to the one Hap and Margie are talking to, Daddy?"

"Uh-huh. Looks a lot like her. Has to be her little sister."

"That's what I was going to say."

At that moment, Hap motioned to one of the women sponsors nearby, who was not occupied at the moment. "Ma'am! My wife and I are ready to sign the papers."

The woman stepped up. "You want to take both Lorraine and Maisie, I assume."

Hap leaned toward Margie, and they talked in a low tone.

The sisters watched as Hap and Margie had their private talk. Maisie tugged at Lorraine's sleeve and rose up on her tiptoes. Lorraine kept her eyes on the Lakins as she bent her head toward her little sister in order to hear what she so desperately wanted to say to her.

Maisie whispered, "Sissy, are they gonna take both of us? They haven't talked to me."

A troubled look claimed Lorraine's features. "I would think so, honey. I told them you're my sister."

"Then why haven't they talked to me?"

"I don't know. I—"

The Lakins were now speaking to the woman with the clipboard.

Fear touched Lorraine's heart. She looked on, eyes wide.

The woman was now asking questions, and when she finished, she handed the Lakins the clipboard and a pencil, so they could sign the papers. Both put their signatures on the papers, then Margie handed the clipboard back to the woman. She made sure the signatures were at each place as directed, then turned to the oldest girl. "Lorraine, this nice family is taking you home with them."

Lorraine frowned. "You *do* mean both of us, don't you?" she asked in a low whisper, her eyes hopeful.

Maisie was able to pick up her sister's words, and her eyes went to the woman. "No, dear. They are only taking you."

"But—but—"

"We can't take both of you, honey," Margie said softly. "We just can't afford to take in two mouths to feed."

Suddenly, Maisie threw herself into her sister's arms and burst into tears. "I have to go with you, Sissy! Please, please take me with you!"

The Lakins exchanged glances, each showing a helpless look.

The woman with the clipboard bent down and stroked the face of the seven-year-old. "Maisie, honey, don't cry. I'm sorry you and Lorraine will have to be separated, but it often has to be this way. Mr. and Mrs. Lakin just can't afford to take in both of you."

Jody Claiborne bit her lips and took hold of her father's arm. "Daddy, this is awful. That poor little Maisie must have already lost her parents, and now she is losing her sister too!"

Sam pulled Jody close and said in a low voice, "I read in the newspaper that quite often brothers and sisters are separated when they are chosen by foster parents. It is better than the children living on the streets of New York in squalor, starving to death or freezing to death."

Jody shuddered, shook her head, and fixed her gaze on little Maisie as Lorraine put an arm around her. "Honey, please don't cry. This is the way it has to be. I have to go with these people. You heard what Mrs. Jackson said."

"But I want to go with you!" wailed Maisie.

Lorraine cupped Maisie's face in her hands. "Honey, someone will take you and give you a good home. I promise." Tears were now streaming down Lorraine's cheeks. "I love you, Maisie. I don't want to leave you, but I have to go with these people. I don't have a choice. It's the rule."

Lorraine stepped back and felt Margie take hold of her hand. "We need to go now, dear."

Hap was looking on, his face pinched as his heart went out to Maisie. "Yes. We need to go."

Margie kept Lorraine's hand in hers and led her away, with Hap at her side.

Maisie was sobbing.

When the Lakins and Lorraine had taken a few steps, Lorraine looked back over her shoulder for one last glimpse of her little sister.

Maisie drew a shuddering breath and reached her thin little arms toward Lorraine. "No, Sissy! You can't leave me! Please don't leave me-e-e!"

Maisie broke from the line and ran after her sister. Mrs. Jackson saw it coming and intercepted her. She took her up in her arms and held her close. "No, Maisie, you can't go with your sister. You must stay in the line." As she spoke, she carried the child back to the line and placed her between two boys. "You stay, here. Someone will choose you soon and take you home with them."

Maisie wept as if her heart was going to break in two.

Jody dashed from Sam's side and ran to Maisie. She put her arms around her, and with tears flowing from her own eyes, said, "Maisie, my name is Jody Claiborne. Please don't cry. My Daddy is here with me. I'll ask him if we can take you home with us."

Sam's head bobbed and he blinked his eyes.

"But I want my Sissy!" sobbed Maisie, looking past Jody to the spot where Hap and Margie Lakin had now stopped a short distance away with Lorraine between them. They were watching the scene. Lorraine's entire body shook as she wept and wiped tears.

Hap shook his head. "Margie, we can't do this. We'll just cinch our belts up tighter and take Maisie too."

A smile broke over Margie's face. "Oh yes! We'll do that!"

Lorraine gasped. "Really? You'll take my little sister, too?"

"We sure will," said Hap. "Come on."

As the three of them headed back toward Maisie, Hap called to Mrs. Jackson, saying they would take Maisie.

Margie took Maisie up in her arms and set her teary eyes on Jody. "Honey, I appreciate your kindness to Maisie. Thank you."

"Yes, thank you, Jody," said Hap.

Lorraine smiled at Jody. "That was nice of you."

Hap said, "Lorraine, Maisie, as you heard her say, this young lady's name is Jody Claiborne. She and her parents live on a ranch near ours. You'll get to see her often."

Lorraine surprised Jody by hugging her. "We're already friends, aren't we, Jody?"

"We sure are!"

Sam was now at Jody's side. He put an arm around her shoulders and squeezed her tight. "You're Daddy's special little girl, darlin'. I think if Hap and Margie hadn't changed their minds, you'd probably have talked me into taking Maisie home with us."

Jody smiled up at him.

The Lakins laughed, and Hap said, "I think she probably would've, Sam."

Jody grinned. "I sure would have tried, Mr. Lakin."

Mrs. Jackson obtained signatures from Hap and Margie and

quickly finished the paperwork.

"Okay, Margie and girls," said Hap, "let's head for the ranch. Jody, Sam, we'll see you later."

As the Lakins walked away with the girls between them, it was a sweet picture to behold, and tears formed again in Jody's eyes while she stood there, watching them. Maisie was chattering happily and doing a skip while holding on to her big sister's hand. Hap and Margie smiled at each other.

When they passed from view, Sam looked down at his daughter with admiring eyes. "Jody, I'm so proud of you. I appreciate the love you always show to others."

She said softly, "You and Mommy taught me."

When father and daughter put their attention once again on the orphans, they saw that the sponsors were ready to put the children back on the train. One of the men said to the others, "Well, we've still got fifty-one to place in homes on down the line."

The remaining boys and girls, their heads hanging low, shuffled back aboard the waiting train. Two of the younger girls were crying because they had not been chosen, and one of the teenage girls was trying to comfort them.

Sam set a hand on Jody's shoulder. "Well, honey, we'd better be going. Your mother is expecting us for lunch in just a little while."

"Daddy, I feel so sorry for those poor children."

"I do too, honey."

She took hold of her father's hand and looked up at him with tender eyes. "I'm so thankful I have you and Mommy and my Christian home."

Sam and Jody reached their horses and mounted up. They put them into motion and soon they were out of town, heading due north.

As they trotted along the road side by side, Jody was unusually quiet. Sam knew she had been touched by the plight of the orphan children, and being so tenderhearted, she couldn't get them out of her mind. He decided not to interrupt her thoughts.

Emma Claiborne was busy in the kitchen, expecting Sam and Jody to arrive any minute. She had baked fresh bread and made roast beef sandwiches from last night's leftovers. They also had wedges of cheese and dishes of canned peaches.

As she was sliding the hissing teapot to the back of the stove, she heard the sound of hoofbeats and looked out the kitchen's side window. Sam and Jody both waved at her, and she called through the open window, "Lunch is ready!"

Father and daughter smiled and veered their mounts toward the back porch. Emma went to the door, opened it, and watched as Sam and Jody dismounted. Sam took the canvas bag containing the groceries from behind Jody's saddle, and they mounted the porch steps together.

Jody moved ahead of him and kissed her mother's cheek. "Hello, Mommy. I sure do love you."

Emma smiled and kissed her daughter's cheek in return. "I sure do love you too."

While Jody crossed the back porch and entered the kitchen, Sam paused to kiss his wife. Emma preceded him through the door, asking over her shoulder how his meeting with the bank president went.

"Went just fine, honey," he replied, setting the canvas bag on the cupboard. "I'll give you the details while we eat lunch."

"Okay. You two get washed up while I pour the tea."

Moments later, the Claibornes sat down to the table. Sam led in prayer, thanking the Lord for the food, and they began eating.

While Sam was telling Emma the details of his meeting with bank president Lyle Wilson, she noticed that Jody seemed preoccupied and was only nibbling at her food.

When Sam finished his story, Emma commented, "Well, I'm glad Mr. Wilson saw it your way, honey. That will help us a great deal." She then put her attention back on Jody. "Sweetheart, what's wrong? You've hardly touched your sandwich, and roast beef is your favorite."

Jody met her mother's gaze. "When Daddy and I were in town, we saw one of those orphan trains, Mommy. Those poor little children. I feel so sorry for them."

"Hap and Margie were there, honey," said Sam. "They chose two little girls and took them home."

Emma's eyes brightened. "Really? Well, I'm so glad for them. You remember that I told you Margie came by to see me last Tuesday. You were out at the barn. Jody was out riding with Betty."

Sam nodded.

"I forgot to tell both of you that Betty's doctor told her she should never try to have another baby."

"I sort of figured that might be the case," said Sam. "And let me tell you something our sweet daughter did."

Emma listened while Sam told her how the Lakins were only going to take the older sister, and of the love and compassion Jody had shown the little one before the Lakins decided to take her too.

Emma commended Jody for this. "But, honey, you shouldn't let that little episode keep you from eating your lunch."

"It's not just that, Mommy," Jody said. "I just can't get those children out of my mind. Especially the little ones. They just look so sad. I…I just hope they all find a wonderful home like I have."

She sniffed and wiped away a tear that was forming at the corner of her eye. "Mommy, some of them were so scared. Even some of those who were my age. I can't even imagine what their lives must have been like back there in New York. I'm so sheltered, cared for, and loved. It would be a wonderful world if every child could have what I have."

Emma left her chair, moved around to Jody, and planted a soft kiss on her dark hair. "God has been so good to give us such a precious daughter."

Sam sighed. "That He has, honey. That He has."

Emma sat down again while Jody said, "Daddy, how and when did these orphan trains get started?"

Sam told her the story of Charles Loring Brace and how he started the Children's Aid Society in the mid-1850s.

"You see, honey," Sam went on, "in the early days of this century, this country began to change in its eastern states from a country in which the greater part of the population lived in rural areas, to an industrial nation with cities on the grow. Farm machines were being invented that replaced workers on the farms. At the same time, factories were being built that put those people to work. Lots of jobs were opening up."

"Right," put in Emma. "I've read the newspaper accounts about it, too. That's why the immigrants from all over Europe began coming to America. Hundreds of thousands of them."

Jody nodded.

"Of course this brought on a problem," said Sam. "The cities were growing by leaps and bounds, and there was not enough housing for everyone. Many of the factory workers—both Americans and immigrants—had large families. Great numbers of them were jammed into tiny apartments that had to be shared with two or three other families. Some families even lived in the alleys in cardboard boxes.

"People who worked in factories and other kinds of jobs often worked ten to twelve hours a day, six days a week. Wages were low, and even with the men working such long hours, many parents could barely feed and clothe themselves and their children."

"And even the children often had to work, Jody," said Emma. "Many of them, as young as five and six years of age, labored long hours in factories, earning only pennies a day."

Sam nodded. "That's right. Other children took to the streets and did what they could to earn money to live on. Others, barely old enough to walk, begged for food and money on the streets."

Jody moved her head slowly, her green eyes wide. "We're so fortunate to live here in the West and have this ranch that makes us a good living."

"That's for sure, honey," said Emma. "The Lord has been so good to us."

"In that newspaper I read last week, Jody," said Sam, "it said even when every member of a family worked, many families still could not make enough money to survive. Many adults and children starved to death. Lots of adults died as alcoholics. Others went insane. Sometimes parents were so upset at the birth of a child that they would abandon the newborn in a church, a store, or a hospital, hoping someone would take the baby and care for it."

"Yes," said Emma, "and there were other parents who didn't even make that effort. Almost every day, the New York police would find the bodies of infants who had been left to die in rain barrels or trash cans. In other families, the parents forced older children to leave the home to make space for a new baby. Sometimes the children who were sent away were no more than six or seven years of age. These children had nowhere to go but to the streets, where great numbers of children whose parents were dead were already struggling to stay alive. Homeless children slept on sidewalk heating grates, doorways, empty buildings, trash receptacles, cardboard boxes, or shipping crates in the alleys. They ate out of garbage cans or stole food from the grocery stores."

Jody's face twisted up. Oh, how awful!"

Sam rose from his chair. "Last week's newspaper is still out on the back porch in the stack we use to start our fires with. I'll get it. There's something in there that Charles Loring Brace wrote. I want to read it to you."

While Sam was out of the room, Jody said, "Mommy, I'm so glad the Lord put me in this family."

Emma smiled. "So am I, sweetheart. What would your daddy and I ever do without you?"

Sam returned with the newspaper in hand. "Jody, when charitable groups began to open orphanages in the large cities back east, most of the children who lived in them were from the slums. Mr. Brace's heart went out to the homeless children. He knew they needed housing, medical care, good food, clothing, and schooling. In this particular article, Mr. Brace is quoted as saying that when he opened the Children's Aid Society, immediately children came to their door, needing help. This is what he wrote about these children."

Sam opened the paper before him. "'It was touching to see the crowds of wandering little ones who were finding their way to our office. Ragged young girls who had nowhere to lay their heads; children driven from drunkards' homes; orphans who slept where they could find a box or stairway; boys cast out by stepmothers or stepfathers; newsboys, whose incessant answer to our question, *Where do you live?* rang in our ears: *Don't live nowhere!*

"'Little bootblacks, young peddlers…pickpockets and petty thieves trying to get honest work; child beggars and flower sellers growing up to enter courses of crime—all this motley throng of infantile misery and childish guilt passed through our doors as those first months came and went, telling their simple stories of suffering, loneliness, and temptation, until our hearts became sick.'"

"I can see why," Jody said, her voice cracking. "Poor children. It makes my heart sick too."

Emma shook her head and looked at her husband. "Sam, if I remember correctly, the article goes on to say that Mr. Brace didn't think orphanages were the best solution for this problem because not only were all of New York City's orphanages over-crowded, but they didn't teach the children to become responsible adults who could take care of themselves."

Sam nodded. "Mr. Brace believed that this would happen only if children had good families of their own. But where would the Children's Aid Society find such families to take so many needy children? There was only one plausible answer—out West. So he created a plan called 'placing out.' And that's how the orphan trains got started. What you saw today, Jody, was Mr. Brace's 'placing out' in action."

"Well, it seems to be working, Daddy. Not long ago, I heard some people at church talking about the orphan trains, and one man said they are now carrying homeless children all the way to California, even up to Oregon and Washington."

Sam nodded. "That's right, sugar. All the way to the Pacific Coast."

Emma smiled. "Well, thank God for Charles Loring Brace! Before this orphan train program is over, I'm sure that hundreds of poor, needy children will be placed in good homes all over the West."

Jody reached across the table and took hold of the hands of her mother and father. "The Lord has been so good to me! How thankful I am to have my precious parents and this wonderful home."

Chapter Three

Warm breezes swirled across New York Harbor, sending the message that spring was coming on in full strength. It was Friday, April 10, and a number of sailboats were in the harbor, as well as fishing boats and ocean liners coming in from the Atlantic Ocean.

On the waterfront in New York Harbor, near the southern tip of Manhattan Island, stood the American Ship Lines building. The executive offices were on the second floor on the south side of the building, which protected them from the noise of the company's ships as they docked and crews loaded and unloaded them on the west side.

In the office of assistant business manager Bob Marston, silver-haired Scott Woodrow, vice president of Manhattan Industries, closed his briefcase and stood. "Mr. Marston, it's a pleasure to deal with you. I'm very happy with this contract, and I know our president and executive board will like it as much as I do. From this day on, American Ship Lines has all of our shipping business north and east on the Atlantic."

Marston rose from his chair and shook Woodrow's hand. "Thank you for coming to us, Mr. Woodrow. We'll look forward to a long and lasting business relationship."

"So will we." Woodrow cocked his head, scrutinizing the young executive. "You're quite young to be holding this position in the company. Have you seen thirty?"

"Yes, sir. I turned thirty last month."

"Aha! I was close, at least. I figured you for twenty-eight or twenty-nine. And you're married, I assume."

"Oh yes. To a lovely lady. Her name is Louise."

"Children?"

"The Lord has blessed Louise and me with three wonderful children. Mary is eight years old, Johnny is six, and the baby is four. Her name is Elizabeth, but we call her Lizzie."

"Sounds like a happy family." Woodrow picked up his briefcase. "Well, I must be going. I'm excited about telling my people at the office about this excellent contract."

Bob Marston opened the office door, and with congenial parting words, Scott Woodrow hurried away.

Bob closed the door and swung a fist through the air. "Yes! Yes! Thank You, Lord!"

He walked to the large open window, where a flood of golden sunshine streamed in, and looked out on to the waters of the harbor. A warm, fragrant breeze came through the window.

He drew the salty air into his lungs. "Thank You, Lord!"

There was a tap at the door.

Bob moved hastily across the office carpet and opened the door. It was Leona Harrison, secretary to the company's business manager. "Mr. Carr is ready to see you now, Mr. Marston. He wants you in his office right away."

A smile spread over Bob's handsome face. "I'm ready!"

He closed the door behind him, and as he and Leona walked down the hall together, she looked at him. "Mr. Woodrow looked happy when he came out of your office, Mr. Marston. I assume we got the contract with Manhattan Industries."

"We sure did!"

"Wonderful! That'll make Mr. Carr happy."

"The one thing I want to do is keep Mr. Carr happy."

They drew up in front of Weldon Carr's office.

Bob smiled as he tapped on the door. "See you later, Leona."

A deep voice inside called, "Come in, Bob!"

When Bob Marston stepped into the office, Carr stood up from the chair behind his desk. "Sit down and tell me!"

Grinning, Bob moved toward the desk. "I'll tell you *before* I sit down, sir. We got the contract!"

"Great! As we wanted it? No changes?"

"No changes," said Bob, sitting down in one of the two chairs positioned in front of the desk.

Carr settled into his chair. "That's going to net us somewhere between five and seven hundred thousand dollars a year, Bob. You just might get a salary raise for landing this one."

"Well, that wouldn't make me mad."

Carr laughed.

"You wanted to see me about something else, I understand."

Carr smiled and picked up a letter that lay before him on the desk.

"Yes. Take a look at this."

Bob took the letter in hand, noting that it was from Albert Clarke, president of Mount Pearl Mining Company in St. John's, Newfoundland. As he read it, he saw that they wanted to negotiate with American Ship Lines on a contract to transport iron ore for them to manufacturers in New England, New York, and New Jersey. He looked at his boss. "I know this company, Mr. Carr. They're big."

"They sure are. If we can land this contract, it'll be a huge account. It'll bring us a great deal of income. I want you to go to St. John's and close the deal with them."

Bob's eyes brightened. "I'd be glad to do that, sir!"

"I figured you would."

"Would it be all right if I took Louise with me?"

"Of course. The trip will be good for both of you. You can go on the *Hampton*. It is scheduled to leave here next Tuesday the fourteenth."

Bob knew the American Ship Lines freighter, *USS Hampton,* did business all along the Atlantic coast of Canada and its eastern provinces. "This will be my first time on the *Hampton,* sir. Many of our crewmen have told me she's quite a vessel."

"That she is. I'll make arrangements for you and Louise to have the executive cabin. It's really nice. The ship will dock in St. John's on Friday and pick you up the next Tuesday, the twenty-first. This will give you Saturday and Monday to negotiate the contract. You'll arrive back here in New York Harbor on Friday. I'll have Leona wire Mr. Clarke and let him know that you and Louise are coming. Leona will also make hotel reservations in St. John's for you."

At the close of the workday, Bob Marston drove his buggy from the docks toward home, which was also in Manhattan. He could hardly wait to tell Louise about the trip. It was set in his mind that since their neighbor, Frances Roberts, had often volunteered to take care of their children anytime they would need to be gone, he would suggest to Louise that they ask Frances to come stay with the children.

Bob passed through the business district in south Manhattan, turned into the residential area where the Marston home was located, and soon pulled the buggy into the driveway. He smiled when he saw his three children standing on the porch—as usual—waiting for him.

The Marstons had a modest frame house whose clapboard

exterior was painted gray with white trim. It sat like a jewel in the middle of a multicolored flower garden. That early in the spring, only the hardiest of plants were in full bloom, but still it was enough to brighten the yard and give a hint of what was to come with the summer weather.

As Bob pulled the buggy to a halt in front of the house, Mary, Johnny, and Lizzie dashed off the porch. When his feet touched ground, little Lizzie was ahead of the other two. "Papa! Papa!" she cried joyfully while lifting her arms in silent supplication for him to pick her up.

Bob swept the little girl into his arms and kissed her cheek, then held her in one arm while embracing Mary and Johnny with the other. Lizzie wrapped her arms around her father's neck, holding him tight, and planted a kiss on his cheek.

Louise appeared on the porch, observing with a smile as her children greeted their father.

As Bob headed toward the porch, the older two clung to his arm. Lizzie's blue eyes were dancing with joy as they climbed the porch steps.

Louise looked at the four-year-old. "Now, little Miss Lizzie, would you please let Mama give Papa a hug and a kiss?"

Lizzie grinned and shook her head. "You can hug and kiss him later." With that, she squeezed her father's neck and planted another kiss on his cheek.

Louise tickled her under the arm, and while the child was giggling, Bob hugged Louise and kissed her. After he had kissed her the second time, he said, "Honey, I've got some good news."

"Oh? Did you land the Manhattan Industries account?"

"Sure did, and that's good news for the company, and according to what Mr. Carr said, possibly a raise in salary for me."

Louise's eyes lit up. "Oh, darling, that's wonderful. I'm so proud of you."

"Thank you, sweetheart. But the good news I was referring to was something else."

"Well, while we head for the kitchen and the supper I've got prepared, tell me."

The children followed close behind their parents as they moved down the hall toward the kitchen. While Bob and Louise walked, holding hands, Bob told her about his upcoming business trip to Newfoundland and that she was going along.

They were just entering the kitchen. All three children hurried around in front of their parents.

Mary bounced on the balls of her feet. "Can we go, too, Papa? Please, oh, please? We'll be good, and we won't be any trouble, I promise! Why, you'll hardly know we're there!" The other two immediately joined in with Mary.

Bob held his hands up. "Wait a minute now, children!" He raised his voice to be heard over the commotion the trio was making in excited chorus. "This is not a vacation. It is a business trip for my company, and children don't go along on business trips."

The excitement died instantly with all three murmuring an "Oh-h-h." Dejection showed on their faces.

Bob gathered them in his arms. "Tell you what, though. We'll plan a nice vacation trip for all five of us this summer. How's that?"

"Well, okay," said Johnny. "But could we do something really exciting, like renting a boat and taking a ride on the East River?" His eyes were large with the prospect.

Bob smiled and messed up Johnny's hair. "Your mother and I will discuss it. I promise."

All three thanked him at the same time. They knew their father always kept his promises.

Bob gave all three a squeeze. "I'm going to ask Mrs. Roberts if she will come and stay with you while Mama and I are gone."

"Oh, goody!" piped up Lizzie. "I love Mrs. Roberts!"

"Me too!" said Johnny.

"And we'll be good for her," chimed in Mary.

"Tell you what," said Bob. "After supper, we'll all go next door and talk to her about it."

When the Marstons knocked on Frances Roberts's door, the widow welcomed them. While the children munched on fresh oatmeal cookies, Bob told Frances about the trip and asked if she would stay in their house with Mary, Johnny, and Lizzie while he and Louise were gone.

Frances hugged the children. "Bob, I'd be glad to. And since Pastor and Mrs. Moore always pick me up for Sunday school and church services, I'm sure they'll be glad to take these precious babies too, especially since their father is one of his deacons."

Bob laughed. "I know Pastor won't mind stuffing these kids in the back of his buggy. I'll talk to him about it Sunday at church."

On Monday evening, April 13, Pastor Darryl Moore and his wife, Dora, came to the Marston home for a visit. As Bob, Louise, and the children sat down with the Moores in the parlor, the pastor said, "Bob, Louise, I want to reconfirm what I told you yesterday at church. Dora and I will pick up Frances and these children for the church services while you are gone."

"We really appreciate it, Pastor," said Bob. "And were you able to contact your Canadian friend today and find out if there is a good Bible-believing church in St. John's?"

The pastor reached into his shirt pocket and pulled out a folded slip of paper. "Yes, and there is. I've written down the church's address and the pastor's name for you. My Canadian friend told me at this church they exalt Jesus and make His gospel plain and clear."

Bob took the paper and thanked Moore for helping him find a place to go to church. The pastor then led in prayer, asking God to watch over Bob and Louise while they were on their journey.

The next morning, an American Ship Lines company carriage came to the Marston home to pick up Bob and Louise and take them to the docks. Hugs and kisses were passed around while Frances Roberts looked on.

While Bob and Johnny were carrying the luggage to the carriage, Lizzie clung tenaciously to her mother with tears coming down her cheeks. Louise hunkered down in front of the trembling child. "Lizzie, sweetheart, it's only for a few days. You'll have so much fun with Mrs. Roberts. Remember all the plans she has for you? Games and baking cookies?"

"Y-yes, I remember," Lizzie said between sniffles.

"All right. Now be a good girl for Mama and enjoy your fun times. Papa and I will be home before you know it."

Mary stepped up and put her hands on Lizzie's shoulders. "She'll be fine, Mama. I'll take good care of her."

Louise stood up and gave Mary a grateful smile. "Thank you, dear. I know I can depend on you."

Bob and Johnny returned to the porch.

Bob hugged his youngest. "You have a nice time with Mrs. Roberts, Lizzie. Mama and I will bring you a present from Newfoundland, and we'll bring presents for Mary and Johnny too."

Lizzie smiled at him through her tears.

Bob patted the top of her head while speaking to all three children. "Be good for Mrs. Roberts, won't you?"

"We will, Papa," said Mary.

The children huddled close to each other while watching their parents hurry to the carriage. They waved as it pulled away, and Bob and Mary waved back.

Trying her best to be brave, Lizzie pressed a smile on her pinched face and kept waving until the carriage turned the corner and passed from view.

Mary held her little sister in her arms and told her Mama and Papa would be back soon. They would have a fun time with Mrs. Roberts while their parents were gone. Frances assured Lizzie they were going to have lots of fun. They would play lots of games, and Lizzie could help her bake cookies.

Lizzie looked at her with an impish grin on her lips. "Mrs. Roberts, can we bake cookies right now?"

"As soon as we get your sister and brother off to school, sweetie."

Frances led them all into the house.

Soon Lizzie's tears were dried up, and the four-year-old was having a good time with Frances in the kitchen while Mary and Johnny went off to school.

At the docks, Bob and Louise boarded the *USS Hampton,* and soon the freighter sailed out of New York Harbor and headed north on the Atlantic Ocean with clouds of black smoke billowing from the two huge smokestacks.

After standing by the rail at the bow on the main deck for almost an hour, Louise said, "Honey, let's go to the cabin and sit down for a while."

As they moved along the swaying deck, they watched the crew moving about the huge crates, checking the canvas covers.

"Why are they doing that?" Louise asked.

"Just need to make sure everything's covered right," said Bob.

"This time of the year, the Atlantic gets some real rainstorms."

"Well, I hope the storms wait till we're back home. I remember some of the storms you've been in at sea. I don't think I'd like that."

"They're no fun, honey, but unless they are especially severe, there's nothing to worry about. Besides, it isn't like we were going to Europe. It's only a few days."

They were almost to the door of their cabin when they saw the ship's captain, Duane Thraxton, coming toward them. Bob had been on other American Ship Lines vessels with him before, but Louise had met him for the first time when they first boarded the ship.

As Thraxton drew up, he said with a smile, "I hope everything's all right in your cabin."

"Couldn't be better," said Bob. "Louise especially likes the vase of flowers."

"Well, we did that especially for her. The flowers don't usually go with the cabin, no matter what American Ship Lines executive is traveling with us. But Mr. Carr told me to order them for her."

Louise smiled. "They sure are pretty. And they make the cabin smell beautiful."

One of the crewmen called for the captain from the bridge. Thraxton gave a signal with his hand, then told the Marstons they would be dining with him in his quarters that evening at six-thirty. He then hurried away.

When Bob and Louise entered their cabin, Louise picked up the small vase, smelled the flowers, then set it down, and looked at her husband with creases on her brow.

"Now, sweetheart, you're not worried about the children, are you?"

"Oh, I wouldn't say I'm worried. How about just concerned? Mainly for Lizzie."

Bob folded her in his arms. "Now, honey, Lizzie will be fine. You know how much she loves Frances. And besides, her big sister and brother will help take care of her. Let's just enjoy the trip."

The creases on Louise's brow disappeared as she smiled. "You're right. I'm just acting like a—"

"Like a mother," he chuckled.

The sky remained clear for the rest of the day, except for a few white clouds on the western horizon. After enjoying a magnificent sunset, the Marstons went to the captain's quarters and relished a delicious meal, prepared especially for the captain and his guests by the ship's cook.

The next morning, a strong wind was blowing across the sea, producing white caps on the surface as Bob and Louise rose to meet the new day. The eastern sky reddened with the rising sun, then blazed in vivid hues during the half hour it took to groom themselves and dress for breakfast, which they were to have with the captain.

As they made their way across the rocking deck toward the captain's quarters, the sky was slowly drained of color while dark clouds thickened overhead.

When they reached Thraxton's quarters, he was standing in his open door, talking to one of the crewmen. He gestured for them to step inside, and as they did, they heard him say to the crewman, "Yes, Arnold, we have a head sea and a fresh breeze."

Louise leaned close to her husband. "Honey, what does that mean?"

"It's seaman's talk for whitecaps and a twenty-knot wind. There just might be a storm coming."

"Oh. I hope not."

"It probably won't be a bad one. Don't worry."

Louise bit her lips as Captain Duane Thraxton stepped in and pulled the door shut.

"What do you think, Captain?" asked Bob. "Have we got a storm coming?"

"Looks like it," replied Thraxton, "but I don't think it's going to amount to anything." Noticing the look on Louise's face, he added, "Really, Mrs. Marston. There's nothing to worry about."

Bob grinned at her. "See there, honey, I told you so."

"Well, let's eat!" said Thraxton.

By the time Bob and Louise had returned to their cabin, the clouds were darker and the wind was stronger. She stood at the window and watched the coal smoke swirling skyward as it cleared the smokestacks and was carried away. She felt the bow of the ship rise and fall with the powerful swell of the ocean.

Bob stepped up behind her while the wind-driven salt spray drifted across the pitching deck and put his arms around her. "Now, honey, you mustn't let this upset you. We both heard Captain Thraxton say there's nothing to worry about. He's an old sea dog. He knows what he's talking about. Tell you what—let's go over here and pray about it."

"That sounds good to me," said Louise. "I just wish we'd see the Lord Jesus walking out there on the deck, and He would calm the storm like He did that day in the boat on the Sea of Galilee."

"You know that's not going to happen, sweetheart, but He is with us in the Person of the Holy Spirit. The storm will pass soon, I'm sure."

That night, the ship pitched and rolled on the rough sea, and the wind howled. Bob and Louise got little sleep.

The next morning, as the *USS Hampton* sailed past the southern tip of Nova Scotia, the Marstons were once again having breakfast with the captain.

As they sat at the table, Louise looked out the porthole. Focusing on the dry land, which was barely visible because of the swirling sea mists, she said, "Captain, wouldn't it be smart just to pull into the nearest port in Nova Scotia and wait this storm out?"

Thraxton grinned. "We would if I thought it was going to get any worse, ma'am, but the barometer in the wheelhouse is starting to rise, which means the storm will soon abate. We'll be out of it, shortly."

Louise ran the back of her hand across her forehead. "Oh, I'm sure glad to hear this. I feel better already."

Bob chuckled. "Good. Now, enjoy your breakfast."

When the Marstons returned to their cabin, the clouds were still low and dark and the wind continued to beat mercilessly against the ship. Louise was skeptical about the captain's barometer reading and told Bob she was still frightened. The storm was not letting up. Bob reminded her that Thraxton was well experienced, then read to her from the Bible and prayed with her. Suddenly, lightning was cracking through the dark black clouds, and thunder followed like bellows of rage.

Fear beat through Louise's chest like the frantic wings of a caged bird. She lunged for her husband and wrapped her arms around his neck. "Bob, I'm scared!"

Bob laid aside the Bible, folded her in his strong embrace, and held her tight, speaking soft words of encouragement.

Soon the rain was coming down in sheets and the wind continued to howl. It seemed that the waves and the dark sky were crashing together. Bob was still holding Louise when they heard loud, panicky shouts outside from the crewmen.

Bob let go of her, telling her he would be right back, and staggered to the cabin door with the ship swaying fiercely. He opened the door, and with the spray hitting his face, called out to a small group of crewmen who were clinging to a railing. "Hey! What's wrong?"

One of the men shouted back, "Some heavy cargo below deck came loose and crashed into the side of the ship! It's taking in water! Cap'n Thraxton has ordered all crewmen to get down there and bail water! We're trying to get there without being washed overboard!"

"I'll come and help!" shouted Bob.

"No, sir!" the man shouted back. "You stay right there with your wife!"

When Bob closed the door, Louise's arms went around him like bands of steel. "Oh, Bob, I heard what he said! We're going to sink! We're going to drown!"

Bob helped her back to the chair where she had been sitting, sat her down, and tried to calm her down, saying they would make it.

She screamed, "The captain shouldn't have believed that barometer! He shouldn't have relied on it!"

Bob could only hold her tight and attempt to relieve her fears.

It only grew worse when the ship started to list to the starboard side. Louise cried out when she looked through the window and saw huge waves washing over the deck, with the crewmen trying to keep from being washed overboard.

Suddenly the engines below went silent. Bob knew the ship was now at the mercy of the angry sea. Louise clung to him, digging her fingernails into his arms.

Waves once split by the prow of the ship were now the size of foothills on the broadsides and came crashing down on top of the *Hampton* from stem to stern. All at once there was a crash so loud, the Marstons thought the ship would head for the bottom of the ocean at once.

Abruptly, the cabin door came open, and Captain Duane

Thraxton was there, clinging to the doorframe. "The ship is sinking!" he shouted. "We've got to get into a lifeboat quick! Come on!"

Louise released a quivering wail of terror as Bob grabbed her, held her tight, and helped her to the door. When they were out on the pitching deck, Thraxton shouted, "Follow me!"

As they struggled across the deck toward the lifeboats on the starboard side, the crewmen were climbing into them as fast as they could.

Bob and Louise could see wooden crates bobbing on the surface of the churning sea, along with pieces of furniture and other debris from the ship.

Suddenly the ship listed so far toward the starboard side that the captain and the Marstons lost their footing. A huge wave broke over the ship and carried them swiftly into the wild, angry sea.

Louise screamed as they plunged into the water.

Bob was still holding her in his arms.

Chapter Four

On Friday afternoon, April 17, Frances Roberts walked little Lizzie Marston into the girls' bedroom. "All right, sweet baby, you have a nice nap now."

Lizzie paused at the side of her bed and looked up at her. "I'm really not sleepy, Mrs. Roberts. Do I have to take a nap if I'm not sleepy?"

Frances smiled and ran her fingers through the girl's curly blonde hair. "Like I told you yesterday, honey, your mama asked me to make sure you get your daily naps. It's good for little girls your age to get a nap in the afternoon. Come on, get up on your bed."

Lizzie obeyed, and when she lay on her back with her head on the pillow, she set her eyes on Frances. "If I should go to sleep, will you wake me up before Mary and Johnny come home from school?"

"I'll do that, sweet baby," she said, bending down and planting a kiss on her forehead. "I have a feeling if you lie here real quietlike, you'll be asleep in no time. Okay?"

"Okay."

Frances crossed the room to the door. She paused and smiled at the little girl. "Sleep tight."

"I'll try."

Frances closed the door and headed down the hall toward the parlor.

She smiled to herself, thinking how much she enjoyed taking care of the Marston children. She loved all three, but little Lizzie had found a very special place in her heart.

Bob and Louise had moved into this house on the day they were married, and Frances had been with Louise at the birth of all three babies. She had come to feel very much a part of the family. As old age had come upon her, she no longer had the energy nor the stamina she once did when caring for the lively youngsters, but since Mary was mature for her eight years, she was a help to her. Even then, by the end of each day since Bob and Louise had been gone, Frances was more than ready for bedtime, when she could crawl into the soft bed in the guest room and indulge in its comfort.

As Frances entered the parlor and eased into the soft overstuffed chair by the window, she thought about Lizzie, and how she had been especially energetic today. It was time for Lizzie's "nanny" to get a little rest too.

It was the sound of a neighbor's dog barking across the street that brought Frances out of her sound sleep. She opened her eyes, rubbed them gently, and looked out the window. Across the street, Mrs. Chelton was scolding her dog for barking, and with a grip on his collar, was leading him back inside the house.

Frances glanced at the grandfather clock on the other side of the room, and noted that it was almost three-thirty. Mary and Johnny would be home from school in less than half an hour. She rubbed her eyes again, and with difficulty—which was now normal—she left the chair.

Moments later, when Frances quietly opened the door of the girls' room and peeked in, she saw Lizzie lying on the bed smiling at her. "I been awake for a while, Mrs. Roberts."

"Well, I'm glad you went to sleep, honey. And that was a good girl to stay on the bed till I came to get you up. Want to go out on the front porch and wait for Mary and Johnny to come home?"

"Uh-huh." Lizzie rolled over on her stomach, slid off the bed, and hurried to Frances's side.

Moments later, they stepped out onto the front porch. Frances stepped to the railing, and leaning on it, ran her gaze over the colorful flowerbeds that surrounded the porch. Lizzie was waiting behind the comfortable canvas chair where Frances liked to sit. When Frances moved to the chair, the girl took hold of it to steady it, which was Johnny's job when he was home.

Secretly, Frances was hoping the older two would do something to occupy Lizzie when they got home, so she could get a few minutes' rest before starting supper.

Smiling, Lizzie stood in front of Frances. "Is there anything I can do for you, Mrs. Roberts?"

Frances smiled. "Not that I can think of, sweet baby. Just sit over here in one of these chairs so you can watch for your brother and sister."

"How about I sing for you?"

"That would be nice, honey."

"I been learning a new song in Sunday school. It's called 'Jesus Loves Me.' Wanna hear it?"

"Sure."

Lizzie took her usual stance for singing—one foot a half-step behind the other—and splayed her fingers, holding her hands at waist level.

Frances smiled. Lizzie loved to entertain, and it showed in her eyes.

"Jesus loves me, this I know;
For the Bible tells me so.
Little ones to Him belong;
They are weak, but He is strong.

Yes, Jesus loves me,
Yes, Jesus loves me,
Yes, Jesus loves me,
The Bible tells me so."

Frances clapped her hands. "That's really good, honey. God has given you such a sweet little voice."

Face beaming, Lizzie said, "I know another verse, Mrs. Roberts!"

"All right. Let's hear it."

Lizzie adjusted her stance slightly, splayed her fingers again, and began:

"Jesus loves me, He who died,
Heaven's gate to open wide;
He will wash away my—"

Lizzie heard a horse blow on the street, and saw a frown crease Frances's brow as she looked that direction. Lizzie pivoted and saw two uniformed policemen dismounting from their horses in front of the house.

As the officers started toward the porch, Lizzie turned to Mrs. Roberts. "How come those policemen are coming here?"

"I don't know, honey." She noted the solemn faces of the officers.

As the officers drew up to the porch steps, they both touched the brims of their caps. One of them said, "Ma'am, I am Officer

Harold Demers, and this is my partner, Officer Ed Holbrook. This is the Marston residence, isn't it?"

"Yes, sir," came France's reply. "But Mr. and Mrs. Marston are not home. They sailed to Newfoundland a few days ago, and won't be home till a week from today. My name is Frances Roberts. I live next door, over here on the east, and I'm staying here with the Marston children while their parents are gone."

Before either officer could speak, Lizzie spotted her brother and sister coming down the street. She dashed off the porch and ran toward them, calling out their names.

Frances looked up at the officers, who both appeared to be in their early thirties. "The two older children are just getting home from school. Is there something wrong?"

Officer Demers nodded and cleared his throat. "Yes, ma'am. We have some bad news, but we'll wait till the children can hear it, too."

Frances's face lost color. "Is it about Bob and Louise?"

Demers cleared his throat again. "Ah…yes, ma'am. But I'll only have to tell it once if we wait till the children are on the porch."

Down on the street, when Lizzie reached her sister and brother, both of them had already noticed the police officers on the porch.

As they continued walking toward the house, Johnny asked, "Lizzie, how come those policemen are on our porch?"

Lizzie shrugged. "I don't know."

Mary frowned. "How long have they been here?"

"Jus' a few minutes."

Mary looked at her brother. "Johnny, I can tell something is wrong by the look on Mrs. Roberts's face."

Johnny focused on Frances. "That's for sure."

Mary took hold of Lizzie's hand and looked at Johnny. "Let's run. Take Lizzie's other hand."

On the porch, the officers were watching the Marston children hurry their direction.

Frances said, "I think it would be best if you tell me what this bad news about Bob and Louise is. If something has happened to them, the bad news could devastate the children."

Officer Ed Holbrook said, "Ma'am, we will be as gentle as possible, but it is our duty to tell them what has happened. We have orders from our chief."

Frances bit her lip.

All three children were puffing as they reached the porch and bounded up the steps, eyes fixed on the uniformed men. Johnny and Mary still gripped their sister's hands.

Demers bent down, hands on his thighs just above the knees. "Children, I am Officer Harold Demers, and this is my partner, Officer Ed Holbrook." His eyes centered on the oldest. "I know your last name is Marston. What is your name, honey?"

"Mary." Her voice quivered slightly.

"And how old are you, Mary?"

"Eight."

He nodded, then set his eyes on the next oldest. "And what is your name, son?"

"Johnny."

"And you're how old?"

"Six. And my little sister's name is Lizzie. She's four."

"What's wrong, Officer Demers?" Mary asked.

Demers looked at Frances. "Could we go inside and sit down?"

"Of course," said Frances, and began her struggle to get out of the chair.

Johnny let go of Lizzie's hand and stepped to Frances, offering both hands. Officer Ed Holbrook stepped up. "I'll help her, Johnny."

The boy moved back and nodded.

When they were in the parlor and seated, the officers were facing Frances and the children. Lizzie sat between Mary and Johnny on the sofa, and Frances was next to Mary. Lizzie reached for her sister's hand, sensing that something bad had happened. The siblings sat close together, their wide, troubled eyes fastened on the two police officers.

Demers sat on the edge of his chair. He cleared his throat, fixing his gaze on the children. "Mary, Johnny, Lizzie…I have some bad news for you. I wish it could be different, but…but I must tell you that the ship your parents were taking to St. John's, Newfoundland, was in a fierce storm on the Atlantic Ocean yesterday, and—"

Demers cleared his throat again. "The ship sank some twenty miles off the coast of Nova Scotia. All but two crewmen were able to get into lifeboats and make it to the Nova Scotia shore. They—they reported to the Nova Scotia authorities that the ship's captain, your parents, and the other two crewmen were thrown into the sea by a huge wave that swept across the deck, and—and went into a watery grave. This information came to police headquarters by wire from the Nova Scotia authorities."

Frances's arm slid around Mary just as she and Johnny burst into tears. Seeing this, little Lizzie did the same, though she did not quite understand what had happened.

With tears flowing down her own wrinkled cheeks, Frances said, "Babies, listen to me. I know this is horrible news, and my heart goes out to you…but you must understand that your mama and papa are in heaven with Jesus."

Suddenly, Johnny jumped off the sofa and dashed out of the

parlor. He bolted through the front door, crossed the porch, and ran around the corner of the house. They all saw Johnny run past the parlor's side window, heading toward the backyard.

Wiping her own tears, Mary said, "Mrs. Roberts, I need to go to Johnny. Lizzie, honey, you stay here with Mrs. Roberts."

Frances valiantly gathered her wits about her. She leaned over, picked Lizzie up, and sat her on her lap. "Go on, Mary. I'll take care of Lizzie."

Mary hurried after her brother.

The officers watched Mary go, then Ed Holbrook set his gaze on Frances. "Mrs. Roberts, are there any relatives who can take the children and raise them?"

"No. There is no one."

Demers and Holbrook looked at each other.

"This is bad," said Demers. "We've got to find someplace for these poor children."

On Frances's lap, a puzzled Lizzie looked up into her face. There was a dull look of sorrow in her faded brown eyes. Frances drew a shuddering breath. "Officers, I would like nothing better than to take these three precious children into my home and finish raising them, but it just isn't possible. I'm almost eighty-two years old. They need someone younger and much more capable than I."

Demers nodded. "Yes, ma'am. We understand. Would you happen to know anyone who might take them in?"

"Only one thought comes to mind. My pastor—who is also the Marstons' pastor—may have someone in the church who could take them."

"All right," said Demers, taking a small paper pad from his shirt pocket, along with a pencil stub. "Would you tell me your pastor's name and where he lives?"

Frances gave him the information, which he wrote down.

Then Holbrook asked if the Marstons owned their house. Frances nodded. "Yes, but there is a mortgage on it."

"I see. Well, we will have to let the court handle it."

Mary caught up to Johnny in the backyard as he stopped and leaned against a tree, still sobbing. She took him in her arms and held him. As he sobbed, he bewailed the fact that their parents were dead, and that the three of them had no one to care for them.

Mary caressed her brother's face. "Johnny, as Mrs. Roberts said, Papa and Mama are in heaven with Jesus. We will be with them someday. The Lord loves us. He will take care of us. Please don't worry."

Johnny looked at her through his tears. "We won't be able to stay in the house. Where will we live?"

Mary bit down on her lower lip. She was trying to fathom the enormity of their predicament, but it was too much for one so young.

Louise had experienced a difficult time giving birth to Lizzie some four years earlier and had never completely regained her strength. From that time, Mary had always been her helper. She had learned to do many things in the past four years that most girls her age would find impossible to handle. Her mother had always been there to guide her, but now, Mary was overwhelmed with the task of comforting both Johnny and Lizzie without that guidance.

"I don't know where we will live, Johnny, but the Lord will see that we have a place to live, food to eat, and clothes to wear."

Johnny looked at her, his eyes puffy and red. "He will do that, won't He?"

"Yes."

Johnny's lower lip quivered. "I miss Papa and Mama."

"Me too. But just think how happy they are now. They are with Jesus."

The boy frowned. "But don't they miss us?"

"Of course they do, but being with Jesus in heaven is the most wonderful place to be. Mama and Papa know that you and I are saved, Johnny. They know that we'll be together with them in heaven someday. And you remember what Pastor Moore preached a few weeks ago about babies and little children going to heaven when they die? You know. It was the Sunday after Mr. and Mrs. Kirtland's little baby boy died."

"Uh-huh."

"Well, if anything happened to Lizzie right now and she were to die, she would go to heaven because she is too young to understand about sin and how to be saved. In his sermon, Pastor Moore showed from the Bible how when Jesus died on the cross and shed His blood, he provided for babies and little innocent children who would die. Mama and Papa know this. And when Lizzie gets old enough to understand these things, you and I will show her in the Bible how to saved, and we'll lead her to the Lord."

Johnny was comforted to a degree by his sister's words. He tried to be brave. "Yes. We'll do that. And…the Lord will take care of us with Mama and Papa gone."

Mary hugged him. "Yes, He will."

"We'd better get back inside, Mary. Lizzie needs us."

"I'm sure she does. Let's go."

When Mary and Johnny entered the house through the back door and walked past the kitchen toward the parlor, they saw the police officers and Frances Roberts go out the front door.

"Come on, Johnny," said Mary, breaking into a run.

Johnny followed on his big sister's heels, and they both moved through the door onto the front porch together.

The officers stopped and turned around, as did Frances, who had Lizzie's hand in her own. Frances looked at Johnny with concern in her eyes. "Are you all right?"

Johnny looked up at her with his reddened eyes. "I'm better, ma'am. Mary helped me. I'm…I'm very sad to know that Mama and Papa won't be coming home, but Mary made me feel better."

Frances pulled him close to her side. "I'm glad, Johnny." Then she said to Mary, "Thank you, sweetheart, for going to your little brother."

In spite of the sadness that was in her heart at the moment, Mary smiled at her, then set her eyes on Johnny. "I had to, Mrs. Roberts, because I love him, and he needed me."

Officer Holbrook had misty eyes as he said, "Children, I'm so sorry for this tragedy. I know how terrible it must be for you."

"Thank you, sir," said Mary.

"I'm sorry about it too," put in Officer Demers. "And I'm sure glad you have this kind lady to take care of you right now. We're going to Pastor Moore's home immediately to let him know what happened to your parents, and to see if he can find a family in the church who will take you in."

The appreciation Mary felt showed in her sky-blue eyes. "Thank you so much for doing what you can to help us."

Officer Demers laid a hand on her shoulder. "It's our pleasure, Mary. We wish we could just snap our fingers and make everything all right for you."

Mary managed another smile.

Demers turned to his partner. "Well, Ed, we'd better head for the parsonage."

Frances and the children looked on as the officers mounted up. Both men touched the brims of their caps and put their horses to a trot.

As they turned the corner, Demers said, "Ed, that little Mary is quite the young lady. What marvelous composure she displayed for an eight-year-old."

Holbrook nodded. "I'll say. Indeed she is quite the young lady. She's hurting every bit as much as her little brother, but she's keeping it inside for his sake, and no doubt for little Lizzie's sake too."

Standing on the front porch of the house, Frances and the children watched the officers until they passed from view.

"Let's go into the parlor," Frances said.

When they entered the parlor, Frances sat on the sofa and took Lizzie into her lap. Johnny snuggled up to her on one side, and Mary did the same.

Frances put an arm around Mary and an arm around Johnny. "Don't you sweet babies worry. The Lord is going to see that you have a home."

"We'll always miss Mama and Papa, though," Johnny said.

"Of course you will, honey. But just think how happy your mama and papa are right now. They are with Jesus. Not only that, but do you realize they are in the presence of all of those beautiful angels?"

Mary's eyes widened. "I hadn't thought of that. Mama and Papa have met Michael and Gabriel, haven't they?"

"They sure have. And you know what else?"

"What?"

"They are also in the presence of all those wonderful Bible saints like Moses, Daniel, Elijah, Paul, Peter, and John."

Johnny's eyes brightened. "Do you suppose they've met Abraham and Sarah?"

Frances smiled. "I'm sure they have."

Mary's eyes showed a glint. "And just think, Johnny: they've met the thief on the cross who got saved. And they've met Mary Magdalene and the woman who got saved at the well, and Nicodemus, and Lazarus, Mary, and Martha, and the Philippian jailer and his family. And they've met Jesus' mother, Mary, and Joseph, and John the Baptist…and—and—"

"The list goes on and on, doesn't it?" said Frances. "I'm glad this is a comfort to you. And something else—from what your mama and papa told me, both sets of your grandparents are in heaven, along with an uncle and three aunts."

Mary nodded. "Uh-huh. And they're all together, now."

"And someday you will see them again," said Frances. She glanced at the grandfather clock across the room. "Tell you what. It's almost suppertime. I know you're probably not feeling hungry after learning about the shipwreck and all, but I know that food helps in any situation. And you have to eat to keep up your strength. How about we go to the kitchen and fix us something to eat?"

Frances led them into the kitchen, and while she sliced brown bread and cheese and set a kettle of soup to heat up on the stove, Mary and Johnny set the table with Lizzie's help.

Mary poured milk in tin cups for herself and her siblings, and Frances brewed a pot of strong tea.

When they sat down at the table, Frances led in prayer, thanking the Lord for the food and that He was going to take care of the Marston children.

It was a somber gathering at the table as each one looked at the chairs that had always been occupied by Bob and Louise. Though the children had little appetite, Frances urged them to eat. There was some sniffling between bites, but Mary, Johnny, and Lizzie obeyed Frances, doing their best to eat enough to satisfy her.

They were just finishing when there was a knock at the front door.

Johnny pushed his chair back, saying he would get it, and hurried to the door. When he opened it, he found Pastor and Mrs. Moore looking at him with tender eyes.

The pastor picked him up and hugged him. "Johnny, the policemen came to see us and told us about your parents. We're so sorry."

Johnny's lips quivered as the sound of footsteps came from the hall and the Moores saw Mary and Lizzie coming their way, with Frances following.

Dora Moore immediately put her arms around the girls, held them tight, and told them she loved them.

They went into the parlor and sat down.

The pastor spoke words of comfort to the children about their parents being in heaven with Jesus. "Frances, tomorrow I'm going to make visits in the homes of the church members and see if any of them would become foster parents to Mary, Johnny, and Lizzie."

Frances nodded. "I'd take them if I could, Pastor, but at my age, I just can't do it. They will have needs that I simply can't provide."

Pastor Moore nodded. "I understand."

Dora sighed. "Pastor and I would love to take them, but as all of you know, we have both of our widowed mothers living with us. There just isn't any more room in the parsonage."

"We understand, Mrs. Moore," said Mary. "But thank you for wanting to."

After Pastor Moore had prayer with Frances and the children, they walked the couple to the door.

As the two of them stepped out onto the porch, the pastor said, "I'll be back sometime tomorrow after making my visits."

Frances thanked them for coming.

Chapter Five

When Frances Roberts awakened, she opened her eyes and glanced toward the window. Just outside the guestroom, sunbeams were filtering through the branches of the trees. The splash of sunlight formed a backdrop of emerald patches and golden bars on the wall opposite the window.

Frances sighed, threw back the covers, and rose wearily from the bed. She yawned, stretched her arms, and hobbled stiffly to the washstand. She looked at herself in the mirror on the wall, noting her tired eyes. After pouring water from a pitcher into the washbasin, she splashed it briskly on her face.

Most of her night had been spent in prayer for the precious Marston children, seeking God's comfort for them in the loss of their parents and asking for the wisdom she needed to give them the help they deserved.

As she dabbed a towel on her face, she looked at her reflection and shook her head. "If only I were younger," she said. "But what I see and feel this morning reaffirms what I said yesterday. Those sweet babies need young parents. People with means, and the energy to care for them and raise them."

Frances hung the towel on its rack and sighed. "Lord, please see that a Christian couple adopts them, even if there's no one in the church who can do it. Keep Your mighty hand of protection on them and guide them in their young lives." She brushed her hair, made the bun at the nape of her neck as usual, then dressed, made her bed, and went to the kitchen.

She built a fire in the cookstove, then took down the iron kettle from the compartment on top of the stove. *Oatmeal this morning,* she thought. *Since I was a small child, oatmeal has been a comfort food for me. And those dear children could use all the comfort available.*

With breakfast cooking, Frances slowly made her way down the hall to the girls' room. She paused at the closed door, listening for any sound from within. She heard the quiet murmur of voices, punctuated periodically with a sniffle.

"Lord, help me," she whispered, and opened the door. The pathetic scene that greeted her brought a lump to her throat. Lizzie was curled up in her sister's lap in the middle of Mary's rumpled bed. Mary had her arms around her and Lizzie's head lay on her chest. They both looked at Frances. Their usually bright eyes were dull and red-rimmed. Tears glistened on their pale cheeks.

Mary's voice cracked as she said, "We talked long into the night, Mrs. Roberts. And…and now Lizzie understands what death means, and that Mama and Papa will never be coming home."

Frances's hand went to her mouth as she hurried to the bed. She lowered her body on the bed and gathered both girls in her arms. She spoke softly to them, attempting to bring comfort to their broken hearts.

Mary was too young to carry this heavy load, and Frances could see that she was trying with everything that was in her to ease her little sister's heartache and give her comfort.

Moments later, Johnny appeared at the door with tears on his face. Mary saw him first, and when Frances noticed her looking toward the door, she turned her gaze. Sympathy lanced her heart and she extended a hand toward the boy. "Come here, Johnny."

As Johnny moved toward the bed, it was evident by the look on his face and the determined set of his jaw that he was trying desperately to do his best to be strong. But when he reached the bed, he began sobbing and crawled up onto the bed. Frances and the girls made room for him. He and his sisters clung to each other, seeking what solace they could find.

"Mary, Johnny," Frances said, her voice raspy, "you won't be going to school today. Lizzie needs you, and I'm sure you wouldn't be able to concentrate on your lessons."

Mary turned sad eyes on her. "Thank you, Mrs. Roberts. You're right. Johnny and I wouldn't be able to concentrate on what our teachers were saying. And we do need to be here with Lizzie. At least in this house, where everything reminds us of Mama and Papa, it makes us feel closer to them. And besides, Johnny and I would like to be here when Pastor Moore comes, so we'll know what happened about finding us a home."

Frances nodded. "Of course, honey."

"I was thinking about Pastor Moore talking to all those people about taking us into their homes to raise us…"

"Yes?"

"Will…will we have any say in the arrangements that are made for us? I mean, if someone wanted to take us, but we didn't think we would be happy there, would we be able to tell Pastor Moore how we felt?"

By the slight tremor in Mary's voice, Frances could tell she was fearful of the answer. She patted her cheek. "Honey, I'm sure Pastor Moore will want to hear how you feel about any home where you are being considered, and he'll take your feelings into consideration. But you must remember he can only do so much."

Mary lowered her eyes. "I know."

Frances put a chipper sound into her voice. "Tell you what, babies—I've made oatmeal for breakfast. Let's all go to the kitchen and I'll serve it up. You can get dressed after we eat."

It was a sad little trio that walked down the hall and found their places at the big round table.

Johnny took one look at the chairs his parents had always occupied, swallowed hard, and said in a squeaky voice, "Mama and Papa will never sit in those chairs again."

In unison, he and his sisters burst into tears.

Frances gathered them in her arms again. "It's all right, babies. Go right on and cry. God gives us tears as a means of helping our broken hearts to heal."

All three clung to her tenaciously while tears flowed.

"Did you know that in the Bible, it says that God puts our tears in a bottle? He keeps our tears and remembers our broken hearts."

Johnny sniffed and looked up with awe in his eyes. "Really?"

"Yes, really. The Lord said He will supply all our needs. You remember that Pastor Moore preached on this subject not long ago, don't you?"

"Yes, ma'am."

"Well, God knows that when we have a broken heart, it has a need. It needs healing. So He has supplied a way to heal it. Somehow, our tears help to heal our broken hearts."

Johnny sniffed again. "Wow! He is a great God, isn't He?"

"Yes, Johnny. Indeed He is."

Frances dished up the hot oatmeal, added a pat of butter and a lump of brown sugar to each bowl, and placed them before the children. Then she put a stack of buttered toast in the middle of the table and a cup of milk at each child's plate.

She brought her own bowl of oatmeal and a cup of coffee and took her seat. Heads were bowed, and Frances prayed over the food. She also asked the Lord to comfort the Marston children in their sorrow.

When she lifted her head and opened her eyes, all three of the children sat staring at their food. "Well, go ahead. Eat your breakfast."

Mary, Johnny, and Lizzie set pain-filled eyes on her.

"Oh. Now, sweet babies, I know it isn't easy to swallow past the lump each of you has in your throat, but please try. You must eat. Your parents would want you to eat. Let's do it for Mama and Papa, okay?"

Mary's voice was strained as she said to her brother and sister, "Let's eat for Mama and Papa."

When breakfast was finished, Mary said, "Mrs. Roberts, I'll do the housecleaning while you and Johnny are washing and drying the dishes."

"I'll help you clean the house, Mary," volunteered Lizzie.

The foursome stayed busy with a variety of chores while they remained alert for the sound of hoofbeats. They were hopeful that when Pastor Moore arrived, he would have good news.

While Mary went about sweeping and dusting, Lizzie was close by, doing what she could to help. Often Lizzie would move up to Mary and cling to her. She would stop her work and simply hold her little sister until once again she was comforted.

It was early afternoon when the buggy came to a halt in front of the house, and all three of the Marston children bolted through the door and onto the porch with Frances not far behind.

A chorus of voices greeted Pastor Darryl Moore, and he greeted them in return as he stepped out of the buggy. Frances could tell by the look in the pastor's eyes that all was not well, but pretending not to notice, she invited him in and they all went into the parlor and sat down. Frances and the children were seated on the sofa, facing the pastor, who was in an overstuffed chair. Lizzie was on Frances's lap, with Mary on one side and Johnny on the other.

Pastor Moore cleared his throat. "Well, my news is not the best. There is no one in the church who can take you children on a permanent basis. We have some families who are willing to take you temporarily, but even then, you will have to be split up. There is no one who has space for all three of you."

Mary leaned forward. "Pastor Moore, is there someone who would take two of us? I have to be with Lizzie, even if Johnny has to stay somewhere else."

Johnny felt a cold ball like ice form in his stomach. He couldn't bear the thought of being separated from his sisters.

Pastor Moore nodded. "I'll see what I can do, Mary. I think there is one family who might take both of you girls. I will talk to them, and let you know as soon as I can."

Frances and the children walked the pastor to the door, and when he was driving away, Johnny began to cry.

Mary looked at him with concern in her eyes. "Johnny, what's wrong?"

"I don't want to be separated from you and Lizzie!" he sobbed. "You two will have each other, but what about me? I'll be alone! I'm only six years old. Mama and Papa are dead. I need to be with my sisters!"

While Frances and Lizzie looked on, Mary wrapped her arms around her little brother. "Johnny, I don't want to be separated, either. The Lord will fix it. He will give us a family somewhere who will take all three of us. We'll try not to be a bother to them. We'll work hard to do our part around their house. Surely there's someone that will understand and let us stay together."

Johnny's entire body shook as he continued to sob.

Mary hugged him tighter. "Please stop crying, Johnny. It's going to be all right. I won't let them separate us."

Johnny's blinked at his tears. A hopeful look came into his eyes. "Promise?"

Mary took a deep breath. Her throat tightened, but she got it out. "I promise." She kissed his cheek and released her hold on him.

Johnny sniffed, ran a shirtsleeve across his face, and looked up at Frances. "Mrs. Roberts, why did God take Mama and Papa to heaven when we need them so much?"

The silver-haired woman met his questioning gaze. "I can't tell you why He took your parents, Johnny. But I can tell you this— God never makes mistakes. He had a reason for doing so, but we might not know what it was till we get to heaven and He explains it to us. Let's go into the parlor. There's a Scripture I want to show you that is related to your question."

Moments later, the children were seated on the sofa, and Frances was on the chair where the pastor had sat earlier. Johnny had gone to the guest room and brought Frances's Bible to her.

She opened the Bible, and while she was flipping pages, she said, "I want to read you a very special verse from Romans chapter 8." She found the page. "It's verse 28. Paul is addressing God's people. Listen. 'And we know that all things work together for good to them that love God, to them who are the called according to his purpose.' Did you notice he said *all* things?"

Mary nodded. "Yes, ma'am. I remember Mama and Papa talking about this verse. Papa pointed out the word *all*. And he pointed out the words *work together*. He said all things that come into our lives are not good, but that they *work together* for our good."

"He was right, honey. And only God could make it work like that. What I wanted to do was to help you understand that *all things*—including this tragedy—will work together for good, and you will see it one day."

Johnny set serious eyes on Frances. "Mrs. Roberts?"

"Yes, honey?"

"Mary told me that God will take care of my sisters and me. She said He will see to it that we have food and clothes and a place to live. Do *you* believe He will?"

Frances smiled. "I sure do, Johnny. Let me read you what the Lord Jesus said about that. It's in Matthew chapter 10."

She flipped pages. "Verses 29 through 31. Listen to Jesus as He talks about little sparrows."

Lizzie's eyes came to life. "I like sparrows, Mrs. Roberts!"

"You do, huh?"

"Mm-hmm. They come into our yard a lot. And doves do too. Sometimes Mama lets me put out bread crumbs for 'em."

Frances nodded. "Well, listen to what Jesus said about those little sparrows, honey. 'Are not two sparrows sold for a farthing? and one of them shall not fall on the ground without your Father. But the very hairs of your head are numbered. Fear not therefore, ye are of more value than many sparrows.' When Jesus said that one of those little sparrows shall not fall to the ground without your Father, He is telling us that those little sparrows are never alone. God is always with them."

"Mrs. Roberts?" Mary said.

"Yes, dear?"

"Didn't Jesus talk about the little sparrows in the book of Luke, too?"

"Yes, He did, honey. He said almost the same thing, but it might be good if I show it to you. The way Jesus put it in Luke's gospel strengthens what I was about to say next." Turning to Luke 12:6–7, she said, "Now, listen closely. 'Are not five sparrows sold for two farthings, and not one of them is forgotten before God? But even the very hairs of your head are all numbered. Fear not therefore: ye are of more value than many sparrows.'

"Now, we saw in Matthew that Jesus spoke of a little sparrow falling to the ground, but that our heavenly Father is right there with him when he does. As I said, He is telling us that those precious little sparrows are never alone. God is always with them. In Luke's account, Jesus said that not one of them is forgotten before God. Sometimes in our lives, things happen that break our hearts. And sometimes we feel so lonely in our troubles that we think God has forsaken us and even forgotten us. But Jesus is trying to get us to see that this will never happen. Notice in both accounts, he tells us not to be afraid because we are of more value than many sparrows.

"Do you see what Jesus is saying, children? God provides nests for little sparrows to live in, food for them to eat, and feathers to clothe them. A sparrow's home is his nest. A human's home is his house. The Lord Jesus, who loves *you*, Mary, Johnny, and Lizzie, is telling you that since God loves little sparrows and always remembers them, He will take care of you. He will provide you a home, food, and clothing because each of you is of more value than many sparrows."

Lizzie picked up on what Frances was telling them. Her eyes brightened as she exclaimed, "Mary! Johnny! We're God's little sparrows!"

In spite of the sorrow in their hearts, this brought a laugh to the others.

The elderly woman left her chair, bent down, wrapped her arms around all three, and hugged them tight. With tears in her eyes, she said, "I love these little sparrows!"

On Sunday afternoon, April 19, a group of older children—seven boys and one girl—were playing roughhouse games on the sidewalk in the 1200 block on Canal Street in south Manhattan. The entire block, on both sides, was made up of tenement houses.

While playing, some of the children noticed a man in his early thirties coming along the sidewalk, but paid him little attention until he drew up and said, "Could I interrupt for a moment?"

One of the boys, who looked to be about thirteen, said, "What can we do for you, mister?"

"Do any of you happen to know which tenement Mr. Curtis Holden lives in?"

All seven boys looked at the girl, who at the moment was measuring the man with her eyes. One of them said, "Mr. Holden lives in this very tenement you are standing in front of, sir." Then pointing to the girl, he added, "This is Josie, Mr. Holden's daughter."

Josie smiled at the man. "What is your name, sir?"

"I'm Matthew Clark, Josie. Perhaps your father has mentioned my name."

Josie's smile broadened. "Yes. Papa has talked a lot about his good friend, Matt Clark. I know you grew up together in Little Rock, Arkansas, and were best friends as boys."

"You're right about that, Josie. It's been too many years since Curtis and I have seen each other. I'm in New York on business. Do you know the name Will Barton?"

"No, sir."

"Well, he's a mutual friend of your papa's and mine in Little Rock. He's had contact with your papa sometime in the not-too-distant past, and told me that he lived on Canal Street here in

Manhattan. I sure want to see him before I head back to Arkansas. Is he home?"

"He sure is. I'll take you up to the apartment."

"I appreciate that."

Josie turned to the boys. "I'll be right back."

With that, she led Matt Clark into the tenement and up to the third floor to apartment number 28. She opened the door and Matt followed her inside.

"Papa!" Josie called. "There's an old friend of yours here to see you!"

Seconds later, Curtis Holden appeared from the rear of the flat, and a smile broke over his face when he saw his old friend. "Matt!"

"Hello, old pal!"

The two men embraced, pounding each other on the back, then Curtis started asking questions about what had brought Matt to New York.

Before Matt could begin his explanation, Josie said, "Papa, excuse me, please."

"Yes, honey?"

"I'll go back down and play with the boys so you and Mr. Clark can talk, okay?"

"Sure. Have fun."

She giggled. "Whipping boys in our games is always fun, Papa." With that, she was gone.

Matt laughed. "That's some kind of girl you've got there, Curtis."

"And don't I know it. Come on. Let's sit down."

The two old friends sat down in chairs close to a window that overlooked the street. Matt explained about the business that brought him to New York, and while doing so, he glanced down on the street and saw Josie appear and join the boys once again in a roughhouse game.

When Matt finished his explanation, Curtis said, "Well, I'm sure glad you looked me up."

"I wouldn't get this close without trying to see my old pal." Matt looked back down at the children at play. "Curtis, that's one pretty little girl. She sure looks like her mother." He chuckled. "And she's holding her own with those boys, too."

"She's quite the tomboy. Yet she is very feminine."

"So Josephine became Josie, eh?"

"Mm-hmm. She picked up the nickname when she was about two years old."

"And she's what, now? Twelve? Thirteen?"

"Twelve."

"Hardly seems possible. Let's see, it's been seven years since Carrie died, hasn't it?"

"It will be in another month. It was just too much for both Josie and me to stay in the apartment where we lived then. Too many things reminded us of Carrie. So we moved here about six weeks after she died. And I want to thank you for the letter you sent when you found out from one of Carrie's childhood friends in Little Rock that she had died giving birth to our little son."

"It was the least I could do. The baby died at the same time, if I remember correctly."

"Yes. Within minutes after Carrie did."

Matt nodded. "Seven years. Do you…ah…have some young lady in your life, now? Any plans to marry?"

Curtis grinned. "Not really. I have some lady friends in the neighborhood, but no one I'm serious about." He chuckled. "If and when I find one I'm really interested in marrying, she will really have to be something to get Josie's approval. I guarantee you, she'll be very picky about a stepmother."

"I tell you, that girl really resembles Carrie. Not only in facial features, but she has the same dark hair and flashing green eyes."

"For sure. And she also has her mother's sweet disposition and tender personality. Now that she's maturing, it's almost like having Carrie with me again." He choked up, swallowed hard, and wiped away a tear from his eye.

"I'm sure that's true," Matt said softly. "So what are you doing for a living?"

"I'm a laborer for the Roebling Construction Company. One of New York's biggest construction companies. Have you heard anything about the Brooklyn Bridge being built here?"

"Why, yes. There was something about it in the *Little Rock News* back when it was first started. That's been a while."

"Mm-hmm. It was first begun back in 1869. By the Roebling Construction Company."

"Really? And are you going to tell me that you are working on that bridge?"

"Sure am."

"Well, I'll be. And this Brooklyn Bridge is from Brooklyn to where?"

"Manhattan Island."

"Oh, sure. Come to think of it, there was an article in the *Little Rock News* about it more recently. Probably a year ago. It spans the East River, doesn't it?"

"Yes, sir. It will when it's finished. That's a long way off, though. We expect it to take us a total of twelve or thirteen years from start to finish. So we've got another seven or eight years to go."

"So how long will the bridge be when it's done?"

"One thousand five hundred and ninety-five feet."

"Wow."

"It'll be the world's largest suspension bridge, Matt."

"Mmm. Sounds like some project."

"It is.

Matt's brow furrowed. "I recall that the more recent article told about some of the construction workers who have been killed. Quite a few, isn't it?"

"Well, it could be a lot worse, but to date, seven men have lost their lives in work accidents. The very first to be killed was John Roebling, who owned the company. He was killed in October 1869. His son, Wash Roebling, has headed up the company since then."

Matt nodded and looked back down on the sidewalk. "Well, lookee there! Josie's wrestling with one of the boys. Hah! He's bigger than she is, and she's got him down on the sidewalk so he can't move!"

Curtis focused on the scene below. He grinned and laughed. "She's some tomboy, all right. When you see her like that, it's hard to believe that she is really very feminine in her ways. I'll have to say, though, that she enjoys doing the small handyman jobs with me that I do around town on my off-hours from the job on the bridge. She can handle a saw, a screwdriver, and a wrench quite well. Josie and I have become very close in these past seven years, Matt."

"I'm glad for that. You need each other."

"Actually, Matt, Josie's tomboyishness developed after her mother and baby brother died. She was trying to fulfill my need for the son I wanted and lost. At the same time, though, Josie takes her mother's place in the home, doing the cooking, the housework, and the sewing, in addition to going to school and doing her homework. She began doing this when she was nine years old."

Matt smiled. "Like I said, old pal, that's some kind of girl you've got there."

Curtis nodded.

Matt took out his pocket watch and looked at it. "Well, I hate to say this, but I've got to be going."

As both men rose to their feet, Curtis said, "I'm just glad you could come by. Thanks for thinking of me."

Matt cuffed him playfully on the shoulder. "Hey, we're pals. I'm just glad you were home."

Curtis walked downstairs with Matt, and when they moved outside, they both laughed when they saw Josie pinning another one of the boys.

They moved to the spot where Josie was holding the boy down. Breathing hard, she looked up at them and grinned. "Hello, Mr. Clark, Papa."

Matt snickered. "I sure wouldn't want to get on your bad side, Josie. You'd probably put me down and pin me too."

Josie let go of the boy, allowing him to get up. Embarrassed, he darted away as she rose to her feet, brushed off her dress, and caught her breath. She giggled. "Well, Mr. Clark, if you want to wrestle, I'm ready."

Matt laughed and shook his head. "Oh no, you don't! I don't want to get embarrassed like that boy did."

Chapter Six

On Monday, April 20, at the West End Orphanage in Manhattan, the playground was busy with children playing hopscotch to tag to baseball under a partly cloudy sky.

In the medical office and examining room, Deborah Williams—the orphanage's new nurse—was busy arranging things to her own liking. It was her first day on the job, and while she worked at the rearrangement task, the pleasant sound of happy children at play came through the open windows.

Moving to one of the windows that overlooked the playground, the young nurse ran her gaze over the running, hopping, jumping, laughing, shouting boys and girls whom she knew ranged in age from four years old to their early teens. Deborah rubbed her chin as she made mental notes of each child. She knew that sooner or later, for one reason or another, she would have to tend to each one of them.

Deborah shook her head in amazement at all the energy they exerted. She smiled to herself and started to turn away from the window, but halted when her attention was drawn to one solitary little figure standing in the far corner of the fenced-in playground. All the other children were playing in groups or teams, except for this pitiful little lad.

The boy was standing with his back pushed tight against the fence, his hands shoved into his pockets. His head was bent low with the warm spring sunshine glinting off his blond hair. He was digging the toe of his right shoe into the dirt.

Deborah frowned. "I don't think I've ever seen such a woebegone little creature in my life."

While she stood there at the window with her gaze fixed on the little boy, it was as if he felt her eyes on him. He raised his head and looked directly at her. Deborah's heart seemed to turn over in her chest when she saw his solemn little face, streaked with tears.

Her hand went to her mouth. "Oh, little fellow, what's wrong?" She wheeled and darted out the door.

The boy saw her coming and kept his eyes on her while wiping tears from his cheeks.

Deborah drew up and laid her hands on his shoulders. "My name is Miss Deborah Williams, honey. I'm the new nurse. What's your name?"

He sniffed, blinking at fresh tears that were welling up in his eyes. "J-Jimmy K-Kirkland."

"How old are you?"

"F-five."

"Jimmy, why are you crying?"

Jimmy's voice quavered as he said, "B-becauthe th-thome of the k-kidth were t-teathing m-me about th-the—th-the way I t-talk."

Deborah's heart went out to little Jimmy because of his speech impediment. His stuttering was emphasized even more by his decided lisp.

"Jimmy, I'm sorry they were teasing you. Do they tease you a lot?"

He sniffed again, clinging to her. "Uh-huh. All th-the t-time."

She picked him up in her arms, carrying him toward the building. "Well, Jimmy, this teasing has got to stop. We're going to go talk to Mr. Myers about it right now."

Two minutes later, with Jimmy still in her arms, Deborah drew up to the office of orphanage superintendent Walter Myers. The door stood open, and Myers looked up from his desk when his attention was drawn to the nurse and the boy. "Yes, Miss Williams?"

"Mr. Myers, I need to talk to you."

Myers stood up and nodded. "Certainly. Come in."

Deborah sat down in front of the desk, holding a sniffling Jimmy Kirkland on her lap.

Myers eased back down onto the desk chair. "Is something wrong with Jimmy?"

"Not physically, sir...but emotionally."

Deborah proceeded to tell the superintendent how she happened to look out the window of the medical office to see Jimmy standing on the playground, crying. She explained that Jimmy told her some of the boys and girls had been teasing him about the way he talked.

Myers, who was in his late fifties, pulled his lips into a thin line and nodded. "Yes, it has happened many times, but never when someone in authority in the orphanage is around to see it. Jimmy has been asked before to name the guilty parties, but has always refused to do so. I know it's because he's afraid what the boys will do to him if he identifies them."

Deborah looked down at the towheaded child on her lap. "Is that true, Jimmy?"

Jimmy nodded, fear showing in his eyes.

Myers lowered his head and looked the boy in the eye. "How about this time, Jimmy? Will you tell Mr. Myers who was teasing you about your stuttering?"

The fear was still in Jimmy's eyes. He shook his head. "Hmmpmm."

"Was it just boys, son?"

Jimmy shook his head again.

"Girls too?"

The boy nodded.

Deborah hugged Jimmy close to her. "Mr. Myers, something has to be done about this."

"I agree, but unless I know who to deal with, it's pretty difficult to stop it."

"How long has Jimmy been here at the orphanage?"

"Since he was no more than two or three days old. We found him on the orphanage doorstep one morning, wrapped in a blanket. A note was pinned to the blanket, saying the baby's name was James Kirkland and that the parents were too poor to keep him."

Deborah bit her lips and laid her cheek in a loving manner against Jimmy's head.

Myers went on. "We contacted the police. They did a search among the city's Kirklands, but no Kirklands were found who could have been the baby's parents. The police concluded that the name was false. But since we needed a name for the little guy, we registered him as James Kirkland, and of course, called him Jimmy."

Deborah kissed the top of Jimmy's blond head. "Well, honey, I'm glad at least that your parents left you on the doorstep of the orphanage, rather than in a trash receptacle in some alley downtown."

Myers leaned toward the boy again. "Jimmy, I want you to know that I understand why you're afraid to name those boys and girls who tease you. They said they would hurt you if you told on them, didn't they?"

Jimmy nodded. "Mm-hmm."

Myers sighed, eased back in the chair, and looked at Deborah. "Well, I've had enough of this. I'm going to have a meeting and do something about it."

After supper that evening, the staff of fourteen men and women and the three hundred and seven orphans met in the orphanage's small auditorium. Walter Myers stood before them on the platform and told them of the incident that day when Miss Williams found Jimmy Kirkland crying on the playground because some of the boys and girls had been teasing him about his speech impediment.

The superintendent had the undivided attention of the crowd as he frowned deeply. "I am thoroughly ashamed of you boys and girls who have made fun of Jimmy's speech problem. He can't help it that he talks the way he does. He was born with the problem, and it is cruel for you guilty ones to tease him about it. Any one of you could have been born with the same impediment. You ought to thank God that you weren't and show kindness and sympathy to Jimmy."

Among the orphans, many were exchanging glances.

Myers went on. "I know that some of you boys who have picked on Jimmy have told him you would hurt him if he told anyone who you are. He has not told anyone. Believe me, if he had, you would be in real trouble. Do you understand that? Every one of you who has teased him should apologize to him."

Staff members were nodding their agreement.

Myers ran his gaze over the young faces. "Listen close, now. Even though Jimmy refuses to tell me who the guilty parties are, sooner or later, I am going to find out. And I assure you, the punishment is going to be severe. Whoever you are, you are mean little cowards and you deserve to be punished. So if you want to face the consequences, just go on being cowards. You will be found out. On the other hand, if you will go to Jimmy and tell him you are sorry for what you have done to him and ask his forgiveness, you will spare yourself the punishment I've got planned for you. You see, when I find out who you are, but Jimmy tells me you came to him for forgiveness, there will be no punishment."

Myers dismissed the meeting and conversed on the platform with some of the staff members.

Jimmy Kirkland was sitting beside Deborah Williams on the front row of seats while the children were milling about the auditorium, talking.

Deborah leaned over and said, "Jimmy, I'm going to leave you now, so if there are any of those who want to ask your forgiveness, they can do so without me listening."

Jimmy nodded. "All r-right."

Deborah mounted the platform steps and joined in the group conversation with the superintendent.

Less than a minute had passed when Jimmy saw two of the girls coming toward him who had teased him that very morning about his speech problem. Leah Penrose was eleven years old and Nadine Sellers was ten.

Jimmy stayed seated as they drew up and looked down at him.

Leah said, "Jimmy, Nadine and I are sorry for teasing you this morning. Will you please forgive us?"

"Please, Jimmy," added Nadine. "We were wrong to do that. We really are sorry, and we want to be forgiven."

Unknown to the girls, the conversation on the platform had been stopped abruptly, and the adults were looking on. The majority of the orphans were also observing the scene.

Jimmy nodded. "Yeth, I f-forgive you, b-both."

Walter Myers stepped to the edge of the platform and spoke so all could hear. "I heard every word you said, Leah and Nadine. I want you to know that I am proud of you for asking Jimmy's forgiveness." He raised his eyes to the rest of the orphans in the auditorium. "Did you all hear that? Leah and Nadine just came to Jimmy and asked him to forgive them for teasing him this morning about his speech impediment. Because they have done this, they will not be punished. Who else wants to come down here and ask Jimmy to forgive them?"

There was dead silence and no movement.

Myers looked down at the boy. "Jimmy, come up here on the platform with me."

Jimmy left his seat, mounted the steps, and halted in front of the superintendent. He looked up at him questioningly.

Myers laid a hand on his shoulder. "Would you like to tell me right now who the others were that teased you?"

Jimmy shook his head. "N-no, thir."

The superintendent ran his gaze over the faces of the orphans. "You all heard that. He still won't tell me who the cowards are. Leah and Nadine did the right thing. Jimmy has forgiven them, and so have I. The other guilty parties have one more chance to make it right. Come on."

Still there was dead silence and nobody moved.

Myers set his jaw. "All right. You can all go to your rooms."

Moments later, when the children were in the halls heading for their rooms, four boys, ranging from ten to twelve years of age made a circle around Jimmy, making sure there were no adults around. A twelve-year-old named Butch Hankins was their leader. Butch stood in front of Jimmy with a hard look in his eyes. "It's a good thing you didn't name us, you stutterin' little weasel. If you had, we'd have beat you to a bloody pulp and told

Myers you fell down the stairs. You ain't gonna tell him, are you?"

Jimmy shook his head. "I w-won't."

The bullies mocked his speech, then one of them punched Jimmy's shoulder hard enough to inflict some pain, and they walked away laughing, looking back at him.

Jimmy fought the tears that were threatening to spill, not wanting them to see him crying.

On that same Monday, Jody Claiborne was riding Queenie at a gallop across the Wyoming plains. Since there would be no school that week due to a teachers' convention in Cheyenne, Jody had plans to visit some of the neighboring ranchers. Wednesday would be a special day. She and Betty Houston had another race planned.

Jody loved to ride. To her, it seemed she had been born on a horse. Her father had often said she could ride like a burr sticking in a horse's mane. While Queenie carried her across the plains along the south bank of the Lodgepole River, Jody let the wind caress her face and breathed the pleasant aroma of the sage.

The scene around her awoke a sweet gratitude to the Lord for the fullness of her life in this vast country. She was rapt with love for all she beheld from her lofty perch: the swift Lodgepole River flowing toward the lower country like a golden ribbon in the Wyoming sun; a bald eagle poised like a feather on the air, silhouetted against the deep velvet azure of the sky; the grazing cattle on the surrounding ranches, making black dots on the sage; and the beckoning range before her that swept into the distance where the majestic Rocky Mountains lifted their proud peaks toward heaven.

Soon the front gate of the *Diamond L* ranch came into view. Moments later, Jody slowed Queenie to a trot, then a walk. She smiled to herself as she turned onto Lakin property. She was eager to see how Lorraine and Maisie were doing since they had come to the Lakin home.

As Jody trotted Queenie down the winding lane that led to the small ranch house, she saw the two girls on the front porch. Suddenly Lorraine dashed to the door, opened it, and shouted something. Seconds later, Hap and Margie appeared. All of them waved to Jody, and Jody waved back. Seconds later, she drew up and slid from the saddle. Both girls bounded off the porch and opened their arms as they ran toward her.

While Lorraine and Maisie hugged Jody, Hap and Margie looked on, smiling. Jody was then invited to sit with them on the porch. Margie and Lorraine went inside while Jody sat down with Hap and Maisie climbed up on her lap.

Moments later, Margie and Lorraine appeared with tea and cookies. When everyone was seated, Jody said, "I wanted to come by and see how these girls are doing."

"We're doing fine, Jody," said Lorraine. "We just love it here with Mama and Papa."

"Yeah!" said Maisie, turning on Jody's lap to look up into her eyes. "And guess what!"

"What?"

"Mama and Papa are gonna 'dopt us!"

Jody looked at Hap and Margie. "Really?"

"Really," said Hap. "We have an appointment with Judge Morton in Cheyenne in just about an hour and a half."

"Oh! Well, you'll have to be leaving pretty soon."

"You finish your tea, honey," said Margie. "We have a few minutes before we have to leave. We're just so glad you came to see us."

Maisie looked up at Jody again. "Yeah! We sure are!"

Hap grinned. "I think you've made a friend for life, Jody.

Maisie talks about you every day. The love you showed her that day at the railroad station has made a deep impression on her."

Maisie twisted around on Jody's lap, raised up on her knees, and planted a kiss on her cheek. "I love you, Jody."

Jody returned the kiss. "I love you too, sweetie."

"Will you come back and see us some more?"

"I sure will, Maisie. I sure will."

Soon the Lakins were in the family wagon, headed toward Cheyenne. Jody rode alongside them until she came to a fork in the road that would lead her home.

Hap and Margie thanked her for the visit, and as she put Queenie to a gallop, Lorraine and Maisie called to her and waved. With her long, dark hair flying in the wind, Jody waved back.

The next evening, Emma Claiborne was busy preparing supper in the kitchen when she happened to glance out the back window while slicing hot bread. She smiled to herself when her eyes focused on Sam and Jody, who were coming toward the house from the barn.

Jody had been helping her father with the evening chores, and Jody was carrying the milk pail. It pleased Emma that Jody was such a tomboy and loved to help her father with the chores. It was their special time together. They were chatting and laughing as they approached the back porch.

Emma carried the plate of fresh bread to the table and smiled as they climbed the porch steps and she heard Jody sniff. "Daddy, do you smell that? I hope it's what I think it is."

Sam chuckled. "Smells like fried chicken and all the trimmings to me. Let's hurry!"

Emma heard Jody pour the milk into the strainer and set the

pail down. They made short work of washing their hands at the galvanized tub on the back porch, then entered the kitchen.

Emma turned from the stove with the plate of crispy fried chicken in her hands, her cheeks rosy from the heat and her eyes sparkling. "Yes, you two, it's your favorite meal. And I sure hope it tastes as good as it smells."

Jody followed her mother, watched her set the plate of chicken on the table, then hugged her. "Mommy, you've never failed yet with your fried chicken dinner! Let's eat!"

The Claiborne family sat down to supper. After thanking the Lord for the food, they began eating. The conversation went to Pastor Dan Forbes and his wife, Clara, who had been talking about the orphan train that was arriving in Cheyenne the next morning. The Forbeses had shared with the Claibornes recently that since Clara could not have any more children, they were praying about taking one of the orphans from the train.

Since they had Peter and Paul, who were twelve and ten, they would like to take in a girl, and they thought they would like to get one who was seven or eight years old. Pastor and Clara had told the Claibornes they felt peace about their decision and knew the Lord was leading them in this matter. Peter and Paul were in full agreement.

The Forbeses said they had spent many hours discussing their desire to take in a girl from the orphan train with their sons. At first, Peter and Paul were reluctant and said they thought their family was fine just the way it was. But as the days passed and prayers of the parents went heavenward, the boys began to see what a blessing a girl would be to their mother. They decided that having a girl in the family wouldn't be so bad after all. This change in the boys' attitude made their parents happy, and now, all four of them were looking forward to finding the little girl God had chosen for them. The boys were glad there was no school tomorrow because of the teachers' convention, so they could go to the depot with their parents.

Later that evening, the Claibornes were sitting in the parlor together, talking about how excited the pastor and his family must be at that moment, knowing they were going to take a daughter into their home tomorrow.

"Just think," said Jody, "right now that train is rolling westward, and that little girl the Lord has picked out for the Forbes family is hoping someone in Cheyenne will choose her and give her a home."

Emma nodded. "That's right, honey."

"And she is a very fortunate little girl," said Jody. "She will be taken into a wonderful Christian home where she will be loved, adored, and given all the care possible. If she isn't a Christian, it won't be long until she becomes one."

Sam smiled. "That's right, sweetheart. In the atmosphere of that home, the little girl will be lovingly given the gospel, and at that young age, will soon open her heart to Jesus."

Emma sighed. "Just think of all those orphans Charles Loring Brace and his Children's Aid Society are placing in homes from Missouri to California. What a marvelous thing it is. I'm sure glad the Lord put it on his heart to do this great work."

"Amen," said Sam.

"And amen," echoed Jody.

At breakfast on Wednesday morning, Sam said, "I'd like to be a fly on the wall in the Forbes house right now. Can you imagine the excitement? I wonder if any of them got any sleep last night."

"Probably not much," said Emma. "This will be a banner day in their lives."

There was a knock at the front door.

Jody shoved her chair back and jumped up. "That'll be Betty. We've got a big race planned."

When Jody opened the door, she found a smiling Betty Houston. "Good morning, Jody! Ready for the race?"

"Of course I am. Queenie and I are going to make you and Millie eat dust today! But my parents and I are not quite finished with breakfast. Come on back."

Betty laughed. "We'll see who eats dust today!"

While they kidded each other about who was going to win today's race, Jody led her best friend to the kitchen. Sam and Emma welcomed Betty, and Emma poured her a cup of hot chocolate.

As the Claibornes were finishing their breakfast and Betty sipped her hot chocolate, Sam said, "So where are you girls going to do your racing today?"

"We've agreed to race each other for that five-mile stretch due east of the *Circle C* to the old Cheyenne Indian burial ground, Daddy," said Jody.

Emma's concern over the girls riding their horses at top speed rose in her heart. Keeping her voice steady, she said, "Please be careful, won't you?"

"Of course, Mommy," Jody said, reaching across the corner of the table to pat her hand. "We're always careful." She giggled. "Queenie and I are going to leave Betty and Millie in the dust."

Betty laughed. "Oh yeah? Well, we'll see about that!"

At ten o'clock that morning, the Forbes family was on the platform in the Cheyenne depot as the train chugged to a halt. The two coaches that were designated for the orphans were at the rear of the train, just ahead of the caboose. They watched as the boys filed out of their coach, which was the one connected to the caboose, and the girls filed out of theirs.

The Children's Aid Society adult escorts lined the children up on the depot platform as the crowd looked on. Many people had gathered to observe as the orphans were put on display—some as prospective foster parents and others who were simply curious.

When the forty-eight children were positioned properly, one of the men in charge explained the procedure to the prospective foster parents, and soon they were filing by to talk to the orphans and look them over.

The Forbes family was in the line, and while they were looking for a girl who was seven or eight years of age, Clara spotted one further down the line. To Clara, the child stood out from the rest of the children. She nudged her husband and drew his attention to the girl.

Her hair was dark and hung down her back in twin braids. Her brown eyes had a definite twinkle as she answered questions of the couple who had stopped to talk to her, and her little jaw was set at an angle that depicted determination. Unlike most of the others, there was not a sad expression on her face, but rather, one of excitement and curiosity at what was happening around her. She was even joking with the prospective foster parents.

Peter whispered, "I like her, Mama."

"Me too," said Paul.

"She's loaded with personality," said the pastor. "I really like her."

There were still three more couples who would reach the little girl before the Forbes family could get to her. Clara prayed in her heart, *Dear Lord, she seems to be just what we're looking for. If she's the one You have chosen for us, please don't let any of these people ahead of us want her.*

Dan was praying exactly the same thing.

The next several minutes seemed agonizingly slow, as they

watched the people ahead of them. The couple that had been talking to the little girl moved on, and each time a different couple paused to look her over and talk to her, Clara held her breath.

Finally, the couple just ahead of them moved on, and the Forbes family stepped up to the little girl. The pastor smiled and said, "Hello, little lady. My name is Dan Forbes. This is my wife, Clara, and these are our sons, Peter and Paul."

The child gave him an impish smile. Using her fingertips to extend her dress on both sides, she curtsied. "I'm glad to meet all of you. My name is Susie Nolan and I'm eight years old."

The pastor and Clara exchanged glances and smiled at each other.

"Where are you from, dear?" asked Clara.

"I'm from Staten Island, New York, ma'am. My father died before I was born, and my mother died three months ago with pneumonia. I've been staying in an orphanage, but it was getting so crowded, the superintendent turned several of us over to the Children's Aid Society so they could put us on this orphan train and send us out West to find homes for us."

Dan said, "Susie, I am the pastor of a church here in Cheyenne. Would it bother you to live in a pastor's home?"

"No, sir. I have never been to church, but I think I would like it. I sure would love to live in your home. And I would really like to learn about God." Susie had been watching this family from the corner of her eye, and had secretly been hoping they would be the ones to choose her.

Peter smiled. "Paul and I really want a little sister. We'd sure like for it to be you."

"We sure would," said Paul.

Susie's heart was banging her ribs.

The pastor looked at Clara. Susie knew they were about to make their decision. Her body stiffened, then relaxed as Clara smiled and nodded. "Yes, Dan. This is the one."

"That's how I feel," he said.

"Me too!" said Peter.

Paul set his eyes on Susie, smiled, then looked at his parents. "Me too!"

Clara immediately leaned over and folded Susie in her arms while the pastor motioned for one of the Children's Aid Society sponsors. "You're going home with us, sweetheart!"

Susie's eyes sparkled. "Oh, thank you, Mrs. Forbes! Thank you for choosing me! I promise you won't be sorry."

A mist of grateful tears welled up in Clara's eyes. She thanked the Lord in her heart, then kissed Susie's cheek. "I'm sure we won't be sorry, dear. We have prayed for the Lord to lead us to the right little girl, and today our prayers were answered."

While their parents were conversing with the man who held a clipboard in his hand, Peter and Paul told Susie how glad they were that she was going to be their little sister. This pleased Susie, who felt like she was dreaming.

When the papers had been signed, Dan and Clara turned back to Susie and the boys, and Dan said, "Well, it's official. Susie is now our foster child."

Peter and Paul both hugged Susie, as did Clara and Dan. Clara then took hold of the little girl's hand and said, "All right, Susie, let's go home."

Pastor Forbes and his boys followed behind Clara and Susie as they headed out of the depot. Each of the three had a satisfied smile on his face.

That evening at the church's midweek service, Pastor Dan Forbes had Clara bring Susie Nolan up on the platform, where he introduced her to the congregation.

When the service was over, the people filed by to meet Susie. When the Claibornes and the Houstons met her, they liked her very much and welcomed her to Wyoming. Jody and Betty both hugged her.

Emma turned to the pastor and Clara. "How about coming to our house for supper on Saturday evening?"

"We sure will!" piped up Paul.

The pastor said, "Well, Emma, I guess Paul has spoken for us. We'll look forward to eating with you again."

Peter smiled at the newest member of the Forbes household. "Oh boy, Susie! You'll really like Mrs. Claiborne's fried chicken."

Emma laughed. "Well, I guess that settles what we're having for supper on Saturday."

Chapter Seven

On Thursday, May 7, Charles Loring Brace was at his desk at the Children's Aid Society headquarters. A smile was on his face as he read the financial report for the month of April. He noted the amounts that had been given by three new churches who had promised to help support the Society, then let his eyes run down the page, taking in the other churches, which had been supporting the Society for some time.

"Bless them, Lord," he said softly. "Without these churches and the businesses and individuals who support us on a monthly basis, we wouldn't be able to send those precious children out west. Thank You, Lord, for the great number of children we've been able to place in homes out there."

Just as Brace laid the papers down, there was a knock at his office door. "Yes?"

The door opened, showing him the face of Tod Owens, one of his assistants. "Mr. Brace, Walter Myers, superintendent of the West End Orphanage, is here to see you. May I show him in?"

"Of course."

Brace rose from his desk chair as his tall, husky friend Walter Myers entered, carrying his briefcase. Brace extended his hand. "Good morning, Walter. Nice to see you."

"You too, Charles," said Myers.

"Sit down, Walter."

"Thank you."

Myers settled onto the chair that stood in front of the desk. As Brace sat down on his desk chair, he smiled. "Do you have more orphans to put on a train?"

"I do. There are six of them this time. There are four girls, ranging from seven to nine, and two boys: one is six years old, and the other is five."

Brace nodded. "And you have the usual papers."

"Yes." Myers opened his briefcase and took out papers, which Brace knew would have the names and ages of each child, along with information on their backgrounds, when the father and mother had died, and how long they had been at the orphanage.

Myers waited while Brace looked over each sheet. When he laid the last one down, Myers said, "The last one there, Charles—Jimmy Kirkland."

Brace picked that sheet up again. "Mm-hmm?"

"You need to know that five-year-old Jimmy has a speech impediment."

Brace looked up. "Oh? What kind?"

"Well, actually, it is a dual impediment. Jimmy stutters and has a very noticeable lisp."

"Is he retarded?"

"Well, not that I can tell. I realize that a lisp, especially, often goes with mental slowness or one limited in intellectual development. Jimmy seems as bright as any normal child his age."

Brace rubbed his temple. "You're aware, though, that when prospective foster parents talk to this boy and ask him questions, they will immediately assume that he is mentally slow."

"Yes, but he's such a sweet little fellow, Charles. My heart is heavy for him. We have a continual problem at the orphanage with the other children making fun of the way he talks. They keep him upset and in tears almost every day. I feel it is best to send Jimmy out west so he can find a good home where there will be no ridicule."

Concern showed in Charles Brace's thin, angular face. "We'll take Jimmy, of course, Walter. But we have found that children with physical disabilities are very difficult to place in homes. Prospective foster parents shy away because they do not want what they feel will be an added burden. It will be even more difficult with Jimmy, because they will hear his stuttering lisp and automatically assume that he is retarded. All we can do is trust God to help my staff on the train as they do their best to find the little fellow a good home."

"Well, God loves Jimmy, Charles. He will find some good family who will take him."

Brace smiled, then opened his top desk drawer and took out a clipboard with papers on it. "Let me check my train schedules." He put a finger on a spot. "All right. I can put all six children on a train on Tuesday, June 16."

"Good! Thanks again, Charles, for the great work you are doing. We'll have the children ready."

"All right. The train will leave Grand Central Station at ten o'clock that morning. We'll need you to have the children here at Society headquarters by seven-thirty. You already know what they are to bring with them and how they are to be dressed."

"Yes. And we'll have them here no later than seven-thirty."

"Fine. Before you leave, Walter, I want to give you a report on some of the previous children you have brought to us in this past year that we have placed in homes."

Myers's face lit up. "Oh, I'd love to hear about them!"

Brace left his chair and went to a file cabinet that stood nearby. He took a folder out of a drawer, sat down again, and began reading from papers that had been put together by his staff, who had been in contact with the children and their foster parents by mail.

When Myers had heard the reports, he said, "Thanks for letting me hear those, Charles. I'm really glad to learn that all of the orphans are in good homes and are happy."

An hour after Walter Myers had left Charles Brace's office, Tod Owens tapped on the door. "Mr. Brace, Pastor Darryl Moore is here to see you. Can you talk to him now?"

"Certainly."

Charles Brace deeply appreciated Moore, who had led his church to generously support the Children's Aid Society. When Moore came through the door, Brace stepped around his desk and shook his hand. "Pastor Moore, it's nice to see you."

"That goes double for me," Moore said, smiling from ear to ear.

"Sit down and make yourself comfortable."

When they were seated, Brace looked at Moore across the desk. "What can I do for you?"

"I want to tell you about three children in our church whose parents were recently killed. The father, Bob Marston, was one of my deacons."

"Oh my." Brace eased back in his chair. "Go ahead."

"Bob and his wife Louise were drowned, Mr. Brace. Bob was employed by American Ship Lines here in Manhattan as assistant business manager. The company put him on one of their freighters, intending to send him to St. John's, Newfoundland, on a business trip. His wife, Louise, was with him. The ship was caught in a storm and went down some twenty miles off the coast of Nova Scotia. All but two crewmen were able to get into the lifeboats, but the captain, those two crewmen, and the Marstons were swept off the deck into the Atlantic and drowned.

"The Marston children had been left in the care of an elderly woman named Frances Roberts, who is also a member of our church. There are no living relatives who can take them and raise them. At her age, Frances is in no position to attempt it. Dora and I would take them, but we have both of our widowed mothers living with us. We simply don't have room for three children.

"Right now, the children are being kept in different homes among my church members, but none of them can take them permanently. I need you to send them west on one of your orphan trains so they can find a permanent home."

Brace leaned forward and put his elbows on the desk. "Pastor Moore, we will gladly put the Marston children on one of our trains, but I need to explain something."

"Yes?"

"Our twenty years of working at finding homes for homeless children have taught us that it is extremely difficult to place three children in the same home. It rarely happens, even with two siblings, but placing three in the same home has only happened twice that I can recall. I just don't want the children to have any false expectations."

Moore rubbed his chin and nodded. "I see. I hadn't realized it would be that difficult."

"Like I said, we'll gladly put them on one of our trains, but I thought I should inform you of this."

"Certainly. I appreciate it."

Brace picked up a pencil and a blank sheet of paper.

"M-A-R-S-T-O-N, right?"

"Yes."

"And what are their names and ages?"

"Mary is the oldest. She's eight. Johnny is six, and little Lizzie is four."

Brace wrote the information down, then said, "The first train that has room for them will leave Grand Central Station on Tuesday, June 16. It is scheduled to leave the depot at ten o'clock that morning. We'll need you to have the children here by seven-thirty at the latest. I need time to talk to all the children who will be going on the train in order to acquaint them with the staff people who will be traveling on the train with them, to lay down the rules, and to answer any questions they might have. We'll also need a good twenty minutes to transport them to Grand Central."

The pastor nodded. "Mr. Brace, I deeply appreciate this. The Marston children are polite and well-behaved. They won't cause you any trouble, I'm sure."

Brace opened a side drawer on the desk. "I wish that were true of all our orphans, Pastor, but once in a while we get some who give us all kinds of trouble." He took out a printed form and handed it to Moore. "This will explain what the Marston children will need to have with them and how they should be dressed. Will there be a problem with buying new dresses for the girls and a suit for the boy, if they don't have them?"

"No. The church will foot the bill."

"All right. Have them here, as I said, not later than seven-thirty on Tuesday morning, June 16."

The two men shook hands, and as Pastor Darryl Moore walked out of the building and headed for his buggy, he said, "Thank You, Lord, that You are looking out for Mary, Johnny, and little Lizzie. When that train takes them out West, please direct them to just the right family. One family, Lord. Please see to it that they are not separated but are placed in the same home."

On Sunday morning, May 17, Pastor Dan Forbes finished a dynamic sermon and began the invitation. While the song leader led them in Charlotte Elliott's "Just as I Am," two young men walked the aisle quickly to receive Jesus Christ as Saviour, followed by a thirteen-year-old girl.

In the pew behind the one where the two young men had been sitting, Sam Claiborne turned and smiled at Emma and Jody. "Praise the Lord!" he said in a whisper. "Those two fellows were under conviction during the whole sermon!"

Emma and Jody returned the smile.

They were still in the first verse when Clara Forbes stepped into the aisle at the second row of pews, holding eight-year-old Susie by the hand. Peter and Paul were on the same pew, and their faces showed the joy they were feeling as they watched their mother and Susie move into the aisle. Together, they walked forward and waited as the pastor was talking to the thirteen-year-old girl while a lady counselor waited to take her to the altar. The two young men were already kneeling at the altar, being counseled by two older men with open Bibles.

When the girl and the counselor went to the altar, Pastor Forbes smiled down at Susie and hugged her. Clara and Susie then sat down on the front row, and Clara filled out a card on Susie.

Another teenage girl came during the last verse of the invitation hymn, and the invitation was closed.

Pastor Forbes took those who had come forward one at a time, gave their names, and had each one give a testimony that they had just received the Lord Jesus Christ as personal Saviour. Forbes announced that each one would be baptized in the evening service. Then, having reserved Susie till last, he asked her to step up beside him, with his wife at her side.

Smiling broadly, the pastor said to the congregation, "All of our people know that Clara and I chose little Susie Nolan off the orphan train almost a month ago. My wife has come forward with Susie this morning to tell you a little story. Honey…"

While holding Susie's hand, Clara ran her gaze over the congregation. "Since Susie has been in our home, and of course, coming to church and Sunday school these past few weeks, she has heard the gospel many times. It really began to take effect about ten days ago. She was showing definite conviction about her lost condition at family altar time and here at church at invitation time. Last night, about an hour after Susie had gone to bed, I was walking down the hall, and as I was passing her bedroom door, I heard her crying.

"Of course, I opened the door and went in. I asked her what she was crying about, and she said she wanted to be saved. My husband and I never pushed the gospel on Susie, but from the day we brought her home from the railroad station, we prayed that the Lord would speak to her heart. God heard our prayers and the precious Holy Spirit went to work on her heart."

There were smiles all over the auditorium with heads nodding.

The Claiborne family had beaming faces, and Jody was wiping tears from her cheeks.

Clara looked down at the little girl with the long twin braids. "Susie, would you like to tell all these people what happened to you last night?"

A bit nervous, Susie smiled up at her and nodded. She then looked out at the audience. "I took Jesus into my heart and He saved me. I've been born again. Now, I'm in God's family."

The pastor laid a hand on Susie's shoulder. "And you want to obey the Lord and be baptized, right?"

Susie smiled up at him. "Yes, Papa."

Keeping his eyes on Susie, the pastor said, "You're right, sweetheart, you are now in God's family. May I tell the people that you are also in another family?"

"Yes, Papa."

Forbes looked at the crowd. "We haven't told anyone this news, yet. We wanted to wait till it was a signed and sealed matter. Just this past Friday, Susie officially became our adopted daughter. Her name is now Susan Mae Forbes!"

There was instant applause and a host of amens.

When the crowd grew quiet again, the pastor said, "Susan Mae Forbes will be baptized this evening, along with these others who have been saved."

On Saturday, May 23, at the *Circle C* ranch, Jody Claiborne was helping her mother prepare breakfast and was talking excitedly about going riding with Betty Houston that morning.

Jody would rather be at the barn doing chores with her father, but since Betty had been invited for the meal, she graciously stayed inside so she would be there when Betty arrived.

The Claiborne kitchen was redolent with the enticing aromas of pancakes, scrambled eggs, sausage, and hot coffee.

While Jody was setting the table, Emma dried her hands on a dish towel. She draped the towel on its rack and stepped up behind her daughter, placing a hand on each shoulder. "Honey…"

Jody put the last piece of silverware at her father's plate. "Yes, Mommy?"

Emma looked in her bright eyes. "Honey, I don't mean to be a nag about your racing with Betty, but I'm asking you to be careful. I wouldn't be so concerned if you were just riding. It's the speed you ride when you're racing that worries me. If Queenie would step in a prairie dog hole—"

"Mommy, I'm always careful. Betty and I know that prairie out there like the back of our hand. We don't ride where we know the prairie dogs live. Please remember I've been riding since I was old enough to sit in a saddle." She grinned, trying to reassure her mother and dispel the frown on her brow. "You don't have to worry about me. I can handle a horse."

Emma kissed her cheek. "All right, dear. I'll try not to be a worrywart."

Jody kissed her mother's cheek and gave her a quick hug. "I love you, Mommy."

"I love you too, honey."

"Hello-o-o-o!" came Betty's voice from the just outside the back window of the kitchen. "Sure smells good from out here! Breakfast ready?"

"Just about!" called Jody, moving up to the window. "Come on in!"

As she spoke, Jody saw her father coming from the barn. She opened the door. "Where's Millie?"

"I have her tied out by the front porch. Just figured I'd save you coming all the way to the front door to let me in."

Emma greeted Betty as Sam came up the steps and entered the kitchen.

He and Betty exchanged good mornings, and as soon as Sam had washed his hands, they sat down at the table. Sam led in prayer, thanking the Lord for the food, and as they began to eat, Sam said, "Well, girls, where's your race going to take you today?"

Betty was drinking milk from a tin cup, so Jody decided to answer the question. "We've agreed to race each other for the seven-mile stretch from here to that rock formation due north. You know, they call it Eagle Rock."

Sam nodded. "You've raced to that spot before."

"Mm-hmm, but it's been a while."

Betty giggled as she set her cup down. "And poor Jody and Queenie are going to get beat again."

Jody shook her head, putting on a mock scowl. "No way, blondie. Since you and Millie beat us the last time we raced to Eagle Rock, I snuck over to your corral last night, and had a heart-to-heart talk with Millie. She told me that she and Queenie had agreed that it was our turn to win the Eagle Rock race."

They all had a good laugh and then talked about last Sunday morning's service when little Susie gave her testimony at the close of the invitation, and her baptism on Sunday evening.

Sam wiped his mouth with a napkin. "While you girls are helping Emma clean up the kitchen and the dishes, I'll go to the barn and saddle up Queenie for you, Jody."

Jody thanked him, and the ladies went to work on the dishes.

By the time Sam came from the barn leading the magnificent bay mare, the dishes were done and the kitchen was clean. Emma and the girls were waiting for him on the front porch.

When Millie caught sight of Queenie, she lifted her head high and whistled. Queenie bobbed her head and whistled back. Her whistle was shrill, clear, and strong.

Jody laughed. "Did you hear that? In horse language, Millie just said that she and Betty are going to win today. But Queenie told her in no uncertain terms that she is wrong. She and I are going to win the race!"

Everybody had a good laugh again.

Jody and Betty mounted up.

As she settled in the saddle, Jody looked at her parents. "We'll be back before noon."

"If you girls aren't something else," said Sam. "Have fun."

Queenie reared up, whistling shrilly, ready for the race. Millie nickered and began to prance.

Jody looked at her best friend. "Betty, we'll have to warm the horses up before we put them to a gallop."

Betty nodded. "We'll trot them for a couple of miles, then start the race."

"All right. Let's go."

As the girls trotted away toward the north, Sam set admiring eyes on his daughter and put his arm around Emma. "You know, honey, that slip of a girl was born to ride a horse. She's as strong and lithe as an Indian, and as I've said before, she rides like a burr sticking in a horse's mane."

Emma chuckled. "You sound just like a father."

Sam and Emma watched the trotting horses until they faded from view, then Sam said, "Well, Mrs. Claiborne, it looks like I have to clean that old barn out there all by myself, since my 'boy' is out there trying to show Betty who's boss of the race track!"

Chapter Eight

When Jody Claiborne and Betty Houston had trotted their horses some two miles from the *Circle C* ranch, they drew rein. When both mares stopped, they tossed their heads and snorted. They knew the race was about to begin.

Jody's attention was drawn to the west. She pointed that direction with her chin. "Look there, Betty."

Betty's gaze followed to the army patrol unit. "Uh-huh. They're probably from Fort Laramie."

"I'd say so. Aren't you glad things have calmed down with the Cheyenne and the Arapaho so we can ride like this without being in danger?"

"Sure am. But it's always nice to see those cavalrymen out patrolling. Makes me feel safe."

Jody patted Queenie's neck. "Well, Miss Lightning, are you ready to run this race?"

Queenie bobbed her head and snorted.

The girls looked at each other. They had set a pattern. To start the race fairly, one of them would toss a stone into the air and when it hit the ground, the race was on.

Betty grinned. "Since it's your turn to start the race, Miss

Slowpoke, I'll wait while you fetch a stone."

Jody snickered as she slipped from the saddle. "Miss Slowpoke, huh? Well, you're about to become an Indian."

Betty's eyebrows arched. "An Indian?"

"Uh-huh. Miss Dust-in-the-Face."

Betty laughed and shook her head. "We'll see about that!"

Jody bent over, picked up a stone a little smaller than her fist, then mounted again. She drew Queenie up close beside Millie and offered her right hand. "Shake?"

"Sure."

Betty gripped her hand and shook it. "Okay, kiddo, let's go."

Jody backed Queenie up, then moved her forward so the horses were some six feet apart and their noses were even.

Millie's sage gray body was as sleek and shiny as satin as she swished her tail.

Queenie tossed her head and champed her bit. Her muscles rippled under her reddish brown coat.

Adjusting herself in the saddle, Jody glanced at Betty, then tossed the stone some thirty feet high so it would land just ahead of them.

The girls bent forward in their saddles and waited for the stone to hit the ground. Both of them felt a thrill in their veins. When the rock plopped in the dust, they put their horses to a gallop instantly, and the race was on to the sound of thundering, rhythmic hoofbeats.

Within half a minute, Jody was two lengths ahead of her best friend.

Betty snapped the reins and called for Millie to go faster, but Queenie seemed determined to win and kept gaining ground. Queenie was running for the love of running as the girl bending over her was riding for the love of riding. Jody's motion was one with the horse. Her long, dark hair flew in the wind.

Betty and Millie were still losing ground as Jody and Queenie pulled farther ahead of them, seemingly with each stride. Betty continued to urge her mare on, bent low, with her long blond hair a bright stream of gold in the wind.

When Eagle Rock came into view, Jody was some twenty yards ahead of Betty, who was still doing her best to get more speed out of her gray roan. By the time they were within a mile of Eagle Rock, Jody was more than thirty yards ahead. There was a creek close by, and both girls saw another army patrol unit. The men in blue were out of their saddles, watering their mounts. The racing horses quickly caught the attention of the majority of them. Some of them pointed, saying something to those who were not yet aware of the race, and quickly, all of them smiled and waved. The girls waved in return.

A moment later, Jody looked back at Betty, who was now gaining on her a little. Directly in Queenie's path, a large diamondback rattler as thick as a man's wrist was swiftly coiling into attack position. Its flat, wide head was pointed directly at the oncoming horse and rider with its greenish black tongue flicking in and out of its mouth menacingly and its angry black eyes flashing. The rattles in its tail were in a steady whir.

Jody was still looking back at Betty when Queenie spotted the snake, which was now no more than a few strides away. Queenie stiffened her legs, but when she saw that she was skidding toward the deadly reptile, she attempted a sidestep to avoid it. Jody was facing forward, her feet pressed hard into the stirrups as she pulled back on the reins. Because of Queenie's speed, the frantic sidestep threw her off balance. She lost her footing and went down headfirst.

Betty jerked back on the reins as she saw Jody fly out of the saddle. She caught a glimpse of the snake as it was slithering off the path toward a large boulder. Jody sailed through the air, her arms and legs flailing, and hit the ground hard. Her momentum sent her rolling helplessly until her head struck a rock that stuck out of the ground.

Queenie struggled to get up, and when she once again had her legs under her, she staggered about unsteadily, then looked back at Betty, who was skidding Millie to a halt. Queenie whinnied softly, shaking her head.

Betty was out of the saddle immediately and knelt down beside the unconscious Jody. There was a deep gash on the side of her head where it had struck the rock and blood was flowing freely. Betty cradled Jody's head and upper body in her lap. She pulled the handkerchief from around her own neck, pressed it against the gash to stay the flow of blood.

"Jody! Jody! Can you hear me? Open your eyes, please! Please, Jody, you've got to be all right!" Jody's lack of response caused panic to set in. "Jody-y-y! Jody-y-y! Wake up! Wake up!"

Suddenly, two of the cavalrymen were at Betty's side while the others were just bringing their mounts to a halt. She looked at them. "Jody's hurt bad! I'm afraid she's going to die!"

One of the men was the officer in charge of the patrol unit. The other was a sergeant. The lieutenant laid a hand on Betty's shoulder and said calmly, "Try to get hold of yourself, little lady. We're going to help you take care of her."

The other men were gathering close as the lieutenant lifted the hand that held the handkerchief against the gash, examined it, and placed Betty's hand on it once again. "Pretty deep, all right. What's your name, little lady?"

"Betty Houston. She's my best friend. Her name is Jody Claiborne. Oh, please don't let her die!"

"We'll get her into town to the clinic." The lieutenant looked up at his men. "The girl is unconscious and bleeding profusely. We've got to get her to the clinic in Cheyenne as soon as possible.

Corporal Hayden, take Private Willis and ride over there to that ranch just beyond the creek. Borrow a team and wagon. Hurry!"

Hayden and Willis wheeled, dashed to their horses, and galloped away.

The lieutenant then called for the sergeant to get his canteen for him from his saddle. It was done quickly, and as the lieutenant bathed Jody's face and the gash with the cool water, he looked at Betty. "What happened? Did her horse stumble?"

"Only when she saw a big rattlesnake and tried to avoid it. The snake was coiled and ready to strike."

All of the men heard Betty's words, and suddenly one of them said, "Lieutenant, I just saw what I thought was a snake slithering over there around the base of that boulder." With that, he dashed to his horse, whipped his rifle out of the saddle boot, and headed toward the boulder.

The lieutenant capped his canteen, handed it to the sergeant, and took his bandanna from his hip pocket. "You did a good job with this kerchief, but since my bandanna's much larger, I'll wrap her head with it. While we ride the borrowed wagon into town, you can press the kerchief against the gash to help keep it from bleeding."

Betty nodded, looked at the pallid face of her unconscious friend. "I'm sure glad you and your men were close. I don't know what I would have done."

At that instant the crack of a rifle split the air, echoing across the prairie. One of the men said, "Clete just killed the rattler, Lieutenant."

The lieutenant nodded and looked back down at the unconscious girl. As he began wrapping Jody's head with the bandanna, he said, "Betty, my name is Tom Bell. The sergeant is Dale Dixon. We're out of Fort Laramie."

"I'm glad to meet both of you."

Bell finished his wrapping job. "Betty, why don't you go ahead and press your kerchief against the gash?"

Betty nodded.

"Where are you girls from?"

"Just south of here a few miles, sir. My parents own the *Box H* ranch and Jody's parents own the *Circle C* ranch. Jody and I race each other a lot on our horses. Today, we were racing to Eagle Rock."

As she spoke, Betty saw one of the men leading Queenie toward them.

When he drew up, he said, "Lieutenant, the girl's mare is all right. As you can see, she scuffed up the side of her head a little when she fell, but she's okay."

Bell nodded. "Good. Thanks for checking on her, Clyde."

"My pleasure, sir."

"Oh, thank the Lord Queenie's all right," said Betty. "Jody loves that horse dearly."

Bell rose to his feet. "Betty, you keep the pressure on the spot. I'm going to have a look at that snake. Those two men ought to be here with a wagon pretty soon."

"I'll take care of her, sir."

While they were waiting for Corporal Rex Hayden and Private George Willis to return with a borrowed wagon, Betty kept the pressure on the gash and looked at Jody's face.

"Jody, please wake up," whispered Betty. "Oh, dear Lord, please make her wake up."

Tears began to flow, and a couple of the men who stood close by moved up to Betty's side. One of them knelt down and laid a hand on her shoulder. "Don't cry, honey. Your friend is going to be all right. We'll get her to the doctor. He'll bring her around."

Betty used her free hand to wipe away the tears on her cheeks. "Thank you for the encouragement, sir."

"Lieutenant, Rex and George are coming!" called one of the men.

Everybody looked to see the wagon coming with the team at a gallop. Corporal Rex Hayden was at the reins. Private George Willis was following on his horse while leading Hayden's riderless mount. When they drew up in a cloud of dust, Lieutenant Tom Bell told two of the men to pick up Jody and carry her to the wagon. With Betty at his side, he rushed ahead, telling her that the two of them would sit in the wagon bed. He would hold Jody in his arms so he could cushion her against the jolts. Betty would sit beside him and keep the pressure on Jody's wound.

When they reached the wagon, Bell picked Betty up and placed her in the wagon bed, then hopped in. While Jody was laid in the lieutenant's arms and Betty pressed the kerchief firmly over the spot where the bandanna was showing some blood, the men mounted up. Three of them were leading Queenie, Millie, and Bell's horse.

The wagon team was put to a gallop, and the rest of the patrol unit followed.

While bouncing in the wagon and doing her job to stay the flow of blood, Betty prayed in her heart, asking the Lord to let Jody live.

All morning long, as Emma Claiborne did her housework and sewed on a new dress for Jody, a heavy sense of foreboding had dominated her mind.

The Wyoming sun was now past its apex in the crystal clear sky as she sat alone in the swing on the front porch of the house, staring across the plains to the north. It was after one o'clock. Jody had assured them that she and Betty would be back before noon.

Sam came out the door and looked to the north. "No sign of them yet, I see."

"Nothing," Emma said. "Sam, I haven't said anything to you about it, but I've had an uneasy feeling for some time about the girls racing. I talked to Jody about it this morning. I told her I wasn't against them riding together, but I was concerned about the speed when they raced. She told me there was nothing to be concerned about because she and Betty were experienced riders. I tried to shrug it off, saying I'm just a worrywart. But with them being late, I'm worrying again."

Emma was wringing her hands while keeping her eyes on the plains to the north.

Sam eased onto the swing beside her. "Now, now, Mother," he said, making his voice calm, "remember the old saying, 'Don't start swimming until you hit the water.' You know those two are very good at losing track of the time when they're out riding. But to ease your mind, I'll go saddle Midnight and see if I can find them."

When he stood up and headed for the porch steps, Sam's attention was drawn to two riders galloping down the road from the south. When he paused to focus on them, Emma turned and looked at him. "What is it?"

"Couple of riders in a big hurry, coming from the south."

Emma left the swing and moved up beside him. "Looks like army men."

"Uh-huh."

When the riders slowed and turned into the *Circle C* gate, Emma grabbed her husband's arm. "Something's wrong."

Sam patted her hand. "Now, honey, don't fret. Let's see what they have to say."

As the riders drew near, Sam and Emma moved down the steps to meet them. When they came to a halt, the man with the lieutenant's insignias on his shirt said, "You're Mr. and Mrs. Claiborne?"

Sam nodded. "Yes."

"I'm Lieutenant Tom Bell, and this is Sergeant Dale Dixon. We're from Fort Laramie."

Fear was an icy stake in Emma's heart. "What's wrong, Lieutenant? Has something happened to our daughter?"

"May we dismount?"

"Of course," said Sam.

Bell and Dixon touched ground. Bell said, "I was leading my regular patrol up north of here this morning. We saw your daughter and her friend racing toward Eagle Rock while we were watering our horses at one of the creeks. They waved to us, and shortly thereafter, we saw your daughter's horse go down."

Emma gasped. "Oh no! Is Jody all right?"

"She's alive, ma'am. Let me explain."

While Sam and Emma clung to each other, Bell told them about the rattlesnake in Queenie's path that coiled up to strike, and how Queenie fell when trying to avoid the snake. He explained that Jody had been thrown from the saddle while Queenie was going down, and that she had struck her head on a rock. He went on to tell them that he had wrapped Jody's head with his bandanna to stay the bleeding as much as possible, and that Betty kept pressure on it while they took Jody to the clinic in Cheyenne in a wagon borrowed from a rancher.

His face solemn, Bell said, "Betty is at the clinic with Jody at the moment, and Dr. John Traynor is working on her."

Sam looked at Emma. "I'll hitch up the team to the wagon, honey. Be back in a couple minutes."

"We'll wait and escort you, Mr. Claiborne," said Bell.

Sam nodded and ran toward the barn.

Emma dashed into the house and hurried to the kitchen. She

took the teakettle off the stove, grabbed a light shawl from a wall hook, and paused to take a breath. "Oh, dear God," she whispered, her voice shaking, "please make my little girl all right. Don't let her die. She's so young. And…and please don't let her have brain damage or anything like that." She burst into tears, and it took her a few minutes to calm herself.

By the time Emma reached the front porch, the two men in blue were astride their mounts, and Sam was guiding the wagon around the corner of the house.

He hopped down, helped her onto the seat, and climbed up beside her. "All right, Lieutenant Bell, let's go."

Sam put the team to a gallop, and the cavalrymen rode alongside the bouncing wagon. Tears streamed down Emma's face once again. As they sat tensely on the wagon seat, both parents prayed to the Great Physician, entreating His mercy on behalf of their beloved child.

When they pulled into Cheyenne and slowed to a trot, Emma gripped Sam's arm. He patted her hand and squeezed it gently. Soon they neared the clinic. A sharp gasp escaped Emma's pinched lips when she saw Queenie at the hitch rail with Millie. The beautiful bay mare seemed to be fine, and for Jody's sake, Emma was grateful the prized horse was uninjured.

Sam drew the wagon to a halt. Bell and Dixon dismounted and tied their horses. Sam helped Emma down from the wagon seat, and the four of them hurried into the clinic.

Betty Houston was in the waiting area and jumped up when she spotted them. She burst into tears when she went into Emma's arms.

Since Dr. John Traynor was the Claibornes' family physician, Joyce Adams, the nurse at the desk, knew them. She left the desk, stepped up to Sam and Emma, and said, "I'm so sorry for what happened. Jody is still unconscious, but Dr. Traynor hasn't left her side since she was brought in. I'll go in and advise him that you're here."

"Thank you, Joyce," said Emma.

When the nurse was gone, Lieutenant Tom Bell said, "Mr. and Mrs. Claiborne, we have to get back to the fort. We'll check with Dr. Traynor later about Jody's condition."

Sam and Emma expressed their deep appreciation for what they had done for Jody.

As the men passed out the door, Sam said, "Let's sit down. Betty, we want to hear every detail about Jody's fall. Lieutenant Bell told us what they saw from where they were by the creek, but you were right behind her, they said. We want to know everything you can tell us." Sam sat down, facing Betty.

Betty worked at calming herself, then began her story. She had barely started when the nurse appeared and said, "Folks, Dr. Traynor will come and talk to you as soon as he can. Right now, he is giving his full attention to Jody."

Sam's brow furrowed. "Has she regained consciousness yet?"

"No, sir. Not yet."

The father leaned forward, took hold of Emma's hand with his right hand, and gripped Betty's hand with the left. "Let's take Jody to the Lord in prayer."

Joyce Adams stood quietly to one side, giving respect to the parents and Betty as they bowed their heads and Sam led them in prayer. Sam poured out his heart, asking God to give the doctor wisdom as he worked on Jody, and imploring Him to let her be all right.

When Sam's amen was said, Joyce moved close again and said, "May I offer you some coffee?"

"That would be great," said Sam.

Emma nodded. "Yes, I'll take some, too. We both like it black."

"All right. And what can I get you, Betty?"

The girl looked up at her with a trace of tears still in her bleary eyes. She gave her a ghost of a smile. "Just a glass of water, please, ma'am."

"Two cups of black coffee and a glass of water coming right up." With that, she hurried down the corridor, her starched dress making a swishing sound with each step.

Betty picked up where she left off on her story. She was interrupted when Joyce returned with the refreshments, which included oatmeal cookies she had made at home the night before. When Joyce returned to her desk and busied herself with paperwork, Betty continued her story. Sam and Emma listened intently.

Almost two hours passed, with patients coming and going, who were being tended to by the clinic's other doctor. Emma happened to be looking toward the door that led to the patients' rooms when it came open, and Dr. John Traynor appeared. She jumped to her feet. Sam and Betty saw him and also stood up.

The doctor looked a bit haggard as he headed toward the spot where the Claibornes and Betty were standing in the waiting area. As he drew up, a weak smile formed on his lips.

Emma spoke before Traynor could get a word out. "Is she awake, Doctor? She's going to be all right, isn't she?"

"She still hasn't regained consciousness. Please sit down, and I'll tell you as much as I know right now."

They sat back down on their chairs, and the doctor sat down next to Sam. "I stitched up the gash in Jody's head. I'm sure it will heal with no problem. The blow left a bump there, but the swelling will go down in a couple of days or so. There doesn't seem to be any damage to her skull. As for her failure to come to,

I can only say that I believe she will do so soon."

Sam's eyes showed his concern as he looked at Traynor. "Doctor, from what Betty has told us, Jody's head hit that rock pretty hard. Do you think there has been damage done to her brain?"

"Well, there's no way to tell for sure until she regains consciousness. I certainly hope not. I think the best thing for you folks to do at this point is to go home and come back in the morning. She certainly should be awake by then. You know that Ellen and I live in the house just behind the clinic. We'll never be far from Jody. I'm going to sleep on the cot in Jody's room tonight, so I'll be right there with her."

"I appreciate that," said Sam.

"May we go in and see her now, Doctor?" asked Emma.

"Yes. You sure can. I'll take you in."

The doctor led them into the back part of the building and up to the door of the small room where Jody lay unconscious on the bed with a bandage wrapped around her head. Her face was devoid of color. On trembling legs, Emma moved into the room first. When she reached the foot of the bed, she stopped abruptly and threw her hands to her mouth, trying to suppress the sob.

Valiantly containing the rush of emotions, Emma moved up to the side of the bed. Tears filled her eyes as she gently caressed her daughter's dark hair and pale cheeks while Sam, Betty, and Dr. Traynor looked on.

Emma took hold of Jody's limp hand, watching for any sign of awareness, as she said in a low voice, "Jody, sweetheart. It's Mommy. Can you hear me? Daddy's here, and so is Betty. We love you."

Sam slipped up beside Emma and put his arm around her shoulders as her tears splashed on Jody's hand.

Emma looked up at her husband, whose eyes were awash with

unshed tears. "Oh, Sam, she will be all right, won't she? The Lord won't take our only child."

Sam looked first at the small form on the bed, then at his wife, whose eyes were pleading for the answer she wanted to hear.

He spoke in a hushed voice that was clogged with tears. "I don't know God's plan in all of this, but I do know that He doeth all things well. We simply must trust our little Jody into His hands and keep praying. He encourages us in His Word to pray without ceasing. He also tells us: 'Be careful for nothing; but in every thing by prayer and supplication with thanksgiving let your requests be made known unto God. And the peace of God, which passeth all understanding, shall keep your hearts and minds through Christ Jesus.'"

Emma nodded. "Let's pray again, honey."

Letting go of Emma, Sam leaned down over his precious daughter and cupped her face in his hands. As he prayed, his voice reflected the courage that the blessed, familiar verses had given him. He thanked the Lord for all His blessings, and thanked Him for blessing Emma and him by giving them Jody twelve years ago, and for what a wonderful daughter she was. He then entreated the Lord that His perfect will be done, adding that he and Emma knew He would do what was right for Jody and for them. When Sam closed his prayer with an amen, Emma embraced him, laying her head on his chest.

The doctor stepped up. "It's good to see a family so close. You two are under a great deal of strain. Go on home and get some rest. I'll see you in the morning."

Emma pulled back from Sam and looked up at him with the pleading look he had learned to read over their years together. "You don't have to say a word, sweetheart. I know what that look means."

Emma drew a shuddering breath. "Oh, Sam, there is no way I

can leave Jody. I *must* be here with her. I don't want her to wake up and not have me at her side. She'll need me, and I'm going to be here. I know you have to go home to take care of the stock and milk the cows. You get a good night's sleep, and I'll see you in the morning."

Sam turned to Dr. Traynor. "Is it all right if she stays?"

The doctor nodded. "Of course. I understand. Emma can sleep on the cot I was going to use. I know she'll rest much easier being here with Jody. I'll bring in another cot for Ellen to sleep on so Emma will have her close. Ellen will bring her some supper too."

"Oh, that'll be great," Sam said, a smile tugging at the corners of his mouth.

Emma set grateful eyes on Traynor. "Thank you, Doctor. "I'll stay out of your way and try not to be any trouble."

The doctor grinned. "You're not going to be any trouble."

Betty had moved up to the opposite side of the bed, and was holding Jody's hand while looking into her still, pallid face.

Sam took Emma into his arms and held her close. "God is near, sweetheart. He's watching over both my girls. Please rest in His gentle care."

"I will, honey. I promise." She rose up on her tiptoes and kissed his rough cheek.

Emma then turned to Betty. "Thank you, sweetie, for being here for Jody."

Betty stepped around the bed and hugged Emma. "Jody is my best friend, Mrs. Claiborne. I'll be back tomorrow morning. If Jody's no worse after I see her, I'll go to church, then come back afterward to check on her again."

"All right, dear. Please ask your parents to pray."

"You can depend on that, ma'am." As she spoke, Betty moved to the door and stepped into the hall. She waited there for Jody's father.

Sam kissed Emma's forehead, then headed for the door, saying over his shoulder that he was going to go by the parsonage and tell Pastor and Mrs. Forbes what had happened to Jody so they could be praying too.

Emma said, "Yes. Please do that." She then moved back to Jody's side. Dr. Traynor was now standing on the other side of the bed, looking down at the unconscious twelve-year-old.

Sam paused at the door and found Emma's eyes on him. "Please get some rest, sweetheart. Jody will need you to be strong when she awakens."

Emma managed a smile. "I'll be fine, dear. See you in the morning."

When Sam and Betty stepped out the front door of the clinic, he tied Queenie's reins to the rear of his wagon.

Betty mounted Millie. "If I don't get home pretty soon, my parents will be getting worried. I'll tell them about Jody, and we'll be praying. See you in the morning, Mr. Claiborne."

"Fine, honey. I'll be here about eight o'clock."

Betty nodded, turned Millie into the street, and trotted away.

Sam reached the parsonage and told Pastor Dan Forbes and his family about what had happened to Jody. The pastor offered prayer then and there.

The pastor and Clara told Sam they would meet him at the clinic at eight o'clock in the morning. This would give them time to look in on Jody and still make it to back to church before Sunday school started.

Chapter Nine

As the Wyoming sun was lowering over the Rocky Mountains west of Cheyenne, Emma Claiborne was keeping up her vigil at Jody's bedside, sitting in a comfortable chair that Dr. Traynor had provided her before going to his house behind the clinic.

The setting sun was filling the room with deep purple shadows as Emma held Jody's hand, her heart feeling like it was made of lead. Jody's breathing was shallow but steady.

The last rays of the sun had disappeared when Emma heard the back door of the clinic open. Seconds later, she looked up to see Dr. Traynor and his wife entering the room. The doctor was carrying a food tray that delicious aromas were coming from.

Ellen Traynor moved ahead of her husband and bent over Emma, embracing her. "I'm so sorry about this, Emma."

Emma patted Ellen's cheek.

Ellen quickly pulled a small cart in front of Emma, and as the doctor set the tray on it, Ellen said, "I made you some bean soup. Actually I made enough for Dr. John and me. We'll have our supper in a moment. I doubt that you feel very hungry, but you must nourish your body in order to hold up under this strain."

Emma's eyes were still on Ellen. "It smells wonderful. I'll get most of it down, I assure you." As she looked at the tray, her eyes went to the small vase with a bright yellow tulip in it. "Oh, thank you, Ellen. How very thoughtful of you."

Ellen smiled. "My pleasure. Now, Dr. John and I will go have our supper and let you eat in peace. I'll be back later to spend the night with you. And Dr. John will take another look at Jody then. If you want to freshen up, there's a washroom back there by the clinic's rear door. Everything you need is there."

Emma thanked both of them; then Ellen moved close to the bed and looked down at Jody. She turned again to Emma. "Honey, don't you give up. Dr. John and I have already prayed for this sweet girl, and we will continue to do so. We will also ask our pastor to put her on the prayer list at church."

"I appreciate that very much. Thank you."

The doctor lit a lantern that sat at the head of the bed. "Eat now, Emma. We'll be back shortly."

When the Traynors had left the room, Emma bowed her head, thanked the Lord for the food, and once again, begged Him to spare her daughter's life.

Emma took up the spoon provided on the tray and dipped it into the thick bean soup. She had barely started eating when she thought, *I didn't realize I was so hungry.*

She enjoyed the soup, along with a slice of cornbread slathered with butter and honey. She sipped on the hot coffee and enjoyed a piece of spice cake to finish off the meal. She wiped her mouth on her napkin and wondered what Sam was having for supper. Knowing he wasn't much on cooking, he probably ate a slice of cheese, along with some bread and a cold chunk of ham. "I'll make it up to you when we get through this hard time," she said in a whisper.

Pushing the cart aside, Emma stood up and looked down at her daughter by the light of the lantern. She stared at her intently, wishing for the smallest flutter of an eyelash. She sat down on the chair again and took hold of Jody's small limp hand.

Emma let her thoughts go back to the day Jody was born. As the next hour passed, she relived many of the wonderful memories and happy moments the precious girl had brought into the Claiborne home in the past twelve years.

She was nodding in the chair from sheer exhaustion when she heard footsteps and looked up to see that the Traynors had returned.

Ellen laid a hand on her shoulder. "Emma, Dr. John wants to check on Jody. Why don't you take a few minutes to go to the washroom and refresh yourself, then step outside and let some of the fresh spring air into your lungs?"

Emma nodded and stood up. "I do need a little break."

The doctor smiled. "We'll be right here with Jody. Go take your little break."

Glancing once more at her daughter, Emma managed a smile for the Traynors, and made her way to the washroom.

When she had finished in the washroom, she stepped outside into the inky darkness. The air was cool and felt good on her face. She looked up into the night sky and marveled at the millions of twinkling stars. "Thank You, Lord, for the beauty you bring even in the midst of such heartache and stress."

After a few minutes, Emma returned to Jody's room. Both the doctor and his wife were standing over the unconscious girl. Emma noted the two cots that stood side by side near the bed, each with blankets and a pillow.

Emma moved up, glanced at her daughter, then at the doctor. "Any change?"

Traynor shook his head slowly. "Not yet. I'm hoping and praying that there will be by morning. I'm going to leave now, and let you ladies get some sleep."

When the doctor was gone, Ellen put an arm around Emma as she stood over her daughter's bed. "Let's have prayer first, Emma."

At dawn on Sunday morning, Emma awakened to see Ellen rising from her cot. Jody's mother had experienced only short snatches of sleep during the night. Her eyes were red and bleary with fatigue as she looked up at Ellen. "Emma, Jody's still unconscious. I'm going to the house to make breakfast. You just lie here and rest. I'll be back with a tray for you in a little while."

When Ellen had left the room, Emma rose from the cot and made her way to the washroom. She washed her face, tidied her hair as well as possible, and tried to smooth some of the wrinkles out of her pale yellow cotton dress.

Upon entering Jody's room once again, Emma found Dr. Traynor listening to Jody's heartbeat with a stethoscope. Ellen had a breakfast tray on the cart in front of Emma's chair.

Ellen smiled at Emma. "Come, dear. Eat your breakfast."

Emma thanked her for the breakfast, then sat down on the chair. The strong coffee helped to revive her. While eating, she kept an eye on the doctor, who was checking Jody's pulse with Ellen at his side. When he finished with the pulse, he bent low over her and pushed the eyelids open.

Emma cringed when she caught sight of her daughter's glazed eyes, which seemed to stare into nothingness. The doctor held the eyes open for several minutes while studying them carefully. When he let them close, his shoulders stiffened.

Ellen looked up into his gray face. Before she could whisper a question, Emma said, "What is it, Doctor? What's wrong?"

The doctor turned slowly. "She's gone into a coma, Emma."

Emma blinked. "A coma? I…I've heard of people being in

comas, but I don't really understand. What does that mean?"

At that instant there was a tap on the door, and when it opened, Joyce Adams appeared. "Dr. Traynor, Mr. Claiborne is here. Pastor and Mrs. Forbes are with him, as well as Betty and her parents."

"All right, Joyce. Tell them I'll be out in a few minutes. I'm going to put a fresh bandage on Jody's head, then I'll bring Emma with me."

Joyce nodded, and was gone.

Dr. Traynor put kind eyes on Emma. "I'll wait to explain about the coma when I can tell you, Sam, and your friends at the same time."

Emma was squeezing her hands together until the knuckles were shiny white. "Does this mean she is going to die?"

The doctor shook his head. "Not necessarily, Emma. Many people who slip into comas come back out of them. Let me change this bandage, and we'll go out and talk to Sam and the others. Ellen will stay here with Jody."

A few minutes had passed when the doctor and Emma left the room and went out to the office and the waiting area.

Sam saw the uneasy look in their eyes. He rushed to Emma and took her hand. "Is it bad?"

She looked up into his face, which was haggard from loss of sleep. Concern was etched in every line. "I'm not sure exactly, dear. Dr. Traynor is going to explain it."

Sam nodded, then kissed her pale cheek. "Did you rest at all?"

"I…well, I snatched a few winks here and there."

The doctor spoke to Pastor Dan Forbes and Clara, Mike and Natalie Houston, as well as Betty. All were his patients, and he knew them well. They all sat down in the waiting area, and Dr. Traynor sat down facing them.

"I just did an examination on Jody. I was so hoping that she would regain consciousness by this morning, but it's worse. I told Emma before we came out here that Jody is now in a coma."

Sam's features were pinched and gray. "Tell us what this means, Doctor. I, at least, know very little about comas."

Dr. Traynor adjusted himself on the chair. "A coma is a deep state of unconsciousness from which a person cannot be aroused even by stimuli that would give them pain. If they're just unconscious, they can be stimulated to consciousness if physical pain is induced. Sometimes even cold water splashed in their face will bring them around. They also will respond to certain commands. But a person in a coma does not respond to any kind of command.

"I don't want to frighten you, but I must be honest about this. Coma is the result of damage to the brain stem or the cerebrum, or both. The cerebrum is that part of the brain that contains higher nervous centers than the stem. This damage can be from a blow to the head—which Jody had—or by cardiac arrest, stroke, shock, or hemorrhage."

Emma was taken aback at the doctor's words. Clara and Sam both tightened their grip on her hands.

"Let me tell you this. Medical science is constantly learning more about coma. They now know that there are various depths of coma, which medical researchers in Switzerland have recently discovered. The nature of the injury determines the depth of the coma. Survival and prognosis depend on the extent of the damage. Sometimes it is very difficult to say whether a person will come out of the coma—and one day awaken—or will die in that state."

Pastor Dan Forbes leaned forward on his chair. "Doctor, in your opinion, what are Jody's chances of coming out of the coma?"

Traynor wiped a palm over his face. "Pastor, I can only guess. We physicians read the depth of the coma mostly by studying the eyes of the patient. The heartbeat and the pulse can tell us a lot, but it's the eyes that tell us the most. I dealt with comas as an army doctor in the Civil War, and my experience in this realm tells me that Jody's chances of awakening are not good."

Emma gasped.

Sam stiffened.

The doctor took a deep, shaky breath. "I wish I could be more optimistic, but based on my experiences in dealing with soldiers in comas, I must come to this conclusion: Jody's eyes don't look good at all. The percentage of people as deep as she is, of ever coming out of it, is very small." Tears misted his eyes. "I'm sorry I can't give you more hope."

Sam pulled Emma's head tight against his chest and held it there as she began to drop silent tears.

Pastor Forbes said, "We must bathe Jody in prayer."

Traynor nodded. "Yes, Pastor. Only God can bring Jody back to her parents and friends, if this is His will. He…He may want her in heaven with Him."

"The only way we can pray in this matter," said the pastor, "is that the Lord will do whatever will bring Him the most glory."

The doctor nodded his agreement, then turned to Sam and Emma. "My experience with comas has taught me that the patient can be kept alive for a matter of a few weeks by feeding them broth and giving them water. Most coma patients will swallow whatever liquid is put in their mouth. If Jody does this, her chances of coming out of it are better."

Emma lifted her head from Sam's chest and drew a shuddering breath. "Doctor, how often should Jody be fed the broth?"

"Five or six times a day, since only small amounts can be given at a time. She should be given water at least a dozen times a day." He added quickly, "It will be best if Jody is kept here at the clinic so the other doctor or one of the nurses can keep watch on her at all times."

Emma nodded. "Doctor, I know the nurses can't stay up all night, and neither can either of you doctors. I will have Sam bring me into town every evening so I can stay with Jody all night and give her water and broth during that time. I'll catch my own sleep during the daytime."

Clara Forbes spoke up. "Emma, that will still be too much for you. An every-night vigil could put you down. I'll alternate nights with you."

"Tell you what," said Natalie Houston, "I'll take my turn too. Let's make it every third night intervals."

Betty shook her head. "Every *fourth* night. I'll do my part. School's out next week, so I'll be able to do it, starting next Thursday."

Emma's eyes were misty. "Thank you, Clara. Thank you, Natalie. Thank you, Betty. I appreciate your willingness to help, and the sacrifice it's going to be on the part of each of you to do so. God bless you."

Clara took hold of Emma's hand. "We wouldn't have it any other way, dear. That's what Christian friends are for. When one of our own is hurting, we should do everything we can to ease that pain. And always remember, Emma: God's grace can make our peace greater than our pain."

Emma squeezed her hand. "Thank you for reminding me, Clara. You are so right. We have a wonderful God whose grace is immeasurable and whose way is always best."

"Amen," said Pastor Dan Forbes. "I'll get more volunteers from among the ladies in the church to stay with Jody at night. Then no one will get worn down by it."

"I appreciate your willingness to do that, Pastor," said Emma.

Dr. Traynor turned to Dan Forbes. "If you don't get enough help from the ladies in your church, Pastor, I'll try to get some of the ladies in our church to help."

Forbes nodded. "I appreciate that, Doctor, more than I can tell you. But I think we'll get enough help from among our ladies. If not, though, I'll let you know."

"You do that."

"You can count on it. Dr. Traynor?"

"Yes?"

"Would it be all right if all of us go into Jody's room to pray over her?"

"Certainly. Let's go."

John Traynor led the group into the room where Jody Claiborne lay in a coma.

The eyes of the Forbeses and the Houstons were fixed on Jody as they drew up to the bed. Betty leaned down and kissed Jody's forehead. "I love you, Jody. Please come back to us."

This brought tears to every eye.

Pastor Forbes said, "Let's make a circle around the bed and join hands. You too, Dr. Traynor. We want you in on this."

When the circle was formed, Pastor Forbes led in prayer, asking the Lord to leave Jody in this world with her family and friends unless He could get more glory to His name by taking her home.

When he finished praying, Sam Claiborne turned to him. "Pastor, I know you understand that Emma and I feel we should stay here with Jody, so we won't be in church today."

Forbes smiled. "Of course I understand, Sam. The Lord understands, too."

In Manhattan, New York, on Monday, May 25, Josie Holden arrived at the tenement house from school at 3:45 in the afternoon. When she stepped into the foyer, the landlord and his wife—both in their early sixties—were in conversation with a couple Josie did not know.

Myrtle Bailey said, "Hello, Josie. I'd like to introduce you to Mr. and Mrs. Claxton. They'll be moving into apartment 22, just down the hall from you. Mr. and Mrs. Claxton, this is Josie Holden. She and her father live in apartment 28."

Josie adjusted the small pack that bore her schoolbooks and curtsied. "I'm glad to meet you."

The Claxtons both smiled, and the lady asked, "How old are you, dear?"

"I'm twelve, ma'am."

Frank Bailey chuckled. "And let me tell you, Mrs. Claxton, this little gal is quite the tomboy. She can throw a baseball as far and as straight as any boy in this neighborhood."

Mrs. Claxton's smile widened. "Really?"

"Really," said Bailey. "And she's quite the wrestler, too. She can pin almost every boy in the neighborhood who's her age or older."

Josie's face tinted. "Now, Mr. Bailey, I can only pin the boys who are my age, or some of them who are thirteen or fourteen. But not those who are fifteen or older."

Mr. Claxton laughed. "Well, Miss Josie Holden, remind me to stay on your good side. I'm only fourteen!"

Josie laughed, as did the others. Then looking at the Baileys, she said, "Well, I need to get upstairs to the apartment. Since Papa doesn't get home from work till six o'clock, I don't need to start supper for another hour and a half. So after I put my books away, I'm going down to the playground. The boys are about to start a baseball game."

"Well, far be it from us to keep you from that game!" Bailey said.

Josie told the Claxtons she was glad to meet them, then hurried up the stairs.

Five minutes later, when she came back downstairs, the

Baileys and the Claxtons were no longer in the vestibule. She ran down Canal Street to the next block where the neighborhood boys had two team captains who were choosing boys to be on their respective teams.

When one of them spotted Josie coming across the playground toward them, he said he wanted her on his team. The other captain immediately argued, saying he wanted Josie on his team. Josie laughed and waited while one of the captains flipped a coin. The team leader who had called tails won the toss, and Josie joined his team.

The game was over shortly before it was time for Josie to go home and start supper. The team she had played on had won the game. Her teammates—all boys—cheered her because on offense, she had knocked two home runs, and on defense, she had helped make a double play.

The boys on her team were still cheering her when she headed down the street toward home.

As Josie drew near the tenement, she saw Frank Bailey talking to a well-dressed man. She did not recognize him. Myrtle was standing with them.

On the front steps of the tenement house, Frank Bailey glanced up the street. "Here she comes."

Myrtle's face pinched. "Oh, I wish this horrible accident hadn't happened. Poor little thing. What's she going to do?"

Bailey shook his head. "I don't know."

Josie was smiling as she neared the porch steps, and since the eyes of all three were on her, she smiled at the Baileys. "Guess what! My team won!"

Frank cleared his throat. "Uh…Josie, this gentleman is here to talk to you."

Puzzlement etched itself on the girl's features as she looked up at the stranger.

His face was pale as he said, "Josie, I'm Wash Roebling."

"Oh, you're my papa's boss at the Roebling Construction Company."

Roebling's throat tightened, and while he was trying to speak, Myrtle stepped up beside Josie and put an arm around her. Josie glanced at Myrtle, then looked back at her father's employer.

Roebling cleared his throat and swallowed hard. "Josie, there was an accident on the construction site at the Brooklyn Bridge just after two o'clock. Your—your father fell from a scaffold, and—and, well, he was killed."

Josie's mouth fell open and her eyes widened. She shook her head in disbelief. "No! It can't be! Not my papa! He can't be dead. No! No-o-o!" Her voice went into a wail. "No-o-o! It isn't so-o-o!"

She burst into tears, and her knees gave way. Myrtle held onto her, keeping her from falling.

"Oh, Mrs. Bailey, what am I going to do? There was only Papa and me!" Josie's voice raised hysterically. "What is going to happen to me? I'm only twelve years old! I have no one!"

Myrtle held her close, saying only, "There, there, honey."

While Myrtle attempted to calm the grieving child, her husband looked at Wash Roebling and said, "Curtis was to pay this week's rent when he came home today. He always paid us on Mondays. I...I've got to rent the apartment to someone else as soon as possible."

Roebling reached into his pocket and took out a wad of currency that was folded under a money clip. "How much is the rent?"

"Three dollars a week."

Roebling took out six one-dollar bills and handed them to him. "This will take care of the rent for last week and next week.

After that, you'll have to decide what to do about the girl."

Josie had observed the transaction. Sniffling, she said, "Thank you, Mr. Roebling."

"I'm glad to do it, Josie. And I'm very sorry about what happened to your father. He was a good worker, and I'll miss him. I...I told Mr. and Mrs. Bailey what funeral home picked up your father's body."

Josie wiped tears. "So there will be a funeral for Papa?"

"My company will pay for the coffin, the burial plot, the digging of the grave, and the burial, but not embalming or a funeral service. His body will be buried at the cemetery on 116th Street, which is the least expensive on Manhattan Island. I will see to it that an inexpensive grave marker is put on the grave."

Josie nodded. "Thank you, sir."

"You're welcome. I informed the Baileys that the body will be buried yet today."

When Wash Roebling had gone, the Baileys took Josie into their apartment and tried to comfort her. When her emotions had settled some, Frank said, "Now, honey, when the rent runs out this coming Monday, I'll have to rent the apartment to someone else. I'll need you to clean up the apartment before you move out. You must take your father's belongings, as well as your own."

Josie was too upset to attend school during the following week. She stayed in the apartment, spending a great deal of time weeping over the loss of her father and the fear of what was going to happen to her. The Baileys had explained that they were in no position to take her into their home. They had brought up that an orphanage would be good if she could find one that had room for her.

Josie had heard much about New York City's overcrowded

orphanages. She knew about the colonies of children who lived on the streets and decided she had no choice but to join them.

When Monday came after long days of grieving over her father and dreading her move to the streets, Josie steeled herself for the pain she would feel when she walked out of the apartment she had shared with her father. Going to her bedroom, she stood at the door and ran her gaze over the room. Reaching down inside herself, she found the courage she knew was there and brought it as a cloak around her.

"I can do whatever I have to. Papa taught me well, and I won't disappoint him."

She went to the bed, knelt down, and pulled out a small satchel.

Placing it on the bed, she filled it with dresses, underclothes, and a spare pair of shoes. She also stuffed in her winter coat. Though it was now May, she knew how severe the Manhattan winters were.

With this done, Josie took her father's clothing and shoes out of his closet and placed them on the bed. Tears welled up in her eyes as she looked at them. Ejecting a sob, she picked up a wad of shirts and pressed them to her face, soaking them with her tears.

When her weeping had subsided, she laid the note she had written the night before next to her father's clothing. In the note, she had told Mr. Bailey that she had nowhere to dispose of her father's belongings, nor her own, and asked if he would do it for her.

She went to the kitchen and filled a canvas bag with as much food as she could carry in one hand, then set it by the front door of the apartment beside the satchel.

Before opening the door, Josie took one last look around the apartment that had been her home for so long. Her shoulders slumped as silent tears flooded her vision, then glided down her drawn face and dripped off her chin.

She wiped away the tears. Squaring her slim shoulders, she opened the door and picked up the satchel in one hand and the canvas bag in the other. She looked up and down the hall to make sure neither of the Baileys was in sight. She took a deep breath. "You can do this, Josie," she said. "Now go."

She closed the door behind her and went down the hall to the back stairs. When she reached the alley, she was thankful that she had not accidentally run into either of the Baileys. Josie reached the end of the alley and told herself she must find her father's grave before taking to the streets.

With her heart fluttering in her chest, she moved out onto the street and started the long walk north toward 116th Street.

Chapter Ten

After walking for nearly two hours, Josie Holden arrived at the cemetery. She had seen it many times, but had never walked onto the grounds. It was large, and she knew it might take a while to find her father's grave.

She passed through the gate and noted the dirt path that was used by hearses, wagons, carriages, and buggies. She made her way along the edge of the path, letting her eyes roam over the grounds as she looked for fresh graves. The cemetery was rich with shade trees that were scattered about, casting their dark shadows on nearby graves. Soon she spotted three fresh graves off to her right and veered across the grass toward them. When she reached the mounds, she read the markers, but none of them bore her father's name.

She kept moving, and after a few minutes, she came to an area where she spotted half a dozen fresh graves. While making her way toward them, her attention was drawn to a hearse and a few buggies and carriages that stood on the dirt path. A few yards away, there was a funeral service in progress at an open grave close by.

When Josie drew up to the mounds, the first grave marker bore the name *Curtis Holden.*

She dropped the satchel and canvas bag. Her hand went to

her mouth, and suddenly a sea of churning emotions made her tremble. Tears gushed from her eyes as she fell to her knees beside the fresh mound. "Oh, Papa, I miss you terribly! I didn't want you to die! I'm all alone now. I have to go live on the streets with other children who have no home."

She buried her face in her hands.

At the nearby graveside service, a young woman happened to catch sight of the girl kneeling beside the fresh grave, her body shaking as she sobbed.

At that moment, the preacher conducting the service closed in prayer. When the young woman lifted her head, she glanced at the sorrowing young girl then quickly made her way to the family of the deceased. She hugged each family member, offering her heartfelt condolences. The young woman stepped to a couple close by. "Wait for me, will you? I'll be back in a moment."

The man nodded. "Of course, Rachel. We'll be right here."

Josie Holden knelt at her father's grave and heard soft footsteps in the grass behind her. She turned and looked up through her tears to see a lovely young woman in her late twenties standing over her.

"Hello," said the young woman. "My name is Rachel Wolford. I was attending the graveside service and I noticed you kneeling beside this fresh grave. What is your name, honey?"

"Josie Holden."

"Can I do anything to help you?"

Josie sniffed and rose to her feet. "There's really nothing you can do for me, ma'am. But thank you for offering."

Rachel looked down at the simple grave marker, which bore

only the name of the deceased. There was no date of birth or death. "Curtis Holden. Was this a relative, Josie?"

"Yes, ma'am. My father."

"Oh, I'm so sorry. How did he die?"

"He was killed in a work accident at the Brooklyn Bridge last Monday. He worked for the company that's building the bridge."

"Where's your mother? You shouldn't be alone like this."

Josie sniffed again. "Mama died seven years ago giving birth to a baby boy. My little brother died too."

Rachel's heart was heavy. "Are you living with relatives now?"

"No, ma'am. I have no relatives. Papa and I lived in an apartment down on Canal Street, and the landlord needed to rent the apartment to someone else, so I left this morning."

"So what are your plans? What are you going to do?"

"I'm going to have to live on the streets like thousands of other children do. As you can see, I have my satchel with some of my clothes, and this canvas bag has food in it. I know the food won't last long. I'll have to try to find work like some of the other children do...or beg for food like so many have to."

Rachel took a step closer. "Josie, have you ever heard of Charles Loring Brace and the Children's Aid Society and the orphan trains?"

"Yes, ma'am."

"Well, I am a certified medical nurse and I work for Mr. Brace. I travel on the orphan trains to care for the children in case they get sick."

"Oh. I didn't know the orphan trains had nurses on them."

Rachel took another step and put her arm around Josie's shoulder. "If you would like, I could put you on one of those orphan trains. Would you rather go out West and be taken into a foster home, than to live on the New York streets?"

Josie thought on it a moment. "A foster home out West

sounds a whole lot better than trying to stay alive on the streets, Miss Wolford."

"All right. I have to leave on an orphan train tomorrow morning. The Children's Aid Society has rooms in their building where children can stay on a temporary basis while they wait to go west on a scheduled orphan train. They are fed and given clothing suitable for traveling on the trains. Since you want to go out west, I will take you to the Society headquarters right now and get you lined up to go on the first train that has space for you."

Josie looked up into Rachel's eyes. "Oh, thank you, Miss Wolford. Thank you so much for caring about me."

"You're a sweet girl. It isn't hard to care what happens to you."

Josie managed a smile. "Miss Wolford, could I have a minute to tell my papa good-bye?"

"Of course."

Rachel took a few steps back. She watched her kneel beside the grave once more.

Josie touched the wooden grave marker. "Papa, this nice lady is going to put me on an orphan train so I can find a home somewhere out West. I…I've always lived here in New York, and the only thing I know about the West comes from the stories I've heard. There are still wild Indians out there and no large cities like I'm used to. Or so I've been told. But it will be a fresh start for me, and I think you would want me to do this, Papa, rather than live here on the streets. Maybe some nice family out there in the wide open spaces can use a tomboy like me. I will always try to make you proud."

Even though she was a few steps back, Rachel could hear every word.

Josie rubbed the grave marker lovingly. "Papa, I won't be able to come and visit you anymore, but I will always carry you in my heart. You will never be out of my thoughts. I love you. I always will."

She rose to her feet, picked up the satchel and canvas bag, and looked at Rachel. "All right, ma'am. I'm ready."

Rachel said, "Let me carry those for you."

"It's all right, Miss Wolford, they're not heavy."

"How about I carry just one, then?"

"All right."

Rachel took the canvas bag and put an arm around the girl. "I have some friends waiting over here. They'll take us to the Society's headquarters."

Josie put her arm around Rachel, and as they made their way across the grass, weaving their way among the grave markers, Rachel said, "I haven't asked your age, but I'm guessing you're going to turn thirteen on your next birthday."

Josie smiled up at her. "As Papa would say, Miss Wolford, you hit the nail right on the head."

Rachel chuckled. "Sometimes I do that."

Josie squeezed her tight with the arm that encircled her waist. She had developed an attachment to Miss Rachel Wolford quickly.

When Rachel and Josie arrived at the Society's headquarters, Rachel took her into the office to register her for a room and establish the date she would be put on a train for her trip west.

Rachel introduced Josie to Mildred Fallon, one of Mr. Brace's assistants, and as they sat down in front of Mildred's desk, Rachel told her how she found Josie at the 116th Street Cemetery, then related Josie's story to her.

Mildred used a hanky to dab at the tears that had filled her eyes. "Well, Josie, we're going to see that you find a good home somewhere out West. The next train that is not yet full will leave

Grand Central Station on Tuesday morning, June 16. I'm placing you on that train."

"Oh, good!" exclaimed Rachel. "That's the one I'm scheduled on after I make this trip that I'm going on tomorrow."

Josie's eyes lit up. "You mean we'll be on the same train when I go?"

"We sure will, sweetie."

"I'll look forward to that!"

"Me too. We'll get better acquainted that way."

When the papers had been completed, Mildred said, "All right, Josie, I'll take you to the room where you'll be staying while you're here. One thing for sure. You won't be lonely. There are five other girls in the room. They will be going west on the same train with you."

Josie smiled. "Oh, boy! A chance to make new friends!"

Rachel hugged Josie, saying she had to get to her apartment and make ready to leave on the train tomorrow morning. Josie hugged her tight, kissed her cheek, and thanked her once again for caring about her.

When Mildred Fallon took Josie Holden into the room where she would be staying, the five girls—ages eleven to fourteen—welcomed her warmly. After Mildred was gone, the girls sat down with Josie and asked about her; why she was going west. Their hearts went out to her while she told them her story.

Josie then asked to hear their stories. Two of the girls had been recently orphaned, like her. The other three told horror stories of having to live on the New York City streets for the past several years—hungry and dressed in rags. They told of friends who starved to death on the streets, and of others who froze to death during the winters. Josie's heart went out to them for what they had suffered. Each one then told how she had been found hungry and in tatters by some member of the Children's Aid

Society and brought to their headquarters. One girl told that it was Charles Loring Brace and his wife who had picked her up off the street and brought her to the Society, telling her they would send her out West on one of the orphan trains so she could find a good home.

The next morning, Rachel Wolford came to the room in her white nurse's uniform to see Josie before heading to the railroad station. Josie assured her she was fine and told her how much she liked the girls with whom she was rooming.

As Rachel was about to leave, Josie hugged her. "Miss Wolford, thank you. I love you."

"I love you too, Josie." Rachel then kissed the girl's forehead and hurried away with tears in her eyes.

As the days came and went in Cheyenne, Jody Claiborne remained in the coma. The women who had volunteered to stay at the girl's side during the nights—including Betty Houston— were faithful to do so. Dr. John Traynor personally oversaw his nurses as they fed broth to Jody and gave her water, and he examined her several times a day, watching her vital signs carefully.

On Wednesday, June 3, Sam and Emma arrived at the clinic just before sundown. Nurse Wilma Harned was at the desk and greeted them. Emma informed her that it was her turn to stay the night with Jody.

"Bless your heart, Emma. You've been so faithful to come here every day and stay by Jody's side. If I didn't have to be here on the job every day, I would offer to take your place for the all-night vigils."

"That's sweet of you, Wilma," said Sam, "but there are other women in our church who have offered to do just that. However, my wife feels she must take her turn at night, too."

Dr. Traynor came through the door at the rear of the waiting area. "Hello, Sam, Emma." He noted that Jody's parents were clearly showing the strain.

Sam smiled. "Hello, Doctor. Any change since we were here to see Jody last evening?"

Traynor shook his head sadly. "No. There hasn't been the slightest change. I'm sorry."

"She's been in that coma almost two weeks, Dr. Traynor," said Emma. "Tell us your honest opinion. Do you think Jody will ever come out of it?"

"Well, with each day that passes, Jody's chances of ever awakening become slimmer. All we can do is keep praying."

Sam nodded. "We will do that. Okay if we go back?"

"Of course."

When Sam and Emma entered Jody's room, they stepped up beside the bed, their faces grim. Sam took hold of Emma's hand as they looked down at Jody's features.

"She's losing weight every day, honey," said Sam.

Emma nodded and sighed. "I know."

Sam let go of Emma's hand, went to the chair she always occupied, and slid it to the side of the bed. "Here, darlin'. Sit down."

When Emma was comfortable, Sam pulled up another chair for himself. They sat side by side, watching for any hint of movement from their daughter, but it did not come. At ten o'clock, Sam said, "Well, honey, guess I'd better head for home."

He stood up, took hold of Emma's hand and Jody's hand, then led in prayer. When he had finished praying, he leaned down and kissed Jody's cheek. "Daddy loves his baby girl. Please, sweetheart, come back to us."

"Yes, Jody," said Emma, "please come back to us. We love you so very much."

Sam kissed Emma, saying he would be back to get her in the morning, and with a heavy heart, made his way to the door. He paused with his hand on the knob. "Good night, darlin'. I love you."

Emma wiped a tear from her eye. "Good night, my precious husband. I love you too."

When the door closed, Emma arose from the chair and stood over her beloved daughter. Looking at Jody's thin features, she said in a low tone, "You've been such a blessing, sweetheart. I'll never forget how happy I was when old Dr. Ben Jones told me I had you in my womb. And how very happy I was the day you were born and I held you in my arms."

Emma's mind flashed back to Wednesday, February 27, 1861. It was a banner day for her. She and Sam had almost despaired of ever being parents. They had prayed earnestly, asking God to give them a child.

Sam was in the waiting room at Dr. Jones's office when Emma was being examined. Emma had hoped that she just might be expecting and felt it was time to see what Dr. Jones could find out.

She pictured the look on his face when he looked down at her as she lay on the examining table and said with a smile, "Emma, your prayers have been answered. You are definitely with child, and should give birth about the last week of September."

Having longed to hear this news from the doctor's lips for what seemed like forever, Emma had said with her heart beating rapidly in her breast, "Are you absolutely sure, Dr. Jones?"

"Yes, my dear, I am absolutely positive. Now get dressed so you can go out there and tell that husband of yours!"

The doctor was out of the room while the nurse helped Emma get dressed and returned just as she was ready to go tell the joyful news to Sam. Emma surprised the aging physician by planting a kiss on his cheek. He and the nurse watched as she literally floated out the door.

Standing over Jody's bed with these sweet memories drifting through her mind, Emma laid a hand on her daughter's cheek. "Oh, Jody, what a happy woman I was!"

Remembering once again, Emma recalled that she had enjoyed a fairly easy pregnancy and was delighted with each sign of the baby growing beneath her heart. She and Sam had spent hours planning their future with the child who was already so dear to them.

Stroking Jody's pallid cheek, Emma smiled as she remembered their conversation one night in March 1861.

Sam and Emma sat on the sofa in the parlor of their farmhouse, holding hands. She turned to him and smiled. "I have a very important question to ask you."

Sam smiled back. "All right. Fire away."

"Do you want a boy or a girl?"

This time the smile was also in Sam's voice. "Well, my love, either is fine, 'cause if it's a girl, I'll make a tomboy out of her, anyway!"

"Oh, you will, huh?"

"Absolutely."

"Well, that's all right as long as you let me teach her to be a lady as well."

"Oh, of course. But I have a feeling it's going to be a boy."

Emma grinned. "You do, eh? Well, we will just wait and see, won't we?"

Emma patted Jody's face as she stood over the bed. "Sweetheart, the moment your daddy saw you on that day you were born, he wouldn't have traded you for a million boys."

Her mind drifted back through time again. She recalled how the long months seemed to pass so slowly as she eagerly awaited the day she could hold her baby in her arms.

Then her thoughts fastened on that marvelous day...

Monday, September 30, 1861, dawned rainy and cold. In the kitchen, Emma stirred up the fire in the cookstove and began her morning routine.

After she and Sam had enjoyed their breakfast and had read their Bibles and prayed together, Emma slowly raised her ungainly body from the chair at the kitchen table and felt a sharp stitch in her left side.

Hmm, she thought to herself as she rubbed the spot. *I wonder...*

Then the pain went away.

Nothing, I guess. "Sam, this is the last day of September. If Dr. Jones is right, and I'm to have a September baby, he or she is going to have to hurry up."

Sam grinned as he pushed his chair back and stood up. "Well, hon, we both know that doctors are only human. Predicting the date of a baby's birth is difficult at best. We'll just have to wait and be patient. I'll be working in the barn if you need me. Just give a holler."

"Don't worry. I will. You come in sometime around mid-morning, and I'll have some hot coffee for you. It's pretty cold out there, with the rain and all."

"Will do, sweetie," Sam said, and taking her in his arms, kissed her soundly.

The day went by as usual, and they both stayed busy with their chores. Emma, of course, took a few minutes to rest periodically. Several times during the day, she stopped and rubbed her aching back, making a fist of her hand and pushing against the offending spot. As the hours passed, she knew she didn't feel just right. She had a few twitches, but nothing to indicate real labor.

The day grew colder and the rain came down steadily.

Late in the afternoon, Sam came in with his milk pail, chilled and damp. Emma was at the cupboard, slicing potatoes. Sam noticed that she was quite pale. He gave her a hand with supper.

When they sat down to eat, Emma toyed with her food, but ate very little.

"Not hungry?"

"Not really. I just don't feel very good. Nothing specific."

After the dishes were washed and put away, they went into the parlor. Sam stirred up the flames in the fireplace while Emma relaxed in her favorite padded rocking chair.

For the past two months, Sam had been rubbing Emma's swollen feet and ankles after supper, and while he was doing so that evening, they spun their dreams of the wonderful future ahead of them.

It wasn't long until Emma was nodding in her rocking chair. Sam took hold of her hand and her eyes popped open. "Honey, I know it's early, but I think you need to get to bed. You go on. I'll stoke the fire and put out the lamps."

Moments later, when Sam entered the bedroom, Emma was already flat on her back and covered. Her swollen midsection made a sizable mound under the covers.

Sam put out the lantern and slipped in beside her.

Shortly after Emma had dropped into a light sleep, a jarring pain gripped her back and shot around to her midsection. She let out a gasp and put her hands on her belly. Sam seemed to be sleeping soundly, and not wanting to awaken him, she lay perfectly still.

However, in a matter of less than five minutes, another pain attacked her. A small moan escaped her tight lips.

Fully aware that Emma could go into labor at any time, Sam was attuned to her every movement and was immediately awake. Turning onto his back, he raised up on an elbow, trying to see her face in the dark room. "What is it, honey? The baby?"

"I think so," she squeaked as another pain began its route through her body.

Sam jumped out of the bed and lit the closest lantern, wanting to better assess the situation.

Wide-eyed, Emma lay on the bed, a sheen of perspiration covering her brow. Her hands were gently rubbing the girth of her belly.

"Should I go for Dr. Jones?"

Emma swallowed. "I…I don't know. It seems so sudden. I was always told that first babies take hours and hours."

She caught her breath after another contraction lanced through her.

"I can't leave you to go for the doctor, sweetheart. Your pains are too close together. What if the baby came while I was gone?"

Emma had no answer.

Sam began pacing the floor like a caged animal. Several minutes passed. The sound of his bare feet on the floor was nearly drowned out by the sound of the steady rain.

Emma dared to take a deep breath. It brought no pain. Looking sheepishly at her pacing husband, she said, "Guess it was a false alarm. No more pains have come. Let's try to go back to sleep."

Sam stopped and shook his head. "Oh no, you don't. My mind's made up. I'm going for the doctor. This may very well be the real thing and the Lord has let your pains slow down so I'll have time to go bring Dr. Jones here. You stay right there in that bed. I'll be back with the doctor soon."

While he was putting on his clothes, Emma said, "All right, dear husband. You be careful riding out there in that rain. Baby and I need you."

As Sam dashed out the bedroom door, Emma said, "Please protect him, Lord. He's just about beside himself right now." She noted by the clock on the wall that it was 9:40.

The patter of the rain lulled Emma into a light sleep. When she woke up, she glanced at the clock and found that she had slept exactly one hour. Sam should be here with the doctor any minute.

While she listened for the sound of her returning husband, a pain assailed her body. She gasped, "Hurry up, Sam! Please hurry!"

One pain after another was upon her, with little time in between to catch her breath.

She was fearful of giving birth while alone, yet knowing that God was in control, she tried to rest in Him. Moaning now with each pain, Emma clamped her teeth together, trying not to scream, but the pains were coming one right after another and a loud scream made its way past her clenched teeth.

Emma heard pounding feet in the hall, and Sam came through the door with Dr. Jones on his heels, black medical bag in hand.

"We heard your wail, honey," said Sam, taking hold of her hand.

"Oh, thank God!" she gasped, squeezing Sam's hand.

Dr. Jones set his medical bag on the small table by the bed. "We're here now, Emma. Everything will be all right. Sam, go get me a pail of warm water from the kitchen, and bring a couple of towels with you." With that he turned, went to the basin by the dresser, and washed his hands.

Sam dashed obediently out the bedroom door, saying they

had bought some soft blankets for the baby.

When the doctor returned to the bed, he said, "Just relax now, Emma, and push for all you're worth when I tell you."

Sam returned with the pail of water, the towels, and a soft baby blanket.

The doctor had prepared Emma for the birth that was about to take place, and after two more contractions, a lusty cry was heard while Sam stood like a statue, his eyes bulging.

Emma gave a huge sigh of relief and satisfaction.

The silver-haired physician put his attention on the wailing baby and said, "You folks have a beautiful daughter!"

Emma was still panting slightly from her exertion. "Is…is… she all right…Doctor?"

Jones chuckled, his attention still on the newborn. "Everything looks to be in working order. Eight fingers and two thumbs. Ten toes, two eyes, two ears, and a cute little nose above a rosebud mouth. Just a moment, I'll let you see for yourself." He looked at the clock on the wall. "By the way, she *is* a September baby! It's fifteen minutes till midnight."

Jones quickly washed the baby with the water Sam had brought and dried her off with a towel. The baby was still crying, but began getting quieter while the doctor wrapped her in the soft blanket and placed her in her mother's waiting arms.

Sam moved up and sat on the edge of the bed beside mother and daughter. Both parents had tears in their eyes as they beheld the blessed gift God had given them, feeling their hearts enlarge to encompass this wonderful little miracle.

Emma kissed a tiny cheek. "Hello, sweetheart. Daddy and I agreed that if you were a girl, your name would be Jody Ann. We love you."

"We sure do, darlin'," said Sam, leaning down to kiss the other cheek.

He then took hold of Emma's free hand and bowed his head. "Thank You, heavenly Father, for this incredible blessing. Right now, we give little Jody Ann back to You, asking that You will use her to glorify Your name. Please give us wisdom as we raise her in Your nurture and admonition. Thank You, again, for this little bundle of love. In Jesus' name, amen."

"Amen," echoed Emma, her voice soft with wonder.

Tears flowed down Emma's cheeks as she stood over the bed in the clinic and stroked Jody's cheek with the precious memories fresh in her mind.

Emma gazed at the form of her daughter on the bed. "Honey, it wasn't in God's plan to give us more than one child, but you have always been enough, and just exactly what we needed."

She bent down and kissed her forehead. "The day of your birth was so marvelous. And so was the day of your new birth. Remember? Mommy had the joy of leading you to Jesus when you were six years old. And what a joy it has been to watch you grow into such a fine Christian young lady."

Emma went on to tell her daughter what a blessing she had been to her daddy, being the tomboy that she was.

All the while, Jody lay still and silent.

Emma's eyes filled with tears. "Lord, You know that Sam and I have agreed on this. We will understand if You decide to take Jody home with You. We will miss her terribly, but we only want Your will to be done. If that is to take her home, I know you will give Sam and me the grace to bear it."

Chapter Eleven

In Manhattan, New York, early on Monday evening, June 15, Johnny Marston was standing on the front porch of the house where he had been staying, watching for Pastor and Mrs. Darryl Moore to arrive.

Seated on the porch behind Johnny were Albert and Susan Snyder, who were in their late fifties.

Albert said, "So you've never been on a train before, eh, Johnny?"

Johnny kept his eyes glued on the street, not wanting to miss the sight of the Moore buggy when it rounded the corner. "No, sir. My sisters and I have never even been up close to a train. We've seen 'em moving on the tracks lots of times, but we've never been up close to one so's we could touch it."

Susan kept her eyes on the boy. "Do you suppose Mary and Lizzie are as excited about riding the train as you are?"

"I think Mary is, Mrs. Snyder, but I don't think Lizzie really understands what it's all about, yet. Mary told me at church yesterday that Lizzie still talks about Mama and Papa coming home. We thought we had made her understand that when people die, they don't come back, but Lizzie still doesn't realize that Mama and Papa will never come home again. At times, it seems she understands, then she says things that tell us she doesn't."

"Well, it will just take time," said Albert. "I imagine when you children get settled in a home out West, Lizzie will get the picture."

"Mm-hmm."

Susan left her chair, moved up beside the boy, and put a hand on his shoulder. "I'm glad you and your sisters will get to spend tonight with Mrs. Roberts. She really loves you."

Johnny nodded, keeping his eyes fixed toward the corner. "She's a real nice lady. She said she would adopt us if she was younger. She— Oh, look! Here come Pastor and Mrs. Moore!"

Albert joined his wife and Johnny at the porch railing, and all three watched as the Moore buggy came down the street toward them.

Johnny dashed down the porch steps. When the Moore buggy came to a halt at the curb, Johnny was there to greet them.

The Snyders watched while Pastor Moore helped Dora from the buggy, then both of them hugged the boy.

Johnny walked between them as they crossed the yard and moved up the steps. The Snyders greeted the Moores, then the pastor said, "Has this kid eaten you out of house and home?"

The Snyders both laughed, then Susan said, "He does have quite an appetite for a six-year-old, but it's been a joy to feed him, Pastor. We both wish we could keep him, but he needs to be with his sisters. And all three of them need a permanent home."

Albert nodded. "Right. I'm sure the Lord is going to give them a good home out West."

Dora smiled. "Well, we really appreciate your keeping him here with you all this time." Then she said to Johnny, "Time to go. Mrs. Roberts is fixing supper for all of us."

Johnny hugged Susan and Albert, thanking them for letting him stay at their house.

The Snyders stood on the porch and waved as the buggy pulled away. Sitting between the pastor and his wife, Johnny waved back.

While Pastor Moore was driving the buggy to where they would pick up Mary and Lizzie, Johnny said excitedly, "Just think! Tomorrow, Mary and Lizzie and I will get on that train! It's gonna be really neat! And when we get out West, I'll get to see lots of cowboys and Indians!"

The Moores looked at each other and smiled. They were glad to see Johnny so happy.

The pastor guided the buggy to a halt in front of the home owned by church members Roger and Lois Neal. The Neals, like the Snyders, were in their late fifties. They stood on the porch and smiled as Mary and Lizzie bounded off the porch and ran across the yard, calling to their brother.

Johnny jumped out of the buggy on the street side behind the pastor, and ran around the horse to greet Mary and Lizzie. While the pastor was helping Dora from the buggy, the Marston children began talking excitedly to each other about their upcoming train ride. Together, they walked with the Moores toward the house.

Once they were on the porch, the Moores and the Neals chatted for a moment, then Dora said, "Well, girls, you'd better tell Mr. and Mrs. Neal good-bye. Mrs. Roberts will be waiting for us."

With Lizzie at her side, Mary said to the Neals, "Thank you for letting us stay with you."

"We enjoyed it, honey," said Lois. "We'd like to keep you forever, but we know you have to be on that train tomorrow."

Lizzie raised her arms to Lois while Mary was hugging Roger.

Lois picked Lizzie up, held her close, and kissed her cheek. "I'll miss you, sweetie."

"Miss you too," said Lizzie. "Thank you for taking care of us."

Lois squeezed her tight. "You're welcome, honey. I love you."

When both girls had hugged Roger and Lois, the Marston children followed the Moores across the yard toward the buggy.

The shadows of the trees and houses stretched eastward as the sun's last golden rays shone over the western horizon. Frances Roberts was looking out her parlor window when the Moore buggy pulled up in front of her house. She moved out onto the front porch.

All three of the Marston children looked sadly at the house next door, where they used to live, and their thoughts went to their dead parents. They had once felt so secure. The house looked the same, but Mary and Johnny knew that nothing would ever be the same again in their lives.

As Johnny was helping Lizzie out of the buggy, the little four-year-old pointed to the house that once was her home. "Want Mama! Want Mama!"

Mary took hold of Lizzie's hand. "Honey, Mama and Papa are in heaven with Jesus. Remember?"

Lizzie looked at her blankly. "Want Mama an' Papa come home."

Mary shook her head. "Mama and Papa don't live in that house anymore. They're way up in the sky with Jesus. Don't you remember? We've talked about it lots of times."

"Oh. Uh-huh."

"That's why we're going to ride the train tomorrow. We're going on a long trip to our new home."

"Oh. Okay."

Frances Roberts greeted the children and the Moores. "Supper's ready, everybody. Let's get inside."

When they were gathered in their chairs at the table, Frances asked the pastor to offer thanks to the Lord for the food. In his prayer, Moore asked the Lord to take care of the Marston children as they boarded the orphan train tomorrow, and to give them a happy home with a good Christian family out West.

While they were eating, Frances ran her gaze over the faces of the three children. "I'm sure going to miss you precious babies. I'm so glad I could have you with me in this house tonight. Like Pastor, I've been praying that the Lord will take care of you."

Lizzie's eyes lit up. "Oh, God will take care of us, Mrs. Roberts. Me an' Mary an' Johnny are God's little sparrows."

Pastor Moore smiled and swallowed a mouthful of mashed potatoes. "Lizzie, how'd you know about your being God's little sparrows?"

Frances set her coffee cup back in its saucer. "Shortly after we received the news about Bob and Louise, I showed these children what Jesus said in Matthew chapter 10 and Luke chapter 12 about God's care of the sparrows, and that those who belong to Him are of more value than many sparrows. Lizzie picked up on it and announced that she and her sister and brother were God's little sparrows."

Dora's eyes misted as she looked at Lizzie. "That's so sweet. You're pretty smart, aren't you?"

"She sure is!" said the pastor. "That's some wisdom you have, Lizzie."

As if it were a settled matter in her own mind, Lizzie said, "Thank you."

Frances chuckled. "Well, if you little sparrows will finish cleaning up your plates, I've got chocolate cake for dessert!"

This announcement compelled the children to hurry and devour the food on their plates.

When supper was over and the kitchen was cleaned up, Frances took the children and showed them the room Johnny would sleep in that night, then showed the girls their room. They returned to the Moores in the parlor, and when they sat down, the pastor said, "Dora and I need to get home and check on our mothers, but before we go, I'd like to have prayer for these three sparrows."

They gathered in a circle, holding hands, and with heads bowed and eyes closed—except for Lizzie, who peeked a few times—Pastor Darryl Moore led in prayer, praising God for the Children's Aid Society and thanking Him that He was going to take care of His little sparrows as they went west on the orphan train to find a new home.

When the Moores were at the front door, ready to leave, the pastor said, "Mary, Johnny, Lizzie: Mrs. Moore and I will pick you up in the morning as planned and take you to the Children's Aid Society headquarters. We'll have to pick you up at six-fifteen in order to be there on time."

"We'll be ready, Pastor," Mary assured him.

Later, when Frances had tucked the children into their feather beds and gone to her own bedroom, Lizzie snuggled up close to her sister in the darkness. "Mary, if we prayed an' asked Jesus to let Papa an' Mama come back from heaven so we could still live in our house next door, He would do it, wouldn't He?"

Mary marveled at the sweet innocence and trusting heart of her little sister. She hugged her tight. "Sweetie, there are some things that just can't happen. Whenever God takes someone to heaven, He keeps them there. He doesn't let them come back down here. But don't you worry. God takes care of His little sparrows, remember?"

"Uh-huh."

"Well, He will take care of us then. You and Johnny and I will always be together."

"Okay. Would you hum me a lullaby so I can go to sleep?"

"Sure."

As Mary began humming one of Lizzie's favorite lullabies, she felt the little body relax, and soon Lizzie was asleep.

Mary was unaware of it, but Lizzie was dreaming that her parents had come back, and that once again the family was living in the house next door.

The next morning at just after seven o'clock, the Moores walked the Marston children into the Children's Aid Society headquarters and approached the first desk they came to.

Mildred Fallon looked up and smiled. "You must be Pastor and Mrs. Moore."

"Yes," said the pastor.

"We've been expecting you." Mildred was still smiling as she ran her gaze over the faces of the three orphans. "And this is Mary, John, and Elizabeth Marston."

"Right," said Mary. "But we call my brother Johnny and my sister Lizzie."

"All right. Mary, Johnny, and Lizzie, it is. I see you are dressed properly for your trip. You need to say your good-byes to Pastor and Mrs. Moore now so I can take you to the auditorium where the children always gather for their meeting with Mr. Brace before being taken to Grand Central Station."

Dora turned to the children. "Well, I want my hugs before we go."

"Me too."

When it came Lizzie's turn to hug Pastor Moore, he held her close and kissed her cheek. "I'll miss you, Lizzie. You are a very special little sparrow."

Dora was fighting tears when she and her husband went out the door.

Mildred led the Marston children toward the auditorium, explaining that the building used to be owned and occupied by the Italian Opera House. Lizzie didn't know what an Italian Opera House was, but decided she wouldn't bother to ask.

When they stepped into the huge auditorium, they saw several of the Society's staff members moving about, speaking to the children who were clustered in the first few rows of the center section. Mildred led them to the second row, where three seats were unoccupied.

The children in the area looked at Mary, Johnny, and Lizzie.

Mildred leaned down close. "Mr. Brace will be here in a few minutes to help you understand all about your train ride and what to expect when you meet the people who are wanting to choose children."

Mary nodded. "All right. Thank you, ma'am."

Lizzie sat between her brother and sister, and as Mildred Fallon walked away, she took hold of their hands.

Just behind them, Jimmy Kirkland was seated between a girl and a boy, who were also five years old. As Jimmy was talking to his two friends, the Marston children picked up on his stuttering lisp.

Johnny leaned past Lizzie and said in a low voice, "Mary, that little boy talks funny."

Mary frowned. "He can't help it, Johnny. It would be very impolite to ever say anything to him about it."

"Oh, I would never do that."

Four rows back, Josie Holden was sitting with the girls who had been her roommates since she came to the Society. Suddenly she spotted the nurse who had brought her there. She hadn't seen Miss Wolford since she had left to ride the orphan train the last time.

Josie jumped up and said to her friends, "There's Miss Wolford! Be back in a minute!"

Rachel had come into the auditorium from a rear door at the back of the stage and spotted Josie the instant she stepped into the aisle. She smiled and opened her arms as she hurried to meet up with Josie.

When the two of them came together, they embraced, then easing back in each other's arms, their eyes met.

"Honey, how are you?" asked Rachel.

"I'm fine, Miss Wolford. And even better now that you're here. Are you still going to be the nurse on our train?"

"I sure am. It's almost seven-thirty. Mr. Brace will be here any minute. You'd better take your seat. I'll see you on the train, if not before."

Josie hugged her again and hurried back to her friends.

The staff members who were going to be on the train were mounting the steps to the stage when everyone saw the small frame of Charles Loring Brace come onto the stage from a side door. The staff quickly sat down on the wooden chairs that were clustered in a group a few feet behind the rostrum.

Brace was smiling as he stepped onto the rostrum. "Good morning!"

Children and staff answered in a chorus of good mornings.

Brace looked down at the children in the seats before him. "Looks like we've got all sixty-one of our passengers here." He looked back at the staff. "Anyone missing?"

"They're all here, sir," one of the men told him.

Turning back to look at the children, Brace said, "I hope all of you will enjoy your trip west. Now let me explain the rules you will abide by once you are on the train."

When he had gone over the rules, Brace explained the procedure that would be followed in the railroad stations when the prospective foster parents would file by them, looking them over and asking them questions. When that was done, he smiled at them. "How many of you have never traveled on a train before?"

The majority raised their hands.

"Well, this will be a new experience for most of you. I want to introduce you to the ladies and gentlemen who will be your sponsors and chaperones on the trip."

This was the cue for the staff behind him to step forward and line up at the edge of the stage.

Brace gestured toward them. "I will introduce them in the order they are standing in line. First are Mr. Gifford Stanfield and his wife, Laura. Next are Mr. Derek Conlan and his wife, Tabitha. There are two coaches for the orphans in the train. One for the boys and one for the girls. Mr. Stanfield and Mr. Conlan will be riding in the boys' coach, and their wives will be riding in the girls' coach. The two coaches will be connected at the rear of the train just ahead of the caboose. The girls' coach will be ahead of the boys' coach. Ladies first, you know."

Laughter swept over the group.

"I want all of you to understand that there will be Bible reading and prayer twice a day in both coaches, as is done here at the Society. And I want to make sure all of you understand that you are to obey your sponsors at all times. Now, let me introduce someone else—this lady in the white uniform. This is Miss Rachel Wolford. She is a certified medical nurse and will be traveling with you in case any of you should become ill on the trip. Miss Wolford will be riding in the girl's coach."

Rachel let her eyes settle on Josie Holden, and found Josie smiling at her and clapping her hands silently.

Charles Brace then explained that the train would have other coaches that carried passengers as usual. He pointed out that the train would be stopping at Cleveland, Chicago, Des Moines, and Omaha, before the first stop where people would be prepared to choose orphans. This would happen at Kearney, Nebraska. At each stop after that, people were expecting the orphan train—Cheyenne, Wyoming; Rawlins, Wyoming; Austin, Nevada; Reno, Nevada; Sacramento, California; and finally, San Francisco, California.

"Now let me say this, boys and girls. Please don't get discouraged if you are passed over time and again. It usually takes the entire trip for us to see all of the orphans chosen by prospective foster parents. Now, if any of you have not been chosen by the time the people in San Francisco have looked you over and talked to you, you will be brought back to New York, and after some time passes, you will be put on another train. The process will continue until every child has been chosen. We've had very few times that children have been brought back here to start over again. And on the second trip, those children have been chosen."

Brace then led in prayer, asking God to give safety to the children, their chaperones, and their nurse on the trip.

The children were then escorted outside, where six wagons waited to carry them to Grand Central Station. When they arrived at the station, the five adults led them to the track where the train was parked that would be taking them west.

The children who had never ridden on a train stared wide-eyed at the engine that was heaving steam from its bowels. Their eyes ran to the coal car, baggage coach, three regular coaches, two that were set aside for the orphans, and the caboose.

The five adults were kept busy quieting the fearful hearts of some of them, assuring them that it was quite safe to travel in the giant vehicle.

Once on board, the boys and girls crowded up to the windows of their respective coaches to observe the crowds of people, including those who were boarding other coaches in their train.

At ten o'clock sharp, the orphan train pulled out of Grand Central Station and headed west.

On Wednesday morning, June 17, at Chicago's Union Station, a carriage bearing two men rolled into the parking lot.

Thirty-five-year-old Lance Adams hopped out, turned, and picked up his briefcase.

The man at the reins, sixty-year-old Harold Fremont, eased out a little slower and tied the reins to the hitching post.

Adams set his eyes on the gray-headed Fremont. "Really, Harold, you don't have to walk me in and wait till my train leaves."

Fremont shook his head. "Oh, but I'm getting to know you, Lance. When I met you at the businessmen's convention, I told myself that I can learn from a man your age who owns the largest department store in San Francisco. My store here in Chicago isn't half the size of yours. And when you were introduced before you spoke to the convention, and I learned that you didn't inherit some large sum of money but started at the bottom and rose to where you are now, I said to myself, 'Harold, offer to take that young genius to the depot when he heads back to California. You can learn something from him.'"

Lance grinned as they headed into the depot. "Harold, let me give you the truth of the matter of my success."

"I'm listening."

"My success has come because the Lord helped me. The glory goes to the God of heaven. He has blessed me in a marvelous way."

"I got that impression when you gave your testimony at the convention on Monday morning. It was a joy to find out that you were my brother in Christ. I can tell you really love the Lord."

"I sure do. Jesus saved me when I was twenty-one years old at a revival meeting, and my life has been wonderful ever since. It hasn't been without trials and troubles, but the Lord has seen me through them all, and I'm confident He will do so in the future. My greatest blessing since being saved is the fine Christian wife God gave me when I was twenty-four. Carol is the most wonderful Christian woman in all the world. The most beautiful one, too."

They passed through the door into the terminal.

"I appreciate your feeling that way about your wife, Lance, but actually my wife, Bertha, is the most wonderful Christian woman in the world and the most beautiful, too."

They agreed that they both should feel that way about their wives.

Harold gestured toward the large chalkboard in the main part of the station. "Let's check and see if your train is leaving on time."

They drew up, and Lance said, "Yep. It's going to arrive on time, and it will leave on time."

They walked to the track where the train from New York's Grand Central Station would be coming in and sat down on one of the benches.

While they were waiting for the train to arrive, Harold Fremont asked question after question to learn all he could about Lance Adams's successful business practices. Soon the train chugged in and squealed to a halt.

Harold thanked Lance for all the excellent information, then frowned as he pointed to the last two coaches. "Look there, Lance. Those two coaches are loaded with children: boys in one and girls in the other. There's nothing but young faces at the windows. Why would those two coaches be filled with children?"

"I don't have any idea. That's strange, isn't it? I wonder— Wait a minute! I know what that is. It's one of those orphan trains I've read about."

"Oh yeah! I've read about those too. This is the first time I've ever seen one. Just look at all those innocent faces."

Chapter Twelve

Lance Adams and Harold Fremont stayed on the bench while the Chicago-bound passengers were getting off the train.

Harold pointed at the girls' coach. "See that little blonde in the second window from the front? The one with the red hair bow?"

"Uh-huh. She's a doll. 'Bout five years old, I'd say. What about her?"

"She reminds me of one of my granddaughters when she was that age. She's seventeen now, but that little girl sure looks like her."

"How many grandchildren do you have, Harold?"

"Six. Three boys. Three girls. I have two daughters and one son. One daughter-in-law. Two sons-in-law. You have any children, Lance?"

"Ah…no. Carol had to have a hysterectomy when she was seventeen. Before we even met."

"Oh. I'm sorry."

"It was tough on her. When we met and found ourselves falling in love, she told me she could never have children, then explained about the hysterectomy. I told her I knew she was the one God had chosen to be my wife and asked her at that moment if she would marry me. She was so overwhelmed at my attitude, it took her a full minute to get hold of herself enough to accept my proposal."

"She sounds like a fine young lady."

"That she is."

Harold's eyes went to the orphans in the two coaches. "Have you considered adopting a child?"

Lance's mind flashed back to a day a few months previously when he had mentioned the idea of adopting a child to Carol. She seemed cold to the idea. By the few words she spoke, Lance figured that Carol felt if she couldn't bear a child, an adopted child would not fulfill her need as a mother. He cleared his throat gently. "We've…ah…talked about it some, but at this point, I guess we're just not ready."

"I see. Well, children are a blessing. I hope someday you will adopt one, or even more than one. Otherwise you'll never have any grandchildren, and believe me, you don't want to miss out on that."

At that instant, the conductor yelled, "All abo-o-oard! All abo-o-oard!"

Lance stood up. "Well, Harold, the man is telling me to get on the train."

The bell on the engine began to clang.

Harold rose to his feet and they shook hands, telling each other good-bye. Lance picked up his briefcase and hurriedly boarded the coach just ahead of the orphan girls' coach. He found an empty seat, and sat down next to the window. He saw Harold Fremont standing close to the coach, looking at him. Harold smiled, waved, then turned and walked away.

As Lance placed his briefcase on the floor next to his feet, he heard other passengers around him talking about the orphans in the last two coaches. Soon the engine whistle sounded, and the train rolled out of the station.

In the boys' coach, little Jimmy Kirkland was alone on his seat as he turned around and rose up on his knees. Smiling at the two six-year-old boys in the seat behind him, he said, "W-won't b-be l-long, now! P-pretty thoon we'll b-be out w-wetht, an' I'm gonna have a m-mama an' a p-papa! I c-c'n hardly w-wait to thee who ch-chootheth me!"

Jimmy wiped a hand over his mouth, removing the saliva that always appeared on his lips when he spoke.

One of the boys laughed gleefully. "I'm excited about who's gonna choose me too, Jimmy!"

"Me too!" said the other boy. "I sure hope the people who choose me will be farmers! I saw some farms one time when my parents took me all the way up to Buffalo. I really like horses and cows. I wanna be a farmer!"

On the seat directly across the aisle from the six-year-olds were two twelve-year-old boys, who had already been teasing Jimmy about his speech impediment. Jason Laird elbowed Rick Schindler with a grin, then looked at Jimmy. "Hey, Jimmy! Nobody's gonna choose you! They wouldn't wanna listen to all that stutterin' and lisp all the time!"

Rick Schindler laughed. "Yeah, *retard!* And they wouldn't wanna clean up that spit all the time, either!"

Jimmy's features twisted up and tears filled his eyes.

"Hah!" Jason laughed. "The lame brain retard's cryin', now!"

Jimmy broke into sobs and buried his face in his hands.

Three seats behind Jason and Rick sat a muscular fifteen-year-old boy named Barry Chandler. His eyes riveted to the backs of their heads. As he stood up in the aisle, he was unaware that Derek Conlan and Gifford Stanfield were entering the coach from the rear door.

Barry moved up to the spot where Jason and Rick sat, laughing, and when they looked up and saw his burning eyes, the laughter died on their lips. Every eye in the coach was on Barry as he leaned down, putting his face close their faces. "You two leave the little guy alone! Do your hear me? I'm not going to put up with it!"

Conlan and Stanfield looked at each other, then hurried down the aisle. As they drew up, Derek Conlan ran his gaze between Barry and the two on the seat. "What's going on here?"

Barry set his jaw. "These two are picking on Jimmy about his speech impediment again."

Both men turned their attention to Jimmy, who was observing the scene with wide, tear-filled eyes.

Stanfield looked back at the offenders. "Stand up!"

At the same instant the train began to curve, and as Jason and Rick rose to their feet, they lost their balance and plopped back down on the seat. Quickly, they scrambled to their feet once more. Fear showed in their eyes.

Stanfield scowled. "I thought we had this issue settled. Is there something you two don't understand about do-not-pick-on-Jimmy?"

The offenders exchanged glances, then Jason looked back at Gifford Stanfield. "No, sir. We…we didn't mean no harm, Mr. Stanfield. We was just funnin' him."

Barry's features tinted. "What do you mean, funning him? It was plain and simple being cruel and mean to him! Jimmy can't help it that he stutters, and he can't help lisping! And he's not retarded, either!"

Derek Conlan's brow furrowed. "Is this what you two said? That Jimmy's retarded?"

Both boys blushed and avoided his steady eyes.

"Is it?" demanded Conlan.

Barry's eyes flared. "Well, tell the truth! Everybody in here heard you say it."

Rick nodded, his head bent forward. "Yes, Mr. Conlan. But

like Jason said, we was only funnin' him."

"Well, it was you who were having the fun. Jimmy certainly wasn't."

Rick swallowed hard. "No, sir."

Gifford Stanfield's face was like stone. "Barry was right. What you two did was cruel and mean. And if you do it again, you're in real trouble. Understand?"

Both boys met his steely gaze but did not speak.

"I said do you understand?"

Both offenders nodded. "Yes, sir."

"All right. Now I want your promise that you won't pick on Jimmy again."

With a sullen look on his face, Rick said, "I promise."

"I'll believe it when you get that sour look off your face."

The sullen look disappeared.

"That's better. Now, Jason, what about you?"

Jason kept a pleasant mien on his face. "I promise."

"Promise *what?*"

There was a brief silence, then Jason said, "I promise I won't pick on Jimmy any more."

Stanfield ran his gaze over the faces that were looking on. "You all heard what Rick and Jason said. Mr. Conlan and I want to know if you ever see them bothering Jimmy again."

Many heads were nodded.

"All right, boys," said Stanfield, "you can sit down now."

Stanfield turned to Conlan. "Let's go sit down."

When the two men headed for the rear of the coach, Barry Chandler leaned over Jason and Rick. "If you do it again, you'll not only have Mr. Stanfield and Mr. Conlan to face, you'll answer to me too. Got that?"

Both boys gave silent nods.

"Good. Now find another way to have your fun."

The boys in the immediate area heard Barry's words, including Jimmy.

Barry then turned to Jimmy, who was alone on his seat. "Hey, little guy, I'm sorry for the way those two have treated you."

The five-year-old managed a smile. "T-thank you f-for being on m-my thide."

Barry tousled his blond hair. "I'm your friend, little pal. I'll always be on your side."

There were tears in Jimmy's eyes as the boy crossed the aisle and sat down. The boy sitting next to Barry smiled at him. "Good for you. Maybe Rick and Jason learned their lesson."

"It'll go better for them if they did."

Johnny Marston was seated with a sixteen-year-old boy three rows behind Jimmy Kirkland. Having observed it all, Johnny said, "I'm gonna go talk to Jimmy."

"Sure," said the older boy, then turned and looked out the window.

Jimmy was sitting next to the window, peering over the bottom edge at the countryside when he heard a voice say, "Hi, Jimmy."

He turned to see a smiling boy who was a bit older than himself. He had observed him at the Children's Aid Society and on the train, but didn't know his name. "Hi."

"My name's Johnny Marston. Could I sit here with you?"

Jimmy smiled and patted the seat. "Th-thure."

Johnny eased onto the seat. "I'm sorry those big boys have been picking on you, Jimmy, but you know what?"

"Wh-what?"

Johnny grinned impishly. "I'd rather be handsome like you and have to stutter and lisp than to be ugly like Jason and Rick and not have to stutter and lisp."

Jimmy giggled. "C-can you th-thit with m-me longer,

Johnny?"

"Sure. I can stay here as long as I want."

"Okay."

"I saw you at the Children's Society, but I never knew your name until we were on the train and those bad guys started picking on you. Are both of your parents dead, Jimmy?"

"I don't know."

"What? You don't know?"

"Huh-uh. I wath l-left on the d-doorthtep of the or-orphanage wh-when I wath a b-baby. They never f-found my p-parent."

"Oh."

"J-Johnny, are y-your parenth d-dead?"

Johnny's countenance sagged. "Yeah. They were on a ship on the Atlantic Ocean. It went down in a storm, and they drowned. I have two sisters in the other coach."

"Oh. I'm th-thorry. F-for you and y-your thithterth. Wath thith very l-long ago?"

"Huh-uh. Not very long."

Jimmy shook his head. "It mutht b-be awful t-to know your p-parenth and have them d-die."

Johnny nodded. "It really is bad. Me and my sisters miss Mama and Papa so much."

"I h-hope you g-get a nithe home out wetht."

"I hope you do too. And that nobody ever picks on you again about the way you talk."

"M-me too."

In the girls' coach, Josie Holden was seated next to a thirteen-year-old girl named Wanda Stevens, whose parents were also dead. They talked about their parents for a while, then told each other how they came to be on the orphan train.

Wanda had lived on the streets in Manhattan for two years before being spotted by Mr. and Mrs. Brace when she was staggering out of an alley. The Braces had stopped their buggy to check on her and learned that she was at the point of starvation. They picked her up, took her to the Society's headquarters, and fed her well for weeks. When she had put some weight back on, they scheduled her to ride this train.

When Josie had finished her story, Wanda said, "I've heard some marvelous things about Miss Wolford, Josie. From what I know about her, I can say it's just like her to approach a girl beside a grave and offer help. She's usually on one of these orphan trains, but what little time she's been at the Society while I've been there, I've grown to like her very much."

Josie sighed. "After what she did for me, I've come to love her a whole lot."

The girls continued to talk, telling each other things from their childhood, as well as more recently. After a while, they saw Rachel Wolford coming down the aisle of the coach. She spoke to girls along the way, showing a cheerful countenance. When Rachel's line of sight fell on Josie, a smile curved her lips. She paused to say something to a teenage girl, then drew up. "Hi, Josie, Wanda."

They both greeted her, then Rachel set her eyes on Josie. "You doing all right, sweetie?"

"Yep. Wanda and I just met this morning and decided to sit together. She and I are becoming friends, and this helps."

"It sure does," said Wanda. "And Miss Wolford?"

"Yes, dear?"

"Josie told me how you two met. I think it's wonderful what you did for Josie by approaching her at the cemetery and then taking her to the Society's headquarters so she could eventually be on this train."

Rachel smiled. "Well, honey, all the praise goes to the Lord. It was Him who guided me to Josie."

Wanda looked at her blankly. "Oh. Of course."

Rachel told the two girls she would see them later, then moved on down the aisle.

Josie turned to Wanda. "I don't understand what Miss Wolford meant, saying the Lord guided her to me."

Wanda shrugged. "I don't understand it, either. Anyway, you were telling me about playing baseball with the boys in your neighborhood. I want to hear some more."

The train made its stop at Des Moines, Iowa, as the sun was setting. From the windows of their coaches, the orphans watched a few people get off the train and a few more get on. By the time the train pulled out of the station, the sun had dropped below the western horizon, leaving a glow in the sky.

In the girls' coach, Mary Marston had her little sister on her lap. Lizzie had tears in her eyes. "But Mary, why can't Mama an' Papa come back? I want 'em to come back." The tears began streaming down her cheeks.

Rachel Wolford was coming along the aisle behind Mary and Lizzie, and heard Mary say, "Lizzie, I keep telling you that Mama and Papa can't come back from heaven. They're with Jesus, and as much as they love us, they want to stay there with Him. They will be there to meet us when we get to heaven someday."

Rachel stopped, leaned down to Lizzie, and wiped away the tears. "There, there, sweetie, don't cry." Then she said to Mary, "Is this your sister? You resemble each other."

"Yes, ma'am. My name is Mary Marston, and this is Lizzie. She's only four years old and is having a hard time understanding that our parents can't come back from heaven and be with us."

Compassion showed in Rachel's eyes. "Mary, did both of your parents die at the same time?"

Mary's voice cracked as she said, "Yes, Miss Wolford. Back in April. Papa worked for American Ship Lines in New York Harbor. He took a business trip on one of the company's ships, and Mama went with him. They were going to St. John's, Newfoundland, but a bad storm came up, and the ship sank in the Atlantic Ocean several miles off the coast of Nova Scotia. Mama and Papa drowned."

"Oh, Mary, I'm so sorry. I'm sure it had to have been horrible for you."

Mary nodded, biting her lower lip. "Yes, ma'am. It was hard for my little brother, Johnny, too. He's six years old."

"And Johnny is in the boys' coach, I assume."

"Uh-huh. But it's really been hard for Lizzie. Johnny and I thought we had finally been able to help her to understand about death, and that Mama and Papa can't come back from heaven, but she still thinks they should be able to come back to us."

"I heard you telling her that your parents are in heaven with Jesus and will be waiting for you when you get to heaven someday."

"Yes, ma'am," said Mary. "I've been telling her this for weeks. Sometimes I think she understands, then when she comes up with it again, I realize she doesn't."

"It's her young age, honey. It will just take time."

"I suppose so. I've prayed a lot lately and asked Jesus to help her to understand so she won't cry like she does."

"Mary?"

"Yes, ma'am?"

"You talk like you know about being saved."

"Mm-hmm. I asked the Lord Jesus to come into my heart and be my Saviour two years ago when I was six. He washed away my sins in His blood, and I was born again."

Rachel's heart seemed to swell within her. "Oh, honey, I'm so glad to hear this. So your parents raised you this way."

"Yes. Mama and Papa were both faithful Christians and loved the Lord with all their hearts. Papa was a deacon in our church. My little brother got saved about six months ago."

"Well, Mary, you and I have something in common. Both of my parents are in heaven too. And what a wonderful moment it will be when we meet our parents in heaven."

Lizzie looked into Rachel's eyes. "I wanna go heaven now. Be with Jesus an' Mama an' Papa."

Rachel kissed her forehead. "That would be wonderful, Lizzie, but Jesus still has plans for us down here. Don't you cry, now. Be a big girl. That will help your sister."

Lizzie nodded slowly. "Big girl. Help Mary."

"That's it. Well, Mary, I have to keep moving. I'm glad I got to meet you and Lizzie, and I'll look forward to meeting Johnny."

When Rachel had gone, Lizzie looked up. "Mary?"

"What, honey?"

"Is the next town where people will look at us?"

"No. It will be the town after that. It's called Kearney. We'll be there tomorrow."

Mary noticed that Laura Stanfield and Tabitha Conlan were out of their seats and moving toward the front of the coach. "Are you hungry, Lizzie?"

The little child's face lit up. "Uh-huh!"

"Well, Mrs. Stanfield and Mrs. Conlan are about to pass out the trays so we can eat. They'll bring the food from the cooks, and we'll have our supper."

"Oh, goody! Will Johnny get supper?"

"Yes, he will."

Supper was over by 7:30, and the train made its stop in Omaha, Nebraska, at 8:45. It pulled out at 9:30. The children were reminded in both coaches that lights-out time was ten o'clock.

By ten o'clock, many of the children were sound asleep, curled up on the seats. The sponsors dimmed the lanterns in the coaches, and began covering them with blankets and placing pillows under their heads as they moved down the aisle. Those who were still awake were handed pillows and blankets.

In the girls' coach, when all the children had been tucked in, Laura Stanfield, Tabitha Conlan, and Rachel Wolford stood at the rear door and ran their eyes over the blanketed forms in the dim light. Some were lying flat on the seats and others were slumped down in a seated position. Sniffles could be heard as some of the lonely little girls were seeking comfort in sleep. Two or three could be heard calling for their mothers.

Rachel looked at Laura and Tabitha and sighed. "I know we're doing all we can, but my heart is so heavy for these dear little ones who are too young to fully understand what has happened in their lives. I know the Lord cares more for them than I do, but it's so hard to hear them cry for their mothers. I wish I could just make one big happy home for all of them." She sighed again. "But that's impossible."

"I know how you feel, Rachel," said Tabitha. "It affects Laura and me the same way."

Laura nodded. "And when we return to New York, there'll be another coach full of them heading west, looking for someone to take them in and give them love and shelter."

In the boys' coach, as Derek Conlan and Gifford Stanfield were moving down the aisle handing out pillows and blankets to the boys who were still awake, Barry Chandler was standing in the aisle speaking to little Jimmy Kirkland. Johnny Marston was curled up beside Jimmy and already asleep.

When the two sponsors drew up, Barry was telling Jimmy good-night. A sleepy-eyed Jimmy was smiling up at him.

Gifford Stanfield said, "Barry, Mr. Conlan and I very much appreciate the interest you've shown in Jimmy and for protecting him from the boys who would pick on him."

Barry was patting Jimmy's head. "I can't stand to see someone with a weakness of any kind be ridiculed for it. My little brother, Billy, also stuttered. He didn't lisp, but so many children used to tease him about his stuttering and make him cry. So I understand how Jimmy feels. This is why I feel a special kinship with him, and why I went to his defense when Jason and Rick were picking on him."

Jimmy looked up at the sponsors. "I really l-like B-Barry."

Conlan smiled down at him. "Well, we can understand why."

Stanfield set his eyes on Barry. "You spoke of your little brother in the past tense."

"Yes, sir. Billy died when my parents died."

Conlan's brow furrowed. "How did it happen?"

Barry's face pinched. "We lived in a tenement in Queens. One night, just two months ago, when I was staying all night at a friend's house a few blocks away, the tenement caught fire. My parents and little brother were trapped on the fourth floor and burned to death."

The two men spoke their condolences to Barry, then Derek Conlan covered the sleeping Johnny Marston and put a pillow under his head.

As Gifford Stanfield was about to take care of Jimmy, Barry took the pillow and blanket from him. "I'll tuck Jimmy in, sir."

Stanfield smiled and nodded silently, then moved on with Conlan beside him.

Barry placed the pillow under Jimmy's head and laid the blanket over him. "Okay, little pal, it's night-night time."

Jimmy nodded, then looked at the sleeping boy beside him. "J-Johnny and I are g-good friendth n-now, Barry."

"I'm glad for that."

Jimmy lifted his arms toward the older boy. When the muscular Barry leaned down and hugged him, Jimmy said, "You are m-my very betht friend."

Touched by this, Barry squeezed him extra tight. "Hey, little pal, you're my best friend, too. Sleep tight."

Barry walked away, and with a smile on his face, Jimmy put his pillow close to Johnny's head, laid a hand on Johnny's shoulder, and fell asleep.

Chapter Thirteen

In the coach just ahead of the girls' car, Lance Adams sat alone on his seat, reading his Bible. The lanterns had not yet been turned down in the regular coaches.

Lance was reading in Genesis 32 where God changed Jacob's name to Israel. "For as a prince hast thou power with God and with men, and hast prevailed."

He grinned to himself. *Yes, sir, Jacob, you were a prince, all right!*

He finished that chapter, then went on into chapter 33, where Jacob and Esau came together and were reconciled. Lance smiled when he read: "And Esau ran to meet him, and embraced him, and fell on his neck, and kissed him: and they wept. And he lifted up his eyes, and saw the women and the children; and said, Who are those with thee? And he said, The children which God hath graciously given thy servant."

Lance paused in his reading and thought about the children in the two coaches behind him. A lump rose in his throat. His mind went to Carol and the fact that she could never bear children. He thought again of the orphans on the train and of the people in towns along the line ahead of them who would choose a child, or even more than one, and take them home. He couldn't help the longing that often arose in his heart to be a father.

Though he could never be the literal father of a child, it would be a pleasure to adopt one—or even more.

His eyes fell on Genesis 33:5 again, and the last nine words seemed to stand out like letters of fire against a night sky: "The children which God hath graciously given thy servant."

The Scripture reference in the margin next to the verse caught his eye. Psalm 127:3–5.

Lance turned to Psalm 127 and read the verses:

Lo, children are an heritage of the Lord: and the fruit of the womb is his reward. As arrows are in the hand of a mighty man; so are children of the youth. Happy is the man that hath his quiver full of them: they shall not be ashamed, but they shall speak with the enemies in the gate.

Lance shook his head. "Happy is the man that hath his quiver full of them. Lord, I don't even ask for a full quiver. I'd just like to have at least one."

His mind went back to that day not so long ago when he mentioned adopting a child to Carol, and how she was cold to the idea. "Lord," he said in a whisper, "You know that I love my precious Carol with all of my heart. She is a wonderful wife. I just—well, I just wish she wanted a child in our home like I do."

He sighed and flipped back to Genesis 33.

After reading for some time, Lance closed the Bible and placed it in his briefcase, pondering what he had read in verse 5 of that chapter, and verses 3 through 5 of Psalm 127.

His attention was drawn to the conductor as he came through the front door of the coach and began dimming the lanterns so the passengers could go to sleep.

Scooting down on the seat, Lance laid his head back, wishing the train had a Pullman car, and closed his eyes. His thoughts went to Carol, who awaited his return in San Francisco. His heart yearned for her and his arms longed to hold her. "Lord, thank You for giving Carol to me for my life's mate."

And soon he drifted to sleep.

In the girls' coach, Rachel Wolford was moving down the aisle toward her seat at the rear. As she came to the seat where Josie Holden and Wanda Stevens were sleeping, she stopped, bent down, and put a soft kiss on the top of Josie's head. Though Rachel did not know it, the twelve-year-old actually was not asleep. And though her eyes were closed, she knew who was kissing her.

As Rachel moved on, Josie opened her eyes and smiled. *Miss Wolford,* she thought, *you are the sweetest person I know.*

Josie's thoughts went to her father, and tears came to her eyes. She moved her lips silently, saying, "Oh, Papa, I miss you so very much! I love you and Mama and my little brother with all of my heart. I always will."

She continued weeping, but soon the steady clicking of the wheels beneath her and the sway of the coach lulled her to sleep.

Upon reaching the rear of the coach, Rachel Wolford had noted that both Laura Stanfield and Tabitha Conlan were asleep. She decided to go into the boys' coach to make sure all was well.

In that coach, she found only Derek Conlan awake, and he assured her all was well.

Satisfied, Rachel returned to the girls' coach. Before sitting down on the seat she occupied by herself, she looked forward to where she could see Josie Holden's dark head lying still by the dim light of the lanterns. She sat down and whispered, "Dear

Lord, that precious girl has stolen my heart. There has been no indication that she knows You, and I am burdened for her. Please help me to reach Josie for You before someone takes her to be their foster child."

Early the next morning, the sponsors moved up and down the aisles calling for the orphans to wake up.

Most of them came awake slowly, rubbing their eyes and stretching arms and legs, stiffened by their cramped positions through the night.

In the girls' coach, Laura, Tabitha, and Rachel moved among the girls, seeing to their personal needs: brushing hair and washing faces.

Most of the younger ones were nervous and a little confused about what was happening to them. Laura and Tabitha carefully explained the procedure for appearing before the people in the railroad station, doing all they could to calm their fears.

Some of the younger ones who had been in orphanages started to cry. They were confused as to why they were on the train in the first place, having been taken from the orphanage, which they had known as home. It seemed they all shared one basic emotion: fear of the unknown. They were going to strange places where they would be taken from the railroad stations by strange people. In the orphanage, they had grown close to one another, forming a bond of sorts. And now, they were facing separation.

The sponsors tried to comfort them and give them hope of a better life and a new family with which to bond.

The sponsors knew that even the older children were nervous

about it all. Everything would be foreign to them. On one hand, they wanted desperately to be chosen and to start a new life in a new home; but on the other hand, they didn't want to be separated from each other and the "family" that they had considered themselves since being at the Children's Aid Society headquarters.

After breakfast, the boys and girls each had a piece of paper pinned on their chests with a number from 1 to 61.

At 10:15 the train pulled into the Kearney, Nebraska, railroad station. Once the Kearney-bound passengers had left the train, the sixty-one children were taken out of their coaches and lined up on the platform. Though they were nervous, all sixty-one presented themselves well, and the sponsors were proud of them.

A small number of potential foster parents were waiting to interview the orphans and look them over.

The other passengers on the train left their coaches to stretch their legs and get some fresh air. A soft breeze was blowing across the Nebraska plains. Most of them were interested in watching the orphan-choosing process and moved up close to look on. Among these was the businessman Lance Adams.

Nurse Rachel Wolford positioned herself quite near to the spot where Josie Holden and Wanda Stevens were standing together in the line, praying that God would not let anyone take Josie until she had the opportunity to talk with her about being saved and had the joy of leading her to Jesus.

The Stanfields and the Conlans moved along the line with clipboards and pencils in hand, ready to question the interested couples about themselves and do the paperwork if they qualified to become foster parents.

Soon two couples showed interest, one in an older boy and the other in an older girl. The couples summoned the sponsors and the questioning began.

Rachel noticed a couple step up to Wanda Stevens and begin

talking to her. She was close enough to hear what was being said, and after a few minutes, it was obvious that they were interested in her.

Josie had a couple talking to her, but they soon passed on down the line. Rachel heaved a sigh of relief. She noticed that as Josie listened to the conversation between Wanda and the couple, she was picking up on the fact that they were interested in taking Wanda home with them. Josie's eyes showed the fear she was feeling. She was disturbed about the prospect of losing Wanda to foster parents.

The man stepped to Tabitha Conlan, who was only a few feet away, and told her they wanted to take Wanda as their foster daughter. Tabitha smiled as she accompanied the man to the spot where his wife stood talking to Wanda.

Instantly, Rachel began to pray, asking the Lord to help Josie to accept it if she lost Wanda so early in the trip; but most of all, that He would not let anyone take Josie until she had the opportunity to talk with her about salvation.

A little farther down the line, Lance Adams was standing near the spot where Jimmy Kirkland was positioned next to Johnny Marston. Johnny's sisters were on his other side.

While observing the scene, Lance's heart grew heavy for all the children, whose faces showed the apprehension they were experiencing. He knew that as orphans and street urchins, their lives were already full of sorrow and uncertainty.

Lance's attention was soon drawn to a couple that had stopped in front of the small, blond boy.

"Hi there, little fellow!" said the man, smiling from ear to ear. "My name is Jack Hankins, and this is my wife, Esther."

"And what is your name, honey?" asked Esther.

The little boy smiled in return. "My n-name ith Jimmy K-Kirkland."

Jack and Esther's smiles vanished as they shot a glance at each other.

Jack said, "Jimmy, are you talking like that because you're nervous and afraid?"

Jimmy shook his head. "N-no, thir. I…I always talk like th-thith."

Jack looked at his wife. "Let's move on, Esther."

When they were out of Jimmy's earshot, Lance heard Esther say, "I couldn't live with the stuttering or the lisp."

"Me, neither," Jack said.

Lance felt his heart grow heavy for little Jimmy Kirkland, who had tears in his eyes as he watched the couple walk away.

Lance watched another couple show interest in the little towheaded boy until they heard him talk. They quickly walked away. Moments later, another couple stopped and began talking to Jimmy. As soon as he responded to them, they walked away discussing the speech impediment, and the woman said, "Ralph, that boy is retarded."

Ralph agreed.

Jimmy was wiping tears.

At the same moment, a man and his wife, who by their clothing were obviously farmers, stepped up to the three children next to Jimmy. The man said, "Mr. Stanfield told us you three are brother and sisters."

The Marston children nodded, and Mary said, "That's right, sir. My brother's name is Johnny. My sister's name is Lizzie. And I'm Mary. What are your names?"

The man's eyes twinkled. "I'm Will Banton, and my wife's name is Leah."

Leah smiled. "And what are your ages?"

Mary swallowed nervously. "Johnny's six. Lizzie's four. And I'm eight."

As the Bantons asked the Marston children questions about their parents and the home in which they were raised, Lance Adams looked back at little Jimmy Kirkland. Tears were streaming down his cheeks, and he had never seen a more dejected look.

Jimmy's head was tilted downward. His lips were quivering and his hands were jammed into his pockets. *Nobody will ever want me. I can't talk right, and I'm too little to be much help to anybody. I'm just no good, I guess.* Jimmy's little body shook as he sobbed.

Unable to stand it any longer, Lance Adams walked up to the pitiful little boy, bent down to look him in the eye. "Hello, little guy. My name is Lance Adams. I'm from California. And your name is Jimmy Kirkland, right?"

Jimmy sniffed, wiped tears, and nodded.

Lance's heart was so sore for the child; he couldn't help but wrap his arms around him. Jimmy offered no resistance, but let the man hold him tight.

"Jimmy, don't be afraid. Somebody along the line will want to take you home with them."

At that instant, Gifford Stanfield drew up. He smiled down at Lance. "Are you interested in taking Jimmy home with you, sir?"

Lance let go of Jimmy and stood up. He took one of the boy's hands in his own. "I'm not a resident. My name is Lance Adams. I'm a passenger on the train on my way home to San Francisco."

"Oh. I see. I…I thought by the way you were hugging him, you just might want to take him. Sorry for the misunderstanding."

Lance grinned. "It's all right. Jimmy looked so sad by the time three couples had talked to him and passed on down the line. I just wanted to try to cheer him up."

Stanfield nodded, and putting the pencil and clipboard in his left hand, offered his right. As their hands met, he said, "I'm

Gifford Stanfield. Maybe you'd like to be Jimmy's foster father, even though you live in San Francisco. The orphans who are left by the time we get there will still need homes. Interested?"

Lance ran a hand briskly over his mouth. "Ah…no, sir. I wouldn't be able to do that."

Stanfield nodded again. "I see. Well, somebody's going to get a real nice boy when they take him."

Lance let go of Jimmy's hand and patted him on the head. "I have no doubt about that. He is indeed a fine boy." He looked down into Jimmy's teary eyes. "Perk up, little pal. Some nice people will come along and choose you."

Jimmy watched the two men walk away together.

When they were out of earshot from the boy, Stanfield leaned close to Adams and spoke in a whisper. "Just between you and me, Mr. Adams, I think the problem is Jimmy's speech impediment. Our director, Mr. Brace, told us it might be difficult to find him a home because of it. Most people equate a stutter and a lisp with retardation."

"Mm-hmm. I've heard that many times before, and one of those couples who stopped to talk to Jimmy, agreed that he was retarded."

"Well, you were talking to him. What do you think? Is he retarded?"

"Not that I can tell. His thinking seems perfectly normal for a child his age. What is he, five?"

"Exactly. And I agree. Jimmy is not retarded."

Someone in the line called for Gifford Stanfield, saying they were interested in one of the teenage boys. He excused himself to Lance Adams. Lance returned to the spot he had occupied before and continued to observe.

By this time, Will and Leah Banton motioned for Laura Stanfield.

"Could we talk to you in private, Mrs. Stanfield?" asked Will.

"Of course."

Laura led them a few paces away, so their conversation could not be heard.

While the Bantons talked to Laura, the Marston trio stood close together. Johnny noted that Jimmy Kirkland was sniffling, and turned to him, placing a hand on his shoulder. "You all right, Jimmy?"

Jimmy wiped a palm over his wet face. "Mm-hmm. That n-nice m-man thaid thomeone will w-want me."

"Well, he was right. It'll happen, you just wait and see."

Johnny turned back to his sisters as they were looking around at the people milling about. Mary had an arm around Lizzie, who obviously was overwhelmed by it all. She leaned into her sister's side and buried her face in Mary's dress.

Mary leaned down and spoke into her ear in her most grown-up voice. "Lizzie, honey, stand up straight, now. We have to make a good impression. I think Mr. and Mrs. Banton are talking to Mrs. Stanfield about taking us."

Johnny voiced his fear. "But what if they only want one or two of us, Mary?"

"Yeah," said Lizzie. "What if they only want you an' Johnny? What if they don't want a girl who's four?"

"Now, sweetie," said Mary, "they will want you too."

"But what if they don't? I want to go with you and Johnny. Please, Sissy, don't let 'em take you an' Johnny away from me." Tears had formed in her eyes.

Mary stroked her little sister's cheek. "Don't you worry, Lizzie. We'll stay together." She wished she felt as sure as she sounded.

Johnny was looking at the Bantons as they continued to talk to Laura Stanfield. Mary's line of sight followed his, and when Lizzie saw it, she looked back at the Bantons.

At the spot where the Marston children's attention was focused, Laura Stanfield was asking the Bantons the normal personal questions required by the Children's Aid Society.

The Bantons told her they owned a 160-acre farm a few miles north of Kearney and made a good living. They explained that Will was forty years old, and Leah was thirty-eight. She could not bear children. They had wanted children in their home since early in their marriage and were thrilled with the prospect of getting all three of the Marston children at once.

Laura felt an electric current of excitement flow through her at these words from the Bantons. "Now, I need to ask about alcoholic beverages. Do you folks imbibe?"

"Absolutely not," responded Will. "We never touch the stuff. There is no liquor and no wine in our house."

"Great!"

Will said, "Mrs. Stanfield, may I butt in here?"

"Of course."

"Mary and Johnny told us their parents drowned off the coast of Nova Scotia when their ship went down in a storm this past April. Is this so?"

"Yes, sir. It is exactly as they told you. I need to ask you something else. How about your church attendance? Are you members of a Bible-believing church, and if so, do you attend faithfully?"

Will's face tinted. He cleared his throat nervously. "We... aren't members anywhere, and we know we should be. We... ah...really need to change that."

"Well, Mr. Brace insists on it. You need to know that from time to time the Children's Aid Society checks up on children they have placed in homes to make sure all is well. We definitely want the children in church and Sunday school."

Will looked at his wife, then at Laura. "I promise, Mrs. Stanfield, we'll start going to church immediately."

Laura smiled. "I'll take your word for that, Mr. Banton."

"We appreciate that, Mrs. Stanfield," said Leah. "We will have those precious children in Sunday school and church on a regular basis."

Satisfied that the Bantons would keep their word, Laura wrote it down on the official papers on the clipboard. "All right," she said, handing Will the clipboard, "I need both of you to sign at the bottom of this page and the transaction will be done."

When Will and Leah had both signed and handed the clipboard back to her, Laura said, "Let's go tell Mary, Johnny, and Lizzie that they are going home with you."

Mary Marston was watching the Bantons and Laura Stanfield. Johnny was talking to Jimmy Kirkland. When Mary saw the Bantons signing something on the clipboard, her heart skipped a beat. They handed it back to Laura and the three of them turned and headed back toward the line. Her heart skipped a beat again.

Mary prayed, "Dear Lord, please keep us together. Don't let them take only one or two of us."

All three of the adults were smiling broadly as they drew near. Johnny turned from Jimmy and looked up at them. Lizzie's eyes were wide with curiosity. Mary put an arm around Lizzie's shoulder, and on the other side, Johnny took Mary's hand. The three of them presented a picture of determination not to be separated.

Leah spoke in a low voice to Laura. "Look at that united front! It's a good thing we're taking all of them. I'd hate to see their dejection if we took only one or two."

"Me too," said Laura. "It's a blessing that they can stay together. They've been through so much sorrow in their young lives."

"We wouldn't have it any other way," said Will.

As they stopped in front of the trio, Laura ran her eyes over the anxious faces. "Mary, Johnny, Lizzie, how would you like to live on a farm and become Mr. and Mrs. Banton's foster children?"

"Oh yes!" exclaimed Mary.

Johnny's eyes were dancing. "We sure would!"

Mary looked down at her little sister. "Lizzie, we're going to go home with Mr. and Mrs. Banton and live on their farm."

Lizzie looked up with worried eyes. "All three of us?"

"Yes."

"Do they have cows and horses?"

"We sure do, sweetheart," said Leah.

"Oh, boy! I like cows an' horses!"

"And we also have pigs and chickens."

"Really?"

"We sure do, honey," said Will.

Lizzie looked up at Mary. "Do they have sparrows on their farm?"

The Bantons and Laura showed their puzzlement at the question, then Mary looked at the Bantons. "Do you?"

Will chuckled. "Lots of them. Why does Lizzie want to know if we have sparrows?"

Mary smiled. "I'll explain it later, Mr. Banton."

"Mary, they're gonna have some more little sparrows on their farm, aren't they?" Lizzie said.

Chapter Fourteen

Laura Stanfield handed an envelope to Will Banton. "Here are copies of the papers you signed, along with official papers that I have signed as an agent of the Children's Aid Society to prove that you and Leah are legally the foster parents of the Marston children."

Will smiled. He handed the envelope to Leah. "Honey, would you put this in your purse till we get home, please?"

"Of course."

As Leah was placing the envelope in her purse, Laura said, "I'm so thrilled that these precious little ones won't be separated. Most of the time it has to be that way. We've had a few instances when one family took two siblings, and only one other time that I can think of when three were taken. Never more than that. But most of the time, a couple only wants one foster child. Usually it's because they can't afford to take more than one into their home."

Leah smiled. "Well, we're glad we can take all three. It would be a tragedy if they were separated. They've had more than enough tragedy in their little lives already."

"Yes," said Will. "Well, Mary, Johnny, and Lizzie, are you ready to go to your new home?"

All three nodded, faces beaming.

Laura held the clipboard close to her chest. "Good-bye, children. I know you will be very happy in your new home." Then she said to the Bantons, "And I know you will be happy to have these three additions to your home."

Will chuckled. "We sure will! And I want to find out what this business is about the little sparrows."

Laura hurried away to take care of another couple down the line.

Suddenly, Jimmy Kirkland began to cry. Johnny turned to him. "What's the matter, Jimmy?"

The eyes of the Bantons and Johnny's sisters were turned to Jimmy, who drew in a shuddering breath and choked on the words. "J-Johnny, I don't want you t-to go away. Pleathe d-don't go!"

Johnny flicked a look of helplessness at Mary, then said, "Jimmy, I have to go. These nice people are taking Mary and Lizzie and me to live with them."

"B-but I'll n-never thee you anymore. You're my f-friend."

Mary moved to the child. "Jimmy, please don't cry. I know this is hard for you, but it's going to be all right. Maybe at the very next stop there'll be a nice man and lady who will choose you and take you home with them."

Jimmy was trying to say something else, but the weeping made it only a muttering.

Will and Leah looked at each other, wondering what to do.

At his original spot close by, Lance Adams was talking to another passenger on the train. Jimmy's outburst drew his attention. "Please excuse me, Mr. Simmons," he said to the man. "I've got to see about this orphan boy."

Simmons nodded and Lance rushed to the boy and picked him up. "Jimmy, what's the matter?"

The Bantons and the Marston children looked on as Jimmy sobbed. "J-Johnny'th my friend, and...and h-he'th g-goin' away!

He and hith thithterth are b-bein' 'dopted by that m-man and lady! I d-don't want Johnny t-to leave me!"

Tears were in Leah's eyes as her husband stepped closer and looked compassionately at the little boy. "Jimmy, we're sorry to take Johnny from you, but he and his sisters are our foster children now. We would take you, too, but three is all we can afford. We have to go now. Johnny, tell your friend good-bye."

Johnny looked up at his little friend in Lance's arms. "Bye, Jimmy. Don't cry anymore. You'll be in a nice home pretty soon too. I'll miss you."

Jimmy drew a shuddering breath as tears spilled down his face. "I-I'll mith you t-too."

As the Bantons and the Marston children walked away, Jimmy cried harder. When they reached the place where they would pass from view, Johnny turned and waved.

Jimmy had one arm around Lance's neck. He waved with the free hand, sobbing as if his heart would break in two. His entire body began to shake as if he was suddenly penetrated to the core by incredible cold. His breathing became rapid and shallow, and he swallowed uncontrollably over and over again.

The child's sorrow touched Lance deeply. Tears misted his eyes as he held Jimmy close and spoke into his ear. "It'll be all right, Jimmy. You'll have more friends when a real nice family takes you home with them."

Jimmy shook his head intensely. "N-nobody wanth me 'cauthe I talk f-funny!"

Lance held Jimmy even tighter and swallowed the lump that had risen in his throat. "Now, Jimmy, that's not so. In some town there'll be some nice people who won't care that you stutter and lisp. They will love you and take you into their home to be their boy."

Jimmy buried his wet face against Lance's neck. "I w-want to go home w-with you and b-be *your* b-boy!"

Lance suddenly felt numb all over. This small lad had already unknowingly captured his heart. His mind went to Carol and the discussion they had about adopting a child. He wanted to tell Jimmy he would take him home, but there was no way he could surprise Carol at the San Francisco depot by leading Jimmy up to her and saying, "Guess what, sweetheart, here's our new son. We're going to adopt him."

Jimmy eased back in Lance's arms and looked into his face through his tears. "W-would you? Would you t-take m-me home w-with y-you tho I could be y-your b-boy?"

Lance bit his lips as the tears coursed down his own cheeks. His voice was tight. "Jimmy, I—I wish I could do that, but I—I can't."

A wistful expression shadowed the boy's countenance. "Why?"

Lance thought his own heart would most certainly shatter inside his chest. He was trying to think how to express it to Jimmy when the boy said, "M-my real m-mommy and d-daddy threw m-me away."

This was like a sledgehammer to Lance's midsection.

Tabitha Conlan had left the couple who were interested in Wanda Stevens, to let them talk for a few minutes, while she entered the girls' coach to get a fresh handkerchief from her overnight bag. When she stepped out of the coach, her attention went to little Jimmy in the arms of the man who was holding him. Frowning, she headed that way while glancing at Wanda and the couple as they chatted.

When she drew up to Lance and Jimmy, Lance was still trying to find a way to get past the blow of Jimmy's latest words.

"Sir," asked Tabitha, "is something wrong? Are you interested in taking Jimmy as your foster son?"

Lance looked at her and took a sharp breath. He was trying

to gain control of his voice when Gifford Stanfield moved up. "Tabitha, this gentleman is Mr. Lance Adams of San Francisco. He's a passenger on our train. I saw him with Jimmy a little while ago and asked him the same question you just did. He is simply touched by Jimmy's plight and wants to make him feel better."

Tabitha's features softened, and she set appreciative eyes on Lance. "Mr. Adams, that's awfully nice of you. Do you have children of your own?"

"Ah…no, ma'am. My wife and I have no children."

Jimmy set his red-rimmed eyes on Tabitha. "Th-thome people took my f-friend, Johnny, from me. B-but nobody wanth m-me 'cauthe I talk f-funny."

Tabitha ran her fingers through his blond hair in a tender manner. "Jimmy, it's going to be all right. Somebody will take you home just like they did Johnny. You just wait and see."

Jimmy tightened his grip on Lance's neck. "I want M-Mr. Adamth t-to take me home. I w-want to be h-hith boy."

Gifford put his face close to the boy's. "Jimmy, Mr. Adams already told me a little while ago that he wouldn't be able to do that. But don't you feel bad, son. We have a long way to go. Somebody in Wyoming, Nevada, or California will want you. They'll love you and give you a good home."

"Mr. Stanfield is right, honey. Someone will take you, I'm sure." Tabitha patted his cheek and walked away.

Jimmy watched her for a few seconds, then looked back into the eyes of the man who was holding him.

Lance met his gaze. "Jimmy, Mr. Stanfield has taken lots of boys and girls on the orphan trains, and you know what?"

"Huh-uh."

"He has seen those boys and girls taken into homes when they thought it would never happen."

Jimmy studied Lance's eyes. "D-did any of 'em talk f-funny like m-me?"

Gifford came to Lance's rescue. "We haven't had any who talked quite like you, Jimmy, but that doesn't make any difference. God has a family ready to take you into their home, and when those people meet you, they'll want you, believe me."

Jimmy frowned. "C-could God make Mr. Adamth w-want to take m-me home?"

Gifford turned his gaze to the man with the dark, wavy hair.

Lance could feel the nerves twitching throughout his body. His eyes turned troubled. "Jimmy, I would love to take you home with me, but I just can't do that. If I explained it to you, you wouldn't understand. You're too young."

"B-but I w-would be good. Really. I p-promithe."

"I know you would, little pal. It's got nothing to do with how you would behave."

"Jimmy," said Gifford, "it's going to be okay. Somewhere down the line, God has people just waiting for a boy like you. Take my word for it. You're going to be taken into a good home where there'll be lots of love, and you'll be very, very happy."

Jimmy looked at Gifford silently for a moment, then set his gaze on the line of children who were being interviewed by the small number of people who were left. He turned his head and met Lance's loving gaze. "Th-thank you for bein' n-nice to me."

Lance smiled and hugged him. "You're easy to be nice to."

Jimmy let go of Lance's neck so he could put him in the line again. Lance then moved back to the spot where he had been standing before.

Cal Simmons was gone, but the conductor, Art Manley, was there. He smiled at Lance, noting the look of anguish on his face. "Pretty sad, isn't it, Mr. Adams?"

Lance looked at him. "You've been observing this scene?"

"Yes. That little fellow is a heart-grabber."

Lance nodded. "Tell me about it."

"Too bad about his speech impediment. It just might keep anyone from wanting him."

"It shouldn't. He certainly can't help it, and contrary to what a lot of people think about a child who lisps and stutters, Jimmy is not retarded. His little mind is sharp. I'd take him home with me quicker than you can snap your fingers if it was possible. But it isn't."

Manley grinned. "Well, it's sure obvious that he'd go with you too, if you could take him." He turned to walk away. "I have to make preparations for pulling out."

Lance watched Art Manley walk toward the engine, where the engineer and the fireman were waiting for him on the platform.

The effect of the sledgehammer to Lance's midsection was still there, and his nerves were wire-tight. He looked at Jimmy, who was standing in the line with his head bent low. "Lord, You knew before it happened that I was going to board this particular train in Chicago, and You knew Jimmy would be among the orphans. Something…something has happened in my heart toward that little boy. You know that I love children and have wanted to adopt at least one I could be a daddy to. Jimmy is—well, he's special, Lord. You know my heart. It isn't just pity that I feel toward him, though that emotion is within me. But every part and particle of me wants to take him home so he can be my little boy. Jimmy certainly wants to be my little boy. But…but I can't upset Carol's life. She made it quite clear that she doesn't want an adopted child. And, Lord, if I took him home to live with us, it would put a load on her. She would be Jimmy's mother and have all the responsibilities that go with motherhood. I just can't do that to her."

At that moment, a couple stepped up to little Jimmy Kirkland and began talking to him. When Jimmy responded to their questions, Lance saw both of them get sour looks on their faces. The man patted Jimmy on the head, said something Lance could not distinguish, then moved away.

Lance shook his head sadly. "Lord, Carol is Your child. You could speak to her. You could change her mind about our adopting a child." He drew a deep breath. "But, of course, by then it would be too late. Certainly somebody will feel toward Jimmy like I do, and they will take him home to be their little boy. By the time this train gets to San Francisco, Jimmy will already be in someone's home. Unless…unless You would work in Carol's heart, and at the same time, keep anyone from taking Jimmy.

"Lord, I just thought of something. In Genesis 18, You visited Abraham at his tent in the plains of Mamre and told him You were going to give him and Sarah a son in their old age. Sarah overheard what You told Abraham and laughed to herself, saying she was beyond childbearing. And Lord, You said to Abraham, 'Wherefore did Sarah laugh, saying, Shall I of a surety bear a child, which am old?'

"And, Lord, You said, 'Is anything too hard for the LORD? At the time appointed I will return unto thee, according to the time of life, and Sarah shall have a son.' O, dear Father, if You want Carol and me to have a son—and I mean, Jimmy Kirkland—You can time it all out and make it happen. Is anything too hard for You? Please work in Carol's heart, and in Your own inimitable way, You can give us Jimmy as surely as you gave Isaac to Abraham and Sarah. You have brought Jimmy into my life and given me a deep love for him. He loves me and has asked to go home with me and be my little boy. Please, Lord, bring it to pass."

Further up the line, Rachel Wolford was standing close to the spot where the interested couple was talking to Wanda Stevens as Tabitha Conlan returned to finish the paperwork. Rachel felt sorry for Josie Holden, who looked on dolefully knowing now that the couple would be taking Wanda with them.

From the corner of her eye, Josie saw Rachel looking at her. She turned her head and her face pinched. Rachel rushed to her and wrapped her in her arms. "I love you, Josie."

"I love you, too, Miss Wolford," came Josie's shaky reply.

"Honey, I know you've gotten close to Wanda, and it's hard to let her go, but she deserves the happiness she'll find with those people. You wouldn't want to take that away from her."

"Of course not. It—it's just so hard, knowing I'll probably never see her again."

"Well, Josie, that's how life is. This kind of thing happens in people's lives somewhere in the world every day. But you keep your chin up. I'm sure you will be chosen by some good family before the train reaches the end of the line."

At that moment, Wanda turned from her new foster parents while they were signing papers and moved to Josie.

Rachel said, "Honey, I'll let you and Wanda have this moment alone."

Josie nodded, her eyes already filmed with tears, then turned to face Wanda.

Wanda wrapped her arms around Josie, and as they embraced, Wanda said, "I love you."

Josie choked on a sob. "I love you too, Wanda."

"I hope you will be chosen before the train reaches the end of the line."

They released each other, and Josie wiped tears from her cheeks. "Thank you, Wanda, for being my friend."

The woman called, "Wanda, dear, we must go now."

The man had the official papers in his hand.

Wanda kissed her friend's cheek. "Good-bye, Josie."

As Wanda walked away between the man and his wife, Josie

struggled to keep from breaking down. Suddenly she felt an arm slip around her waist, and turned to see Rachel Wolford looking at her with eyes of compassion.

Tabitha Conlan observed with a smile as Rachel and Josie embraced. Tabitha walked toward her husband, who was standing close by, holding his clipboard. Derek said, "Apparently those two girls had become quite close in this short time."

Tabitha looked back at Josie. "That they did, darling. That they did."

While holding Josie close, Rachel said, "Honey, I know you'll miss Wanda, but I'll try to take her place."

Josie eased back and looked her in the eye. "Oh, thank you, Miss Wolford. I'd love to be close friends with you."

At that instant, Gifford Stanfield rushed up and said, "Rachel, we've got a boy over here with a nosebleed."

Rachel nodded and looked at Josie. "We'll spend time together on the train." With that, she hurried away on Gifford's heels.

Barry Chandler was in the line close to where Josie was standing and had observed the scene when she and Wanda parted. Since the last couple moving along the line had already passed him, Barry moved to where Josie stood. "Hi. We haven't met, but my name is Barry Chandler. I saw how it affected you when that couple took Wanda. Is there anything I can do to help you?"

Josie managed a smile. "Thank you, Barry, but there is really nothing you can do. Wanda and I have become friends on the trip, and I'm just having a hard time letting her go. Oh. My name is—"

"Josie Holden," cut in Barry, a wide smile spreading over his face. "I asked Miss Wolford what your name was way back in New York, and she told me."

A bit off balance, Josie kept her smile and nodded. "Oh."

There was obvious admiration in Barry's eyes. "Josie is such a pretty name. Is it a nickname?"

"Mm-hmm. My real name is Josephine."

"Well, that's a pretty name too."

Barry ran his gaze around them. "It looks like there are no more people coming along to talk to us."

"Looks like it," Josie said sadly. "If no one adopts me by the time we get to San Francisco, I'll have to go back to New York and start over again."

"Well, Miss Josie, we've got a lot of stops before we get to San Francisco. I'm sure both of us will be chosen by then."

"I sure hope so."

"Where did you live in New York?"

"Manhattan. Where did you live?"

"Queens."

"Are you actually an orphan, Miss Josie, or were you put on the streets because your parents couldn't afford to keep you?"

"I'm an orphan. My parents are both dead."

"I'm sorry. Would you mind telling me about it?"

Pleased that the handsome boy was interested, Josie told him her story in brief. When she finished, Barry said, "I'm sorry you've had so much heartache, Miss Josie."

She thanked him for his concern, then asked about him, and he quickly told her his story.

Josie looked up at him with her soft, tender eyes. "I'm sorry you've had so much heartache too, Barry."

"We both know what that's all about. You needn't worry about finding a home. As sweet and pretty as you are, I'm sure some fine family will take you home with them."

A tiny smile appeared at the corners of Josie's mouth. Barry's heart did a flip-flop in his chest, and he said suddenly, "Miss

Josie, if I was older and looking for a girl to adopt, I would take you in an instant." Suddenly, he clamped a palm over his mouth. "Oh! I let my tongue get ahead of my brain. Please forgive me for speaking so boldly."

Josie patted his arm. "You don't need to apologize. That was a very nice thing to say."

Suddenly Gifford Stanfield's voice cut the air. "All right, boys and girls, it's time to reboard the train! Five boys and three girls were taken by foster parents. That leaves fifty-three to move on down the line. Don't any of you be discouraged. This was only the first stop. We've got plenty more. All aboard!"

Lance Adams moved up quickly to Jimmy Kirkland. "Hey, little pal, don't be discouraged. Everything is going to be all right."

Jimmy's big blue eyes fastened on him. "You p-promithe, M-Mr. Adamth?"

Lance forced a wide smile. "Sure, Jimmy. I promise." In his heart, he said, *Lord, that promise is based on my faith. Is anything too hard for You?*

Jimmy nodded. "Okay, M-Mr. Adamth. Thee you l-later."

"See you later."

Lance watched until Jimmy had boarded the boys' coach, then headed for his own.

Barry Chandler boarded the boys' coach, feeling a strange sensation in his heart. Without a doubt, he had an attraction for pretty Josie Holden.

When Josie Holden sat down on her regular seat in the girls' coach, her heart lurched at the absence of Wanda Stevens. At the same time, she felt warm feelings as Barry Chandler came to mind. She told herself he was the nicest and most handsome boy she had ever met.

Chapter Fifteen

Outside the railroad station, Will and Leah Banton led their new foster children into the parking lot and drew up to the family buggy, which was parked between two buckboards.

Johnny sized up the husky draft horse that was hitched to the buggy.

"Wow! What a big horse, Mr. Banton! I've never seen one as big as him. It *is* a him, isn't it?"

"Yes, Johnny, it's a him…otherwise known as a gelding."

Johnny frowned. "I thought a he horse was a st—stal—uh…"

"A stallion?"

"Yeah. That's it. A stallion."

"Well, a male horse is a stallion unless he's fixed so he can't be a daddy."

"Huh?"

"I'll explain it to you when you get a little older, okay?"

Johnny shrugged. "Okay."

"Johnny, would you like to ride on the driver's seat with Papa Will?" Leah said.

Johnny's eyes lit up. "I sure would!"

Will extended his arms toward the boy. "Here, I'll help you."

"I can do it, Mr. Banton," said Johnny, and quickly climbed up onto the seat.

"Well, I guess you can!"

Leah snickered. "It's the male ego at work."

Lizzie's ears perked up. "A eagle? I love birds, but I never seen a eagle. Where's the eagle?"

Mary looked at Leah and shook her head, grinning. "Lizzie, Mrs. Banton didn't say *eagle*. She said ego. It has to do with what you think of yourself. I remember my teacher, Mrs. Childress, saying in class that boys and men have a problem with their ego."

Lizzie's face twisted. "Huh?"

"Forget it, honey. Mr. and Mrs. Banton want to get going."

Will helped Leah and the girls into the rear seat of the buggy. Lizzie was positioned between her sister and Leah.

While Will was releasing the reins from the hitching post, Leah said, "Children, we will now go to the general store to buy groceries. We waited on this to see if we would find the child or children we wanted, then we would buy groceries and supplies as needed for the new addition or additions to our family."

Will climbed into the driver's seat and put the buggy in motion. As the big horse pulled the vehicle down the street toward Kearney's business district, Leah said, "And tomorrow, we will bring you back into town and buy all three of you new clothes and shoes."

Johnny twisted around in the seat. "Wow! Really?"

Leah smiled at him. "Really. We're going to see that our foster children have everything they need to make them happy and comfortable. And come fall, we'll outfit you for winter with coats, mittens, stocking caps, and overshoes."

Lizzie's eyes were sparkling. "Will I get a new dress, Mrs. Banton?"

"You'll get more than one, honey."

"Oh, boy! Will Mary get new dresses too?"

"She sure will. And like you and Johnny, she'll get new shoes."

Sitting next to Will, Johnny let his eyes drift to the clapboard buildings on both sides of the dusty street. Some had small balconies on the second level. Others were single stories with flat roofs. Signs above the doors revealed what type of business was inside. People milled about the town on foot, while others were in horse-drawn wagons, buggies, and carriages.

Soon they pulled up in front of Hanson's General Store and the children were led inside. Their eyes widened instantly. They had never been in a store like this one. The long rows of shelves were loaded with everything imaginable, and what items wouldn't fit on the shelves were piled in neat stacks on the floor.

Leah said, "Now, children, if you see something on the shelves that you would like to have for meals, just point them out. I'll cook anything you like."

The children stared in amazement as they followed Will and Leah through the store. Lizzie moved close to Mary and grasped her hand tightly. Her eyes took in everything.

The Bantons came upon people they knew and introduced Mary, Johnny, and Lizzie as their new foster children whom they had just chosen from the orphan train at the railroad station. Every man and woman showed warmth toward them.

Soon everyone in the Banton family except Lizzie was carrying grocery items, and as they headed toward the counter, Johnny said, "I sure like it, here! I really do. I like it here!"

Will chuckled as they drew up to the counter. "Well, I'm sure glad, Johnny. We want you to be happy here."

"I like it here too, Johnny," said Mary.

The Bantons both smiled at Mary.

Will greeted Clyde and Geraldine Hanson, who stood behind the counter. As he placed his armful of goods on the counter, he told the Hansons that he and Leah had chosen the three children off the orphan train, and introduced Mary, Johnny, and Lizzie to them. Again, the children found a friendly welcome.

While the items were being tabulated and the adults were talking, Lizzie's eyes went to the two big jars of candy that sat on the end of the counter. She tugged at Mary's arm and pointed at the jars. "Look, Mary!"

Leah turned to see what Lizzie was pointing at. "Aha! Candy, eh?"

"Mm-hmm. Could I have some please, Mrs. Banton?"

"Of course, sweetheart. We'll buy a good supply, but you must understand that you can only have a couple of pieces in a day. We don't want your teeth to decay."

Lizzie nodded. "Okay."

Moments later, when they were walking out the door with everyone carrying grocery sacks except the little one with a piece of hard candy in her mouth, Lizzie spoke around it. "Yeah, Johnny! I really do like it here too!"

At that moment, they all heard the shrill sound of a train whistle.

Their attention was drawn to the orphan train as it was pulling out of town.

A pang of sadness penetrated Mary's tender heart. "Johnny, Lizzie, the Lord has been so good to us. Most of those boys and girls are still on the train, I'm sure. They didn't get chosen today. I just hope all of them are chosen by the time the train gets to California."

Johnny grinned at his big sister. "You're right, Mary. We sure have been blessed. I know we're gonna be happy with Mr. and Mrs. Banton."

Mary lifted her eyes skyward. "Dear Lord Jesus, thank You for giving us Mr. and Mrs. Banton to be our foster parents."

Will looked down at her and smiled. "Mary, you can call us Mama and Papa now."

Mary giggled and looked heavenward again. "Excuse me, Lord Jesus. Thank You for giving us Mama and Papa Banton to be our foster parents."

Will laughed. "Now that's more like it, honey!"

"Yes," said Leah.

The groceries were piled in the rear of the buggy, and they all climbed in and headed north on Main Street. They were almost out of town when Will pointed to a white frame building. "Hey, kids, see that church?"

All three set their eyes on it.

"Yeah," said Johnny.

"That's where we'll take you to Sunday school and church services."

"Have you gone there before?" asked Mary.

"Yes. A couple of times."

Soon they were out of town, moving along a dusty country road. There were several farms that came into view, with cattle and horses dotting the pastures.

Lizzie jumped up from her place between Leah and Mary. "Look! Cows and horses! Lots of 'em!"

"Sure enough," said Mary. "We've never seen anything like this before, have we?"

"Huh-uh. It's neat!"

Johnny was studying the livestock in the pastures on both sides of the road. "Mr. Ban—I mean, Papa, what kind of horses and cattle are those?"

Will smiled at him. "Well, let's take the horses first. You see that some of them are big and thick-bodied like our horse?"

"Yes, sir."

"Well, those are draft horses. They pull plows, hay mowing,

raking, and stacking equipment, and hay wagons, as well as regular wagons and buggies like this one."

"Uh-huh."

"And then you see the horses that are much slimmer."

"Uh-huh."

"Those are saddle horses. They couldn't pull the kind of weight the draft horses do, but they are much faster."

Johnny nodded.

"Let me direct your attention to the cattle. You see those cattle with dark red hides and white faces?"

"Yes, sir."

"And those solid black ones in that pasture over there on the other side of the road?"

"Uh-huh."

"Well, the red ones with the white faces are called Herefords. They are beef cattle. As are those black ones over there. They're called Black Angus. So both the Hereford and the Angus are raised strictly to provide meat for our tables."

"Yes, sir."

"Now notice the cattle that are white with black markings."

"Okay."

"And those that are a light reddish brown with white markings."

"Yes, sir."

"Well, both of those are milk producers. The white ones with black markings are called Holsteins. The others are called Guernseys. The Holsteins give the most milk, but the Guernseys give the richest milk. So most of us own both kinds. That way we mix the milk and have a whole lot of rich milk!"

Johnny laughed. "That's pretty neat, Papa."

Mary pointed to a nearby farm. "Papa, what's that tall round building next to the barn over there?"

"That's called a silo."

"What's it for?"

"We store fodder in there. Fodder is hay or cornstalks. The silo keeps the fodder dry and fresh all winter long, which helps us to feed our livestock sufficiently when there is no grass for them to eat in pastures."

"Wow!" said Johnny. "This is really interesting! We're gonna learn a lot here, Mary."

"We sure will," agreed his sister.

Johnny ran his gaze across the Nebraska plains. "I've never been able to see so far before."

"Me, either," said Mary. "It seems like there's no end to all the land."

Moments later, Leah said, "Look up there on the right, children. See that farmhouse with the cottonwood trees in the front yard and the big red barn out back with the white silo beside it?"

All three nodded.

"Well, that's our place."

The Marston three focused harder on it.

"Wow!" said Johnny. "That's really a neat farm!"

As they drew closer, they saw the beef cattle and milk cows, and Johnny said, "You've got Herefords, don't you?"

Will grinned. "Sure do."

"And you've got both kinds of milk cows. And I see another draft horse. Do you have saddle horses, Papa?"

"Mm-hmm. Two of them. They're probably in the corral over by the barn, standing where we can't see them right now."

"Can I ride one of them?"

"Of course, but you'll have to let me teach you how, first."

"Okay!"

"Me too!" chimed in Lizzie.

Leah laughed. "You'll have to get bigger first, sweetheart."

Lizzie rubbed her nose. "Okay."

They pulled up to the gate, drove over the cattle guard between the posts, and headed toward the buildings.

The large two-story white frame house, which stood partially in the shade of the cottonwoods, was situated in the midst of the prettiest flower garden the Marston three had ever seen. The windows—upstairs and down—sparkled in the afternoon sunshine, and the breeze moved the swing on the wide front porch.

Mary studied the house. *It looks like a happy house.*

Suddenly there was movement on the porch, and a large dog with a deep red coat bounded down the steps, wagging his tail and barking his welcome.

Lizzie's eyes widened. "Oh! A doggie!"

"What's the doggie's name?" asked Mary.

"His name is Red, honey," replied Leah.

Johnny laughed. "What kind is he, Papa?"

"Irish setter."

"Oh yeah. I should've known that. I saw one at Central Park one time."

Red jumped up and down as Will stepped from the buggy and petted him. He quickly spotted the children as they left the buggy and responded quickly to their attention. After Red had met Mary, Johnny, and Lizzie, licked their hands, and had been petted by all three, Leah said, "All right, children, let's go in the house."

When they went inside—with Red following—Mary told herself the house looked as happy inside as it did outside. The spacious house had four bedrooms upstairs. The master bedroom belonged to Will and Leah, and Leah explained that the girls would have one bedroom together, and Johnny would have his own bedroom. This would allow the Bantons to still have one spare bedroom when company came to stay all night.

Mary put her arm around her little sister and looked at the Bantons. "I'm glad Lizzie and I will be in the same room so I can take care of her."

Lizzie's eyes were dancing. "Me too!"

They were taken to the girls' room first, which was simple but quite cozy. The twin beds were covered with blue and white quilts. A dresser and washstand took up the greater part of one wall. A rolltop desk sat in a corner of the room. Mary was fascinated with the wide, cushioned window seat. She pictured herself whiling the hours away while sitting in that comfortable spot and enjoying the scenery in view through the large window.

The girls followed as Johnny was led down the hall to his room.

When Johnny stepped into his room, it reminded him somewhat of his bedroom at home in Manhattan, though it was much larger. A colorful patchwork quilt covered his bed, and the afternoon sun made a pattern on the glossy wood floor. A rag rug of many hues lay in the middle of the room, and a white dresser and washstand stood against one wall. He had a large window, like the one in his sisters' room.

Will ran his gaze over the three bright faces. "Well, kids, what do you think?"

"We love it, Papa," said Mary.

Johnny and Lizzie spoke their agreement. Red was at Johnny's side and enjoyed the attention his new friend was giving him.

Having caught the mood of the children, Leah smiled. "We want you to be very happy here."

Mary moved to her and hugged her. "Oh, Mama, we will be happy living here with you and Papa. It's all new and different, but everything is perfect. Thank you for choosing us."

"Thank all three of you for wanting to come and live with us," Will said.

Leah smiled, a feeling of satisfaction growing in her heart. "Sounds like we're all pretty happy. Well, Will, let's show them through the rest of the house, then give them the grand tour of the rest of the place."

After being shown through the rest of the house, the children were taken on a tour of the barn and outbuildings. They were able to see the saddle horses and pet them, which was a thrill. The tour also included a walk for some distance in the pastures and the cornfields and hayfields. Red, of course, tagged along, happy to be petted by his new friends.

That evening at suppertime, the family gathered in the large kitchen at the round oak table. The kitchen had lots of cupboards. There were windows on two sides, looking out onto the yard and the fields and pastures beyond.

Will glanced at the fully loaded table. "What's for supper, honey?"

"Pork chops with mashed potatoes and gravy, fresh green beans, and tomatoes. Mary and Lizzie helped me prepare it."

Johnny smacked his lips. "Smells good to me!"

As they all sat down, Leah said, "Now, children, if I should put food before you at meals that you don't like, please tell me. It will take a while for me to know your likes and dislikes. Papa and I are happy to have you in our home, which is now your home too."

Mary smiled at her. "We are very happy that it is, Mama. We will help around here any way we can. Just let us know what you want us to do. We are pretty hard workers, even though we are young. Our parents believed that everyone in the house who was old enough should do their part of the work. Lizzie's only four, but she can help out in many ways."

"Your parents were wise people, honey, and they have raised three special children," said Will. "Well, let's eat!"

As was usual for him, Will picked up one of the bowls and started to scoop potatoes on to his plate.

Johnny looked at Mary, then at Leah. "Aren't we going to offer thanks to the Lord for the food?"

Embarrassed, Leah cleared her throat. "Papa Will must be so hungry, he forgot."

Will's face tinted. "Uh…let's bow our heads and close our eyes."

He waited till all had complied, then bowed his head and closed his own eyes. "We thank You for this food, God. And thank You for bringing Mary, Johnny, and Lizzie into this home. Amen."

When Will opened his eyes, he found Mary and Johnny looking at him quizzically. "What's wrong?"

Johnny frowned. "Papa, you're supposed to close your prayer in Jesus' name."

Will's features turned crimson. "Oh. I'm sorry. I forgot. I'll remember next time."

After the meal was over and the kitchen was cleaned up, they all sat down in the parlor—including Red, who was happy to have Johnny sitting on the floor with him.

Will and Leah, wanting to learn all they could about the Marston children's background, carefully asked questions, trying not to upset them over the loss of their parents. The conversation soon led, however, to their parents and their death in the Atlantic Ocean. Mary and Johnny began to cry, and this caused Lizzie to do the same.

Will took Johnny on his lap and Leah gathered the girls to herself.

When the weeping subsided, Will kept Johnny on his lap. "Mary, Lizzie, Johnny: we're so sorry for this terrible tragedy happening in your lives, but let me say again that we are happy to have you in our home. We promise that we will take good care of you. And whenever you need to talk to either of us, we want you to feel free to do so. Okay?"

Mary and Johnny both nodded, and Leah kissed Lizzie on top of her head. "Children, like I said, we'll take you into town tomorrow and buy you new clothes and shoes."

Lizzie rose up on her knees and planted a kiss on Leah's cheek. Then she ran her gaze back and forth between her sister, who sat on Leah's other side, and to Johnny, who sat on Will's lap. "Mrs. Roberts was right. God does take care of His little sparrows."

Mary's brow furrowed as she looked at her little sister. "What do you mean, Lizzie?"

"Papa Will an' Mama Leah are gonna let us live here in their house. They're gonna feed us, an' they're gonna buy us new clothes. God gave 'em to us."

Mary and Johnny agreed and that made Will remember Lizzie's comment about having little sparrows on their farm.

"Exactly what did Lizzie mean by having little sparrows?"

"Yes," said Leah. "I'd like to know."

Mary said, "Mrs. Roberts is the neighbor lady who took care of us when Mama and Papa went on their trip. And when the policemen came and told us that our parents had drowned in the ocean, Mrs. Roberts tried to encourage us by showing us in the Bible how God loves little sparrows and takes care of them. She showed us that Jesus said those of us who belong to Him are more valuable to Him than many sparrows."

Leah's eyes widened. "Really? Jesus said that?"

"Mm-hmm. If you will let me use your Bible, Mama, I'll show you."

Will and Leah exchanged glances.

Leah stood up, leaving the girls on the sofa. "I...ah—we...

ah—have a Bible in one of the closets upstairs. I'll be right back."

After a few minutes, Leah came down the stairs, carrying a Bible and wiping dust from its cover with her hand. When she entered the parlor, she handed it to Mary. "Here you go, sweetie."

Mary accepted the Bible, and while Leah sat down once again between her and Lizzie, she opened it to Matthew chapter 10. "Here it is. It's Jesus speaking. 'Are not two sparrows sold for a farthing? and one of them shall not fall on the ground without your Father. But the very hairs of your head are all numbered. Fear not therefore, ye are of more value than many sparrows.'"

Leah shook her head in wonderment. "Isn't that interesting? I sure didn't know that was in the Bible. Did you, Will?"

"Ah…no. I sure didn't."

"It's also in the book of Luke, too," said Mary. "And when Mrs. Roberts read us both passages, our Lizzie got all excited and said, 'Mary, Johnny, we're God's little sparrows!'"

Will gave Lizzie a tender look. "Well, sweetheart, it seems to me that you understood exactly what Jesus was saying, didn't you?"

Lizzie smiled at him. "Uh-huh."

Leah pulled her close once again and kissed her cheek. "Sweetheart, Papa Will and I are so glad that we have God's little sparrows in our home!"

The Bantons asked more questions of Mary and Johnny, and as the night drew its curtain of darkness over the land, Lizzie began to yawn and rub her eyes.

Leah noted it. "Okay, little ones, I see Lizzie about to fall asleep, and her sister and brother look pretty tired too. It's been a big, exciting day, and I think it's bedtime for all of us."

In Johnny's room, he patted Red's head, told him good night, and doused the lantern. Seconds later, the happy Irish setter hopped up on the bed and went to sleep, folded in Johnny's arm.

In the girl's room, Mary helped Lizzie into her nightgown, which they had brought with them on the train, then pulled her own over her head. Using a brush provided by Leah, she stroked Lizzie's hair and asked, "Which bed do you want?"

Standing in her bare feet, Lizzie ran her gaze to one bed, then the other. "I'll take that one by the wall, an' you can have the one by the window."

"You sure you wouldn't rather have the one by the window?"

Lizzie shook her head. "I like the one by the wall."

"All right. That's fine with me."

Mary brushed her own hair, then turned down Lizzie's covers. When she had turned her own covers down, she took hold of Lizzie's hand, and they knelt down together at Mary's bed. Mary led them in prayer. She thanked the Lord for the Bantons, and for giving them a home so soon.

Just as Mary finished praying, she felt Lizzie's little body begin to tremble. "Lizzie, what's wrong?"

Lizzie sniffed and choked on the lump in her throat. "I...I miss our real Mama an' Papa."

Mary hugged her. "Johnny and I miss them too. But we must make them proud of us. We have to be strong and realize that our real Mama and Papa are in heaven, and they want us to treat our new Mama and Papa right. They want us to be happy. God has given us this nice new home, with people who love us. It'll get better as time goes on. I promise." Mary was fighting a lump in her own throat.

When they stood up, Mary cupped Lizzie's little round face in her hands. "Tell you what, sweetheart: how about you just sleep with me in my bed tonight?"

Lizzie's eyes widened. "Really?"

"Yes. Come on. Climb in."

When little sister was in the bed and under the covers, Mary doused the lantern and crawled in beside her. Lizzie snuggled up close, and Mary put an arm around her. "All right, go to sleep."

Lizzie clung to Mary, sniffling. It took only a few minutes for the little girl to cry herself to sleep.

Lying in the darkness, Mary let her mind go over all that had happened to Lizzie, Johnny, and her since their parents had drowned in the ocean. Her own eyes began to grow heavy as she heard Lizzie's deep, even breathing. She kissed the sleeping child's cheek. "I love you."

Then like Lizzie, Mary cried herself to sleep.

Chapter Sixteen

On the westbound train that evening after supper, Josie Holden was sitting alone on the seat in the girls' coach, watching darkness fall over the Nebraska plains. Outside the window was a huge dark space of cool, windy emptiness, stretching seemingly into infinity under great winking silver stars.

Suddenly Josie sensed someone behind her. She pulled away from the window, looking up to see the smiling face of Rachel Wolford. A smile broke over her own face. "Hi."

"Hello, sweet girl. Remember I told you we'd get together this evening?"

"Mm-hmm."

"May I sit down?"

Josie straightened up on the seat. "Oh yes! Please do."

When Rachel sat down, Josie hugged her and kissed her cheek. "Thank you for coming to sit by me."

Rachel returned the hug and kissed Josie's cheek. "Pleasure's mine, honey. How are you doing?"

"Better than I was a minute ago. I miss Wanda so much, but now that you're here, the loneliness went away."

"I'm glad, honey."

At that moment both of them were aware of Laura and Tabitha standing in the aisle beside them.

Tabitha leaned past Rachel. "How are you doing, Josie? I imagine you're missing Wanda, aren't you?"

Josie nodded. "I miss Wanda very much, Mrs. Conlan, but Miss Wolford told me right after Wanda left with her new foster parents that she would try to take Wanda's place, and she is already doing it."

Laura laid a hand on Rachel's shoulder. "Bless you for that."

Rachel smiled up at her. "This child is easy to love."

Both women agreed with that statement and moved on toward the rear of the coach to sit down.

Rachel was praying in her heart that the Lord would now give her the opportunity she had been seeking. "Well, honey, have you been thinking a lot about the prospect of what lies ahead of you?"

"Mm-hmm. It's exciting, but it's scary too. You know. Just who will take me, and what they will be like. And what kind of home I will have."

"Sure. I can understand why you would be apprehensive about your future and all that it holds." She paused, then said, "Honey, you are uncertain about what lies ahead of you in this life, but may I ask you something?"

Josie smiled. "Of course."

"What about when this life is over? Are you certain about where you will spend eternity?"

Josie's smile drained away and a blank look took its place. "I…I'm not sure. You mean will I go to heaven?"

"Exactly. Will you?"

"Well, I don't know. I guess it depends on how good a life I live."

"If you didn't live a life good enough to satisfy God, then what?"

"I…ah…I would go to hell."

"Would you want to go to hell?"

"Oh no! I've heard people talk about hell all my life, and even use it as a curse word, but I really didn't know what it was till Mr. Brace read about it from the Bible in those times at the Society. It's a place of fire and torment. I sure wouldn't want to go there."

"Tell me this, sweetie. Just how good would you have to live to go to heaven when you die?"

The blank look came back. "I…well, I don't know. Does the Bible tell us?"

Rachel opened her purse and took out a small Bible. She began flipping pages. "Let me show you what the Bible says on that subject. Do you know what it means to be righteous?"

"I didn't till Mr. Brace talked about it. He said to be righteous is to be blameless and worthy of God's blessing."

"Right. Now, you just said you didn't know how good you would have to be to go to heaven."

"Uh-huh."

"You would have to be righteous, wouldn't you? Blameless before the holy God of heaven and worthy of His blessing you by giving you a place in heaven."

Josie blinked. "You would have to be."

"Right," she said, holding her Bible so Josie could see the page. "Look here in Romans chapter 3 and verse 10. 'As it is written, There is none righteous, no, not one.' That includes you and me, doesn't it?"

Josie swallowed hard. "Yes."

"Then there is not one person on earth who is blameless before God and worthy of His blessing. So there is nobody who is worthy to go to heaven. Right?"

"Yes."

"Look here at verses 11 and 12. 'There is none that understandeth, there is none that seeketh after God. They are all gone out of the way, they are together become unprofitable; there is none that doeth good, no, not one.' Pretty sad commentary on this human race, isn't it?"

Josie nodded.

"Now look over here in verse 23. 'For all have sinned and come short of the glory of God.' That would include the whole human race, wouldn't it?"

"Yes."

"You and me, too?"

"Yes."

"So if it depended on how good we live to get us to heaven and keep us from hell, would we make it?"

Josie's head moved back and forth slowly. "No. We'd go to hell." She took a shaky breath. "So how can we go to heaven?"

"By putting our faith in God's only begotten Son, the Lord Jesus Christ." She flipped a couple of pages. "Look here in Romans chapter 6 and verse 23. 'For the wages of sin is death; but the gift of God is eternal life through Jesus Christ our Lord.' The opposite of death is life, right?"

"Right."

"The Bible makes it clear that hell, in its final state, is the lake of fire. In Revelation we are told that the lake of fire is the second death. This is where all people who leave this life on earth without Jesus Christ will spend eternity. When the Bible speaks of death concerning human beings, it never means to go out of existence. It means a separation. When people die physically, they are separated from the living here on earth, but they are not out of existence. So it is of those who go to the lake of fire. They are separated from the living who are in heaven, but they never go out of existence. Revelation 14:11 says the smoke of their torment ascends up forever. So you see, honey, it's eternal death or eternal life for every human being.

"We just saw here in Romans 6:23 that eternal life is the gift of God. It is a gift, so it can't be earned. And it comes in only one way—through Jesus Christ. If we have eternal life, we will live forever with Him in heaven. Do you understand that?"

"Yes. I remember Mr. Brace telling us some of this you are telling me. And I remember that he told us in order to have salvation, forgiveness for our sins, and eternal life, we must repent of our sin and receive Jesus into our hearts as our personal Saviour. It is all coming back to me."

Rachel's heart was racing. "That's it, honey. In Mark 1:15, Jesus said, 'Repent ye, and believe the gospel.' "And according to the apostle Paul, the gospel is that Christ died for our sins, was buried, and rose again the third day. On the cross, Jesus shed His precious blood and died. He paid the full price for our sins. He arose from the grave as He said He would, and is alive to save every person who will repent and believe the gospel.

"John 1:12 tells us we must *receive* Jesus to become a child of God. We do that according to what Romans chapter 10 tells us."

Rachel turned to Romans 10. "Look here, sweetie. Verses 9 and 10. 'That if thou shalt confess with thy mouth the Lord Jesus, and shall believe in thine heart that God hath raised him from the dead, thou shalt be saved. For with the heart man believeth unto righteousness; and with the mouth confession is made unto salvation.' Please note that it is with the *heart* that we believe. That's receiving Jesus into your heart and that's what makes us children of God. Do you understand?"

"Yes, I do."

"And look at this. It says with the heart we believe unto *righteousness*. Remember, this is what we lack in ourselves—righteousness."

"Yes."

"But when we repent of our sin, believing the gospel, calling on Jesus, receiving Him into our heart, and believing that He does all the saving all by Himself; He comes into our heart, washes our sins away in His precious blood, makes us a child of God, imparts *His* righteousness to us, and gives us eternal life. This is the guarantee that we will be with Him in heaven forever. Do you understand?"

Tears were coming down Josie's cheeks. "Yes, oh yes! Will you help me? I want to receive Jesus into my heart right now!"

Rachel Wolford had the joy of leading Josie Holden to Jesus. After the twelve-year-old had called on Jesus to save her and received Him into her heart, she threw her arms around Rachel. "Oh, thank you, Miss Wolford, for showing me how to be saved! My sins are forgiven and washed away in Jesus' blood, and whenever I leave this world, I know I'll go to heaven to be with Him!"

On Tuesday afternoon, June 23, Sam and Emma Claiborne were in their wagon, heading for Cheyenne. They would go to the general store to pick up groceries and household supplies, stop by the post office, then have their daily visit with Jody at the clinic.

It was a beautiful early summer day. Not a cloud could be seen in the cerulean sky. A gentle breeze played with the leaves on the trees, and wildflowers along the road were showing off their glossy new blossoms.

Holding on to her husband's arm, Emma sighed. "What a lovely day the Lord has given us, honey. I just love this time of year when everything is alive and fresh again."

Sam turned and smiled at her. "Yes, sweetheart, and after the long, hard winter we just endured, it is especially welcome."

She ran her gaze over the lush prairie. "I only wish Jody could enjoy it. She loves summertime so much, riding Queenie across the land and spending the days in the fields working with you." The tears spilled over and streamed down her cheeks.

Sam put his arm around her and pulled her tight against him. This was all he could do at the moment. His throat was too constricted to allow words to be spoken.

Soon they arrived in town and entered the general store. Immediately, they were approached by people they knew, who wanted to know about Jody's condition. Others gathered around to hear about Jody. Sam and Emma told the group that as of their visit to Jody at the clinic yesterday, Dr. John Traynor was losing his optimism that Jody would ever come out of her coma. When Sam asked him if he honestly thought Jody had a chance of living, he told them he didn't think she would live much longer.

One widow woman from their church, whose name was Oralee Baldwin, took hold of Emma's hand. "I'm so sorry, dear."

Emma squeezed Oralee's hand. Her throat tightened, but she forced the words out. "It...it looks like the Lord is going to take our little girl to heaven to be with Him."

She burst into tears. Oralee put her arms around her. "Don't give up, honey. As long as she's alive, there is still hope."

Hardly able to comprehend the possibility that Jody might still live, Emma choked on a sob. "Sam and I— Sam and I are still asking the Lord to do that which will bring Him the most glory. If...He decides to take her to be with Him, heaven will be a brighter place with Jody's presence there, but the sunshine in Sam's life and mine will be very dim."

Oralee squeezed her tight. "Emma, as you and Sam know, Pastor Forbes has asked all the members of the church to continue to hold Jody up in prayer. I for one promise I will do so."

"Thank you for caring, Oralee. It means more than Sam or I can say."

"Yes," said Sam. "It sure does."

The others in the group assured the Claibornes that they were pulling for Jody and were praying that she would come out of the coma and be able to live out her life.

The purchases were made, and Emma was still wiping tears as she and Sam left the store, both carrying grocery bags. When they stepped up to the wagon, Sam placed the bags he was carrying into the wagon bed, then took those Emma carried and did the same. He helped her up into the seat, climbed up beside her, and headed down the street for the post office.

Emma waited in the wagon while Sam went inside the post office to pick up the mail. It seemed that he was in there longer than usual, but he had her attention when he came out, holding the bundle of mail in one hand and waving an envelope in the other. As he drew up to the wagon, he said, "Letter from Ed and Sarah, sweetheart. I couldn't wait till I got out here to open it."

Emma dearly loved Sam's brother and sister-in-law, who lived in Omaha, Nebraska. She and Sam had sent them a letter recently, advising them of Jody's worsening condition. "What did they say, honey?"

"They are coming so they can be with us when—when—well, when Jody goes to heaven. They will arrive at the depot on the eleven o'clock train tomorrow morning."

Emma's eyes brightened. "Oh, I'm glad! It will be so good to see them again. You know how much Sarah and I always enjoy being together. I could really use her company. Especially when Jody—" She burst into tears.

Sam climbed into the wagon seat quickly and took Emma in his arms. He held her and spoke in soft tones, doing his best to comfort her.

When Emma's emotions had subsided, Sam kissed her cheek.

"Let's go to the clinic, sweetheart."

He was about to put the wagon into motion when he saw Pastor Dan Forbes hurrying toward them on the boardwalk. When he drew up, he saw Emma dabbing at her cheeks with a handkerchief. "Are you all right, Emma?"

"I'm just having a hard time over Jody's condition, Pastor."

"I understand. I saw Sam holding you up there in the seat, and thought maybe—well, you know—Jody…"

"As far as we know, she's still alive, Pastor," said Sam. "We're on our way to the clinic."

"Oh. I thought maybe you had just been there, and—"

"We're still holding on, Pastor."

"Good. I was at the clinic about two hours ago to check on her. Dr. Traynor told me that he had expressed his fear to you yesterday that Jody won't ever come out of the coma. But listen to me: as long as Jody is breathing, there is hope."

"We just saw Oralee Baldwin at the general store, Pastor," said Emma. "She said essentially the same thing."

Sam looked down at Forbes. "Pastor, you remember meeting my brother Ed and his wife Sarah when they visited us a couple of years ago?"

"Yes. They live in Omaha, don't they?"

"Right. Well, we just got a letter from them, and they are going to be on the eleven o'clock train from Chicago tomorrow morning."

"Oh, wonderful! I know they'll be a source of strength to you."

"Yes. Especially if—"

"Sam, don't give up now."

Sam bit his lips. "It's pretty hard, Pastor."

"I know. Before you go to the clinic, could we pray together?"

"Of course."

Standing close to Sam's side of the wagon, Pastor Dan Forbes led them in prayer, asking God to strengthen the parents and to comfort them in this time of great trial. He also asked the Lord to do that which would bring the most glory to His name. Before walking on down the boardwalk, he reminded Sam and Emma once again that as long as Jody was still breathing, there was hope.

As Sam drove the wagon down the street toward the clinic, fighting his own tears, he looked at the weeping Emma. "Sweetheart, I appreciate Pastor Forbes so much."

"Me too. I wish I had his optimism about Jody, but it just isn't in me."

"Me, either. I have to say that from all appearances, it looks like it's almost God's time to take her home to heaven."

"That's the way it looks. And if so, honey, we will still love and serve Him with all our hearts. He knows best, and we must trust if He does, that taking her home will glorify Him the most."

They arrived at the clinic and were soon standing over Jody's bed in her small room. She was still breathing shallowly but steadily.

Sam stood beside Emma as she took hold of Jody's frail hand, raised it a little and said, "Look, Sam. She's lost so much weight that her little hands are almost skeletal."

Sam swallowed the lump in his throat and nodded.

Keeping the hand in hers, Emma leaned closer to her daughter and spoke in a soft tone. "Jody, sweetheart, Daddy and Mommy are here with you. And you know what? Queenie is chomping at the bit at home, wanting a good gallop across the prairie."

Sam's heart went out to his dear wife. Emma talked to Jody just like this on each visit, hoping that her words would finally penetrate the veil that kept her in its grip. For both of them, it was hard to leave her, knowing that word could come at any time that she had slipped away. But after over an hour at her side, they knew it was time to head for home.

They both kissed her forehead, and as they stepped into the hall, Dr. John Traynor appeared. "The nurses told me you were here. There's nothing different, as you have seen, but I just wanted to tell you that our church is still praying for her."

"We appreciate that, Doctor," Sam said with strained voice.

"I can't give you any encouragement, but how I wish I could."

Sam nodded. "Well, we very much appreciate the excellent care Jody's getting here, Doctor. Thank you for that."

Sam and Emma slowly left the clinic and moved toward the wagon. She looked up at him and said, "You know, honey, soon I'm going to be staying at the clinic with Jody around the clock. I can't bear to think of her dying without one of us at her side."

"I know, sweetheart, but right now you are a shadow of yourself. You need to rest. I don't want something happening to you. We'll just take it one step at a time and trust the dear Lord for His matchless grace, okay?"

"Of course. I don't mean to be so despondent. I'm really trying to trust the Lord and wait on Him."

"I know you are. Me too. We've never had to deal with anything of this magnitude before. But even though we get despondent, His promise is still true. He will never leave us nor forsake us."

As Sam helped her up onto the wagon seat, she gave him a watery smile. "Praise His precious name for that."

Sam rounded the wagon, climbed up, and sat down beside her. As he put the team in motion and the wagon headed northward, Emma gripped the hand closest to her. "Well, God's been good in sending Ed and Sarah to us. At least they'll be here when—when—" And she began weeping again.

It was ten minutes before eleven o'clock on June 24 when Sam and Emma arrived at the Cheyenne railroad station. This time they were in the family buggy since they were picking up Ed and Sarah.

Sam parked the buggy in the depot's parking lot and gave Emma his arm as they walked inside.

At that very moment, the train was chugging into the station with the bell on the engine clanging.

"Come on, sweetheart. Let's be right there on the platform when they get off," Sam said.

As they walked to the platform where the train would roll to a halt, Emma said, "Oh, Sam, I'm so glad they're going to be here with us."

"Me too."

Many people were waiting on the platform, watching the big engine hiss steam from its sides as it chugged to a halt. Sam and Emma squeezed past some of the people so they could have a full view of the coaches. They were eager to lay eyes on Ed and Sarah Claiborne.

While they waited and watched, a man and woman moved past them toward the rear of the train. They heard the man say, "The ticket agent out front said the orphans are in the last two cars."

Sam looked down at Emma. "Hmm. Looks like this is one of the orphan trains."

Emma nodded, looking toward the last two coaches. "Look at all those sweet, innocent faces in the windows."

Sam set his eyes on the faces in both orphan coaches. "Poor kids. Has to be rough."

"I'll say."

At that instant a young rancher and his wife stopped beside the Claibornes, and the woman said to her husband, "I was told that the adult escorts on the orphan trains always let the regular passengers who are getting off do so before they take the orphans out and line them up for inspection by the prospective foster parents."

"Makes sense," said her husband. "Get the traffic out of the way so people like us can look over the orphans and talk to them without hindrance."

Several minutes passed as Sam and Emma watched for Ed and Sarah to appear from one of the three cars ahead of the orphan coaches while passengers got off, greeted relatives and friends, and walked away, chatting happily.

Suddenly Emma gripped Sam's arm and pointed toward the front platform of coach number two. "There they are!"

They hurried toward Ed and Sarah, who saw them coming and smiled broadly.

Emma broke into tears as Sarah opened her arms to her. They stood, holding on to each other, while the brothers embraced, both pounding the other on the back.

Sam then hugged Sarah while Ed did the same with Emma.

Ed asked, "What can you tell us about Jody?"

"Well, praise the Lord, she's still alive," said Sam.

Sarah's eyes brightened. "Is there any noticeable change in her condition?"

Sam shook his head. "It is only getting worse."

Ed and Sarah showed the disappointment they felt. Sarah held on to Emma. "Oh, honey, I'm so glad Ed and I could come."

"Sam and I appreciate your coming more than we can say."

Sam nodded. "That's for sure."

Emma wiped away the tears. "God sent both of you to us. We need you more than you could ever know. We have wonderful friends here that we love dearly, but there is just something so very special about family. Some of my burden has already been lifted."

"No need to thank us," said Ed. "Wild Indians couldn't have kept us away."

Sarah looked into Emma's sorrowful eyes, so full of pain and discouragement. "Emma, I'm here for you as long as you need me. Ed has to go back in ten days, but I'll stay until you tell me you can get along without me. Just tell me what you need, and I'll do my best to take care of it."

Once again, Emma embraced her sister-in-law. A full smile graced Emma's pretty face, the first in a long time. "Oh, Sarah, I can't tell you how much this means to me…to both of us."

At that moment the orphans were being led out of their coaches and forming a long line. Several couples were there, waiting to look them over and talk to them. Other passengers, bound for points west, were getting off simply to stretch their legs.

Ed looked that way and said, "Sam, Emma, when Sarah and I watched the orphans being interviewed and chosen in Kearney, we found it quite interesting. Since it will take a little while for the baggage handlers to get our baggage unloaded, why don't we watch?"

"Fine with me," said Sam. "Jody and I watched them for a while when an orphan train was here a couple of months ago. Jody felt so sorry for the orphans. You know how tender she is."

Ed and Sarah both nodded.

"In fact," said Sam, "when Jody and I were here that day, some neighbors of ours took two little girls home with them."

"Oh. Is it working out all right?"

"Perfectly," said Emma. "Both the girls and the parents are happy with each other."

Sam grinned. "Jody was so happy for those little girls."

Ed snapped his fingers. "Speaking of Jody, Sarah and I noticed an orphan girl just about her age in Kearney who looks a lot like her. Nobody took the girl. We saw her get back on the train when the interviews were over."

As Ed was speaking, Sarah was running her eyes down the line of orphans. "Yes! There she is. Look, Emma. The dark-haired girl who is talking to that husky boy. He's also one of the orphans."

Emma's mouth fell open and her eyes widened. Before she could speak, Sam said, "I can't believe it! Do you see that, Emma? She looks enough like Jody that she could be her sister."

Emma gasped. "Does she ever! I want to get a closer look at her."

Sam's features lit up, "I do, too!"

Ed and Sarah followed them as they headed toward the pretty, dark-haired girl.

Chapter Seventeen

Josie Holden smiled at Barry Chandler, who had stepped out of the line briefly to check on her. "I'm all right, Barry. Thank you for asking. Yes, it was very hard to let Wanda go, but Miss Wolford sat with me in the coach last night and made me feel lots better."

"I'm glad, Miss Josie. Miss Wolford is such a nice lady. And I have to say, she *really* must have been a help to you, because you've got a sparkle in your eyes that I haven't seen before."

Josie's smile brightened. "Well, Barry, when Miss Wolford was sitting with me in the coach last night, something wonderful happened."

"What was that?"

"Miss Wolford talked to me about where I would spend eternity. She showed me from the Bible that I'm a sinner before God, and if I died without having my sins forgiven and washed away in the blood of Jesus Christ, I would go to hell. When I fully understood how and why Jesus went to the cross and died for me, I opened my heart to Him and received Him as my Saviour."

Barry's face lit up. "That's wonderful, Josie! I was saved at the Children's Aid Society right after Bible study just two days before we boarded the train to come west. Do you know who Mr.

Markum is? He's on the staff there."

"Yes."

"Well, Mr. Markum was leading the boys' Bible study, and he was showing us from the Bible that if we died in our sins, we would spend eternity in hell. When the session was over, I was really miserable and afraid, because I knew I wasn't saved. Mr. Markum could tell I was upset. He talked to me alone and asked what I was upset about. Of course, he really knew. Anyway, he led me to the Lord then and there."

"Oh, Barry! I'm so glad for you. Now we're both children of God."

Barry was about to say something else, but was interrupted as Gifford Stanfield moved up. "Barry, you need to get back in line. You're keeping people from passing along here."

Barry looked up to see several men and women standing still in the line, not wanting to interrupt his conversation with Josie. His face blanched. "Oh, I'm sorry, Mr. Stanfield. Please excuse me, Josie. I'll see you later."

Josie warmed him with another smile, and Barry hurried back to where he had been placed in the line by the sponsors.

The prospective foster parents resumed their slow movement along the line of orphans.

Sam and Emma, and Ed and Sarah positioned themselves a few feet from where the dark-haired girl stood and watched as the men and women filed by, talking to the boys and girls. The Stanfields and the Conlans waited close by, clipboards in hand.

Sam noticed Emma's hand go to her chin. "Honey, this girl has to be very close to the same age as Jody, and I can hardly believe how much she resembles her."

Sam nodded. "Her hair is exactly the same color as Jody's, and her facial features are remarkably similar. Like I said, she could be Jody's sister."

"That's for sure," put in Ed. "The resemblance is striking."

Emma shook her head in wonderment. "And she's exactly the same height. She probably weighs what Jody did before she fell off of Queenie and went into the coma."

Ed and Sarah looked at each other, held the gaze for a few seconds, then put their attention back on the dark-haired girl.

At the Cheyenne Clinic, nurse Joyce Adams looked up from the desk in the office to see Pastor Dan Forbes and Clara enter. "Good morning, folks. You're here to see Jody Claiborne again, I imagine."

"Yes," said the pastor. "Any change at all?"

"No, sir. She's still deep in the coma. I'll have to ask you to wait a few minutes. Mike and Natalie Houston and their daughter, Betty, are in there with her at the moment. They're members of your church, aren't they?"

"Yes. I know they come quite often to see Jody. Betty even comes by herself sometimes, doesn't she?"

"Quite often. Betty is a true friend if I've ever seen one."

Suddenly the door to the rear of the building burst open, and Mike Houston appeared, his face sheet white. "Joyce, Dr. Traynor needs you right now! I'm afraid Jody's dying!"

Natalie and Betty appeared behind him as the nurse jumped up and headed for the door.

Dan Forbes moved that direction. "Anything I can do to help?"

The nurse paused and shook her head. "Dr. Traynor wouldn't want you in the room right now, Pastor."

Mike stepped aside and held the door open so Joyce could pass through. She headed down the hall at a run.

Natalie moved past her husband, followed by Betty, whose hands were clamped over her mouth. She, too, was pasty white.

Mike closed the door and followed his wife and daughter as they headed for the spot where the Forbeses were standing.

"What happened?" asked Clara.

Natalie was first to find her voice. "W-we were s-standing beside Jody's bed, looking down at her as Dr. Traynor was checking her heartbeat with his stethoscope, and suddenly she stopped breathing."

"Oh no!" said the pastor. "What did the doctor say?"

"He just told us to leave the room, and asked that we send Joyce back there as fast as possible."

Dan Forbes rubbed the back of his neck. "Then Dr. Traynor must have known that Jody was still alive, or he wouldn't have needed his nurse to help him."

"I would say so," said Mike.

The pastor gestured toward the waiting area. "Let's sit down and go to prayer."

They had been praying for some fifteen or twenty minutes when they heard the door at the rear of the office come open. Every head came up, and they saw the doctor step into the office.

Clara Forbes murmured, "Oh no."

At the railroad station, while the prospective foster parents interviewed the orphans all along the line, Lance Adams again stood near the spot where Jimmy Kirkland was.

He saw and heard the same thing as in Kearney, Nebraska. People showed interest in Jimmy until they heard the stuttering lisp, then lost interest immediately.

The fourth couple had just drawn up. The man smiled as he bent down and said, "Hello there, young man. What's your name?"

Jimmy was fearful of giving a reply, which was evident to Lance Adams.

The woman bent down. "What's the matter, honey? Cat got your tongue?"

Jimmy's head was tilted down. He shook his head.

"Well then tell us what your name is."

The boy nervously shifted his weight from one foot to the other and finally raised his head. "M-my n-name ith J-Jimmy Kirkland."

The man and woman looked at each other, frowning, then the man said, "How old are you, Jimmy?"

"F-five y-yearth old, th-thir." Jimmy's hand went to his mouth to wipe away the excess saliva on his lower lip.

The man looked at his wife. "Let's move on, Shirley."

As the couple stepped away from Jimmy, he began to cry.

Lanced rushed to him, picked him up, and held him close. "It's all right, Jimmy. Don't cry."

The couple paused in front of a teenage boy and the man looked back. When he saw Jimmy in the arms of Lance, he shrugged and began talking to the boy.

Patting Jimmy's back tenderly, Lance said, "Don't you worry about it, Jimmy. Some nice people will take you home with them at one of these stops."

Jimmy threw his arms around Lance's neck and sobbed, "I w-wanna g-go home with y-you, M-Mithter Adamth. Pleathe t-take me h-home with y-you."

People who were passing along the line looked on as Lance held the sobbing boy.

With Jimmy's plea burning his ears, Lance said in his heart, *Dear Lord, I can't make a move to take this precious child until You show me that it's what You want for sure. Please help me. I have no way of knowing if You have done a work in Carol's heart. You can do a miracle; I know it. You did it for Abraham and Sarah and gave them a son when it looked impossible. Is anything too hard for the Lord?*

With the boy's arms locked tight around his neck, Lance said, "Jimmy, I told you before that I would love to take you home with me, but I can't."

Jimmy sniffled and eased back in Lance's arms so he could look into his eyes. "B-but you d-didn't tell m-me why."

"Jimmy, you simply wouldn't understand. You're just too young." *I'm going to put him back in the line, Lord. If You let some-one else choose him, I'll know my thinking on this was wrong.*

As he placed Jimmy's feet back on the platform floor, he said, "Maybe one of these couples yet in line will take you."

Jimmy looked up at him with pleading eyes. Lance felt like his heart was going to break in two. As he stepped back to his previous spot, he said in his heart, *Please, Lord. Do Your miracle. Lead me so I'll know Your will.*

Farther up the line, Emma Claiborne had her eyes riveted on the dark-haired girl who so strongly resembled the daughter she feared was soon going to die.

Sam, Ed, and Sarah saw clearly that Emma was totally fasci-nated by the girl. They looked at each other questioningly, then Sam silently mouthed, *Are you thinking what I'm thinking?*

Ed and Sarah exchanged glances and smiled at each other. Sarah leaned close and whispered in his ear, "We think Emma wants to take that girl home. Probably because she is about to lose Jody and she feels the need to have a foster daughter who resembles her. You know…to keep Jody alive in a sense."

Sam nodded. "That's exactly what I'm thinking."

He turned back to Emma. She still held her eyes on the girl, who at the moment had a couple talking to her. He leaned close and spoke in a whisper. "Honey, you seem to be mesmerized by that girl."

Emma looked at him with tears in her eyes. "I am, darling. I was just thinking that she could be a real strength to us when—when Jody goes to heaven. Not that she could ever take Jody's place, of course, but the house wouldn't seem so empty if we had her living with us. Especially since she looks so much like our Jody."

As those words came out of her mouth, Emma noticed that the couple talking to the dark-haired girl was moving on.

Sam wiped a hand over his face. "Honey, this is all so sudden. Are you sure you wouldn't regret it later? You know—feeling guilty that you would take a girl who strongly resembles Jody, then wondering if you really weren't trying to put her in Jody's place."

Emma shook her head. "No. That would never happen because I know how much I love Jody, and that I would never let anybody take her place. Sam, that girl needs a home. Who knows what terrible grief and heartaches she has gone through, losing her parents and her home."

"Well, I—"

"Sam, that girl has so captured my heart that even if Jody was in perfect health, I would still want to take her home. These poor orphans are so pitiful. All of them have had such sadness in their young lives. I wish we could take them all home, but that's impossible. And even if it were possible, I still wouldn't do it because I wouldn't want to rob others of the blessing of having these children in their homes. I just hope they will all be loved and treated well."

Sam smiled. "Your soft heart is showing, sweetie, and I love you for it. I...well, I—"

"What?" Her eyes were twinkling.

"I sense something happening in my heart. Like the Lord is speaking to me about this."

She touched his hand. "Really?"

"Mm-hmm. I don't think our seeing this girl was merely coincidence. With Christians there is no such thing as coincidence. We've talked about that before."

"Yes, we have."

"Honey, the Lord has a plan for each life of those who belong to Him, and He has His own way of fulfilling that plan. I...I think we should go talk to her."

Emma's eyes filmed with tears. "Sam, we must make a quick decision I know, but I have to tell you...I have such a peace about this girl. We could be such a blessing to her. She needs a home. A few people have passed her by. That couple who were talking to her a moment ago have moved on."

Ed and Sarah had been silent while listening to Sam and Emma's conversation. They looked at each other, nodding. Ed ran his gaze over their faces. "Sam, Emma, if our opinion means anything in this matter, we both believe you should take that girl home with you."

Emma smiled. "Really?"

"Really," said Sarah.

Emma looked up at her husband. "I feel so positive about this. Let's go talk to her."

Ed and Sarah clasped hands and watched with keen interest as Sam and Emma headed toward the dark-haired girl.

Josie Holden smiled at them. "Hello!"

Both Sam and Emma were smiling as Sam said, "What's your name, little lady?"

"Josie Holden."

Sam and Emma looked at each other in amazement.

Sam swallowed hard. "Honey, can you believe it? Her name is so close to Jody's."

Emma nodded, her eyes wide. "It…it's unbelievable."

"How old are you, honey?" queried Sam.

"Twelve, sir. I'll turn thirteen on October 2."

"Just two days difference," said Emma. "Can you believe this?"

"I think I'm dreaming," said Sam, shaking his head.

Emma looked at Josie, then back at Sam. "She even sounds a little like Jody."

"She sure does. I can't believe it. Honey, this absolutely can't be just coincidence."

Josie's eyelids fluttered and her brow puckered. "Who's Jody?"

Tears misted the eyes of both Sam and Emma.

Sam cleared his throat gently. "She's…she's our daughter, Josie. Our only child. My name is Sam Claiborne, and my wife's name is Emma. We own the *Circle C* ranch a few miles north of town."

Josie's eyes brightened. "A ranch! That sounds interesting."

Emma smiled at the girl. "Josie, were you raised in the country?"

"No, ma'am. I was raised in New York City on Manhattan Island. I'm a city girl. But I've read about ranch life here in the West and it has very much interested me. My papa always called me a tomboy. I think I'd really like ranch life."

Sam and Emma looked at each other. The word *tomboy* rang a bell with both of them. Their Jody and this girl from New York City were amazingly alike. They were both thinking that this had to be God's seal of approval on their taking Josie Holden home with them.

At that moment, Josie noticed that the couple who had interviewed her just before the Claibornes had returned and were looking at her. By the look on both of their faces, she knew they had decided she was their choice.

Sam and Emma also noticed that the couple had returned and were waiting for them to move on so they could approach Josie once again.

Emma moved closer to Josie and whispered, "I think these folks want to talk to you again."

Josie whispered so both Sam and Emma could hear her. "They weren't sure they wanted a girl quite as old as I am. They were going to talk to a girl down the line who is nine years old. It looks like maybe they have decided to take me."

Sam noted Emma's body stiffen. "Josie, do you want us to move on so these people can talk to you again?"

Josie spoke in a normal voice. "No, sir. I want to talk to you some more."

Sam noted that Emma relaxed at Josie's words.

"Please tell me about Jody," said Josie. "Would she feel all right about me living in your home?"

Sam pulled at an ear. "Well, honey, let me explain about Jody. She fell off her horse a month ago yesterday and struck her head on a rock that was sticking up out of the ground. It wasn't her fault. She and her best friend were racing their horses, which they often do, and her horse was frightened by a rattlesnake. The mare tried to avoid the snake and lost her footing. As she was going down, Jody flew out of the saddle and struck her head on the rock."

Josie's face pinched. "Oh, I'm sorry. Is she all right?"

"No, she's not. Jody has been in a coma ever since. We have her in the Cheyenne Clinic, and our doctor isn't giving us any hope that she will ever come out of the coma. He's expecting her to die soon."

The girl saw the tears in Emma's eyes. "I'm so sorry, Mrs.

Claiborne. This must be terrible for both of you."

"It is," said Emma, "but we have the Lord and He is helping us in this most difficult time."

Sam looked down at Emma. "Honey, I am as sure as you are that the Lord wants us to take Josie as our foster daughter."

Emma nodded. "I have no doubt of it, sweetheart."

Both of them saw Josie's eyes brighten. "Could I ask you something?"

"Of course, dear," said Emma.

"Both of you have just mentioned the Lord. Are...are you Christians?"

Sam's face beamed. "We sure are, honey; born again and washed in the blood of the Lamb. We have a Christian home and are regular in Sunday school and church right here in Cheyenne."

Emma smiled. "You must be a Christian too."

"Yes, ma'am! Just last night, the nurse who travels with the orphans on the train led me to Jesus. I received Him into my heart as my Saviour."

Sam took hold of Emma's hand. "Honey, can you believe this? Could it be more perfect?"

"Absolutely not. This is God's hand. There's no other way to explain it."

Sam bent down close to the dark-haired girl. "Josie, would you like to come and live with us?"

A smile spread over the girl's face, but they could see that she was a bit nervous.

Emma laid a hand on her arm. "Josie, is something wrong?"

Josie bent her head down a little. "Mr. and Mrs. Claiborne, I...I wouldn't try to take your daughter's place. I know I couldn't do that. But since Jody and I seem to look and sound so much alike, and we're the same age, could you just think of me as her sister?"

Tears were filling Emma's eyes. She wrapped her arms around Josie and held her close. "That's it! We'll think of you as Jody's sister! Will you come and live with us?"

"Oh yes! I want to with all my heart!"

"Good!" said Sam. "And Josie?"

"Yes, sir?"

"You asked if Jody would feel all right about you living in our home. Honey, if God should decide to perform a miracle and let her live, I can tell you for sure that Jody would love to have you for her sister."

Josie smiled. "I hope the Lord will perform that miracle, Mr. Claiborne."

"Josie," said Sam, "which of these officials should we talk to? Let's make this official."

Josie ran her gaze to Tabitha Conlan, who happened to be free at the moment and was in conversation with Rachel Wolford.

"That lady there with the clipboard, Mr. Claiborne. Her name is Tabitha Conlan. And the lady with Mrs. Conlan in the nurse's uniform is Miss Rachel Wolford, the one who led me to the Lord last night."

Sam glanced at Emma. "I'll be right back."

As Sam headed for the spot where Tabitha and Rachel were standing, the couple who had returned to talk to Josie looked at each other with disappointment obvious on their faces, turned, and walked away.

Both Emma and Josie had their attention on Sam. Emma put an arm around the girl. "Oh, Josie, this makes me so happy. We'll do everything possible to make you glad you decided to become our foster daughter."

"I'm sure you will," replied Josie, "and I'll do everything possible to make you and Mr. Claiborne glad that you took me in."

Sam drew up to Tabitha and Rachel. "My name is Sam Claiborne, ladies. My wife and I own the *Circle C* ranch a few miles north of Cheyenne. We have been talking to Josie Holden, and we want to become her foster parents."

Tabitha looked at a sheet of paper on her clipboard. "I don't have your names here, Mr. Claiborne, as prospective foster parents. Did you talk to one of the other sponsors?"

"Uh…no, ma'am. I didn't realize we had to do that first. We…well, we actually came to the station to meet my brother and sister-in-law who came on the train from Omaha. It wasn't until we happened to see Josie that we decided to take her home with us."

Tabitha smiled. "Well, it'll only take a moment for me to ask some questions and see if you and Mrs. Claiborne qualify to take one of our orphans. Could you have Mrs. Claiborne come over here?"

"Of course." Sam motioned for Emma, and she headed that way.

While they were waiting for Emma, Sam looked at the nurse. "Miss Wolford, Josie told us that you led her to Jesus last night."

Rachel's eyes lit up. "I sure did! Are you folks Christians?"

"We sure are, ma'am! Born again and washed in the blood of the Lamb!"

"Wonderful! I've been praying that the Lord would put Josie in a Christian home."

"This is marvelous," said Tabitha.

Emma drew up, and Sam introduced her to both Tabitha and Rachel. Emma expressed her appreciation to Rachel that she had led Josie to the Lord, then Tabitha asked the questions that were needed to qualify the Claibornes as foster parents. They passed with flying colors, and Tabitha led Sam and Emma to Josie with Rachel following.

Tabitha told Josie that the Claibornes were now approved as foster parents, and asked if she was in agreement to go home with them. Josie assured her enthusiastically that she was in total agreement.

While Tabitha was completing the official papers and getting signatures from Sam and Emma, Josie turned to Rachel. "Oh, Miss Wolford, I don't know how to thank you for all that you have done for me. Especially for caring about my soul, and for leading me to Jesus."

Josie hugged Rachel and kissed her cheek. "I'll see you one day in heaven."

Rachel kissed Josie's cheek. "I'll be looking forward to spending eternity with you, sweetie. Have a wonderful life."

"Oh, I will! I will!"

When the official papers were in Sam's hand, and Rachel and Tabitha were walking away, he motioned to Ed and Sarah, who were standing close by. When they stepped up, he introduced Josie to them.

Josie smiled and curtsied. "I'm so happy to meet Mr. Claiborne's brother and sister-in-law."

"You see, Josie," said Sam, "the reason we were here at the depot when the train came in was to meet Ed and Sarah. Their home is in Omaha, Nebraska. They came here to be with us when Jody—when Jody goes to heaven."

Josie smiled at Ed and Sarah again. "That is very kind and thoughtful of you."

"So you see, honey," said Emma, "we didn't even know this was an orphan train. We had no idea that we would see you and the Lord would give you to us to take home as our foster daughter. But how we praise Him for being so good to us."

Josie's eyes misted. "He has been very, very good to me, too, Mrs. Claiborne. I'm so happy that I can live in your home."

Sam took a deep breath. "Well, time to go! Ed, let's you and I go get your luggage while the ladies take Josie to the buggy."

Josie ran her gaze down the line of orphans. "Ah…Mr. Claiborne, would you let me tell a special boy good-bye?"

"Of course, honey. One of the orphan boys?"

"Yes. His name is Barry Chandler, and he has been so good to me on this trip."

Emma smiled. "Is it that handsome boy you were talking to earlier, honey?"

Josie giggled. "That's him. I'll be right back."

The foursome watched as Josie hurried down the line and drew up to Barry Chandler. She was talking to him while bouncing up and down on the balls of her feet.

Chapter Eighteen

Barry Chandler was feeling mixed emotions at Josie Holden's announcement that a couple had just chosen her, but showed only elation. "Really? Josie, that's wonderful!"

"And Barry, they are Christians! I'm going to live in a Christian home!"

"Oh, that's double wonderful!"

She stopped bouncing. "They are ranchers. Their names are Sam and Emma Claiborne. They own the *Circle C* ranch a few miles north of Cheyenne. They have a daughter my age named Jody."

Barry's eyebrows arched. *"Jody!* That's pretty close to your name."

She nodded. "But it's a sad situation. Jody fell off her horse and hit her head on a rock. She's been in a coma for a month. They have her at a clinic here in Cheyenne, and she isn't expected to live."

"Oh, that *is* sad."

"I would like for them to meet you. Would you come with me?"

"Sure."

All four Claibornes were watching as Josie led Barry to them.

Josie said, "Barry, these are my new foster parents, Sam and Emma Claiborne. And these nice people are Ed and Sarah Claiborne, my foster father's brother and sister-in-law. And everybody...this is Barry Chandler."

Each of the Claibornes greeted Barry, and Sam and Ed shook hands with him.

Barry said, "Josie just told me about your daughter, Jody. I'm so sorry."

They both nodded silently.

Josie touched the boy's arm and said to the adults, "Barry has been very good to me on the trip. He's been a real friend. And he's a Christian! He was saved at the Children's Aid Society shortly before we left."

"That's great, Barry," said Sam. "We're happy to know that you're saved."

"We certainly are," put in Emma. "And thank you for your kindness to Josie."

Barry smiled. "She's a sweet girl, ma'am. I'm going to miss her."

Josie set her eyes on him. "Barry, has anyone shown interest in you?"

"Well, one couple seemed interested, but they chose Jason Laird instead. He's twelve. I guess they wanted a younger boy."

"Oh. I'm sorry."

"It's all right. There are five more stops, yet. Certainly someone will take me."

"I'll be praying that will happen, Barry. Well, I mustn't keep Mr. and Mrs. Claiborne waiting."

Barry nodded. "Sure. Ah...Josie..."

"Mm-hmm?"

"Could—could I hug you before you go?"

Tears misted Josie's eyes. "Of course."

When he folded her in his arms, she hugged him back.

Sam said, "I want to thank you too, Barry, for being a friend to Josie."

Barry released Josie. "My pleasure, sir."

Josie laid a hand on Barry's arm. "I know you have no idea where you will be living, Barry, but if you ever get back this way, will you look me up? It's the *Circle C* ranch a few miles north of here."

"I sure will."

"And if it wouldn't be too much trouble, would you write to me when you're chosen, and let me know where you are?"

"Be glad to."

Sam stepped closer. "Just write her in care of Sam Claiborne, *Circle C* ranch, Cheyenne, Wyoming. C-L-A-I-B-O-R-N-E. We pick up the mail at the post office here in town two or three times a week."

"Thank you, Mr. Claiborne. I'll do that." Then to Josie he said, "Bye for now." A hot lump formed quickly in his throat. Swallowing hard, he turned and walked slowly back toward the line.

"Nice boy," said Sam. "Well, let's go."

Josie walked between her new foster parents as they headed for the terminal with Ed and Sarah beside them. Just before they passed through the terminal doors, Josie looked back to see the orphans climbing aboard their coaches. Barry was just about to board the boys' coach. He paused and looked back.

Josie waved and Barry waved in return.

Ed and Sarah's luggage was waiting in a rack outside the terminal. Sam went to the parking lot and drove the buggy up to the rack. He and Ed loaded the luggage in the back of the buggy, then helped the women climb aboard. The women sat on the rear seat with Josie between them.

As Ed and Sam were settling on the front seat, Ed asked, "Are we going to go see Jody now?"

"We'll go on out to the ranch first so we can get Josie settled in her room and you and Sarah settled in the guest room. We'll have lunch, then we'll come back to town this afternoon so you can see Jody."

Sam snapped the reins, putting the horse into motion, and drove onto the street, heading north.

Emma turned to Josie. "Do you want to go in and see Jody when we look in on her at the clinic?"

Josie met her gaze. "Why, ah…yes. I would like to see her."

"All right. Even though she's very thin now, you will see how much you two look alike."

"Yes, ma'am."

"Josie…"

"Yes, ma'am?"

"Will you mind occupying Jody's room at home and calling it your own?"

"I won't mind at all."

"It has two beds because Jody often had her best friend, Betty Houston, stay all night with her."

Josie thought on it for a few seconds. "It would probably be easiest on everybody if I use the bed Betty slept in."

Emma smiled. "I hadn't thought of that, honey. I appreciate your sweet attitude, and I understand how you feel."

When the train pulled out of Cheyenne, in both orphan coaches the sponsors announced that nine of the orphans had been chosen by foster parents, leaving forty-four to travel on. The sponsors spoke encouraging words as they pointed out that there were plenty of stops ahead where prospective foster parents would be choosing the rest of them.

In the boys' coach, Jimmy Kirkland listened to these words

come from the lips of Gifford Stanfield as he stood in the aisle at the front of the coach. He turned to Barry Chandler, who had chosen to sit beside him. "N-nobody'th gonna choothe m-me 'c-cauthe I talk f-funny."

Barry slipped an arm around him. "Don't you worry about it, little pal. There are some nice people up ahead who won't care how you talk. They'll just love you and take you into their home."

Jimmy bent his head down and mumbled, "I w-with it w-would b-be Mr. Adamth."

Barry leaned closer to him. "What did you say? I couldn't hear you clearly."

Jimmy looked up at him. "I'm g-gonna t-take a n-nap. I'm th-thleepy."

"Oh. Well, here. Stretch out and put your head on my lap."

Soon Jimmy was asleep. Barry put his head back and closed his eyes. He whispered, "Lord, I'm glad You gave Josie a Christian home. Please do that for me, too, will You? And Lord, please let me see her again. She's—well, she's really special."

In the girls' coach, Rachel Wolford sat alone on the seat that she and Josie had occupied together. Lord, thank You that Josie was chosen by a Christian couple. And please let that sweet girl have a full and happy life.

In his coach, Lance Adams gazed out the window at the vast Wyoming prairie as the train rolled westward. A small herd of antelope were running away from the sound of the engine, splashing across a wide stream. He thought of Jimmy Kirkland and the sad look he had on his face when the choosing of orphans was over in Cheyenne.

He sighed and whispered, "Heavenly Father, I'm looking to You for this miracle. You gave Abraham and Sarah a son when it seemed impossible. Is anything too hard for You? No. It is not. Help me to trust You as You work it out."

While the Claiborne buggy moved along the road on the undulating prairie, Josie's head swiveled back and forth on her neck as she happily absorbed all she could of her new surroundings.

Emma patted her hand. "Not quite like New York City, is it, dear?"

"No, ma'am. Not at all. Out here you can just about see forever."

"Just about. Given time, these wide open spaces will grow on you, and you'll love Wyoming just like we do."

"I have no doubt of that," Josie responded, her voice full of wonder. "I'm so used to living in a crowded apartment building on a noisy street, where all you can see when you look out the window is another apartment building just like the one you live in. I've never lived in a house, but I'm sure looking forward to it."

Soon the buggy topped a rise and Emma pointed ahead, off to the right side of the road. "There's the *Circle C* gate."

Josie's eyes were wide. "Oh my! That's really something!"

A moment later, Sam slowed the buggy, and as they drew up to the gate, Josie saw the sign on the crosspiece overhead denoting that it was indeed the *Circle C* ranch. She ran her gaze down the tree-lined lane that led toward the buildings, and focused on the two-story ranch house, the barn, the corral, and other outbuildings.

"Oh!" she said. "What a beautiful place!"

Sam looked over his shoulder as he guided the buggy down the lane. "You really think so?"

"I sure do! I know I'm going to be very happy here."

"Well, we're glad to have you, honey. We want you to be happy in your new home."

Josie took hold of Emma's hand. "Mrs. Claiborne, I'm so sorry about what happened to Jody."

Tears filmed Emma's eyes. She squeezed Josie's hand. "Thank you, sweetie." After swallowing with difficulty, she added, "Jody has always called us Daddy and Mommy. You can call us by those names."

Josie thought about it. She didn't want to infringe too much on the relationship Jody had with her parents. "May I suggest something?"

"Of course, dear."

"Maybe it would be easier on both of you if I called you Mama and Papa, instead. That's what I called my parents, but they're gone now. If I used the same names Jody has used for you all these years, it might be very difficult for you."

Sam turned in the seat and looked at Josie over his shoulder again. "Josie, you are such a sweet girl. Thank you for considering us like this. We'd be happy to have you call us Mama and Papa."

Emma leaned over and kissed Josie's cheek. "We sure would. We're honored to be your foster parents."

As Sam was straightening himself on the seat, Ed pointed straight ahead. "Sam, there's a rider just pulling away from the front of your house."

Sam focused on the rider. "I can't tell who it is."

All eyes were now fixed on the rider, who had spotted the buggy and was putting his horse to a gallop.

Emma raised up between Sam and Ed, squinting as she peered at the man on the galloping horse. "Can you tell who he is yet, honey?"

"No, I can't tell for sure, but I think it's—"

"Who?"

Sam waited a few seconds. His whole body jerked. "It's…it's T-Tommy Wentworth."

"Oh no!" cried Emma, throwing her hands to her mouth.

Ed frowned and looked at Sam. "Who's Tommy Wentworth?"

"He's a neighbor to Jody's doctor in town—Dr. John Traynor. Tommy's sixteen. He often runs errands for Dr. Traynor. I'm afraid he—he is trying to find us to tell us—"

Sarah put an arm around Emma.

Josie tensed up. *Dear God, help me. I want to be a strength to my new foster parents in the grief that is about to come on them.*

Sam pulled the buggy to a halt with his heart in his throat as Tommy brought his horse to a stop. His eyes were shining and there was a wide smile on his face. "Dr. Traynor sent me to tell you that Jody is awake! He says she is going to be all right!"

Everyone in the buggy sat in stunned silence.

Tommy ran his gaze from one face to the other, waiting for some reaction. He raised his voice a notch. "Did you hear what I said?"

Emma sat in Sarah's grasp, unable to move or speak.

In the driver's seat, Sam blinked his eyes and shook his head as though coming out of a coma himself. His voice was weak as he said, "D-did I hear you right, Tommy? Jody…has come out of the coma?"

"Yes, sir! She's awake and has been talking to Dr. Traynor and one of the nurses. Dr. Traynor sent me out here to tell you the good news! You must've been in town but didn't stop at the clinic."

"Uh…well, we…uh…picked up my brother and sister-in-law at the depot," Sam said. "We were planning to go back into town after lunch to check on Jody."

Tommy's eyes went to Josie. "She must be Jody's cousin. They really look alike."

Josie tried to smile, but was in a state of shock herself.

Sam turned around on the seat to look at Emma. She stared back at him, tears cascading down her cheeks, and reached toward him.

He took hold of her hands. "Sweetheart, our baby is awake! Did you hear that? She's talking! Dr. Traynor says she is going to be all right!"

"I...I heard, honey. I'm just having a hard time believing it."

"Well, you can believe it, Mrs. Claiborne!" said Tommy. "Jody's awake! And Dr. Traynor said she's asking for her parents."

Emma raised her eyes skyward. "Oh, thank You, heavenly Father! Thank You!"

Suddenly, Sam, Ed, and Sarah erupted in praise to the Lord.

Emma let go of Sam's hands. "Turn the buggy around, honey! Hurry! Our little girl is waiting for us!"

"We're on our way!" Sam shouted in jubilation as he snapped the reins and guided the horse in a circle. Tommy trotted his gelding ahead of the wagon and put him to a gallop as Sam quickly put his own horse to his fastest pace.

All four Claibornes were celebrating the good news as the dust flew up in roiling clouds behind the buggy. No one noticed how subdued and quiet Josie had become. Her mind was in a virtual turmoil. She was glad to know that Jody had come out of the coma, and would live...but now, what would happen to her? The Claibornes had their daughter back. They wouldn't need a foster daughter.

When the Claiborne buggy pulled up in front of the clinic, Tommy dashed to the door and held it open while Sam, Emma, Ed, Sarah, and Josie filed inside.

They were surprised to find Dr. John Traynor in conversation in the waiting area with Pastor Forbes, Clara, Mike, Natalie, and Betty.

Instantly Clara, Natalie, and Betty rushed to Emma, and Mike went to Sam. Having met Ed and Sarah when they were in Cheyenne before, the Forbeses and the Houstons greeted them and spoke their delight over the good news about Jody. Josie remained in the background beside Tommy Wentworth, silently looking on.

When the rejoicing subsided, Sam said, "Dr. Traynor, Ed and Sarah came here from their home in Omaha so they could be with us in our sorrow when Jody died."

Traynor smiled. "How much better to be with you in your joy!"

"Oh yes! And what joy we have!"

"God does indeed answer prayer."

"Amen!" said Sam.

Dr. Traynor ran his gaze between Sam and Emma. "Joyce is with Jody at the moment. I want to tell you about her recovery."

"Oh, her recovery is beyond wonderful!" exclaimed Emma. "Can I see her now, Doctor? I've been waiting for this day for what seems like forever!" Even as she spoke, she started for the door at the rear of the room.

Sam reached out and seized her arm. "Wait a minute, sweetheart. Let's hear what Dr. Traynor wants to tell us. We don't want to do anything that might jeopardize her full recovery."

Emma turned back to the doctor.

Traynor smiled. "Let's sit down over here. I've already told the Forbeses and the Houstons this story, but I imagine they'd like to hear it again."

Tommy quietly backed away and slipped out the door.

As the adults headed for the chairs, Betty Houston spotted Josie Holden for the first time. Puzzlement etched itself on her face. "Who's this?"

Emma wheeled around. "Oh! Josie, come over here and sit beside me, honey."

Pastor Forbes looked at Josie as she was heading toward Emma, then set his eyes on Ed and Sarah. "Well, I didn't know you two had a daughter! Doesn't she look like her cousin Jody?"

Sam said, "This little lady isn't Jody's cousin, Pastor. She does resemble her remarkably, but her name is Josie Holden. She's from New York. When we went to the depot to pick up Ed and Sarah this morning, we found that it was also an orphan train. We'll give all of you more details later, but suffice it to say that Emma and I both felt the Lord leading us to choose Josie from among the orphans and to become her foster parents. We signed the papers right then and there."

Forbes said, "Well, isn't that something? Welcome to Cheyenne, Josie."

Josie forced a smile. "Thank you, sir."

Sam then explained that just last night, the nurse who traveled with the orphans had led Josie to the Lord. This brought joyful comments from the Forbeses, the Houstons, and the doctor.

Dr. Traynor thought to himself that this sudden turn of events might put a different light on the Claibornes taking Josie Holden into their home.

Sam quickly introduced everyone to Josie, adding to the Houstons that they had told Josie about Betty being Jody's best friend.

Betty gave her a pleasant look. "I'm glad you're here, Josie."

Josie made another smile. "Thank you."

Sam said, "Now, Doctor, tell us about Jody's coming out of the coma."

Dr. Traynor told them about Jody's heart stopping almost two hours ago, and that he thought they had lost her. He explained that he began massaging her heart while Joyce Adams was at his side, and suddenly Jody opened her eyes, gasping for breath. He listened to the heart with his stethoscope and it was beating normally again. Within about twenty minutes, Jody was focusing on him and his nurse, and asked why she was at the clinic. He explained about her fall from the horse that had taken place a month ago and that she had been in a coma until now. Jody then asked to see her parents. It was then that he sent for Tommy. He told the boy that Jody had come out of the coma, and asked him to ride out to the *Circle C* and tell her parents the good news.

Sam and Emma wept for joy while praising God that He gave Dr. Traynor the wisdom he needed. They thanked Him for the way He had answered all the prayers that had been offered by so many people on Jody's behalf.

While this praise was in process, Emma glanced at Josie two or three times, and noticed the strained look on her face. However, it didn't register in Emma's whirling mind what might be causing the look.

Sam said, "Doctor, Tommy told us you said that Jody is going to be all right. She struck her head plenty hard on that rock. Could there be brain damage?"

"That certainly would have been a possibility, but there doesn't appear to be any brain damage at all. Her mind is sharp and clear. She can think rationally, her speech is quite normal, and she can focus her eyes perfectly. Once she came out of the coma, it was like she had only taken a nap."

"Praise God!" said Emma. "Only He could have done this!"

The adults and Betty spoke their agreement. Josie smiled, but remained silent.

The doctor said, "Sam, Emma, when you take her home, Jody will require a lot of care to help her regain her strength and to gain back the weight she has lost. But before I release her, I would like to keep her here at the clinic another twenty-four hours for observation."

Emma nodded. "I understand that, Doctor. We want you to make certain she's ready to go home before we take her there. I assure you, though, that when we do take her home, she will get all the care she needs. Ah…can we see her now?"

"Just you and Sam. It is best right now that only the two of you go in."

Dan Forbes set his eyes on Sam and Emma. "I know you're eager to get in there and see Jody, but could we have prayer first?"

"Of course," said Sam.

The pastor offered praise to the Lord for sparing Jody's life. He also asked that the Lord would bless Sam and Emma for taking Josie into their home, and that Jody and Josie would each be a blessing to the other.

When the prayer was finished, Dr. Traynor said to Sam and Emma, "It's best at this point that you stay no more than ten minutes. She's very weak, and we don't want to tire her. Joyce will come out so you can have some privacy for your reunion."

"Thank you, Doctor," said Sam, and with an arm around Emma, guided her through the door at the rear of the office.

As the adults chatted about Jody's recovery, Betty went to Josie and said, "I'm so glad you're here. You'll really love Jody, and I'm sure she'll love you. I'm her best friend, but I envy you."

Josie looked a bit surprised. "You do?"

Betty smiled. "Uh-huh. You get to be her sister."

Josie's features flushed. "Oh. Maybe she'll wish *you* could be her sister."

Betty touched Josie's hand. "I'm sure Jody will be happy with things just as they are."

Josie did not voice it, but she seriously wondered if that would be so.

As Sam and Emma made their way down the hall toward Jody's room, Sam said, "Sweetheart, should we tell Jody about Josie?"

Emma thought on it briefly. "I don't think we should, honey. It might very well be too much for her right now. In fact, I don't think we should tell her about Ed and Sarah being here. Let's just have our reunion with her. We'll leave them at home with Josie when we come to get Jody tomorrow. We can tell her about Josie on the way home, and that her aunt and uncle are here to visit too."

"I agree. Let's do it that way."

When the anxious parents stepped through the door, they saw Joyce Adams standing at the bed, looking down at Jody, whose eyes were closed.

Joyce smiled and tiptoed toward them. "She's resting, but she's awake. I'll leave you with her."

With that, Joyce stepped into the hall and quietly closed the door.

Holding hands, the parents moved up slowly toward the bed. Jody's eyes were still closed.

Never in her life had Emma ever experienced such a moment as this. The loving Father had given back to them their precious daughter who had been all but lost to them. With a prayer of gratitude in her heart and tears in her eyes, she clung to Sam's hand as they drew up to the side of the bed.

Emma's eyes never left Jody's face as Sam leaned close to his daughter and said softly, "Jody, darlin'. Mommy and Daddy are here."

Jody's eyelids fluttered briefly, then she opened her eyes and looked up at the faces of her parents. They saw that her eyes were clear and focused as a weak but brilliant smile crossed her features. Her voice was barely more than a whisper as she raised her shaky arms toward them. "Mommy...Daddy..."

Sam took a step back to allow Emma to bend down and embrace Jody, then hurried around to the other side of the bed where he would have room to do so. Both of them bent down and kissed a sallow cheek, then took their daughter into their arms, which only yesterday had been so empty.

All three wept and clung to each other for better than a minute, then as the parents stood up, Jody said, "I...I was so surprised when I woke up and Dr. Traynor told me I had been in a coma for a month. He told me about my fall from Queenie, but I don't remember it. I remember riding toward Eagle Rock with Betty, but that's where it stops."

Sam patted her hand. "It'll come back to you, sweetie. It'll just take time."

"That's what Dr. Traynor said."

Emma wiped fresh tears that were spilling down her face. "The Lord has been so good, Jody. We thought we had lost you."

Another weak smile graced Jody's face. "Jesus wanted me to stay here with you. Is—is Queenie all right?"

"She's fine, honey," said Sam. "No injuries at all from the fall."

"Is Betty all right? Dr. Traynor told me that she had been here many times to check on me."

"She's fine," replied Emma. "She and her parents are out in the waiting room right now. So are Pastor and Mrs. Forbes. Dr. Traynor won't let them come in and see you because he thinks it would be too much for you right now."

Jody nodded slowly.

Sam smiled and leaned down close. "Honey, Dr. Traynor is going to keep you here till tomorrow. He wants to make sure everything is all right before he lets us take you home. When you get home and settled down, everybody who wants to can come and see you."

Jody smiled weakly again. "I want to see all of them too. But most of all I want to be with my mommy and daddy."

Sam and Emma both choked up and wiped tears away from their faces. They talked to Jody for a few more minutes, then Sam looked at the clock on the wall. "Jody, darlin', Dr. Traynor said we should only stay in here for ten minutes. Time's up."

The parents both kissed their daughter one more time. Saying they would see her tomorrow, they went to the door. Sam opened it, and they paused to look at God's miracle one more time.

Jody smiled and gave a faint wave. "I love you."

Both parents choked up again, squeaked out their "I love you's", and headed up the hall.

Chapter Nineteen

When Sam and Emma Claiborne entered the office, their faces were beaming. Everyone gathered around, their eyes focused on the parents. Josie stood slightly aloof.

"What do you think?" asked Dr. Traynor.

"God has truly done a miracle," Sam replied in a steady voice. "He has brought our little girl back from the very edge of death. Other than the loss of weight and the obvious weariness she is experiencing, she's as normal as can be."

Emma's eyes were dancing with joy. "Oh, praise God! Praise His precious name!"

Sam grasped Traynor's hand. "Thank you, Doctor, for the excellent care you gave Jody. God used you to save her life."

"Oh yes!" said Emma. "Dr. Traynor, if you hadn't massaged her heart when it stopped, she certainly would have died. Thank you."

Traynor let a smile curve his lips. "It's times like this when my line of work is really worth it."

Sam turned to his pastor and shook his hand. "And thank *you*, Pastor, for never giving up. You had more faith than Emma and I did that Jody was going to live."

"Yes!" Emma said. "You sure did. Thank you for not giving

up." Then she looked around at Clara, Ed and Sarah, and the Houstons. "And thank each of you for praying for Jody."

There was a smile on each face.

Sam drew a deep breath. "Well, we'd better get on out to the ranch so Josie can get settled in the room that she and Jody will share, and Ed and Sarah can unpack their luggage in the guest room." Then to the doctor he said, "Emma and I will be back this evening to look in on Jody again. What time shall we plan on being here tomorrow to pick her up?"

"Let's make it exactly twenty-four hours from now. Two o'clock."

"All right. Two o'clock it is."

Josie was still slightly in the background.

To the others, Traynor said, "When you go to the *Circle C* to visit Jody, try not to stay too long the first time or two. She'll tire out easily."

Moments later, with Sam and Ed on the driver's seat and the women in the rear seat, the buggy headed northward out of town. There was indescribable joy in the hearts of Jody's parents and her aunt and uncle. Josie sat between Emma and Sarah, a smile on her face, but a measure of fear in her heart.

Ed turned about on the seat. "Sarah and I will stay a week or so if it's all right."

Sam chuckled. "You can stay a year or so, if you want to!"

"Or even longer!" Emma said with a lilt in her voice.

Ed matched his brother's chuckle. "We wouldn't want to wear out our welcome."

Emma laughed. "You could *never* do that!"

Josie tried to show that she was also happy over Jody's recovery, and joined them in their laughter, but in her heart lay the fear that she might possibly have already worn out her welcome. She pictured herself boarding the next orphan train heading west and trying once again to find someone who would take her in.

Soon the buggy was moving down the lane on the Claiborne ranch, and when they drove up to the front of the house, Josie's fear grew stronger. *What a lovely place.* The white ranch house was trimmed in dark green and nestled in row after row of jewel-toned flowers on three sides. The front porch was wide and wrapped around three sides. A porch swing and several chairs seemed to be just waiting for occupation. Sheer lace curtains rustled in the breeze from the windows both upstairs and downstairs.

Josie bit her lips. *This is so different than where I lived before, but I could have been so happy here.* She followed the adults up on to the porch and paused to take in the rolling prairie all around her, then lifted her eyes to the seemingly endless blue sky.

Emma took hold of Josie's arm. "Come on, honey. Let's go inside."

Josie obediently followed as she went inside and they walked up the stairs together. Emma was chatting happily about Jody's remarkable recovery all the way.

Sam helped Ed carry the luggage upstairs while Sarah followed them to the guest room where they had stayed before. Leaving them to unpack and get settled, Sam hurried down the hall to join Emma and Josie in Jody's room.

Josie had stopped at the door while Emma had proceeded into the room, still chatting. From where Josie stood, she observed the pretty room. Everything from wallpaper to the bedspreads was done in various shades of pink with white trimming. A colorful rag rug covered much of the floor space, and sheer pink-and-white lace curtains framed the two large windows.

While Emma was pointing to the spare bed, saying it was

now Josie's, she turned to find her standing just inside the doorway, her face a picture of dejection. Josie's eyes were misty.

Emma had no idea what could be wrong on such a glorious day. She hurried to Josie and took her hands in her own. "What is it, dear? You seem upset."

At that moment, Sam drew up and stepped through the doorway. He noted the concerned look on Emma's features, then turned and saw Josie's sad countenance. "Hey, gals, what's wrong?"

"I was just asking Josie that question," said Emma. "Something's troubling her."

"Josie, what is it?"

Josie's lips trembled, and the mist in her eyes grew thicker. She was fighting to keep tears from forming. "Mr. and Mrs. Claiborne, I'm so glad that Jody has come out of the coma and is going to be all right. I—I—well, now that Jody is coming home, you probably won't want me." While the Claibornes were exchanging perplexed glances, Josie went on. "I—I want you to know that I understand. You thought your daughter was going to die. If I could just stay here till the next orphan train comes through—"

"Oh no, sweet Josie!" Emma said. "It isn't like that at all. Papa and I know the Lord put it in our hearts to take you into our home, and when He did it, He already knew that He was going to spare Jody's life. We want you to stay."

"Yes, we do, sweetie," said Sam. "The thought of sending you away when we received the incredible news about Jody never entered our minds."

Emma squeezed Josie's hands. "Papa and I know you are a gift from God. He put a love in our hearts the moment we laid eyes on you at the depot. You are a part of this family now. This is your home until you marry someday and have a home of your own."

At these words, Josie lost the battle with the mist in her eyes.

Tears began streaming down her cheeks. "Really? You actually still want me even though Jody is going to be all right?"

Sam laid a hand on her shoulder. "Of course we do, sweetie. God gave us two very special blessings today, and we're not giving either one of them back. You can rest assured of that."

A grin split Josie's pretty face from ear to ear, then disappeared as fast as it had come.

Emma frowned. "What is it, Josie? What's troubling you now?"

"Did you tell Jody about me?"

"No, we didn't. Since we had such a short time with her, we didn't think we should. We didn't even tell her about her aunt and uncle being here. We plan on telling her tomorrow on the way home, then you girls can meet as soon as we arrive home."

Josie wiped tears from her cheek and drew a shuddering breath.

Sam frowned. "What is it, Josie?"

"Wh-what if Jody doesn't want me invading her home? She has been an only child all of her life. Maybe she won't want to share her parents with someone else."

While Sam was trying to find the proper words to put Josie's fears to rest, Emma said, "You're right, honey. Jody has been an only child for all of her twelve years, but let me tell you something. When she was no more than five years old, she began saying that she wanted a sister. By the time she was seven, she always asked God to give her a sister. You are the answer to those prayers, and I know she will love you as we do. You'll have to take my word for it now, but you'll see it for yourself tomorrow."

Josie threw her arms around Emma. "Oh, Mama, I'm so happy!" She squeezed hard, kissed Emma's cheek, then let go and opened her arms to Sam, who folded her to his chest.

She rose up on her tiptoes, and he bent down so she could

kiss his cheek. "Thank you, Papa!"

Sam chuckled around the lump in his throat. "That's better! No more of this Mr. and Mrs. Claiborne stuff. From now on, it's Mama and Papa, understand?"

She nodded, smiling through her tears. "I understand, Papa!"

Emma moved close, and the three of them used their arms to make a circle of love. Josie said joyfully, "This has been one of the happiest days of my life!"

"Mine too! It's been a long, emotional day for all of us," Emma said. "Let's get your bag unpacked and put your things away. I'll free up a drawer for you in the dresser."

Sam said to Emma, "I'll go see if Ed and Sarah are settled in."

While Josie was opening the small canvas bag, Emma moved some of Jody's things from one drawer to another. "There you go, sweetie. There should be plenty of room for you."

Josie put her personal items in the drawer, then slid it closed. "Thank you, Mama."

Emma hugged her again and held her at arm's length. "Tell you what. I'll head for the kitchen, but you stay here and acquaint yourself with the room for a while. There's a washroom a little further down the hall. Wash up and come on down whenever you want. You can help me with supper. Is that okay with you?"

"It's more than okay, Mama. It's absolutely perfect!"

It was just past 11:00 P.M. when the orphan train chugged into the Rawlins, Wyoming, railroad station. Most of the children were fast asleep, and only a few stirred when the train ground to a halt.

While a few people alighted from the coaches ahead of those that carried the orphans, Gifford and Laura Stanfield stood on the rear platform of the girls' coach, making plans for the lineup that would take place in the depot at nine o'clock the next morning.

Inside the girls' coach, Rachel Wolford moved up the aisle toward the front, making sure every girl was comfortable. When she reached the front of the coach, she sat down on the seat beside Tabitha Conlan and sighed.

By the dim light from the few low-burning lanterns, Tabitha looked at Rachel and said, "Tired?"

"A little bit."

Tabitha frowned. "Something's bothering you. It's more than just being tired. Want to talk about it?"

Rachel sighed again, but before she could speak, Tabitha said, "I know. It's Josie Holden, isn't it?"

Rachel nodded. "Mm-hmm. I try not to let myself get attached to the children on these trips, and for the most part I do all right. But it seems like on every trip west, there's at least one that manages to crawl down into my heart. On this trip, it was Josie. My attachment to her started out special because of the way the Lord brought us together at the cemetery. Here was that little twelve-year-old girl weeping over her father's grave. And I just… well, I just—"

Tears spilled from Rachel's eyes.

Tabitha took hold of her hand. "You just have such a tender heart, Rachel. You couldn't let that little girl weep without trying to comfort her."

Rachel brushed the tears from her cheeks. "My relationship with Josie started out in a heart-wrenching moment, but what made it so very, very special was that I had the joy of leading her to Jesus. Oh, what a blessing!"

Tabitha smiled. "Can't top that with anything, honey. I know Josie will always be in your heart as the years go by, and you'll wonder how she's doing and who she marries and how many children she has, and whether they are boys or girls. But one day you will meet her in heaven, and you'll have all eternity to be together. And think of that golden moment when you first see each other up there! Oh-h-h! It gives me goose bumps!"

Rachel rubbed her arms. "Me too. Thank God that for His born-again children, there is such a great future!"

Lance Adams sat in his seat, legs stretched out in front of him, and his head on a small pillow.

His thoughts were on Carol, and he anticipated the moment he would step off the train in San Francisco and fold her into his arms. Every time he made a trip like this, he missed her worse.

For a moment he envisioned what it would be like if after he had kissed her upon alighting from the coach, then said, "Honey, I have a little boy I want you to meet."

A shiver slid down his back. "Oh, dear Lord, what a wonderful thing it would be if You had spoken to Carol's heart, and she had already planned to talk to me about the adoption matter I had introduced back in March." He sighed. "Well, Lord, that's my imagination working overtime again. However You choose to do it, *if* I've been praying within the confines of Your will, You will do it just right."

In the boys' coach, Gifford Stanfield and Derek Conlan finished their final walk up the aisle for the night and sat down on the front seats, opposite each other. Both of them glanced back to see if any of the boys were stirring, and seeing that all was still, they settled back on their seats to get some sleep.

Barry Chandler was still awake with little Jimmy Kirkland

asleep on the seat beside him. Barry was stretched out with his head on a pillow and his eyes closed. His mind was on Josie Holden, and his heart was heavy. His lips barely moved and his words were a slight whisper. "Even when I write to Josie after I am settled in my own foster home, it won't mean that we'll ever be together again. I…I'll never see her again in this world. In heaven, yes…but not here on earth. I could end up somewhere in Nevada or California; a long way from Cheyenne, Wyoming."

Barry found himself wishing that he and Josie could finish growing up together, and one day she could become his wife.

Jimmy moved on the seat, rolled onto his side, and went still again.

Barry looked down at him in the vague light. His heart was heavy for the little boy. He had been passed up again today because of his stuttering and his lisp. He laid a hand gently on Jimmy's foot. "Lord Jesus, please let Jimmy be taken into a good Christian home where he will be loved and wanted in spite of his speech problem. And…and Lord, I need Your guidance in my own life. Please let me be taken into a good Christian home where I can be happy, and where I can be a blessing to my foster parents."

At nine o'clock the next morning, the orphans were lined up on the platform beside the train. A large group of interested people stood as the other sponsors waited close by with clipboards in hand. Gifford Stanfield faced them and said, "Ladies and gentlemen, we're glad you want to interview these children in view of taking some of them into your homes as their foster parents. One of us four has already talked to you to make sure you can qualify as foster parents according to the Children's Aid Society rules."

He pointed to Laura. "So that all of you will know, this lady is my wife, and this is Mr. and Mrs. Derek and Tabitha Conlan. We are here to answer any questions for you, and if and when you decide you want to become foster parents to a certain child, or even more than one, you can talk to any of us, even if we weren't the sponsor who first interviewed you. Are there any questions at this point?"

Silence.

"All right. Line up and talk to the children as much as you want."

Hardly had the prospective foster parents started down the line when a couple in their late thirties stepped up to Barry Chandler.

"Hello, young man," said the husband. "My name is Charles Tracy, and this is my wife, Evelyn. I see you have number nine pinned to your shirt, but what is your name?"

"Barry Chandler, sir. I'm fifteen years old. I'll be sixteen in November."

The lady smiled. "You already know the obvious questions, don't you, Barry?"

"Yes, ma'am. And I'll answer the next question for you. I'm from Queens, New York, and I am an actual orphan. My parents and my little brother are dead. One night this past April, when I was staying at a friend's house a few blocks away, our tenement caught on fire. Mom, Dad, and Billy were trapped on the fourth floor and burned to death, along with several other people."

"I'm so sorry," said Evelyn. "So this left you totally without family?"

"Yes, ma'am. There is no one else to take me in."

Charles set admiring eyes on the boy. "Barry, Evelyn and I own a large cattle ranch a few miles south of Rawlins. We're interested in being foster parents to a young man about your age who would like to come live with us. We have six ranch hands, but the young man we choose will be asked to do work on the ranch the same as if he was our natural son. Does this sound appealing to you?"

A smile broke over Barry's young features. "Yes, sir! I'm not afraid of hard work, Mr. Tracy. I worked as assistant to the janitor at a department store in downtown Queens to help bring in more income for my parents. I did that for two years."

"Sounds good to me! What do you think, honey?"

Evelyn's eyes were bright. "Looks to me like this boy is the answer to our prayers."

Barry liked these people and thought that possibly they were the answer to his own prayers.

Charles said, "Barry, we want you to know up front that we are Christians. Would it bother you to be in a home where your foster parents have prayer and Bible study time every day, and are faithful in church and Sunday school?"

"Not at all, sir. When you say 'Christians,' do you mean that you have received the Lord Jesus into your hearts as your personal Saviour?"

Charles grinned at Evelyn. "That's exactly what we mean, son. Born again and washed in the blood of the Lamb. Sounds to me like you are too."

"I sure am, Mr. Tracy. I received Jesus into my heart while staying at the Children's Aid Society, shortly before we started on this trip."

"Wonderful!" exclaimed Evelyn, and gave him a quick hug. "You most certainly are the answer to our prayers!"

"Mr. and Mrs. Tracy, I have been praying that the Lord would give me born-again foster parents. I would love to live and work on your ranch."

"Well, sweetheart," said Charles, "it's plain to see that the

Lord has worked this out perfectly."

"He most certainly has, honey," said Evelyn. "This is the boy He has chosen for us."

Charles looked around to see if any of the sponsors were unoccupied, and found that Gifford Stanfield was available. He motioned to him, and Stanfield hurried to him. "Yes, sir?"

"We want to take Barry home with us, Mr. Stanfield."

Gifford looked at Barry. "Are you willing to go with them and become their foster son?"

A broad grin etched itself on Barry's face. "Yes, sir! I sure am!"

While Stanfield was asking the Tracys the necessary questions for finalizing the transaction, Rachel Wolford was looking on. She had been there long enough to overhear the entire conversation between Barry and the Tracys. She was glad they were going to take him.

When Charles and Evelyn had signed the official papers, and they were ready to go, Rachel stepped up to Barry. "I was standing close over here and sort of eavesdropped on all that was being said. I'm so happy for you. I know you'll have a wonderful life with these dear Christian people."

Barry's face was beaming. "Thank you, Miss Wolford."

"Yes, thank you," said Charles. "I see by your white uniform that you are a nurse. Are you part of the Children's Aid Society team on this train?"

"I sure am, sir. I've gotten attached to this boy. He's a wonderful young man."

"We'll give him a good home," said Evelyn.

"I have no doubt of that."

With that, Rachel embraced Barry, kissed his cheek, and walked away.

Charles looked at Barry, who was watching the nurse walk away. "Well, son, ready to go?"

"Uh…sir, could I have a minute to say good-bye to a little boy over here?"

"Of course."

The Tracys followed as Barry moved down the line to a small, blond little lad, who was being interviewed by a young couple. Barry stopped short, and the Tracys stayed at his side. "Someone's talking to him right now," whispered Barry.

"We'll wait," Charles said.

Jimmy Kirkland was answering the couple in response to a question one of them had asked. Barry and the Tracys could hear the stuttering lisp. When Jimmy finished his answer and ran a sleeve over his mouth to wipe away the saliva, the man and woman looked at each other and frowned. As they walked away, they heard the woman use the word *retarded*.

Lance Adams was also observing the scene.

Barry hurried to Jimmy, who had a look of hopelessness on his face.

The child's features brightened some when he saw Barry, who bent down to put his face level with Jimmy's.

"Don't you worry, little guy. God has somebody very special somewhere along the line for you. As I said before, the ones He has chosen for you will love you and want you, no matter what."

"You r-really th-think tho?"

"I *know* so. Now, little pal, I have to leave. A family has chosen me, and we have to head home."

Jimmy's features fell. "Y-you mean you w-won't be on the t-train anymore?"

"That's right. They live on a ranch, and I'm going home with them right now. I wanted to tell you good-bye before we go."

Jimmy lunged for Barry and wrapped his arms around his neck.

Barry talked to him for a few seconds, encouraging him once

more that it was going to work out real good for him. Jimmy squeezed Barry's neck hard, then let go and looked at him through his tears. "G-good-bye, B-Barry."

Barry hugged his little friend, told him good-bye, and walked away quickly with his new foster parents flanking him. Jimmy was crying as he watched Barry go.

Lance Adams was about to go to Jimmy when another couple drew up to him. The woman leaned over, put an arm around him, and asked, "Why are you crying, little fellow?"

Jimmy wiped tears from his eyes and focused on her. He pointed to Barry, who was still in sight. "Th-that boy ith my friend. H-he wath jutht 'dopted b-by thome n-nithe people. I gonna m-mith him."

As Jimmy sleeved saliva from the corners of his mouth, the woman looked at her husband, whose face was showing the same aversion she was feeling. He shook his head.

The woman said, "Sorry, little boy. We were actually wanting a girl."

They walked away quickly.

Lance rushed to him and picked him up in his arms. Jimmy clung to him, sniffling. "Th-they d-don't want m-me either, 'cauthe I talk f-funny."

Lance spoke in a soft, level voice. "Jimmy, it's going to be all right. There are still four more stops. Someone will take you."

"I h-hope tho. I d-don't wanna go b-back to th-the orphan-age. B-boyth and girlth pick on m-me there."

"You won't have to go back there, Jimmy. It's going to be all right, believe me."

Jimmy looked him in the eye. "I kn-know it would b-be all right if I c-could g-go home w-with y-you."

"Jimmy, I told you that I can't take you home with me, and that if I tried to explain it to you, you wouldn't understand."

"I kn-know I talk f-funny, M-Mithter Adamth, b-but I alwayth t-try to b-be a g-good boy. If y-you t-took me home, I'd b-be good."

Lance was battling his own emotions again.

Jimmy was still in Lance's arms as the passengers began boarding the train, and Gifford Stanfield called for the orphans to move back into their coaches. He announced that twelve children were taken by foster parents in Rawlins, leaving thirty-two on the train.

Lance carried Jimmy to the boys' coach, mounted the steps of the small platform, and carried him inside. "Do you have a seat that you always sit in, Jimmy?"

"Yeth," said the boy, pointing to the seat he had occupied up till now with Barry Chandler.

Lance placed him on the seat and patted his head. "I'll see you at the next stop."

Jimmy nodded. "Okay."

As Lance left the coach and headed for his own, he said, "Is there anything too hard for You, Lord? Absolutely not. I'm still trusting You to perform Your mighty miracle."

Chapter Twenty

When Barry Chandler opened his eyes on Thursday morning, June 25, a flood of golden sunlight streamed through the open window of his room. His first thought was one of wondering where he was.

Then, in a flash, it came to him. He was in his new home on the *Box T* ranch ten miles south of Rawlins, Wyoming. A warm feeling washed over him as he pictured the faces of Charles and Evelyn Tracy, who had chosen him to be their foster son.

His mind went to Josie Holden, and his heart yearned for her. Pop Tracy had told him the ranch was a hundred and fifty miles from Cheyenne. He had promised to write Josie and let her know where he was living once he had been chosen as a foster child. He would do that soon.

He rolled out of the bed and went to the window, which was on the east side of the house. A warm, dry, fragrant breeze came through the window, carrying the sweet scent of sagebrush. A small creek wended its way through the low spots on the ranch, and ran close to the house. Barry heard the murmuring of the running water, the fluttering of leaves from the cottonwood trees in the yard, and the twittering of happy birds as they welcomed the new day.

Looking eastward across the rolling plains, Barry said aloud,

"A hundred and fifty miles, Josie. It's not like I was a thousand miles away in California. Someday—someday, you'll see a guy on a horse riding onto the *Circle C* ranch."

On that same June 25, it was late morning as Sam Claiborne and Hap Lakin carried the spare feather mattress from the Lakin house as Margie followed them to the *Circle C* wagon. Lorraine and Maisie walked beside their adoptive mother, happy to know that Jody Claiborne had survived the coma and was coming home today.

When the two men had placed the thick mattress in the wagon bed, Sam said, "Folks, I really appreciate your letting me borrow this mattress so Jody will have a comfortable ride home from the clinic."

"Our pleasure," said Hap. "Why should you have to take a mattress off one of your beds when this one was in our attic?"

Margie held her adopted daughters close to her and smiled at Sam.

"You tell Jody we'll be over to see her in a few days. And tell Josie we are looking forward to meeting her."

Sam grinned as he climbed onto the wagon seat. "I will convey those messages, Margie, and we'll look forward to having the Lakin family visit us."

It was just after lunch at the *Circle C* when Sam helped Emma onto the wagon seat, then climbed up beside her and took hold of the reins.

Emma glanced back at the mattress. "It sure was nice of the Lakins to loan the mattress to us, honey."

"Sure was," said Sam.

Ed, Sarah, and Josie stood beside the wagon.

Ed said, "Sam, I'll go to work on that broken gate on the west side of the corral."

"Just wait on that, Ed. You and I can work on it together later, after we have Jody home."

"Papa, I'll help Uncle Ed fix the gate," Josie said.

Sam grinned, thinking that his tomboy, Jody, would have offered to help Ed. But not wanting to make Josie feel unneeded, he said, "Okay, honey, you help Uncle Ed."

The trio stood together in the Wyoming sunlight and watched the wagon pull away, then Ed said, "Well, Miss Josie, let's go fix that gate."

"I'm ready!"

Sarah laughed. "You two have fun. In the meantime, I'll do some work around the house."

"I'll help you, Aunt Sarah," said Josie, "as soon as Uncle Ed and I get the gate fixed."

Sarah grinned and patted her new "niece" on the back. "You're an industrious little squirt. Maybe after you and Uncle Ed get the gate fixed, you should sit out here on the porch swing and rest a while."

"If I help you with the housework, then we'll both be able to sit out here on the porch swing and rest."

Sarah pinched her cheek. "We'll see. Go on now and help your uncle."

When Ed and Josie were heading around the corner of the house, Sarah went inside and paused to consider what she might do first. She knew that a great deal of Emma's time the last month had been taken up with the care of Jody at the clinic. She decided her first priority would be to set some bread dough rising, and while that was in process, she would make sure everything was ready in the girls' room.

A quarter-hour later, with the bread dough in a large bowl on the cupboard, Sarah went upstairs and entered the room Jody had occupied alone since she was very small. She set her eyes on Jody's bed and smiled at the image she got of Jody back in her home where she had been so sorely missed the past month. She decided the furniture in the room could use some polish and the floor could use a scrubbing.

For the next hour—while humming a nameless tune—Sarah polished the furniture to a glossy shine, then picked up the throw rugs and mopped the hardwood floor.

She went outside to tend to Emma's flower garden. After hoeing some weeds, she pumped water into a bucket from the well behind the house and watered all the flowers. While enjoying the beauty of the prairie around her, she picked a bouquet of bright-colored flowers for Jody's room. She put them in a vase, added some water, and carried the vase upstairs to Jody's room.

After positioning the flowers where she felt they would best be seen, she put the throw rugs back in place on the floor and looked the room over once more. Satisfied that the room was ready for the girls to occupy, she returned to the kitchen.

The yeasty scent of the bread greeted her. She formed several loaves, placed them in pans, covered them with a clean tea towel, and left them to rise.

Sarah took stock of what was in the pantry, and set about preparing a celebration dinner in honor of Jody's return home. Knowing that Jody's diet would of necessity have to be quite simple, she would cook up a kettle of chicken broth and a custard pudding. She remembered that custard pudding was Jody's favorite dessert.

For the rest of the family, she would make her special chicken and dumplings and chocolate cake. Humming her tune once again, she went to work.

Three hours had passed when Ed and Josie walked together toward the back porch of the house from the toolshed. When they stepped up on the porch, the sumptuous aromas coming through the kitchen windows met their nostrils.

Josie smacked her lips. "Mmm! Sure smells good, Uncle Ed."

"That it does, my little tomboy! That it does."

Sarah was at the stove when she turned to look at the pair, and noticed Ed shaking his head in wonderment and grinning. "Get the gate fixed?"

"Sure did," replied Ed.

Sarah frowned. "What is it, honey? What's got you looking like that?"

"Not *what,* sweetie…*who.*"

"Pardon me?"

"It's Josie. You talk about a tomboy! I mean a genuine, down-to-earth, lock-stock-and-barrel tomboy. This little gal is the real thing!"

Josie smiled.

Sarah was still frowning. "Ed, what do you mean?"

"Honey, this girl actually knew some things about repairing a gate that I didn't know. And she's good with a hammer and a screwdriver."

Surprised, Sarah looked at Josie. "How do you know about repairing gates?"

"Well, Aunt Sarah, as I explained to Uncle Ed out at the corral, my papa was not only a construction worker on bridges and such, but he also did odd jobs on the side, repairing just about anything that needed repairing around the neighborhood. I worked with him a lot, and believe me, yard gates need a lot of repairing in New York City. I learned by working with Papa."

Ed grinned and shook his head in wonderment again. "What do you think of that, honey?"

"I think it's marvelous. And Sam and Emma will too."

"While Josie and I were working on the corral gate out there, I jokingly called her a tomboy. She told me about herself. She told me all about how she played roughhouse games with the boys in her neighborhood—including wrestling matches—and informed me of a bunch of other tomboyish things that were part of her life."

Josie set her bright eyes on Sarah. "I know Jody and I are going to get along good, Aunt Sarah, because Uncle Ed told me what a tomboy she is!"

At that moment, they heard the pounding of hooves and the rattle of a wagon out front. They rushed through the house and out onto the front porch. Sam was pulling rein, with Emma sitting in the wagon bed beside Jody, who lay on the mattress.

Josie looked down at her soiled dress. *Oh, this is just a great way to meet my new sister! My hands are dirty and my face is sweaty.*

Trying desperately to put some order to her tousled hair, she took a deep breath, trying to calm her fluttering heart. *Oh, well, she'll see me at my worst...but it can only get better from there. Jody will understand, I'm sure, because she would've been working on the gate if she were here.*

Putting on her brightest smile, Josie stepped off the porch with Ed and Sarah, and approached the wagon.

Sam hopped to the ground, opened the tailgate, and helped Emma out. He reached into the wagon, picked Jody up, and cradled her in his arms. "Dr. Traynor says she's doing well."

"Praise the Lord!" Ed and Sarah said in unison.

Jody's smile was a bit weak, but it was there as she said, "Aunt Sarah! Uncle Ed!"

Both of them stepped up close. Sarah kissed Jody's cheek, and Ed did the same.

Josie could hardly believe how much she and Jody resembled each other, though Jody's face was obviously thinner than usual. Their hair was the same color and the same length, and their eyes were almost the same color.

Emma's face was beaming as she took Josie by the hand and led her up to the girl in Sam's arms. "Jody, here's your new sister!"

Josie felt tremendous relief when Jody smiled at her. "Josie, Mommy and Daddy told me all about you. And we sure do look alike! People who don't know us will think we're sisters for sure. I'm so glad the Lord sent you to live with us!" Even as she spoke, Jody extended her frail arms toward Josie.

Josie stepped up and hugged her. "Oh, Jody, I have always wanted a sister. And I'm so happy that I have one now!"

"Me too!" said Jody. "I've prayed for a sister for a long, long time."

Sam waited till Josie stepped back. "Well, let's get this sweet little girl in the house!"

Ed said, "There is something else Sarah and I learned about Josie today. She is a tomboy, just like Jody."

Jody set her tired eyes on him. "I want to hear about it, Uncle Ed."

Emma patted Jody's arm. "He can tell you after we get you on your bed, sweetheart."

When they entered the girls' room and Sam laid Jody on the bed, he said, "All right, Ed, let's hear about this tomboy named Josie."

Everybody gathered around the bed.

When Ed was finished telling how Josie helped him repair the corral gate—and even knew some things he didn't—and told them Josie's tomboy story, Jody lifted her arms to Josie.

"Oh, Josie, it's so wonderful to have you for my sister! We're going to be so happy together!"

Sam took hold of Jody's thin hand, and while holding Josie's hand too, said with a smile, "Isn't God good? Now I have *two* tomboys!"

A day and a half after the orphan train had stopped in Rawlins, Wyoming, it rolled into Austin, Nevada.

A relatively small group of prospective foster parents were waiting to interview the orphans and look them over. When they had passed inspection by the sponsors, the children were placed in line as usual, and the interviewing began.

True to form, Lance Adams stood close by Jimmy Kirkland.

As one young couple came upon Jimmy, the woman smiled and said, "Oh, Ben, look at this darling little boy!"

Ben smiled from ear to ear, bent over, and put his palms on his knees. "He's a handsome one, all right. What's your name, sonny?"

Jimmy was hesitant to speak, knowing from past experience that it would cause the man and woman to pass him by.

"Come on, honey," said the woman, "tell us your name."

Lance's heart went out to Jimmy as he said, "M-my n-name ith J-Jimmy Kirkland."

The brows of both people furrowed.

"And how old are you?" queried the man.

Jimmy held up five fingers. "F-five y-yearth old." He ran a sleeve across his mouth to wipe away the saliva.

The man stood erect and looked at his wife, shaking his head. She nodded, and they walked on.

Lance saw Jimmy's face twist up and redden. He stepped to him, wrapped his arms around him, and picked him up. Jimmy began to cry.

Patting his back as he held him, Lance said, "Don't cry, little pal. The Lord is going to give you a good home."

Jimmy started to say he wanted to go home with him, but was cut off as Gifford Stanfield's voice filled the air: "Okay, everybody, that's it! Let's get back on the train. We had three more children chosen by foster parents. That means there are twenty-nine left. But don't any of you worry now. We still have three stops!"

Lance carried the child into the boys' coach and put him on his usual seat. "There you are, Jimmy. Now, like Mr. Stanfield just said, don't you worry. There are three more stops."

Jimmy was staring at the floor.

"I'll see you at the next stop."

Jimmy nodded and looked up at him, his features pinched.

As Lance left the coach and headed for his own, he said, "Lord, I remember what Job said when he was perplexed and needed to know Your mind: 'Oh that I knew where I might find him! that I might come even to his seat!' He wanted to come to Your very throne, Lord, and talk to You face to face so he could get his questions answered. So, You know how it is with us humans. I'm wishing that I could talk to You face to face, so You could tell me if You are working on Carol's heart. Jimmy's still on the train. I know if You wanted it differently, he would have been chosen by someone. Please, Lord, help me not to waiver in this, but to trust You completely, even though I don't know what Your will is about Jimmy coming into our home."

When he was back in his seat, Lance took out his Bible and turned to the book of Job.

The next day at Reno, Nevada, the foster parents took home eight children, leaving twenty-one on the train. Lance Adams tried to comfort little Jimmy Kirkland, who had been spurned once again.

When the train crossed the California border, Lance was silently begging God to change Carol's mind about adopting a child, so if Jimmy was still on the train when it arrived in San Francisco, she would agree with him to take Jimmy into their home.

The train made its slow crawl over the towering Sierra Nevada Mountains and arrived in Sacramento on Friday evening, June 26.

The next morning, the twenty-one orphans lined up once again to be interviewed and inspected by prospective foster parents. Lance Adams was on the platform a few feet away from Jimmy Kirkland, as usual.

Every time the train had stopped and the children had been interviewed and inspected, Lance had watched the sweet little boy put his best foot forward. On that morning, there seemed to be a fresh supply of hope and anticipation in his eyes.

Lance watched as three couples paused to talk to Jimmy, and each couple passed on when they heard him stutter and lisp. By then the light of hope in Jimmy's eyes had vanished.

A fourth couple stepped up. They both bent down closer to Jimmy's eye level, and the man said, "Hello, there. My name is Howard Wells. What's yours?"

Fear was evident on Jimmy's face as he met the man's gaze. "J-Jimmy Kirkland."

"How old are you, Jimmy?"

The child held up five fingers once again, but refrained to give his verbal answer.

"Five? Is that how old you are, Jimmy?"

Jimmy nodded.

The woman smiled. "I'm Jeanne Wells. Are you nervous, honey?"

Jimmy nodded, his eyes avoiding contact with hers.

Jeanne cupped his chin in her hand and tilted his face

upward. "You don't need to be nervous with us, honey. We love children, and we want to take one home today to live at our house. Tell me what your favorite food is."

Lance felt sorry for the child as he finally had to speak more than his name.

Jimmy licked his lips. "I—I like j-jutht about any k-kind of f-food, ma'am."

Jeanne's brow furrowed. "Do you like soup?"

"Uh-huh."

She looked at her husband, then back at Jimmy. "Say it for me: 'I like soup.'"

"I—I l-like th-thoup."

Standing erect, Jeanne met her husband's hard gaze. "He's a precious boy, Howard. He can't help he has this impediment."

Howard pulled his lips tight. "Yeah, but—"

"Being Christians, we can be such a blessing to this child, Howard. Remember how we've prayed ever since we knew this orphan train was coming? And we prayed this morning before coming here that the Lord would guide us to the child He had chosen for us. I believe this is that child, honey. I want to take Jimmy home."

Jimmy's heart jumped in his chest at her words.

Lance kept his eyes on the couple as Howard shook his head vigorously. "Jeannie, do you realize the problems we're facing if we take him?"

"God can overcome problems, dear. I really believe this is the child we are to take home with us."

Howard looked down at the boy, then at his wife. "I really doubt that it's supposed to be him. I say let's go back and talk to Freddie."

While this discussion was going on, Lance saw that Jimmy's face showed the familiar fear that he was going to be rejected, that

Howard Wells was going to win out.

Lance whispered, "Lord, I want Your will to be done."

Suddenly the discussion was over, and Howard wheeled and moved back up the line to one of the older boys they had talked to earlier.

Jeanne bent down to Jimmy's level again. "I'm sorry, honey." With that, she turned and followed her husband to the older boy.

Jimmy began to whimper, and instantly Lance had him in his arms.

The boy wrapped his arms around Lance's neck and wept, with his tears moistening Lance's face. While holding Jimmy and speaking words to comfort and encourage him, Lance saw Howard and Jeanne Wells talking to Tabitha Conlan, who was making notes on her clipboard. It was evident that they were taking the older boy.

Jimmy was still in Lance's arms a few minutes later, when the Wellses walked away with the older boy, along with a number of other foster parents who were taking orphans with them.

Lance let his eyes run the line and he could tell that the choosing in Sacramento was over. *Lord, You could have let Mrs. Wells convince her husband to take Jimmy home with them if You wanted to. But You didn't. The next stop is home. Are You going to let Carol and me have him?*

Chapter Twenty-one

The four sponsors and Rachel Wolford gathered at the spot on the depot platform where the two orphan coaches connected.

Laura Stanfield's attention was on Lance Adams as he held little Jimmy Kirkland in his arms.

Gifford raised his voice and said, "All right, children, it's time to get back aboard the train. Things went well, as you can see. Fourteen orphans were taken into foster homes. We now have seven of you left: four boys and three girls. I have no doubt that all of you will find homes in San Francisco. Let's get aboard."

Laura was still watching Lance and Jimmy as Lance carried him toward the boys' coach.

Holding the boy close, Lance said, "Jimmy, I'm sure someone in San Francisco will take you, even as Mr. Stanfield just said."

Jimmy looked at Lance through a film of tears. "Y-you live in Than F-Franthithco, Mithter Adamth. Pleathe. Won't y-you t-take me? I want t-to g-go to y-your houthe and l-live with you."

Once again, Lance relived that day in March when he suggested the idea to Carol that they adopt a child, and the way she looked at him and spoke in return. There was no way he could know at this time if God had done a miracle in Carol's heart and changed her attitude about it. "Jimmy, I really wish I could take you home, but I can't."

"B-but nobody h-hath taken me in the other t-townth. Nobody will t-take me in Th-Than Franthithco, either." He choked on a sob. "N-nobody wanth me 'cauthe I talk f-funny."

Laura had heard Jimmy's words. She moved up to meet them, and Lance stopped. Laura caressed Jimmy's cheek, wiping away tears. "Jimmy, honey, I'm sure there'll be someone in San Francisco who will take you. You're a sweet little boy, and they won't care how you talk."

Jimmy shook his head. "No th-they won't. N-nobody wanth me 'cauthe I thtutter an' lithp when I t-talk."

Laura's throat constricted. "Don't give up, Jimmy. I'm sure God has someone who lives in San Francisco who will take you."

Jimmy sniffed and knuckled tears from his eyes. His lower lip quivered. "M-Mithter Adamth liveth in Th-Than Franthithco. I w-want him to take me, but he c-can't."

She said to Lance, "I've noticed that you two have become pretty close."

Lance nodded. "That we have, Mrs. Stanfield." Then he said to Jimmy, "Well, little pal, I'd better get you aboard."

Laura pinched Jimmy's cheek playfully. "It'll be all right, honey. You just cheer up now."

Lance smiled at her and headed for the front platform of the boys' coach. "See you later, Mrs. Stanfield."

As Lance mounted the steps, he sensed a strange stirring in his heart and mind. If asked to describe it, he would be at a loss to do so, but it was as real as could be.

He placed Jimmy down on the seat, patted his cheek, and said, "I'll see you later, little pal."

Jimmy grabbed his hand and looked up at him with pleading eyes.

"What is it, Jimmy?"

"M-Mithter Adamth, if thomebody in Than F-Franthithco doeth take me an' let m-me live with th-them, will y-you come an' thee m-me?"

The conductor's final call for boarding echoed past the window.

Lance swallowed hard. "I sure will, Jimmy." With that, he hurried up the aisle toward the front door of the coach, leaving behind a brokenhearted little boy who desperately wanted to be his foster son.

When Lance stepped out onto the coach's platform, he found Laura Stanfield waiting for him. The engine's whistle sent a shrill message into the air, and the big engine's wheels spun on the tracks. The train lurched forward, with the couplings between cars giving off a series of thumping sounds.

As both Laura and Lance grasped the railings to steady themselves, she said, "Could I talk to you, Mr. Adams?"

"Of course, but—"

"You can pass through the girls' coach to get to yours."

"Oh. Okay."

The train was rolling slowly out of the railroad station.

"Mr. Adams, I don't mean to interfere in your business, nor to be nosy, but could I ask you something?"

"Of course."

"Well, since you and Jimmy have become so close, and he has spoken his desire to go home with you, isn't it possible for you to take him?"

Lance moved his head back and forth. "No, it isn't, Mrs. Stanfield. You see, there are some circumstances that make it impossible. Circumstances that only God could alter."

"Oh. I'm sorry. It's just that—well, that precious little boy seems to love you very much, and even though I tried to show a positive attitude about his being chosen in San Francisco, I'm actually afraid he will be the only one left when the choosing is over. I'd hate for Jimmy to have to go back to New York and start over. That would be terribly devastating to him. Then when the Society puts him on another train, he will have to go through all of this again."

Lance lowered his head. "Yes. I know."

"Mr. Adams, Gifford and I would take Jimmy if our situation was different, but traveling on these orphan trains is how we make our living. It wouldn't be right for us to take Jimmy in then leave him weeks on end with someone else."

"Of course not. And if our situation was different, I'd take that little guy in an instant. You see, Carol—my wife—is unable to bear children, and she has an aversion to the idea of our adopting a child. Somehow she feels she would not have the fulfillment of being a mother unless she could give birth to the child. I must admit that I don't understand it, but I certainly can't get off the train with Jimmy in my arms and say, 'Here, Carol, whether you like it or not, I've brought you a little boy to raise.'"

Laura shook her head. "Of course not."

"Believe me, Mrs. Stanfield, I wish it were different. I've really developed a strong attachment to that little boy and would love to take him home and be his daddy, but I can't violate Carol's right to live her life in the way that will make her happy."

"I understand that," said Laura. "Is your wife meeting you at the station in San Francisco?"

"Yes."

"It's only two hours to San Francisco. Is it all right if between here and there, I pray that the Lord will change Carol's mind?"

A smile tugged at the corners of Lance's mouth. "It sure *would* be all right! I've been praying the same way, myself. Like I said, only God can alter these circumstances." Even as he spoke, Lance was aware of the strange, indescribable stirring in his heart and mind. Was this stirring coming from the Holy Spirit?

"Well," said Laura, moving toward the platform of the girls' coach, "I'll let you get to your coach, and I'll take a seat in here and start praying."

Lance followed her onto the rocking, swaying platform, then moved ahead and opened the door for her, allowing her to enter first. Laura chose a seat at the rear of the coach and sat down.

Lance smiled. "I don't know how to thank you for your concern for Jimmy. Pray hard, okay?"

"I sure will."

Lance hurried through the girls' coach. As he was moving up the aisle toward his seat in his coach, the same strange stirring was in his heart and mind.

He sat down and glanced at the countryside as the train headed southwest toward San Francisco. While he kept his eyes on the grassy, rolling hills, suddenly Laura's words to Jimmy a few minutes ago echoed through his head: *"Don't give up, Jimmy. I'm sure God has someone who lives in San Francisco who will take you."*

"M-Mithter Adamth liveth in Th-Than Franthithco. I w-want him to take me, but he c-can't."

A lump rose up in his throat and he felt tears forming at the back of his eyes. The strange sensation was still within him, tugging at his very being. He thought of his prayer in Cheyenne when Jimmy had once again been rejected by prospective foster parents and begged him to take him home with him. *Dear Lord, I can't make a move to take this precious child until You show me that it's what You want for sure. Please help me. I have no way of knowing if You have done a work in Carol's heart. You can do a miracle, I know it. You did it for Abraham and Sarah, and gave them a son when it looked impossible. Is anything too hard for the Lord?*

Lance tried to swallow the lump; the tears were now welling

up in his eyes. "Lord, this feeling inside me…is it You speaking to me?" He ran splayed fingers through his hair. "Are You telling me that You *have* done a work in Carol's heart? Are You telling me that You are working on a miracle in our lives like You did for Abraham and Sarah and gave them a son even when it seemed impossible?"

The stirring in his heart and mind grew stronger as his last seven words echoed through his head: *a son even when it seemed impossible…a son even when it seemed impossible…a son even when it seemed impossible.*

He wiped the tears from his eyes and looked around to see if any of the passengers were looking at him.

He took his Bible out of his briefcase. As he turned to Genesis 18, his own words were still emblazoned on the walls of his brain—*a son even when it seemed impossible.*

He focused on God's words to Abraham in verse fourteen. "Is any thing too hard for the LORD? At the time appointed I will return unto thee, according to the time of life, and Sarah shall have a son."

His eyes brightened as he thought of a related passage. Quickly, he turned to Genesis 21 and let his eyes fall on the first two verses: "And the LORD visited Sarah as he had said, and the LORD did unto Sarah as he had spoken. For Sarah conceived, and bare Abraham a son in his old age, at the set time of which God had spoken to him."

Lance smiled. "At the set time. At the appointed time. Lord, is this stirring inside me Your way of saying You had it planned all the time that Carol and I would have a son and his name is Jimmy?"

His mind went back to that day when the train pulled out of Cheyenne: He was gazing through the window at the vast Wyoming prairie as a small herd of antelope splashed across a stream not far from the tracks. He recalled his prayer at that moment: *Heavenly Father, I'm looking to You for this miracle. You gave Abraham and Sarah a son when it seemed impossible. Is anything too hard for You? No. It is not. Help me to trust You as You work it out.*

He bent his head down and looked at the floor. "Lord," he whispered, "I know what's going on inside me. You are speaking to me about Jimmy. I want to take that precious little guy home with me to be my son. You have a set time…an appointed time to complete Your plan. I don't know if You have dealt yet with Carol. You know that You will have to speak to her heart so she will want Jimmy as her son too."

Lance was aware of someone standing over him in the aisle. He looked up to see the conductor standing over him. "Mr. Adams, are you all right?"

Lance nodded. "Yes, sir. I'm fine. Just doing some praying."

The conductor's eyebrows arched. "Oh. I'm sorry for disturbing you, Mr. Adams. I didn't realize—"

"It's all right. You didn't know whether I was ill, or something like that. I appreciate your concern."

The conductor smiled. "I'll move on so you can proceed."

Lance eased back on the seat, closed his eyes, and whispered, "Lord, when those seven remaining orphans are being inspected and interviewed at the San Francisco depot, I could tell Carol that You spoke to my heart about Jimmy, and we're taking him home whether she likes it or not, but that wouldn't be fair to her. With a foster child comes much responsibility. It wouldn't be right for me to force him on her. In Your Word, You said, 'Husbands, love your wives, even as Christ also loved the church, and gave himself for it.' You know how very much I love Carol, and because I do, I can't do something that would make her miserable and unhappy. I've got to know that You have dealt with her on this issue before I can tell the Stanfields and the Conlans that we want to take Jimmy home with us."

He took a deep breath and let it out without opening his eyes.

"Lord, I'm trusting that You are working in Carol's heart, even as You have been working in mine. You know that we walk by faith and not by sight. So I won't know for sure when we pull into the depot that You have prepared Carol to be Jimmy's mother like You've prepared me to be his father. I'm just asking You to give me wisdom when I meet Carol and talk to her."

He thought of Laura Stanfield and the fact that she was in the girls' coach, praying that the Lord would work in Carol's heart. He smiled to himself as the sensation in his heart and mind continued to make its presence known.

In the boys' coach, Jimmy Kirkland sat alone, staring out the window. He missed Barry Chandler and wondered if he liked his new home. Fear chilled Jimmy's mind as he thought about the many couples who showed interest in him in all those depots… until they heard him talk.

His lips quivered and tears filled his eyes as he whispered, "M-Mithter Adamth wanth me. He really doeth. B-but he keepth th-thaying he can't t-take me home to live with h-him."

Jimmy felt sure that Mr. Adams had a wife, but he wondered if he had children and couldn't take him because he had no room for him.

His mind went back to the orphanage and how the children picked on him there. He drew a shaky breath and whispered, "I w-would rather live with M-Mithter Adamth and hith f-family, even if I h-had to thleep on the f-floor. I know M-Mithter Adamth would'n' let n-nobody pick on me becauthe I talk f-funny."

Jimmy looked up to see Gifford Stanfield coming down the aisle. He stopped to talk to the other three boys in the coach, who were purposely cramped together on one seat several rows ahead. Alex Geisler, Jared Rice, and Perry Dugan had become good friends on the trip.

Jimmy knew they were ten or eleven years of age and wanted nothing to do with him. This did not bother him. At least they hadn't picked on him like Jason Laird and Rick Schindler did. He was glad that Jason and Rick were gone.

After a few minutes, Stanfield left the three boys and moved on down the aisle. Jimmy managed to make a smile for the man.

Stanfield matched the smile and leaned over the boy. "How you doing, Jimmy?"

Jimmy shrugged.

"Hey, partner, it's going to be all right. San Francisco is a big city. Lots of people live there. There'll be some man and woman who will see what a fine boy you are and they'll come to me and say, 'Mr. Stanfield, we want that handsome boy with the blond hair and the big blue eyes.'"

"B-but when they hear me t-talk, they'll l-look at me funny an' w-walk away. Juth' l-like they alwayth d-do." He wiped saliva from his lips and chin.

Stanfield laid a steady hand on the boy's thin shoulder. "Now, Jimmy, don't you give up. God's got a family in San Francisco who will want you."

Jimmy nodded. "Th-that'th what Mithuth Th-Thtanfield thaid t-too."

"Well, she's a real smart lady. You keep in mind what she said."

Jimmy nodded again, but did not comment.

"Well, I'll see you later."

"Yeth, th-thir."

Jimmy watched Gifford Stanfield turn around, walk back to the front of the coach, and sit down across the aisle from Derek Conlan. They were chatting happily about something.

Jimmy wished he had something to be happy about. He turned on the seat, leaned against the coach wall just below the window, and closed his eyes.

Soon the steady clicking of the wheels beneath him and the rhythmic sway of the coach lulled him into slumber.

Chapter Twenty-two

J immy Kirkland awakened and drowsily sat up on the seat. The train was slowing down. He looked out the window and saw that they were pulling into a big railroad station. He had overheard Mr. Conlan telling some of the other boys yesterday that San Francisco's station was quite large.

Jimmy looked around and saw that the other three boys were now sitting in separate seats near the front of the coach, pushing their faces out the open windows while Mr. Stanfield and Mr. Conlan were rising from their seats close by them.

Jared Rice said excitedly, "I'm gonna get chosen here, I know it!"

"Yeah, me too!" Perry Dugan said.

Alex Geisler laughed. "I'll get chosen first!"

Gifford Stanfield stood over them with Derek Conlan at his side and smiled down at the boys. "Well, no matter who gets chosen first, the rest of you will be chosen before it's over."

Derek Conlan looked back at the little boy and chuckled. "And that includes you, Jimmy!"

Jimmy smiled back at him.

The train came to a halt. Gifford Stanfield said, "I want all four of you boys to sit tight, as usual. It'll be a little longer this time because all the regular passengers are getting off here.

Mr. Conlan and I will be back in a little while to take you to the platform for the lineup."

When the two men were gone, Jimmy saw the other three boys leave their seats and head down the aisle toward him. They stopped at Jimmy's seat and all three looked down at him. He blinked and frowned at them questioningly.

Alex Geisler made a face at him, bugging his eyes. "You're goin' back to the orphanage 'cause nobody wants a kid who spits and stutters when he talks."

The other two laughed, and Perry Dugan said, "If you'd keep your mouth shut and never talk, maybe somebody would choose you."

Jimmy's countenance fell. He was surprised at this behavior by these three boys. They had never picked on him before. They had always been nice to him.

Jared Rice chuckled. "Too bad, stuttermouth! You might as well plan on goin' back to the orphanage. Nobody wants a boy who can't talk without slobberin' all over himself."

Flame leaped into Jimmy's eyes. He slid off the seat and pushed past them into the aisle. He said in a high-pitched voice, "Oh y-yeah? Well, you'll f-find out! Thomebody ith g-gonna take m-me home!"

Jared sneered. "Sure, spitmouth, and just who'll that be?"

Jimmy stiffened his back and squared his shoulders. "Mither Adamth, th-thath who! I'm gonna g-go to hith houthe and live w-with him!"

Alex gave Jimmy a stiff push with the heel of his hand, sending him flying backwards. Jimmy fell flat on his back in the aisle. Tears were forming in his eyes as he looked up at Alex and the other two beside him, peering down with a wicked glint in their eyes.

Alex stuck his tongue out at Jimmy. "You're lyin', slobber-mouth! Mr. Adams ain't takin' you home! He's got better sense than that!"

"Yeah!" said Jared. "Your slobberin' would ruin the rugs and the furniture in Mr. Adams's house!"

Jimmy summoned the necessary strength and sprang to his feet. "I'm not l-lyin'! Mithter Adamth ith g-gonna 'dopt m-me!"

Perry made a face at him. "He ain't, neither! You're lyin'!"

Jimmy made a wild wordless shout and jumped at all three, fists swinging....

Suddenly a voice penetrated Jimmy's dream. He opened his eyes to see Derek Conlan bending over him where he lay on the seat, grasping for his swinging fists.

"Jimmy!" Conlan was saying. "Wake up! Wake up!"

Jimmy blinked, shook his head to clear it, and saw the three boys and Gifford Stanfield draw up. He could feel the train slowing down on the tracks.

Alex Geisler said, "He must've been havin' a bad dream."

Conlan released the boy's fists. "Is that it, Jimmy? Were you having a bad dream?"

Jimmy nodded and rubbed his eyes. "Yeth, thir."

Conlan reached into his shirt pocket and took out a comb. "Here, Jimmy, let me comb your hair. You've got it all messed up. I want you to look nice, because we're about to pull into San Francisco."

Lance Adams's nerves were taut across his back and shoulders while he looked out the window as the train ground to a halt in the San Francisco terminal. He spotted the blonde he loved so much standing on the platform among a crowd of people, waiting for him.

His heart began pounding in his chest. "Dear Lord," he

whispered, "the moment has come. I'll know for sure that You want us to have Jimmy if I find Carol willing to take him, once she has heard his story."

Lance purposely waited until all the other passengers had left the coach, then picked up his briefcase and headed toward the rear exit. A glance out the window showed him Carol craning her neck while searching the faces of the passengers as they alighted from the other cars.

When he moved out onto the coach's small platform and started down the steps, Carol saw him and hurried through the dwindling crowd with open arms.

Carol's lovely features were lit up with a smile. "Welcome home, darling!"

They embraced for a brief moment, then Lance kissed her soundly, told her he loved her, and held her tight once again.

She breathed into his ear, "I missed you so much, darling! I don't know if I'll ever let you go to one of those conventions again!"

Lance laughed, eased back, and looked her in the eye. "But I always learn a lot at the businessmen's conventions."

Carol giggled. "I don't know about that, but I'm sure when you gave your lecture, they all learned things they'd never heard of before."

He smiled and kissed the tip of her nose. "You're not just a little bit prejudiced on your husband's behalf, are you?"

"Why, of course not! I can't help it if the Lord gave me the world's smartest businessman to be my husband, can I?"

Lance saw Rachel Wolford lining up the three girls and the four boys. At the same time, the Stanfields and the Conlans were talking with prospective foster parents, making their approvals, and getting them ready to begin the interviews.

Carol took hold of Lance's arm. "Well, darling, let's be going."

Lance's arm stiffened. "Honey, we can't leave yet."

Carol blinked and looked at him questioningly. "Why not?"

Lance took her hand. "Come over here with me."

She frowned as Lance led her toward a cluster of people on the depot platform who were gathered close to some children who stood in a straight line.

I wonder what's going on? she thought. *Something is in the air with Lance. I felt it the instant I saw him get off the train. For one thing, he's always among the first passengers to leave the coach he's been riding in. Just now, he was the last. He seems a bit distracted. I wonder if something went wrong at the convention. Or maybe he's worried about something. Maybe he's—*

They came to an abrupt halt quite near the spot where the children stood.

Carol ran her gaze over the seven children, then noted the people standing around, and the two women and two men who held clipboards while talking to some of them. "What's this, Lance?"

"Honey, this is an orphan train."

"Oh, really?"

"Mm-hmm. I've been watching people take orphans as foster children in railroad depots ever since Kearney, Nebraska. There were sixty-one to begin with. It's been something to behold."

Lance saw curiosity in Carol's eyes. "That's interesting," she said, looking back at the children.

Lance pointed at the Stanfields and the Conlans, who were each engaged in conversation with a couple. "See those four people with clipboards?"

"Yes."

"They're the officials on this train from the Children's Aid Society. Right now, they're talking to couples who are interested in becoming foster parents to these children. They have many questions to ask them so they can make sure they qualify."

Carol nodded. "I see. Guess they have to be careful."

"Those precious boys and girls have already been through horrible times in their lives. The sponsors want to do the best they can to see that they are placed in the right kind of homes."

"Mm-hmm. I've read about Charles Loring Brace's burden for the orphans, and I know these people from the Society have to feel the same way."

Lance gestured toward Rachel Wolford. "See that nurse over there?"

"Yes."

"She travels with the children so if any of them get sick, she's right there to take care of them."

"Oh yes. I recall reading about the nurses on the orphan trains."

At that moment, the prospective foster parents began moving along the short line, of which Jimmy Kirkland was last.

Lance pointed to him. "Honey, see that little blond boy at the end of the line?"

"Mm-hmm. He looks a little frightened. Isn't he cute? Look at those big blue eyes."

"His name is Jimmy Kirkland. His parents abandoned him on the doorstep of one of New York City's orphanages when he was only a few days old."

Carol's brow furrowed. "Oh. Poor little fellow."

Lance felt his pulse quicken. "I've gotten to know Jimmy pretty well. Such a precious little boy. But so far nobody has chosen him."

A smile curved Carol's lips. "Well, tell you what, if I was looking to take one of them home, he'd be the one I'd choose. He looks so scared, but isn't he cute?"

Lance's pulse throbbed the more. "He *is* scared, honey."

"Well, he can't be more than five years old. He's pretty young for an experience like this. It's only natural that he be frightened."

"There's more to it than that."

Carol looked at her husband. "What do you mean?"

"Well, you're right. He's exactly five years old. But Jimmy has a speech impediment, honey. He stutters and lisps. I've watched people ever since Kearney show interest in him until they start asking questions. When he answers them, they always look at him like he's a freak. Some people, I understand, think a child who stutters and lisps is retarded. It's been really something to watch their reactions when Jimmy answers their questions."

Carol frowned, her eyes fixed on Jimmy. She noticed that he looked at Lance, kept his eyes on him for a few seconds, then looked away. "Well just because he stutters and lisps doesn't mean he's mentally slow." She paused. "But now that you mention it, I *have* heard that even some people in medical science believe that. Personally, I can't see how a person could come to that conclusion without more to go on than a stuttering lisp."

"My sentiments exactly." Lance's hopes were rising.

At that moment, a couple stopped in front of Jimmy, smiling down at him. The man hunkered down and asked a question that Lance and Carol could not distinguish because he spoke too low for them to hear his words.

When Jimmy replied, it was to give the man his name, which they could both hear and understand. He stuttered on both names.

The man frowned and asked another question. This one required an answer with words that brought out the lisp in Jimmy's speech too.

The man stood up, shaking his head, and said something to his wife.

She nodded. Together, they walked away.

Carol laid a hand on Lance's arm as she saw Jimmy swing his

gaze on him once again. This time there was a pleading look in the boy's misty eyes. His little lips began to quiver. She noted the longing look in Lance's eyes. The fact that Jimmy was looking to her husband in his grief at being rejected by the couple and that Lance was eyeing him with compassion, told Carol that the two of them were well acquainted. The look of adoration toward Lance and the pleading in his blue eyes captured her heart. She squeezed her husband's arm. "Darling, little Jimmy's asking for your help."

Lance nodded. "I know, honey. I—"

At that instant another couple stepped up to Jimmy, who still had his eyes on Lance.

The Adamses watched with bated breath.

The young woman smiled as she beheld Jimmy's innocent face and big blue eyes. "Oh, Max, just look at him! Isn't he a doll? What's your name, honey?"

Jimmy dropped his eyes to the platform floor. "J-Jimmy."

The woman put fingers under his chin and lifted his face toward her. "Don't be afraid now, Jimmy. What's your last name?"

Carol's heart went out to the boy as he looked at the woman with fear in his eyes, but did not respond.

The man bent over. "Son, you're supposed to answer us when we ask you questions. Now what is your last name?"

Jimmy licked his lips and swallowed hard. "K-Kirkland."

The man tousled Jimmy's hair. "Don't stutter now. There's nothing to be afraid of. Your name is Jimmy Kirkland, right?"

Jimmy nodded, meeting his gaze.

The man's voice took on a hard tone. "Little boy, when you are asked a question by an adult, you're supposed to answer, 'Yes, sir' or 'No, sir,' 'Yes, ma'am,' or 'No, ma'am.' Now answer me correctly. Is your name Jimmy Kirkland?"

Carol felt Lance stiffen, but kept her attention on the scene before them.

Jimmy's face went pale. His voice sounded small and insignificant as he said, "Y-Yeth, th-thir."

The man glanced at his wife, then set his eyes once again on the boy. "How old are you, Jimmy?"

The little lad swallowed hard, showing his fear. "I'm five y-yearth old, th-thir." He used his sleeve to wipe away the saliva from the corners of his mouth.

Carol could tell that Lance was ready to rush to the spot if one more thing was said to frighten Jimmy.

The man looked at his wife. "Are you thinking what I'm thinking?"

Her face was sour. "Yes. Let's go."

Lance's body relaxed and he sighed as the couple walked away. Carol saw Jimmy send another pleading look to him. Lance was about to go to the boy when another couple approached him.

Carol squeezed her husband's arm again. "You okay, honey?"

"I am now."

While Lance's eyes were fixed on Jimmy and the new couple, Carol squeezed his arm another time. "Darling, there's something I should tell you right now."

He glanced at her. "What's that, sweetheart?"

"Well, while you've been gone I've been giving much thought to the suggestion you made a few months ago that we should consider adopting a child."

Lance felt a jolt like an electric shock spear through his body. "You have?"

"Uh-huh. Honey, I was completely wrong. My attitude and the way I cut you off in that conversation was wrong."

This time, Lance's heart jumped in his chest. "Really?"

"Really. Want to know when I realized it?"

"S-sure."

"At the very moment your coach pulled away from the platform that day I put you on the train to Chicago."

"Really?"

"Yes, darling, and while I was riding home in that carriage you hired, I started praying about it. I've prayed about it over these days you've been gone, and I believe the Lord would have us look into adopting a child. He spoke to me in a way I could not misunderstand."

"Really?"

"Really. It was all I could think about when I pillowed my head at night, and it was the first thing on my mind when I woke up every morning. I was planning to talk to you about it when you got home—you know, to the house."

Lance's breath was coming in short spurts. "You were?"

"Yes."

"Wonderful!"

Carol's line of sight went back to Jimmy, who was talking to the couple who were now showing interest in him. "And darling, I didn't even know you were going to be on an orphan train."

Lance's pulse was throbbing on both sides of his neck, in unison with the thunderous beats of his heart. That familiar stirring was making itself known again in his mind and heart. He knew he had his answer from God.

At that moment, the man and woman who were talking to Jimmy walked away, saying something to each other and shaking their heads.

Lance looked at where the line of children had been. Three of the other six children were gone, and the remaining three were walking away with their new foster parents.

Jimmy Kirkland was the only one left.

He stood there, his head bent down, wiping tears.

Lance took hold of Carol's shoulders, looking straight into her eyes. "Sweetheart, could you be Mommy to a little boy who stutters and lisps?"

A smile spread over Carol's beautiful face. "Darling, as far as I'm concerned, that isn't even a factor. I could, and I *will!* Let's take him!"

Lance's heart felt like it was going to plow right through the wall of his chest. He let go of Carol and dashed to the little towheaded boy.

Jimmy was looking straight at him.

Lance bent over Jimmy, hugged him, then drew back so he could look into his eyes. Jimmy, do you still want to go home with me and be my little boy?"

Jimmy's eyes brightened. "I thure d-do! I n-never had a d-daddy!"

"You never had a mommy, either. Do you want a mommy too?"

The boy jumped up and down excitedly. "I th-thure do!"

Lance took hold of Jimmy's hand, turned him toward Carol, and pointed to her. "Well, that's her, right over there."

Jimmy fixed his gaze on the blond lady who was looking at him and smiling.

"Come on." Lance led the boy to Carol. "Jimmy, this is your new mommy. Mommy, this is your new little boy!"

Lance still had hold of Jimmy's hand.

For a moment, Jimmy and Carol looked at each other, smiling. Then Carol opened her arms to him. "Come here, Jimmy, and let Mommy hug you!"

As Jimmy let go of Lance's hand and dashed into Carol's embrace, Lance wiped happy tears from his eyes and looked toward heaven. "Oh, dear Lord, thank You for answered prayer!"

Still looking toward heaven, he heard Carol speaking sweet

words to Jimmy and recalled that God had said in Isaiah 65:24, "And it shall come to pass, that before they call, I will answer; and while they are yet speaking, I will hear."

Lance drew a shaky breath. "Precious Lord, thank You! Thank You that even before I ever saw Jimmy for the first time on this trip, You were already working in Carol's heart, and answering prayers that I began uttering after I saw Jimmy and he crawled into my heart!"

At that moment, Laura Stanfield stepped up. She looked at Lance, then at Carol and Jimmy, who were hugging. A smile lit up her face as she looked back at Lance. "Does this mean what I think it does?"

"Yes, it sure does! Thank you for praying, Mrs. Stanfield!"

Carol took hold of Jimmy's hand and held it as she glanced at Laura, then looked at her husband.

"Mrs. Stanfield, I want you to meet my wife, Carol. Carol, this is Laura Stanfield." Lance chuckled. "It just so happens that I have had Mrs. Stanfield praying about Jimmy becoming our little boy."

Carol smiled, let go of Jimmy's hand, and put her arms around Laura.

"Thank you, Mrs. Stanfield. God, indeed, answers prayer— sometimes even before we offer the prayer."

"Yes, He does! He makes that clear in His Word."

The women let go of each other, and Laura said, "Let's get the paperwork done so you two can take Jimmy home!"

Jimmy stood between Lance and Carol as they talked with Laura Stanfield and answered her questions. Soon, the Adamses were signing official papers. When it was done, Laura fastened the Children's Aid Society's papers to the clipboard, then handed Lance his copies that made it official. "There you are, Mr. Adams. You and Mrs. Adams are now Jimmy's legal guardians and foster parents. Congratulations!"

Lance thanked her and looked down at the bright-eyed lad. "Well, Jimmy, Mommy and I are now your parents!"

Laura bent down, hugged the boy, and kissed his cheek. "Congratulations, Jimmy! God has given you a mommy and daddy who love you. Always be happy, won't you?"

Jimmy nodded. "I will. I h-have a home n-now."

Carol picked Jimmy up, squeezed him tight, and planted a kiss on his cheek. "I'll be happy too, sweetheart, because I get to be your mommy!"

Jimmy wrapped his arms around her neck. "I l-love you, M-Mommy."

Carol's eyes were now swimming in tears. "And I love you, sweetheart."

She kissed his cheek again, then turned to look at her husband.

Lance gave her a watery smile. "My turn."

Carol let Lance take Jimmy into his arms and looked on with pleasure as he held him close. Jimmy put a powerful hold on Lance's neck, held it for a brief moment, then eased back. "You're my d-daddy, now. I l-love you, D-Daddy!"

"I love you too, son," Lance said past the tightness in his throat. "More than you will ever know."

Jimmy's smile faded away. "Are y-you thure you w-want a boy who t-talkth funny?"

Lance pinched Jimmy's little nose playfully. "I know I want *you*. The way you talk is part of you, Jimmy. God made you the way He did for a very special reason, and I wouldn't change one thing about you."

Jimmy's winsome smile was back in place and a serene look of contentment settled over his shining face.

Chapter Twenty-three

On Thursday, July 16, the Nebraska sun stared down out of a blue sky above the Banton farm a few miles north of Kearney.

Will and Leah had been up since well before dawn in order to get as much of the daily work done as possible while the night's coolness remained in the air. Mary, Johnny, and Lizzie Marston had left their beds just before breakfast, at Leah's call.

After breakfast, Johnny joined his foster father to help him with work that needed to be done in the barn.

The girls had helped Leah with the housework and in the vegetable garden during the morning, and at noon, they had lunch ready. All three stood on the back porch as Leah called toward the barn, "Will! Johnny! Lunch is ready!"

Inside the barn, Will laid down his hammer. "Sounds good to me. I'm hungry."

Johnny had several nails in his hand. He placed them back in the paper sack and laid it next to Will's hammer. "Me too, Papa Will. Let's go."

Red was lying on his belly in the straw and raised his head as Will and Johnny headed for the open barn door. When they reached the sunlight that struck the ground just outside the door,

Johnny looked up at Will and grinned. "Race you to the house, Papa!"

Will set loving eyes on the six-year-old boy. "It's hot out here, son. We'll just get hotter if we run."

"Aw, come on now! You're just afraid I'll beat you again."

Will lifted his hat and wiped his bandanna across his brow. "You couldn't beat me again."

"Oh yeah?" Johnny took his ready-to-race stance.

Red knew what was coming.

Suddenly Will darted for the house, leaving boy and dog behind.

Johnny sprang forward. "That ain't fair, Papa! You got a head start!"

In a flash, Red passed Will, aiming for the back porch where Leah and the girls stood, barking all the way.

Acting as if he was running as fast as possible, Will purposely let Johnny catch up to him and pass him. Johnny was laughing gleefully.

"C'mon, Papa Will!" he called over his shoulder. "Can't you run any faster than that?"

Lizzie shouted, "Hurry, Papa! Johnny's gonna beat you again!"

Red reached the porch ten seconds ahead of Johnny, who was some forty feet ahead of his foster father.

Mary cried out, "Red won! Red won the race!" The dog was jumping up and licking her face.

Johnny bounded up the porch steps, waving his hands in victory. "I won! I won!"

Lizzie giggled. "No, you didn't, Johnny! Red won!"

"Red doesn't count! He has four legs!"

Will drew up, acting disappointed, and letting his tongue hang out. "I don't know…where that boy gets so…much speed, Mama!"

Leah gave him a sly grin. "Maybe he has help."

"What do you…mean?"

Leah looked at Johnny. "Johnny, have you been taking lessons from Red?"

Will grinned, relieved that Leah hadn't given away his secret.

Johnny shook his head. "No, ma'am, but maybe that would be a good idea. Then I could beat Papa even worse!"

Leah and the girls laughed, then Leah said, "Lunch is ready, you two. Get washed up."

Will and Johnny quickly made their way to the small galvanized tub that stood in a shady section of the porch. They splashed water on their sweaty faces and over their heads, letting it run down their necks and soak their shirts while Leah and the girls went into the kitchen.

"Boy, it's a hot one today," said Will, taking a towel from the rack above the tub to dry his face. "We sure could use some rain, but there isn't a cloud in the sky." He dabbed the towel on his face and head. "Oh, well, not much we can do about the weather. We'll just have to endure it. After all, it's summertime in Nebraska. I should be used to this after all these years."

Leah appeared with Red on her heels, carrying his food bowl. "Yes, Will, we should both be used to it by now." She set the bowl down, and the Irish setter began chomping on the food. "We complain about the heat in the summer, and in the winter, we complain about the cold. But it's still a mighty good place to live. That's why we stay here, isn't it?"

"Sure is," said Will as he hung up the towel.

"Come on, boys. A little food and rest will do us all good."

Red looked up at her. She grinned at him. "You just stay out here and eat your lunch, big guy. We both know that Lizzie will slip you food under the table if you're in there whining."

Red went back to his food, and Will and Johnny followed her

into the kitchen. Will closed the door behind them.

As everyone was gathering at the table, Lizzie waited for Johnny to pull out her chair, which Will had taught him was the gentlemanly thing to do.

Johnny grinned as he pulled the chair from under the table. "There you are, baby sister."

Lizzie flapped her arms like wings. "Thank you, big brother. This little sparrow is gonna fly into her chair!" She made motions like she was flying and landed on the chair.

Johnny then seated his big sister, who said, "Thank you, little brother, for being such a gentleman."

Johnny bowed at the waist. "My pleasure, Miss Marston."

Will went to Leah and seated her. When he sat down on his own chair, he looked at Johnny. Since the Bantons had never prayed before meals until the Marston children came into their home, Will had assigned Johnny to lead in prayer before all meals.

They bowed their heads, and Johnny first thanked the Lord for the food, asking Him to bless it to the nourishment of their bodies, then said, "I also want to thank You, Lord, for watching over Your little sparrows, and for giving us a home with Papa Will and Mama Leah. In Jesus' name, amen."

Will and Leah were deeply touched by Johnny's words, and it showed on both of their faces when the children looked at them.

"Mary, Johnny, Lizzie, I want to tell you something. Even though I have fields of hay to mow, rake, and stack, and a lot of other work to do that comes with summer, I am going to make time for you and Mama Leah so we can take in the county fair in Kearney."

"Oh, that's neat!" said Mary.

Johnny's face was beaming. "Yeah! That's really neat! When I saw in town that there was gonna be a fair, I really wanted to go, but I didn't ask 'cause I knew you had a lotta work to do here on the farm. Thank you, Papa Will."

Lizzie frowned. "What's a fair?"

Leah smiled at Lizzie. "I'll tell you about it later, honey. It's all about animals and food and lots of fun things to do."

"Oh. Okay."

Mary laid her fork down and ran her gaze from Will to Leah. "Mama, Papa, you have been so good to us. I am so happy living here with you. And I'm so glad we're going to church regularly."

"Yeah, me too," said Johnny. "I really like everybody at church. I like my Sunday school teacher. Mr. Jones can really make the Bible stories easy to understand; almost as good as Pastor Blevins."

Johnny looked at Mary, and she smiled at him.

Mary and Johnny had talked privately about their concern that the Bantons were not saved and had been praying about it together. Pastor Mark Blevins preached straight from the Bible, and Mary and Johnny had seen conviction on the Bantons' faces in the services—especially at invitation time—and were optimistic that soon they would open their hearts to Jesus.

Lunch was almost over. Will finished his cup of coffee, set it down, and looked at Johnny. "Well, partner, are you about ready to go back to the barn and help me finish repairing that milking stanchion?"

Johnny grinned. "Sure am. Soon's I eat this last bite of potatoes. Wanna race to the barn?"

Will chuckled. "Not this time. It's too hot. I'll race you when—"

There was a knock at the front door of the house.

Will pushed his chair back and stood up. "I'll see who it is. The rest of you go on and finish eating."

"Probably one of the neighbors," said Leah.

Will nodded, left the kitchen, and went to the front door. When he opened it, he found a young couple on the porch. Red was wagging his tail, and the man was stroking his head. Will eyed the buggy parked at the hitching post and said, "Howdy, folks." There was a perplexed look on his suntanned face. "We don't often get visitors out this way. What can I do for you?"

The man asked, "Are you Will Banton?"

"Yes."

"Well, sir, my name is Bob Marston, and this is my wife, Louise. We're Mary, Johnny, and Lizzie's parents."

Will's jaw slacked. He stared at them, unable to believe what he had just heard. "You—you—are—"

"Yes, sir. We knew this would come as a shock to you and your wife, as well as our children. The people at the Children's Aid Society in New York informed us that you and Mrs. Banton had taken Mary, Johnny, and Lizzie as your foster children when the orphan train was in Kearney."

Bob extended his hand. Will took it in his grasp. "Shock? You can say that again. We were told that you drowned when the ship you were on went down in a storm."

"It's quite a story, Mr. Banton. The Lord graciously saved us from death, though we were swept overboard in that storm. We'll explain it when we have the children present."

"Well, come on in. You must be very anxious to see them."

"You can't even imagine how anxious, Mr. Banton," said Louise. "We know this is going to be a jolt to them, but we can hardly wait to let them know we're alive."

Red slipped past them and ran down the hall toward the kitchen.

"Let me take you into the parlor," said Will. "Leah and the children are just finishing lunch." As they passed through the parlor door, he said, "You wait here. I'll go get them."

Will's knees felt weak as he hurried down the hall and entered the kitchen. Red was at Lizzie's chair, looking at her expectantly for something to eat.

Leah noted that her husband's face was pale. "Honey, what's wrong? Who was at the door?"

Will drew a shaky breath and looked at the children. "Mary, Johnny, Lizzie, there's someone here to see you. I took them into the parlor."

The children looked at each other quizzically, then Mary's brow furrowed as she asked, "Is it somebody from church, Papa Will?"

Will looked at Mary, and said, "No, honey. It's not someone from church."

"But we don't know anybody else around here yet."

A thin smile curved Will's lips. "You're right, Mary, but you know these people. Go on to the parlor. We'll follow you."

As the children hurried down the hall with Red at Lizzie's side, Will and Leah followed. Leah looked up at her husband. "Who is it?"

He leaned close to her and whispered in her ear, "It's their parents! They didn't drown in that storm."

Leah felt an unbelievable hot flash start at her neck and flow in waves over her face. Her mouth fell open.

Will took hold of her hand and they drew up behind the children, who were now at the open door of the parlor.

When Mary, Johnny, and Lizzie stopped at the door, Bob and Louise were standing by the sofa with tears in their eyes.

The children's eyes widened and a look of disbelief appeared on each little face. Absolutely stunned into frozen silence, they stared at the man and woman standing before them.

Lizzie was the first to overcome the shock and find her tongue. She broke from her siblings and ran toward her parents.

"Mama! Papa! You came back from heaven!"

Louise scooped her up into her arms.

At the same instant, Mary squealed and dashed toward them. Johnny gasped, and on Mary's heels, darted toward them.

Will and Leah hung on to each other as they beheld the scene. The parents and children were hugging and crying while everyone talked at once, filled with the joy of being together.

When the emotion of the moment had subsided some, Will introduced the Marstons to Leah, who urged them to sit down so they could talk. The children sat on the sofa with their parents, and Will and Leah each sat in an overstuffed chair, facing them. Red planted himself on the floor in front of the sofa and looked up at the children.

Bob Marston smiled down at his children, then looked at the Bantons.

"Let me explain what happened so you can see how marvelously God protected us and spared our lives in that awful storm that sank the ship we were on."

Sitting beside her mother, Lizzie scooted as close to her as possible. Louise's arm was around her. Tears were in Louise's eyes as she smiled down at her baby and pulled her tight against her side.

Bob explained about how the storm came up at sea, and how at first, the captain and his crew thought it would not be a serious one. He went on to tell them that by the time the full force of the storm was upon them, it was too late to head for the nearest shore.

"We were in our cabin as the ship tossed wildly on the sea, listing dangerously. All at once, there was a loud crash. We didn't know what it was, but we were afraid the ship would sink in a hurry. Suddenly the cabin door came open, and the captain was there, clinging to the doorframe. He told us the ship was sinking, and we needed to get to the lifeboats fast."

Lizzie looked up at her mother. "Were you scared, Mama?"

"I sure was, honey."

Bob smiled at Lizzie, then looked back at the Bantons. "Louise and I clung to each other as we followed the captain across the slanted deck. The crewmen were climbing into the lifeboats, and we could see furniture and wooden crates from the ship bobbing on the surface of the ocean. Suddenly, the ship listed severely, and at the same time, a huge wave broke over the deck and swept us and the captain into the ocean."

Leah was shaking her head. "It must have taken a miracle for you to survive that!"

Louise nodded. *"Miracle* is the right word for it, Mrs. Banton."

"The captain went down, and we never saw him again," Bob said. "No question about it. He drowned. Louise and I were still clinging to each other when a large wooden crate floated right up to us. She clung to me while I got a firm hold on the crate, and we hung on till we were swept away from the center of the storm to calmer waters. We watched the ship go down. About an hour later, we were picked up by the crew of a ship from Greenland that was on its way to Halifax, Nova Scotia. Both of us were in serious condition, having been in that cold water for so long. They took us to a medical clinic in Halifax, where we spent several weeks recovering."

Will shook his head in amazement. "Wow! You talk about a miracle. God was sure looking after you!"

"He sure was. We learned later that all of the crewmen made it to shore in the lifeboats. Upon returning to New York, we learned from our pastor that Mary, Johnny, and Lizzie had been put on an orphan train by the Children's Aid Society. We went to their headquarters, and as I told you, that's where we learned that you two wonderful people had taken all three of our children into your home as their foster parents."

Louise smiled and looked at the Bantons, as tears of joy came down her cheeks. "We can never express our deep gratitude for your taking our children in and giving them a home."

"Yes," said Bob. "They've only been here a few weeks, but we can tell that you care for them very much. I know this must stagger you to have us show up out of the blue to reclaim our children."

Louise wiped tears. "I hope it won't hurt you to give them up."

"Stagger us, yes," said Will. "But you are their parents. It's only right that you have them back."

"Of course," said Leah. "Now, I'll tell you, we fell in love with them at the railroad station, and even though there were three of them, we weren't about to let them be separated. We sincerely wanted to give them a loving home. We'll miss them terribly, but as Will said, their place is with you. We're very happy that you didn't drown, and it's wonderful to see your family together. There will be many more little ones coming through Kearney on those orphan trains, looking for a home. You can be assured that we will be in town to meet the very next one."

"We appreciate your sweet attitude," Louise said. "We're just so thankful that the Lord placed our children with you."

"Mama, Mary an' Johnny an' me were tooken care of 'cause we're God's little sparrows."

Bob reached over and tweaked her nose. "And just how do you know you're God's little sparrows, sweet stuff?"

"'Cause Jesus said it in the Bible."

"Well, your papa and I know about it, honey," said Louise, looking at Bob, then back at Lizzie, "but how do you know about it?"

"Mrs. Roberts showed it to us in the Bible, Mama," spoke up Mary. "It was when we were so upset and afraid because the policemen came and told us that you and Papa were dead. She read it to us in Matthew and in Luke and showed us that Jesus said we are of more value than many sparrows. When Lizzie heard it, she blurted out that the three of us were God's little sparrows."

Bob looked at Lizzie. "You're pretty smart, sweetie. That's exactly what you are."

Louise kissed the top of Lizzie's head. "That's pretty good thinking for a four-year-old!"

Will said, "I never knew Jesus talked about sparrows till these precious children came home with us. At that time, now that I recall it, Lizzie asked if we had sparrows here on the farm. That's what led to the children telling us that it was in the Bible."

Bob frowned. "I take it that you and Mrs. Banton are fairly new Christians then."

Will and Leah looked at each other, then Will said, "Mr. Marston, Leah and I have never been real churchgoers—until these little sparrows came to live with us. In order to become their foster parents, we had to promise to take them regularly to Sunday school and church services."

"And they have, Papa," said Mary. "Pastor Blevins preaches just like Pastor Moore. He makes it clear that if people don't come to Jesus for salvation, trusting only Him to save them, they will go to hell when they die."

Louise ran her gaze between Will and Leah. "Then, Mr. and Mrs. Banton, have you come to know the Lord?"

Will cleared his throat and adjusted his position on the chair. "No, we haven't. But after every sermon, we've talked about it privately here in the house. And…well, last Sunday night we agreed that we would walk the aisle after the sermon next Sunday morning and tell the preacher we want to be saved."

Louise smiled.

Bob set serious eyes on them. "What if one or both of you should die before next Sunday morning?"

Will and Leah looked at him blankly, then Will said, "We'd… ah…we'd go to hell."

"Right. You don't have to be in a church building to be saved. You can settle that right here and now, if you will. Proverbs 27:1 says, 'Boast not thyself of tomorrow; for thou knowest not what a day may bring forth.' Every day in this world people die. You should settle this right now."

"Will you help us?" asked Will.

"Be happy to."

Johnny was sent to fetch a Bible, and it took only a few minutes in the Scriptures to bring Will and Leah to the place that they clearly understood how to be saved, and Bob and Louise had the joy of leading them to the Lord.

There was joy on both faces as the Bantons rejoiced in their salvation.

Will wiped tears with his handkerchief. "I know now why God let it appear that you two had drowned in the shipwreck. If He hadn't, Leah and I wouldn't have had these precious children to choose at the depot; we wouldn't have been under Pastor Blevins's preaching; and you wouldn't be here today to lead us to Jesus. I doubt we would ever have been saved. We would have died and gone to hell."

Louise laughed joyfully. "Well, praise the Lord for the way He works in the lives of His children!"

After several minutes of rejoicing, Bob told the Bantons they were to catch an eastbound train in Kearney the next morning. They would let the children stay the night with the Bantons. He and Louise would stay at one of Kearney's hotels tonight and come back to pick up the children in the rented buggy in the morning.

"Well, Mr. Marston, we have a guest room," Will said, "You two are welcome to sleep there tonight."

Bob looked at Louise. "Sounds good to me."

Louise smiled and a sigh escaped her lips. "Oh yes! Now that we have found our children, it would be very difficult to part with them, even for the night."

"That's understandable," said Leah. "And Will and I would enjoy having your company for the rest of the day. Besides, I'm sure you're both tired from your journey. I'm sure you'll rest better being under the same roof with your children."

Louise nodded. "You're right. I still tire quite easily, since we spent that time in the cold waters of the Atlantic Ocean. Even the recovery time was an ordeal. But praise the Lord, He brought something so beautiful out of what could have been such a tragedy. He is always so faithful and good to us."

Leah rose from her chair. "Tell you what, Louise— May I call you Louise?"

"Of course. We should be on a first-name basis. You were saying?"

"I was going to show you the washroom that goes with the guest room. Maybe you'd like to freshen up a bit."

"I could use that, yes."

The two women excused themselves and Leah led Louise up the stairs and down the hall. When they came to the guest room, the door stood open. "Here it is, Louise. And the washroom is right there. You'll find everything in there you need. When you've refreshed yourself, you can lie down on the bed and rest for a while, if you wish. Take a little nap if you want to. You looked pretty tuckered."

"Oh no. I'm fine, but thank you," said Louise while looking at the bed yearningly. "I should spend more time with you."

"Honey, we'll have plenty of time to talk over supper and

afterward. Now please do as I say. You have a long trip ahead of you, starting tomorrow morning."

"All right, Leah. You win. I really am pretty tired."

"Good girl. If you do find that you need something, just give a holler. And rest as long as you want to."

Louise hugged her. "Thank you, my friend."

Supper at the Banton house was a happy celebration. With help from Mary and Lizzie, Leah had prepared a virtual feast, and there was much joy and laughter around the table.

During the meal, Bob bragged to Louise about the work Johnny had been doing with Will. He explained that he was given a tour of the barn and outbuildings, and Will had pointed out the things that had been done with Johnny's help.

Johnny also took opportunity to brag about how he always beat Papa Will when they ran their races.

Will, Bob, and Johnny retired to the front porch while Leah, Louise, and the girls washed and dried the dishes and tidied up the kitchen.

When that was done, the ladies joined the men on the porch, with Leah and Louise each carrying a tray. Leah's tray bore a slice of apple pie for each person. Louise carried coffee for the adults and milk for the children.

When everyone had their fill, Louise leaned back in the porch swing, with Lizzie next to her mother's side. Even though the day had been hot, there was now a cool breeze that refreshed the small group assembled on the front porch.

The sun went down and twilight spread over the Nebraska plains. Soon lulled by the gentle sway of the swing, Lizzie's head began to droop against her mother's arm.

Louise looked up and smiled at the others, who had become

rather quiet. "Well, this has been one very exciting, emotional day. I think we're all about ready to make it an early night."

Leah chuckled. "You are so right, Louise. Let's head toward the stairs."

The weary group trooped into the house, each seeking out their own beds, just as a huge silver moon peeped over the eastern horizon.

The next morning, there were tearful good-byes as the little sparrows climbed into the rented buggy. Lizzie was last to get in for taking extra time to tell Red good-bye.

Bob and Louise once again expressed their deep appreciation for how the Bantons had so unselfishly taken the children from the orphan train, gave them a home, and were willing to raise them as their own.

Will and Louise thanked the Marstons for leading them to the Lord, assuring them that they would walk the aisle, give their testimony of being saved in their home on Thursday, and present themselves for baptism.

The Bantons then stood with tears on their cheeks as the buggy drove away. The children turned around and waved, as did their parents. The Bantons waved back, and Red barked his farewell.

On a hot day in Wyoming that following August, Jody Claiborne sat on the front porch of the *Circle C* ranch house with her parents as they watched Josie Holden Claiborne and Betty Houston riding close by on the prairie.

Betty had also become Josie's best friend and was teaching her to ride. Josie was riding Queenie at the moment, but Sam had promised to buy Josie her own horse within the next few days. After a while, the girls trotted the horses up to the porch.

Sam grinned. "Josie, you're doing all right. You'll soon be a real horsewoman."

"That's for sure!" said Emma. "You're doing great."

Josie smiled. "That's because I have such a good teacher." With that, she dismounted, looked at Jody, and said, "Okay, sis, it's your turn."

Jody had regained much of her weight and had rosy cheeks. Sam took her by the hand, helped her down the porch steps, and walked her toward Queenie. The mare tossed her head, swished her tail, and whinnied a greeting to her mistress.

Jody stroked her long face and kissed it. "I missed you too, sweet girl. Pretty soon Josie will have her own horse, and we can ride together."

Queenie whinnied again.

Sam lifted Jody into the saddle. As she settled on the mare's back, she giggled and looked at Betty. "And in a few weeks, I'll be able to race you again."

Emma jumped out of her chair. "Jody Claiborne, haven't you learned your lesson, yet? Your father and I told you no more racing!"

Jody giggled again. "I was just kidding, Mommy. From now on, I won't be riding Queenie at full speed."

"Okay. That's better."

Sam took the reins and led Queenie at a walk, with Betty riding her mare alongside them.

While Jody was getting her first ride since coming out of the coma—with her father leading the horse—Josie and Emma sat on the porch in the shade.

Josie took hold of Emma's hand. "Thank you, Mama, for letting me stay and be part of the family."

Emma squeezed the girl's hand. "Honey, you've probably thanked us a thousand times already. Papa and I know you're very appreciative, and we wouldn't have it any other way. We love having you as our daughter."

Some twenty minutes later, the girls returned on horseback at their walking pace, with Sam still leading Queenie. When they drew up to the porch, Betty said, "I have to be heading for home now. I'll see all of you in church on Sunday."

Josie thanked her for the riding lesson, and Betty said there would be more to follow.

As Betty rode away, Sam helped Jody down from the saddle, then led the mare around the corner of the house toward the barn.

Josie hurried off the porch to help Jody climb the steps.

Emma looked at them and smiled to herself. The more Jody's health returned to her, the more she and Josie looked alike. Even though they were born and raised in totally different parts of the country, Josie had taken to ranch life as if she had been born in Wyoming. Emma knew she still missed her father terribly, but Josie had made it clear that she loved her new family very much. Josie had commented a few days ago that her natural father would be so pleased if he knew how well everything in her life had turned out.

Josie still read the letter that had come from Barry Chandler in July, every day. She often talked about how she was praying that someday the Lord would let her see Barry again.

When Josie drew up to her, Jody put her arms around her. "Josie, I'm so glad Mommy and Daddy decided to adopt you. I know Daddy is superbly happy to have two tomboys! But I don't even think of you as an adopted sister. As far as I'm concerned, since some people say we could almost be twins, you are my *real* sister!"

Chapter Twenty-four

Some seven years passed. It was Saturday, June 11, 1881. At Wyoming's leading Bible-believing church, a large crowd was gathering in the auditorium while the pump organ played various hymns.

In a Sunday school room just off the vestibule, Josie Holden Claiborne was in a lovely white wedding dress. Emma Claiborne was doing a last-minute touch-up on Josie's long dark hair while two young women, dressed in pink gowns, looked on. Jody Claiborne was Josie's maid of honor and Betty Houston Williams was her matron of honor.

Satisfied with Josie's hair, Emma took a step back and looked her up and down. "My, what a beautiful bride!"

Josie and Emma had spent many happy hours in the evenings for the past two months, sewing on her wedding dress. As the years had passed, Josie had lost some of her tomboy traits, and she now was a lovely, feminine young woman. Jody still would rather ride her horse and help her father mend fence and work around the barn, but things were slowly changing there too.

Emma slipped up and kissed Josie's cheek. "All right, honey, it's time."

Josie kissed Emma's cheek. "Yes, Mama, it's time. I love you."

"I love you too, precious girl."

Jody and Betty were all smiles as they moved to the door ahead of Josie, holding their small bouquets. Emma moved away hurriedly through the classroom's back door.

When Betty opened the door and she and Jody stepped out into the vestibule, Sam Claiborne stood there, smiling. Jody and Betty smiled at him, moved a few steps past him, and stopped.

One of the ushers stood at the auditorium door, ready to open it.

Sam set admiring eyes on his adopted daughter. Josie presented a beautiful picture in her white gown of delicate organdy, trimmed with lace and pink rosebuds. "Well, honey, are you ready?"

"Yes, Papa," she said, slipping her hand into the crook of his arm.

She paused, took a deep breath, and looked up at him through the tears that misted her eyes. "Thank you for being my papa all of these years. I love you so very much."

"I'm honored to be your papa," he replied. "Thank you for all that you are to your mama, to me, and to Jody."

Josie rose up on her tiptoes and kissed Sam's cheek, then squeezed his arm tightly.

Sam nodded at the usher, and he swung the door open. At the same instant, the organist moved into the wedding march. Sitting in the second row of pews at the front of the auditorium, Emma rose to her feet, and the wedding guests followed suit.

Josie closed her eyes and silently told her dead parents and little brother she loved them.

Jody started slowly down the aisle first, with Betty close behind.

Sam and Josie followed, and the bride let her eyes go first to the handsome young man who stood near the steps that led up to the platform, where the pastor waited with a Bible in his hand.

Josie looked at the faces on both sides of the aisle, then let her gaze go to Emma, at the second row of pews. Emma was smiling through her tears.

Across the aisle from Emma stood Charles and Evelyn Tracy, smiling at her.

Josie set loving eyes on the groom again, and her mind flashed back to that day in July 1874 when she received the letter from him, explaining that he had been chosen at the Rawlins depot by Christian ranchers Charles and Evelyn Tracy, who owned the *Box T* ranch a few miles from Rawlins.

Then she thought of that wonderful day two months later— September 16, to be exact—when Barry Chandler rode onto the *Circle C* ranch. As she joyfully stood looking into his face after he dismounted, he explained that he couldn't wait any longer to come and see her, so he rode the one hundred fifty miles from the *Box T* to the *Circle C*. He told Josie he couldn't get her out of his mind, and Josie admitted that it was the same with her.

As time passed, Barry visited Josie as often as he could, with Sam and Emma's permission. By May 1879, with Barry twenty years old and Josie seventeen, they confessed their deep love to each other. In June 1880, Barry talked to Sam and received permission to ask Josie to marry him, which he did on the same day.

And now, on June 11, 1881, Josie was about to become Mrs. Barry Chandler.

As Sam and Josie drew up in front of Barry, the young couple smiled at each other. Barry took a step closer.

From the platform, the pastor asked so that all could hear, "Who gives this woman to be married to this man?"

Sam swallowed hard. "Her mother and I do."

Josie let go of Sam's arm. He took her hand and placed it in the hand of the groom, then moved toward the spot where Emma sat.

While the guests looked on, Barry kissed Josie's hand, then released it. They smiled at each other as she slid her hand into the crook of his arm, and together they mounted the steps of the platform to take their vows.

Some eighteen years passed. It was Sunday morning, June 11, 1899.

Lance and Carol Adams were in their carriage as they moved down San Francisco's Hillside Boulevard.

One by one, the vehicles ahead of them turned into the parking lot where an impressive white frame church building stood. It had a tall steeple with a cross at the top. As they drew up to the front of the property and waited for their turn to enter the parking lot, they both looked proudly at the sign.

Beneath the name of the church, it read: *James Kirkland Adams, Th.D., Pastor.*

When Lance guided the carriage into the already crowded parking lot, he said, "I was just thinking of the day we dedicated Jimmy to the Lord."

Both of their minds flashed back to the very first Sunday after they had taken Jimmy into their home. They had walked the aisle at the close of the sermon, and in front of the congregation, had dedicated him to the Lord. Their daily prayer to God from that time on was for God to give them wisdom as they raised the boy for His glory, and that He would use Jimmy as He saw best, to serve Him all of his life.

Carol smiled. "I was thinking of the night Jimmy was saved."

This time, both of their minds flashed back to January 1875, when their little adopted son received Jesus into his heart one night at bedtime. He was under conviction and told them he wanted to be saved.

Lance pulled the carriage to a halt in front of a hitching post. "And of course, this will lead to that wonderful night in February 1887."

Carol smiled, and both their minds went back to that night when eighteen-year-old Jimmy walked down the aisle at invitation time in the church where they were members at that time. Jimmy told the pastor that God had called him to preach. The pastor, in turn, announced it to the congregation. The adoptive parents had known that something had been going on in Jimmy's heart for several months. But this came as a shock.

Knowing that some members of the church would be skeptical because of Jimmy's speech impediment, the pastor asked Jimmy to tell the congregation about his call from God.

Stuttering and lisping as usual, Jimmy told how the Lord had been dealing with him for the past eight months about being a preacher. At first, Jimmy told them, he explained to God that because of his speech problem, he could not preach for Him. The Lord then directed him to the argument Moses gave Him in Exodus 4:10, when God called him to be Israel's leader, and Moses said he couldn't do it because of a speech problem.

Jimmy then quoted God's reply in verses 11 and 12: "And the LORD said unto him, Who hath made man's mouth? or who maketh the dumb, or deaf, or the seeing, or the blind? have not I the LORD? Now therefore go, and I will be with thy mouth, and teach thee what thou shalt say."

Lance and Carol remembered how Jimmy closed off his testimony of God's call to preach by telling the congregation that when the Lord's powerful words from these verses took hold of his heart, he surrendered because Jesus said in both Matthew and Mark that with God all things are possible.

This brought to their minds how Jimmy did his Bible college and graduate work in a study-packed five years, and at the age of twenty-three in the summer of 1892, he was sent by his home church to start a new church on the other side of the growing city of San Francisco.

Taking the gospel from door to door in his part of the city, Dr. Jim Adams won souls to Christ consistently, got them into the new church, and trained them to be soul winners. The church grew and blossomed for the next seven years, until it was now—in 1899—San Francisco's largest Bible-preaching, missions-minded, soul-winning church.

Lance looked at his wife. "And today is the church's seventh anniversary, sweetheart."

There were happy tears in Carol's eyes. "Yes, and where have the years gone? It seems like only yesterday we dedicated Jimmy to the Lord. And now, he's married to Belinda, and they have four-year-old Lance and two-year-old Carol."

Lance stepped out of the carriage. "Praise the Lord! Two marvelous grandchildren! Isn't it wonderful?"

"It sure is. God's merciful blessings are unending."

Lance headed for her side of the carriage to help her out. "That they are, and He has only just begun! I know Jim will weave his testimony into the sermon this morning, as he has done on each preceding anniversary. He'll tell again how God has blessed his ministry in spite of his speech impediment because he surrendered his stuttering, lisping tongue to Him."

Carol's eyes were bright. "Oh yes! And then he'll tell his marvelous story of how within six months after starting the church, the stuttering all but disappeared."

Lance chuckled. "Yes, and praise God, after all these years, the lisp is hardly noticeable. Is anything too hard for our wonderful Lord?"

"Absolutely not!"

He took hold of Carol's hand to help her out. "All right, sweetheart, let's go hear some more of that good preaching!"

Orphan Train Trilogy

The Little Sparrows
#1 The Orphan Train Trilogy

Follow the orphan train out West as children's hearts are mended and God's hand restores laughter to grieving families...in a marvelous story of His perfect providence.

ISBN 1-59052-063-7

All My Tomorrows
#2 The Orphan Train Trilogy

Sixty-two abandoned children leave New York on a train headed west, oblivious of what's in store. But their paths are being watched by someone who carefully plans all their tomorrows.

ISBN 1-59052-130-7

Whispers in the Wind
#3 The Orphan Train Trilogy

Dane Weston's dream is to become a doctor. Then his family is murdered and he ends up in a colony of street waifs begging for food...

ISBN 1-59052-169-2

Frontier Doctor Trilogy

ONE MORE SUNRISE
Frontier Doctor trilogy, book one
Countless perils menaced the early settlers of the Wild West—and not the least of them was the lack of medical care. Dr. Dane Logan, a former street waif puts his lifelong dream to work filling this need. His renown as a surgeon spreads throughout the frontier, even while his love grows for the beautiful Tharyn, an orphan he lost contact with when he left New York City as a child. Will happiness in love ever come to Dane—or will the roving Tag Moran gang bring his hopes to a dark end?

ISBN 1-59052-308-3

BELOVED PHYSICIAN
Frontier Doctor trilogy, book two
Dane and Tharyn Logan, back from their honeymoon, take over a medical practice in Central City and join the church there. It's not long before Dane establishes a name for himself. After he risks his life to rescue the mayor, the townspeople officially dub Dane the "beloved physician of Central City." Nurse Tharyn faces a challenge of her own when her dear friend Melinda is captured by the local band of renegade Utes. Melinda's friends and fiancé don't know any better than to give her up for dead…

ISBN 1-59052-313-X

Angel of Mercy Series

Post–Civil War nurse Breanna Baylor uses her professional skill to bring healing to the body, and her faith in the Redeemer to bring comfort to thirsty souls, valiantly serving God on the dangerous frontier.

#1	*A Promise for Breanna*	ISBN 0-88070-797-6
#2	*Faithful Heart*	ISBN 0-88070-835-2
#3	*Captive Set Free*	ISBN 0-88070-872-7
#4	*A Dream Fulfilled*	ISBN 0-88070-940-5
#5	*Suffer the Little Children*	ISBN 1-57673-039-5
#6	*Whither Thou Goest*	ISBN 1-57673-078-6
#7	*Final Justice*	ISBN 1-57673-260-6
#8	*Not By Might*	ISBN 1-57673-242-8
#9	*Things Not Seen*	ISBN 1-57673-413-7
#10	*Far Above Rubies*	ISBN 1-57673-499-4

Shadow of Liberty Series

Let Freedom Ring
#1 in the Shadow of Liberty Series

It is January 1886 in Russia. Vladimir Petrovna, a Christian husband and father of three, faces bankruptcy, persecution for his beliefs, and despair. The solutions lie across a perilous sea.

ISBN 1-57673-756-X

The Secret Place
#2 in the Shadow of Liberty Series

Popular authors Al and JoAnna Lacy offer a compelling question: As two young people cope with love's longings on opposite shores, can they find the serenity of God's covering in *The Secret Place?*

ISBN 1-57673-800-0

A Prince Among Them
#3 in the Shadow of Liberty Series

A bitter enemy of Queen Victoria kidnaps her favorite great-grandson. Emigrants Jeremy and Cecelia Barlow book passage on the same ship to America, facing a complex dilemma that only all-knowing God can set right.

ISBN 1-57673-880-9

Undying Love
#4 in the Shadow of Liberty Series

19-year-old Stephan Varda flees his own guilt and his father's rage in Hungary, finding undying love from his heavenly Father—and a beautiful girl—across the ocean in America.

ISBN 1-57673-930-9

Mail Order Bride Series

Desperate men who settled the West resorted to unconventional measures in their quest for companionship, advertising for and marrying women they'd never even met! Read about a unique and adventurous period in the history of romance.

#1	Secrets of the Heart	ISBN 1-57673-278-9
#2	A Time to Love	ISBN 1-57673-284-3
#3	The Tender Flame	ISBN 1-57673-399-8
#4	Blessed are the Merciful	ISBN 1-57673-417-X
#5	Ransom of Love	ISBN 1-57673-609-1
#6	Until the Daybreak	ISBN 1-57673-624-5
#7	Sincerely Yours	ISBN 1-57673-572-9
#8	A Measure of Grace	ISBN 1-57673-808-6
#9	So Little Time	ISBN 1-57673-898-1

Hannah of Fort Bridger Series

Hannah Cooper's husband dies on the dusty Oregon Trail, leaving her in charge of five children and a general store in Fort Bridger. Dependence on God fortifies her against grueling challenges and bitter tragedies.

#1	Under the Distant Sky	ISBN 1-57673-033-6
#2	Consider the Lilies	ISBN 1-57673-049-2
#3	No Place for Fear	ISBN 1-57673-083-2
#4	Pillow of Stone	ISBN 1-57673-234-7
#5	The Perfect Gift	ISBN 1-57673-407-2
#6	Touch of Compassion	ISBN 1-57673-422-6
#7	Beyond the Valley	ISBN 1-57673-618-0
#8	Damascus Journey	ISBN 1-57673-630-X